KINDLE ALEXANDER

TEXAS PRIDE

Edited by Armi Krankkala
Cover design by Reese Dante
http://www.reesedante.com

First Edition March, 2013
ISBN: 978-0-9891173-1-9

Published by: The Kindle Alexander Collection LLC

This book is a work of fiction. Names, characters, places and incidents are either the product of the author's imagination or are used fictitiously, and any resemblance to any actual persons, living or dead, events, or locales is entirely coincidental.

WARNING
This book contains material that maybe offensive to some:
graphic language, homosexual relations, adult situations.

Dedication

This book is dedicated to my Kindle.
I miss you every minute of every day.
I love you beyond reason.
I'll see you soon.

Robert, I couldn't ask for a better son and I will be that mom that kisses you in public forever! I love you!

Angie, Julie, Teri, VR, Armi, Melanie, Lisa J, Deborah, April, Caigh, Stephanie, Soxie (you've been with me from the start) and every single one of my online friends, words can't describe how thankful I am to know you and get to spend time with you every day. Thank you for all the encouragement, laughter and love. Well, except Gio, he just needs to put some clothes on!

Rhonda, I hope I did the boys proud.
Keagan and Aidan, you healed my heart.

http://mmgoodbookreviews.wordpress.com/ - Thank you for my first glowing review of Texas Pride and your great site!

Chapter 1

"Austin! Austin! Over here!" The deafening roars of his name sounded from every direction as he made his way up the theoretical red carpet of the Kodak Theater in sunny California. With a slight lift of his hand, he waved while inclining his head in the general direction of the screams without cracking a smile. Actually, Austin worked hard to keep his sneered frown from showing the disgust resonating deep inside his soul. Nothing more than years of training had him extending a hand down to his date's lower back to gently guide her to the first interview stop along the way to the front doors. The sooner they made it through the line of national media, the closer he got to the end of this evening.

The event's itinerary was set in stone. It was the same dog and pony show at every one of these award ceremonies. Austin had done this for years, too many years, and it never ever changed. There were several media stops all along the route to the front doors of the theater. Each one required them to step in a certain spot and pose prettily in what felt like an incredibly awkward position that somehow magically looked like a normal stance in the printed picture. Then, the cameras blinded the eyes with thousands and thousands of flashes before they gave a meaningless, uninformative, random interview. Once all of the ridiculous questions had been asked and answered, they did it over again until they made it inside the darkened front doors of the theater and out of the public's ever focused eye.

Tonight, Austin's date, who also played the critical role of his assistant and future wife, ate up the cameras. The pair of them were considered the "it" couple of the evening. A role they'd easily held for more years than he could count. No matter how angry or antisocial he became, they were the couple everyone wanted to interview and all the paparazzi stalked to photograph. She played her part with the grace and ease of a trained actress, readily overcompensating for his increasingly disagreeable disposition which technically was exactly what he paid her to do. He let that thought slide by as they stepped up to their first interview.

"Austin, Cara, good to see you again! Cara, you look lovely. Who are you wearing tonight?" Ryan Palmer of *Entertainment Television* started right in on them. They were only allotted two minutes at each interview, and Ryan made the most of it by immediately hurling questions their way as the cameras panned into their faces.

"I'm wearing Vera Wang tonight. She designed this especially for me. What do you think, do I look alright?" Cara linked her arm with Austin's, turning her charming smile in Ryan's direction.

"You look stunning, but that's nothing new," Ryan said with a good natured Texas size grin that he instantly toned down when he faced Austin. He wasted no time in shoving the microphone into Austin's face.

"This could be back to back Oscars for you tonight, Austin, which would put you in a category very few actors have ever achieved. How does that feel?" Ryan angled the microphone to catch Austin's response.

Austin watched Ryan with a distant mild interest, not paying any attention to the question. But, he almost cracked his first smile of the evening. Ryan stood five feet nothing tall, and compared to Austin's six foot two inch frame, he had to really lift the microphone to reach Austin's face. Out of nothing more than morbid curiosity, Austin cast his gaze down to see Ryan already stood on a step stool and was reaching up on his tip toes trying to make them appear closer in height.

"I'm happy with the decision," Austin finally replied after an extended pause. He gave in to the chuckle he'd been holding back, and hoped his response came close to answering the question he hadn't even tried to hear.

"You still plan the extended sabbatical after tonight's ceremony?" Ryan asked.

Austin focused on the way Ryan jerked his hand back and forth between their lips, trying to get in all the questions he could during the short interview. For some reason, the movement tickled his funny bone and provided a bit of comic relief to his way past sick of all this, hardened heart.

"Yes, I am," he said, again not giving anything back in his response while resisting the urge to lift his hand and mimic Ryan in the universal hand gesture of jacking off. It was in that moment, with all the fans surrounding him, all the movie stars taking shape on the red carpet and all the cameras capturing everything, when Austin realized that without question he'd made the right decision to leave behind the extreme celebrity world of Hollywood.

The event aired on national prime time television and he couldn't help but think about jacking off! Damn if this wasn't some major boring bullshit. If they would just come up with something new to ask, something relevant to anything happening in the world, but they didn't. He'd answered all these same questions hundreds of times in the press circuits. Hell, a trained monkey could answer their questions. It was either lift his hand and pretend to jerk off, or make a gun out of his forefinger and thumb to shoot himself in the head. Both would be appropriate responses to this prick's questions.

"I've heard some speculations on your impending departure, saying it's the wrong time, that it'll destroy your career. You're the favorite tonight and if you win, it'll be a clean sweep across the board. You'll have won every major best actor award given this year. Do you think it'll all still be here waiting for you when you come back?" Ryan quickly shoved the microphone back in his face. The question pissed Austin off. He didn't even do the moody contemplation he'd done for years. Instead, he raised an irritated eyebrow ready to tell Ryan exactly what he could do with the microphone.

"Wrap it. We need to move on." Seth Walker, Austin's agent, came from out of nowhere and ended the interview.

"Ryan, my honey here's giving me time to spread my wings in this acting world. We're so diverse in our investment holdings that Austin's going to run that show for a while, freeing me up to give it a go. He's truly one of the most special men alive. I'm lucky to have him." Cara cut in, clearly seeing the direction Austin planned to take the interview. She said it all with her sweet smile in place. He knew every dime he paid her was well worth the cost.

"One last question: when are you two getting married?" The big Texas size grin was back in place on Ryan's face.

"You know the answer to that! When it's legal for everyone to marry, regardless of their sexual orientation, then we'll be the first in line at the altar," Cara said. With that, Seth whisked them away to the next stop. It was all very much like lather, rinse, repeat until they were almost to the front doors of the theater.

Cara took over the interviews, staying on point and letting Austin center back into himself where he liked to be the most. He watched the last few steps to the theater's front doors much as an outsider looking in, a very unimpressed observer while Cara was regal in her role of arm candy at his side. She was long, blond and thin, matching him on every level. Her hair swept up in some classic updo, and her gown was long and flowed around her slender frame. She looked classically elegant and had the rare ability of looking at home and comfortable in this made up world of glitz and glamour. But, maybe that was because she was at home here; she fit perfectly in this world.

Now, at the end of his career, Austin was incredibly grateful he'd found her. No way could he have done any of this without her. He prayed he'd set her up for success when he left it all behind. She deserved to have everything she wanted, as long as she kept it all in perspective.

"This way." A theater staff member held open a door leading them inside.

Without a backward glance, Austin guided Cara inside and walked in after her. The doors closed behind them, effectively shutting out the noise and constant flash of the cameras. Relief coursed through his veins as he ignored the opulence of the theater's entry. This was it, his last time to ever go through this charade, because what the mini sabbatical really meant was an early retirement. One he couldn't wait to begin. T-minus eight hours and the chains of this excessive celebrity lifestyle would be forever broken. Good riddance!

~~~~~~~

Friends in Low Places by Garth Brooks blared from an old jukebox in the only bar in a sixty mile radius of Cedarville, Texas. Kitt Kelly sat on his barstool, his well-worn boots anchored on the first rail of the stool, and his cowboy hat pushed back on his head. He took a deep swig from the longneck Bud Light he held in his hand. His pool stick rested between his legs, and he watched his lifelong best friend, Jimmy Latham, walk the pool table calculating his next shot.

"Kitt, you need another?" A dainty little waitress asked. In a small town everybody knew everybody, and he nodded at his little sister's best friend, handing over the now empty beer bottle.

"One more, then that's it. I gotta get goin'," Kitt said in his cultured Texas accent.

"Sure thing. I talked to Kylie today. It's a real good thing you did for her, Kitt."

"Nah, it wasn't me. Kylie earned her way into that school and got a good scholarship to go with it all on her own. I didn't do anything." He cut his eyes back to the pool table, hoping she'd pick up the subtle hint he didn't want any part of this conversation.

"Whatever! She told me what you did and I totally wish you were my brother! I'll be right back with your beer." She turned on her heel and headed back to the bar, throwing the last comment over her shoulder.

Kitt sat there quietly. He stared at the aging pool table and wondered how many people knew he'd sold a chunk of his daddy's land to pay for his sister's education. The idea anyone might know sure didn't sit well with him, and he suspected this tight knit community wouldn't appreciate him letting the highest bidder just come in and take up residence.

That land had been in the Kelly family for a hundred and thirty years. Kitt certainly hadn't told a soul about what he did, but keeping secrets in a small town like this seemed to equal hiding an elephant in a sheep pin. Pretty much next to impossible. There was only one way to keep a secret: tell no one. He knew that rule for fact, and it looked like he needed to remind Kylie to keep things a little more quiet.

"Kitt, come dance with me..." JoLynne Rogers slid her body between his parted thighs. She was one of the twenty-five girls in his high school graduating class, and he'd known her for most of his life.

"I can't right now. I'm waitin' for Jimmy to fail at his last shot so I can win this game and collect my money," Kitt said loud enough for Jimmy to hear and casually wrapped an arm around her waist. She'd been drinking quite a bit and already swayed on her feet.

"Jimmy, hurry up and lose! Kitt's the best dancer here. We need him on the dance floor!" JoLynne directed her whiny words toward Jimmy who was leaning awkwardly over the pool table.

"He just thinks he has me. I found my shot, I'm comin' back. JoJo, just stay there and keep him occupied." Jimmy positioned himself for the perfect shot. He aimed, lined the ball up and shot. The ball hit just right of the pocket, knocking Kitt's last ball in. "Damn it!"

"Yeah! Now come dance!" JoLynne pulled Kitt off the barstool. The waitress handed him a new beer as JoLynne tugged them out on the small dance floor with a slow moving Carrie Underwood song beginning to play.

"I love this song! No matter how many times I hear it, I love it!"

JoLynne came straight into his arms. She molded her body against his and began to move around the dance floor in a slow, tricked up two-step. Kitt never had a choice. He wrapped one arm around her thin waist and took a long drink of his new Bud Light before discarding it on a random table.

"I'll be back for that," Kitt called out to the couple at the table. It freed him up to twist and turn her to the beat of the music. They danced well together, and after a couple of faster songs, they finally took it slower when Willy began to play. JoLynne came back into his arms all hot, sweaty, and still tipsy as hell. They were back to a simple two-step together. On the pass back around, Kitt grabbed his beer with a nod and took a long swig. He started to give JoLynne a drink, but stopped.

"How're you gettin' home?" He eyed her close.

"I'm not drivin', I'm here with Rae-Anne. But you know I'd go home with you if you asked." There wasn't even a blush at the words. He guessed they were too old now for hesitations and innuendos. The game was gone. Apparently, they just said it plainly and just like every other time she'd asked, there was no way he would be going there with her. Instead of answering, he handed her his beer, and she drained it down.

"I'm guessin' that's a no, like usual. At some point Kitt Kelly, a hot guy like you's gonna need some in town lovin'. When that time comes, you promise to call me." She moved back into their dance embrace with her body molded against his. She spoke more in his ear, and her breath tickled his neck as she rested her head against his shoulder.

"JoLynne..."

"I know, you don't shit where you eat. I heard it all from Jimmy, but just know there's a big Kitt Kelly fan club ready to step in and make you a fine wife for that big ole ranch you got out there. And you aren't gettin' any younger. Twenty-eight's pretty old around these parts to never been married."

"I know and you make it look like so much fun. When's divorce number two final?" Kitt shot back. He kept their feet moving together instinctively. JoLynne was still inappropriately pressed against him from head to toe, and she grinned, gripping his ass when she answered.

"Soon as he gives me the trailer and stops fightin' me on the flat screen. Until then, he can just keep payin' for it all, and I'll keep livin' there without him anyways."

"Hmm…" It was all Kitt said as he felt his phone vibrate at his belt. He anchored her slightly to his left, never stopping their steps around the dance floor as he palmed his phone to read the text. It was the one he'd been waiting for all night. With one hand, he texted back a quick, *I'm on my way* and began to pry JoLynne off his body.

"Honey, I gotta drive to Dallas tonight. I just got the call. Thanks for dancin' with me." He saw her wobble a little and turned his head to see if Rae-Anne was in any better condition to drive them home.

"Kitt! Why're you leavin'! You never come into town anymore!" JoLynne stomped her foot as she spoke.

"Sorry, babe, it's an emergency. I gotta roll. Tell Jimmy bye for me."

He left the dance floor, texting Jimmy to make sure the two women got home safely. Kitt pulled out his wallet, paid his tab at the bar and strolled right out the front door without a backward glance. All of a sudden, the night started looking up in a major way.

It was at least a ninety minute drive to Dallas, but his fuck buddy had gotten free after all, and the lord knew he needed to get laid in the worst way possible. As he used the side step to his F250 pick-up truck, Kitt palmed his phone again. He quickly sent a text to his ranch foreman, letting him know he would be back about mid-morning and to begin the day without him. His truck was in gear and already pulling forward before he even got the door fully shut.

~~~~~~

Four hours into the awards ceremony, Austin wanted to hang himself. The never-ending tears of acceptance speeches rang like a sledge hammer through his head giving him one hell of a splitting headache. At least at the other award shows, they served alcohol to help take the edge off the tedious boredom and in your face egomaniacs. Seriously, the whole industry just thought too highly of themselves. In what world was it ever okay to have a room full of people sit for hours, stewing in their own greatness? All while they waited to see if they'd won a trophy of a naked man with no dick… It was such a joke.

Austin didn't have to worry about his appearance tonight. His hair was sculpted in place, designed not to move even in gale force winds. He didn't have to worry about the make-up either because much to his staff's regret, he'd refused to wear any tonight. Austin drew the line at make-up after he was spray tanned, clean shaven, and if he was willing to admit it, even waxed.

To top it all off, Austin was brawny and built with muscle. The idea of wearing a form fitted tuxedo with a stupidly tight silk necktie that seriously limited his breathing by half was just plain crazy. The seating in this old building was impossible. These tiny seats had to have been made for children, not for grown ass men.

Nearly an hour later, the night finally began to wear down with only three awards left: Best Actor, Best Director and Best Movie. Austin was nominated for his role as a down on his luck guy who turned multi-millionaire, only to lose it all on a sick son he didn't know he had. He wasn't sure the simple, low budget role truly rang award worthy, yet the entire cast sat behind him. He could hear their giddy whispers buzz through the air, but he just wasn't emotionally in the same place with them.

He felt like a caged animal begging to be set free.

The Best Actor nominees were announced while scenes from their films were shown. It took several minutes to get through it all. The regulars were there: Clooney, Pitt, Penn. As Austin's name was read, the cast sitting behind him clapped a little louder throwing in a few whoops and hollers. Cara leaned in to whisper in his ear as the camera panned in on him.

"Focus in, Austin. They're reading your name. It's almost over." She kissed his cheek. He smiled the smile he knew people loved and lifted his head to watch the clip of the movie. The actress giving the award, Meryl Streep, fanned herself after watching him cry by his dying son's hospital bed before she opened the envelope and grinned.

"And the Oscar goes to... Austin Grainger!"

He kept the smile on his face and stood. Cara stood with him. It was like he was in robot mode. She kissed him lightly on the lips before he turned to have the young director hug him tight.

"You deserve this, Austin." The director held him a moment longer in the tight embrace. Austin pulled back to see tears in the young man's eyes. He forced himself to turn, reminding his brain this meant so much to so many.

Austin took the steps up to the stage as various well-wishers congratulated him along the way. Meryl stood waiting for him and handed him the trophy before hugging and kissing him on the cheek. She'd been one of his mentors from the very beginning when he'd played her son in one of his very first roles.

He accepted the award and turned to the audience united in a standing ovation still clapping wildly for him. The fact that he couldn't even muster a serious emotion at winning this award and having his colleagues and peers cheer him on proved beyond any doubt he was more than just burned out.

Austin was a man in hiding and past tired of it all. A stray thought occurred to him as he took a deep breath, preparing to speak. He wondered if he would be standing here right now if anyone in this room knew the truth about him.

"Thank you, Meryl. This is such an honor. I want to thank…" And then he started the long list of acknowledgments in the memorized acceptance speech he'd prepared. When he was done, they kept him back stage. It seemed the organizers finally clued in on just how late they ran.

Next, the winner of the Director's award was announced. Not surprising, his film's director won. Immediately following that presentation, they won the award for Best Picture, requiring the entire crew to go up on stage. Austin stood in the back, letting everyone else involved in the film have their moment.

~~~~~~

"This is it for you. You're ending your career, leaving it all behind. I understand you're taking off right after this interview?" Katie Seymour of *Good Morning America* asked. They sat together in the back of the cleared out Kodak Theater. It was four in the morning, and Austin had done the entire press circuit just like his contract required him to do.

"Yes. I'm done, this is it for me. It's time to get back to the basics." Austin perched on his director's style chair gently bouncing his leg. He was antsy to be done, counting the minutes until he never ever in his life had to do this again.

"It's hard being this famous? Maybe not cracked up to be what everyone thinks it is?"

"It's hard when you can't leave your house without the constant flash of cameras following you everywhere you go." Austin nodded as he spoke. "I love so many parts of all this. The professionals I've met along the way, and my fans, but the media's become too tough, too aggressive. It's no kind of life."

"What about the rumors? Are any of those hard to deal with, Austin?" Katie leaned forward, getting more serious as she spoke, but he didn't bite. He leaned back and became more casual as he sat there.

"Nah, not at all. I don't listen to any of that mess." Austin forced his leg to still and put his game face on as he answered that question. He was an award winning actor; surely he could pull off passive.

"None?" she persisted.

"No, not any. I won't let anyone tell me about them either. I stay away from all that. The gossip, the made-up stories, reviews…I don't pay attention to any of it," Austin replied.

"So there's no chance I can ask you about some of them now, or the constant speculation on your sexuality." The way she said it, it was a question as well as a statement.

"No, I don't address any of it." It was the absolute truth.

"It's four in the morning here in California, but seven in New York. You've been so gracious to stay up and talk to us. Thank you so much, and we wish you well on your future endeavors. But, I have to say that you will be missed. And, I for one will be looking forward to your return."

Austin stayed quiet, letting the anchor finish while the screen went black before he stood up.

Katie got up to shake his hand. "Good luck."

Austin's tie hung open around his neck, along with the first few buttons on his dress shirt. He held his Oscar in his hand as they expected him to do. His agent stood off to the side like he'd done most of the night. Now, he came forward to take the trophy. "Thank you for signing all those photos. My nieces will love them."

"Anytime," Austin said as he tried to distance himself from the situation by taking a couple of steps backward toward the dressing rooms.

"Good luck! You deserve to find that peace you're looking for," Katie called after him. Her gaze never left his. But Katie was gay. She got it, and it was clear in her eyes.

10

"Thank you," he muttered with a nod. The sentiment felt sincere, so sincere it caught him off guard. He turned away, his legs eating up the distance to the dressing room he'd been assigned for the night. Seth's legs worked double time to stay caught up with him.

"Austin, a car's waiting to take you to the airport." They walked briskly, now side by side as he shrugged off his jacket handing it over to his agent.

"Where's Cara?" Austin loosened the cuff links on his shirt as he entered the small room.

"She's at one of the parties." Seth reached for the shirt before it hit the floor.

"Is she being watched?" Austin asked. He dropped his slacks, looking Seth directly in the eye.

"Yep," Seth said. "She's got a couple of guards on her. I'll go there when we're done."

Austin didn't say anything more. Instead, he turned to dig through the small backpack for his jeans. As good as Cara was at putting on airs in this fake world of Hollywood, she had also entrenched herself deeply in its culture. Up until recently, she'd always been discreet with her partying, but lately, things had changed. Her drug and alcohol use spiraled out of control. Her bed partners changed weekly, causing a new cast of characters to constantly filter through their lives. It was risky and the leaks were starting to fill the tabloids. They were watched too closely for it not to be noticed.

Austin's game plan involved getting her acting jobs in the majors. She wasn't ready for the big roles, but she could handle the romantic comedies, no problem. Austin called in favors signing her on to several back to back films. He hoped it might push her back to getting control over some of her wayward ways. Seth agreed to be her agent. He'd watch her, keep her focused and on task.

"Stay with her all the time and let me know if I need to get involved. I'm hoping it calms when she gets on set and I get gone," Austin said shrugging his jeans up over his hips.

"You know I will." Seth nodded keeping it brief. He didn't agree with Austin taking off like this. They'd been over it so many times, but Seth never could sway him from his course. Austin needed this too badly to let anything stand in his way.

Austin tugged on his t-shirt while walking out the back doors of the studio to his waiting car. For the first time in ten years, the clothes he wore were his choice, not from the collection of the highest bidding designer who paid him to wear their clothes anytime a camera might be around. It felt good to wear a pair of Wranglers and a vintage MTV t-shirt he'd owned before he ever got started acting.

The back door of the Kodak Theater opened to a parking lot. A chain link fence surrounded the lot where about a hundred fans stood behind security waiting for him. Austin took the rare minute and went over to the fence. These times were too few anymore when he just got to be one on one with his fans.

Austin stayed and signed every last autograph. He spoke quietly with each fan. Seth and his bodyguards stood close by waiting for him, but no one rushed him. They let him have this moment. When he got through it all, he slid in the backseat of his car. He watched the crowd as he pulled away and gave a wave. Without question, Austin knew this would be the only thing he missed in leaving Hollywood behind.

Chapter 2

A vibration jarred Kitt awake and it took him a second to acclimate to his surroundings. White and black chrome took shape as he opened his eyes, not the polished finish of his hand built log cabin back on the farm. The bed felt about the same – or maybe not. Kitt had just spent lots of time in this bed over the last few years; maybe that's why it felt like home.

Kitt turned his head to look over at the nightstand. The alarm clock read a quarter after six in the morning. He was alone in bed so he took the minute to stretch his long body out. A smile came to his lips at the rolling ache in his sore muscles after hours of deeply gratifying marathon style sex he'd shared with his super hot bed partner. Sean knew him well and easily manipulated him with all the right moves. Sean also loved to bottom letting Kitt bend, torture and dominate him in every way.

"Good morning. I knew you would want to get on the road. I made coffee and have a bagel wrapped and ready to go." Sean came through the bedroom door carrying two cups of steaming hot coffee. Kitt scooted up on the bed, leaning against the headboard to take the cup, not quite ready to give up the comfort of the moment. Sean sat on the end of the bed, tucking one of his long legs underneath him. He was tall, dark and exceedingly handsome. There had to be some Spanish or Mediterranean deep his ancestry. Over all the years spent together, Kitt had never asked about it, but saw it so clearly in the deep dark chocolate eyes and olive complexion. Sean also had a thick brush of long eyelashes sweeping up and down every time he blinked. Kitt's arousal stirred to life just looking at the man.

"You were incredible last night, Kitt. I'm glad you finally got the time to come up and see me," Sean said before taking a sip of his coffee.

"I've been busy. I needed it though. Thanks for fittin' me in." He gave a small kick in Sean's direction and brushed a hand through his light brown hair.

"You've been spending time in the sun with no sunscreen, Kitt. I keep telling you it's bad for your skin. You need to spray tan, it's healthier and everyone's doing it." Sean eyed Kitt closely. "The sun's changed your hair color, I like the gold and auburn highlights. It's longer than I've ever seen you wear it. I like this new look, but you need sunscreen!" Sean scooted closer to Kitt as he spoke. He laid his coffee on the night stand. They had been in this relationship for the past five years, ever since meeting when Kitt was on spring break from Grad school, floating the river in New Braunfels.

"I need to take the time to get it cut. It's in the way." Kitt let Sean take his cup, and watched him sweep a hand down Kitt's chest. Sean lowered the sheet covering his half aroused cock.

"I think you need one for the road. Maybe it'll entice you back to my bed sooner. You know you're my favorite bed partner. No one's built like you. I guess it's just that home grown, corn fed thing I keep hearing about with you farm boys." Sean took Kitt's dick in his hand, skillfully bringing it fully back to life.

"Hmm…" Kitt sucked his breath in at the feel of Sean's hands moving on him. "We went all night. I can't believe you want more." He rolled his hips forward, his cock begging for Sean's tongue.

"I always want you, Kitt. I never turn you down. Besides, all these committed relationships and marriage fighters are really putting a damper on the available men out there," Sean said leaning in to slant his mouth over Kitt's. He opened immediately for Sean's sensual assault, snaking his hands up Sean's back to pull him against his chest.

It became a battle of tongues as Kitt reached his hands low sliding them in the waistband of Sean's workout shorts. As he'd expected, there was no underwear in the way, just Sean, hard and ready. Sean tore from the kiss, licking and nibbling his way to softly whisper in Kitt's ear. "Let me suck you just the way you like it before you go. Something to remember me by."

Sean pulled away, looking Kitt in the eyes. "Come in my mouth…don't push me away. I know you're clean and I love your taste. No one tastes like you."

He didn't wait for an answer, but trailed kisses down Kitt's chest, taking special care around each nipple. He worked his tongue slowly, licking over each defined abdominal muscle in Kitt's stomach. God, how Kitt loved that move! He tightened his grip in Sean's thick, silky black hair, and pushed him lower. The chuckling coming from below had Kitt again rolling his hips forward as his dick was lifted to position. Sean placed a simple, firm kiss on his broad head, and then slid Kitt's hard as steel cock deep into his mouth.

Sean had a way with blow jobs. He rolled his tongue around Kitt's dick, sucking him in deeply until he hit the back of Sean's throat. The gentle scrape of teeth, along with a swirl of his tongue caused Kitt to buck his hips forward, to thrust himself deeper inside Sean's mouth. Sean never failed to take him as far as he needed to go, deep throating him time and time again.

It didn't take long before Kitt's spine began to tingle. He bucked his hips now in earnest as he fucked Sean's mouth. Kitt rolled his head back, exhaling sharply. He tightened his hold on Sean's hair, keeping him right there as Kitt fucked him hard with his hips. Kitt's heart pounded when wave after wave of hot, creamy release exploded from his body. True to Sean's word, he drank it all down, never pulling away from the deep thrusting Kitt continued to make until there was nothing left but the sated feelings taking over his body.

Sean stayed on him. He cleaned Kitt's cock with his tongue before releasing him to kiss his way back up Kitt's chest. Kitt slid his hand up to cover his nipple as Sean's tongue tried to slide across it. Every nerve ending in his body was in overload and his nipples were just too sensitive to allow Sean to suck on them like he liked to do after sex. Another one of those sexy chuckles sounded off as Sean rose from the bed. Kitt opened one eye and watched Sean walk across the bedroom, dropping his workout shorts as he went.

"I have work this morning, and you need to get back on the road, or so you told me several times last night."

Kitt watched the enticingly hot bubble butt bounce back and forth as Sean strutted into his closet. It took him a minute longer to finally look over at the clock to see it was already a quarter to seven, fifteen minutes later than he'd intended to leave. Kitt forced his sated body to move. He took a moment, just placing both feet on the plush rug before he pushed himself up, relieved when he stayed on his feet. The ache from earlier made itself known. His thighs hurt from the hours of thrusting he'd done, and his arms were sore from holding Sean's ass and legs just the way he wanted them. The best part though, his ass hurt. He'd been used pretty solidly last night which was a little different for him and Sean.

Kitt moved his sore limbs across the room to a chair where his clothes were discarded last night. Sean was a clean freak, and even as the clothes were torn away, he always took the minute to fold them neatly on the chair. Everything had a place in Sean's life, and Kitt wondered about the workout shorts still lying in the middle of the floor. Kitt assumed he left them there to prove he could, but it had to be eating Sean up inside.

He decided to give Sean a break and picked up the shorts, casually folding them before dropping them on the dresser where the television sat. He turned the TV on, hoping to catch a few minutes of local news to get an idea on the traffic this morning.

All Kitt had was the clothes he'd worn last night. He began to dress, pulling on his plaid button down with one eye focused on the television. Sean reappeared from the closet wearing dark slacks, a crisp white dress shirt, a crimson silk tie hanging around his shoulders, and some sort of matching expensive looking loafers. His sexy fuck buddy was hot as hell, and tying his tie as he spoke.

"You know him, don't you?" Sean nodded toward the television. It took Kitt a second to focus his eyes back on the screen and not leer at the overly handsome man stepping from the closet.

"Yep, well, no. Austin Grainger went to my high school. He's three or four years older than me. I wouldn't say I know him." Kitt was now fully focused on the sexiest man alive. Literally, per *People Magazine*.

"They say he likes the boys. Did he like you back then? Maybe you shared some of this tight ass of yours with him in that high school Ag barn you're so proud of?" Sean patted Kitt's ass as he walked by.

"Nah, I don't think he's gay. He dated the head cheerleader back then. They got caught on my dad's land together." Kitt's eyes stayed glued to the television screen.

"Doesn't mean he doesn't like a guy now and then." Sean looked at himself in the dresser mirror as he adjusted his tie before placing the cuff links to his wrists.

"Maybe, but I don't think so. I never saw it," Kitt said and stepped closer to the TV.

Austin had aged well and was still as hot as ever. There weren't too many men better looking than Sean, but Austin easily ranked higher. When Kitt was a teenager, no other person on the planet starred in his daydreams as frequently as Austin Grainger. At fifteen years old, he'd woken up plenty of mornings all sticky wet after dreaming some of the most erotic dreams a boy could have, and they all centered on Austin.

"You know. I was thinking with all this talk of commitment and marriage...we aren't getting any younger, you and I," Sean said as he watched Kitt from his dresser's mirror.

Kitt glanced up, but quickly turned his eyes back down at the screen. "Whatever, you're the old man out of the two of us. I'm still in my twenties."

Kitt sat down on the side of the bed to slide on his socks and boots. Whatever show Austin was on had finished airing, freeing Kitt from watching the screen. He looked back up at Sean. Something serious crossed his face, a point he was trying to make, and Kitt's mind raced to remember what they were talking about.

"...and I sure like the way you fuck. Clearly, I do. I've known you for five years, and I only have to see your text, and I start backing out of whatever I've got going on. Maybe, we should consider making this more permanent." Sean finally turned toward him, leaning back against the dresser and stared at Kitt.

"You don't have to cancel plans for me. Just tell me when's good." Kitt tugged hard at the leather loops at the top of his boot until his heel slid inside.

"You're missing my point, Kitt. Let me try again. There's a bigger picture here. While you were buried deep inside my ass last night, I realized how much I like you there. I'm thirty-five, not a kid anymore. Perhaps it's time I settle down...with you."

The words stopped Kitt cold while he pushed the tails of his shirt into his blue jeans. He looked over at Sean with surprise evident on his face. Never, did he ever think Sean would say something like this. Sean was a stereotypical gay man. Stockbroker by day, man whore by night. Kitt narrowed his eyes and watched him closely, wondering if he could have interpreted the words incorrectly. Sean chose then to leave his spot by the dresser to come to Kitt. He wrapped his arms around Kitt and tucked his shirt in from the back.

"I see you're as surprised by my suggestion as I am. It's not such a crazy idea if you think about it. You're about the hottest guy I've ever seen. I've told you over and over you're like a smoke free version of the Marlboro man." Sean stopped speaking and looked up at Kitt's face while wrapping his arms tighter, tugging them closer together.

"I can see by the look in your eyes you never believe me…Kitt, it's time for you to think better of yourself. You're gorgeous, babe. You've got a strong jaw, high cheek bones, sexy full lips and that slightly crooked nose turns my shit on. You rock these Wranglers like they were made just for your body, but I digress. Say you'll think about it." Sean slid his hands along Kitt's arms hanging loosely at his sides and wrapped them around his waist in the same manner he held Kitt.

They were about the same height, about the same build; muscular, but not too bulky. It felt right to hold Sean, especially when he lowered his hands down on Kitt's ass, tugging their hips tighter together. Kitt felt Sean grow harder as he spoke, and the realization hit him: this conversation turned Sean on. He was serious.

"What about the problem of the hour and a half between our houses? I can't come up here much more than I already do." Kitt stopped, shocked at his own words. Was he really considering it?

"You could let me come to you." Sean's stare never faltered.

"Sean…" The thought made Kitt cringe. Secrets only held when nothing broke through the carefully planned lies.

"No, I see that look in your eyes. I could be discreet for a while. Keep it hidden while we decide if it's working," Sean said.

"Yeah, no…You don't have a discreet bone in your body." Kitt laughed at the thought. "No way. It's impossible, Sean. You drive a Fisker. You look like a male model! You draw attention like honey draws flies, and you do it on purpose."

Sean completely ignored him, holding him in place as Kitt tried to pull free.

"I was thinking. If you came up here once a week, and I came to you once a week, we could make it work until one of us gives and moves to the other."

Okay, well *that* sentence just proved to Kitt this was more than a spur of the moment thought, and way more than just bumping up the regularity of their sex partnership. Sean had to have been thinking about this for a while. It left Kitt with no words.

Every part of this conversation hit him completely unexpectedly and just grew crazier by the second. He would never give up the farm, and no way would Sean fit in his world. Besides, there was a much bigger issue. Kitt had never considered long term with Sean. Hell, he'd never thought in long term about anyone. He was a confirmed bachelor for life. He knew his plight, owned it, and planned to live just like this forever. It was the exact reason he thought he and Sean were such a perfect match.

"Kitt, just think about it. I know I'm your only partner. It's obvious, and with a little more regularity, you could be mine. I love having sex with you, that's all I'm saying. I'll give you a few days, but promise me you'll think about it. And, I will be discreet. I can buy one of those big pickup trucks to drive down and see you." Sean finally pulled away from Kitt handing him his wallet and cowboy hat before walking back across the room to the closet to grab a suit jacket.

"I have an appointment this morning. You could stay, but I know you would rather get on the road."

Sean never said another word about commitments or long term relationships as they left his apartment. They rode the elevator down the high rise to the underground garage. Kitt had parked his truck next to Sean's shiny, new Fisker sports car when he arrived last night. He went directly to it, and Sean followed behind him, not going to his car like he usually did when they left together.

"I love watching you back this massive vehicle into this small space. It reminds me of us having sex." Sean chuckled and pushed Kitt against the side of the truck. He was bold this morning, leaning into Kitt for all his neighbors to see. These public displays weren't something Kitt did, and he never got used to it when Sean made the move. It was hard to hide when you were so public with what you were doing. He couldn't help but cut his eyes around to see who might be watching. Sean gripped his jaw, flipping his head back to look only at him.

"It's okay to be gay, Kitt. I don't know why you won't just go with what's natural for you. Think about what I said. We connect well together, and you'd be good on my arm. I'm getting a promotion to Senior Vice President. You wouldn't have to work yourself into an early grave out there, trying to make your dad's place what it once was a hundred years ago. Promise me you'll think about it." Sean leaned in and placed his lips on Kitt's for a quick chaste kiss before he turned and walked away. "Now drive away in that big ass truck. I love to watch you go."

Kitt didn't say a word. He clicked the key remote to unlock the doors before he used the side step to lift himself inside to the driver's seat. He sat still completely shocked at the turn of events between them. Kitt searched his frantic brain, but couldn't figure out what happened in their night to cause Sean to think in terms of exclusivity – with him. It wasn't just that, because hell, Kitt already *was* exclusive to Sean. He lived out in the country. Three thousand people lived in a sixty square mile radius of the farm, and as best he could tell, not one of them was a gay man. Hell, if there was someone, he'd be finding a way to fuck them along with Sean.

"Exclusive…damn it," Kitt muttered driving from the underground garage. This was going to fuck their relationship up. Kitt didn't want an obligation and he sure didn't want to explain Sean's presence to anyone down on the farm. It had taken him a long time to earn the respect of his ranch hands after his father's sudden heart attack. He'd just now proved he could run the place; that everything he'd learned in college, the progressive way of farming and ranching could work better than his dad's old school ways. If his employees learned the truth about whose bed his boots had been under…Yeah, *no way!* Kitt knew he could never come out in the agriculture world. The heavy hitters of the industry overflowed with rednecks and homophobes. No way could he ever come out.

Kitt pushed, no *shoved,* Sean's idea out of his mind. He decided he would deal with it later. If he needed to find a new fuck buddy, fine, he would. Dallas was full of gay men. Maybe, switching to Houston or Austin might produce better results, a change of pace. Proximity wise, they were further away from the farm, even less chance of him getting caught. Surely, he still had connections close to Houston. His alma mater was only about an hour away from there. Besides, even with everything else against them, relationships required a time commitment to be successful, and time wasn't something Kitt had to spare right now.

Kitt easily navigated his oversized pick-up through the crowded downtown streets of Dallas, not letting himself consider Sean's proposal any longer – his mind was made up. He'd find a way to tell Sean 'no' and keep them going just like they had been, or end it all together. His hip vibrated. It reminded Kitt he'd silenced the phone the previous night. He palmed it at a stop light.

'I know you better than anyone does. We've been together too long. We can make it work. I'm willing to stay hidden for a while, and having sex with you a couple of times a week will hold me over, I'm sure. I love our sex…sucking you, swallowing you…don't deny us. I'll keep things like we have them for now, but I'll be working my way in

that direction. You're suddenly very important to me. Actually Kitt, you have been for some time now, I've just kept it quiet.'

Kitt didn't respond but scanned the message a couple of times until the stop light turned green. He turned up the volume on the radio and tossed the phone in the cup holder it usually rested in. One thing he knew without question, he didn't have time for all this right now. If Sean was willing to give him time, he'd take it and pray Sean changed his mind. Kitt liked their sex too, always had, but no way was he ready for any sort of relationship. That wasn't going to change, not for anyone.

As he wound his way through the extreme downtown traffic, Kitt forced his thoughts away from Sean to focus on monumentally more important things. Like his new colt. Or rather the prospect of his new colt. Kitt had taken out loans and invested in four registered mares. Over the next few weeks, the first of four artificially inseminated quarter horses would give birth on the farm. His father had only run cattle on the ranch, but Kitt took a chance. All four mares had been successfully impregnated and were stabled on the farm right now. If things worked out like he hoped, their newborn foals could easily sell for thousands and thousands of dollars, changing everything for him, his stepmom and two little sisters.

Kitt felt much more on solid ground mentally. No, personal relationships meant very little to him right now. He stood on the edge. He needed to stay focused and on target. One wrong move could ruin everything. The sounds of the *Kidd Kraddick Morning Show* filled his mind and he ignored everything as he hit Interstate 20 to make the long drive home.

Chapter 3

The newly built, single story ranch style house sat close to dead center of the fifteen hundred acres Austin had purchased a couple of months ago under the disguise of one of his obscure companies. He knew he couldn't stay hidden forever, but the first twenty-four hours of solitude rocked. He just wasn't of a mindset to let it go easily.

The original plan had been to throw the media off his tracks by flying north to the Cape Cod area after the Academy Awards. He'd stay a few weeks before secretly making his way back here. As it turned out, he couldn't wait to be back home, and came straight to Texas. He arrived yesterday about noon, and as he'd driven up the property, the modernized architecture of his new home blew him away. He'd sat through plenty of conference calls and planning sessions over the last few months, but to see the structure come to life was more than he ever expected.

Nothing was ready for his arrival. The compact, yet spectacular house he had built was in the final stages of completion. The touch up work was just now being done. The house combined a beautiful blend of pine, stone and brick. The workers diligently hammered away at the oversized tin roof covering the large wraparound porches on both the front and the back of the house.

Austin instructed his driver to pick up a blow up mattress for him to sleep on until his furniture began to arrive over the next few days. He planned to have everything arrive on a slow scale so not to draw too much attention to who might be taking up residence in this small farming community.

Austin opted for a three bedroom, one-story ranch style house. The rooms were large and designed to be used, nothing like the show places he'd lived over the last ten years. The one thing he loved most about his new home was the large floor to ceiling windows. They ran the entire length of the living room along the back of the house. He could see everything for miles and miles and would never feel caged again.

The icing on his cake was the completely covered, full length back porch complete with a fireplace and a stone walkway leading down to a barely started deck and brand new swimming pool. Austin loved to swim, but rarely got the time or chance. All that would be changing now.

To the left of the back door, a few hundred feet away from the house, sat a brand new horse stable about four times the size of his house. Apparently, in today's farming world, horses and cattle no longer mixed. The cattle barn loomed straight out in the distance, much further away. Both sported the same design as his home. The place was the most beautiful he'd ever seen. In his heart, he knew that wasn't true, but he was so happy to be here, alone in all this quiet.

Yesterday, during his first meeting with his new ranch foreman, Austin learned that several hundred head of mixed breed cattle were currently en route to the farm. He'd also purchased five purebred appaloosas scheduled to arrive later next week. His new ranch foreman, Mike Cisneros, had a plan for the farm, and after he got past the initial shock of finding out the new ranch owner wasn't actually a rancher from the north, he sat Austin down and explained it all to him.

Mike was young. Newly graduated from Texas A&M and ready to put his new agriculture degree to good use. To Austin, he seemed to be a kid, but he came highly recommended by the previous land owner. Mike appeared more than ready to bring his expertise to the farm. The new foreman took his job seriously and wanted the place to thrive. To Mike's credit, he'd only been momentarily startled to see Austin.

From the beginning, Austin gave Mike carte blanche on everything. All Austin required of Mike was a productive working farm that he could jump in and work when he felt like getting his hands dirty. Well, he cared about that and the iron clad confidentiality agreement he'd made everyone in his employment sign. He'd also included the same confidentiality agreement in the contract when he bought this land. If he ran into the neighbors, the contract prohibited them from talking about who lived here.

Austin installed security cameras around the entire place. His security guards posed as ranch hands. Housed in a newly built building on the southeast end of the ranch's property line, they monitored every angle of the farm. The outside of the building looked very much like every other building on the property, but the inside housed a hi-tech security control panel that rivaled that of NASA's in its ability to monitor every inch of his land. No one knew they were here, including Mike, until yesterday.

To help with the oddity of being so fully staffed without much more than a couple of horses on the property, the ranch hands spent their time fencing the place, separating the different pastures. They also installed more surveillance devices. Mike unwittingly helped the security team by designing a pasture system perfect for rotating cattle and horses and growing hay. The fences provided extra surveillance from every angle.

Austin's persona for the area, what all of his staff were required to say if asked, was that he was a wealthy older Northerner who never planned to live on the ranch, but might visit once or twice a year when he felt like playing cowboy. His family bought the land as an investment. Mike ran the show, and that's all the town needed to know.

Austin hadn't been back in this part of the world since he'd left right out of high school. It was the biggest reason he'd chosen to come back in the first place. No one would suspect it. He'd never spoken highly of the years he grew up on a farm.

The back breaking hard work and hot summer sun had pushed him away to begin with. Yet, he knew these roads like the back of his hand. The wide open range allowed his security team to easily locate and apprehend anyone coming in while letting Austin roam freely within its borders. They all went out of their way to make Austin fully secure here. He had check points installed and monitored along the only two routes leading up to his farm. To get this far back, a person would either have to come through town or come in the back through miles and miles of nothing but rugged terrain. That would require a trained tracker and none of the soft paparazzi he knew could tough it out in the Texas wilderness.

Yesterday, while Austin drove through the small town, it struck him as funny how things hadn't changed since he left well over fourteen years ago. He'd moved his parents to far northern California soon after he'd made some real money, getting them out of the hot desert of Texas that they still called home. Growing up, Austin had always felt a little stifled here. When he was young, he resented the hell out of everyone knowing his business, always telling his dad when he'd done wrong. But, now that he'd been on the true side of hateful, mean spirited gossip, he realized these people down here were the salt of the Earth and never meant him any harm. They just tried to keep him from making too many mistakes, even if their interference sometimes caused his father to take it out on his hide.

There was a time Austin knew what it meant to shine in this town. He'd been the local sports hero, for as much as that said at the time. Their little Division Two school district bussed in kids from as far as sixty miles away. Less than forty kids graduated in Austin's class. To play football, basketball as well as baseball was nothing for the boys out here. To do it well didn't really mean much except to the older population who took pride in their school sports. It provided the only real entertainment around. They considered Austin a star even back in his high school days, betting he'd make it to the Pro's someday. It was those accolades that gave Austin a false sense of confidence, making him think he could handle Hollywood. That he could even belong there. The entire time he grew up, he'd baled his fair share of hay and woken up hours before school to help feed the animals. It taught him the work ethic that made him the movie star he was today.

As he stood out on his back porch breathing in the clean dry air, something from the corner of his eye caught his attention. He took the steps down two at a time. Yesterday, he found out that he'd apparently bought several four-wheelers, and now, two of his crew drove around from behind the barn toward him. He planned to ride out today with his foreman to check the property lines.

The one rule he made clear last night, he didn't want to be treated any different from anyone else on the ranch. He wanted to be held responsible, and his goal was to work alongside them. A frown furrowed his brow. If he intended to pull his own weight like everyone else, his ride wasn't supposed to be made ready and brought to him. He'd do it on his own.

The scowl Austin wore said it all as he stalked toward the two riding up. One of the ranch hands jumped off a four-wheeler, tossing him the helmet and took off running back to the barn.

"Mike, I told you, no special treatment!" Austin yelled over the engine.

"Then catch me if you can, old man!" Mike yelled back and tore off on the four-wheeler. In that moment, Austin knew he'd hired the perfect foreman. He slid on his ride, fastened the helmet and took off. He was a little rusty in controlling the vehicle, but quickly got the hang of it, barreling after his foreman.

~~~~~~~

The fence line looked good. It wasn't the standard hand stretched barb wire surrounding the property line like on other ranches. Instead, they'd used a rod iron design, snaking surveillance equipment all along the way. There was a definite difference in the look. Austin hoped anyone who saw it would think 'successful rancher', not that Austin Grainger hid inside. Austin took a long drink from his water bottle. It was early October, but still hot as hell. He wiped his bandana across his face, ignoring his foreman's mocking laughter.

"You know, it's only eighty-seven degrees out here. I think someone got soft out there in Hollywood." Mike yelled over the hum of the engine of the idle four-wheeler.

"Yeah, what the fuck ever," Austin yelled back, and just in case Mike couldn't hear him, he flipped him the bird while resisting the urge to dump the contents of the water bottle directly on top of Mike's head as he walked by. "Where's this pond I bought that jacked up the price so much higher than any other land in the area?"

"We're on our way to it. It's on the west side of the property. Runs the length of that pasture. You share it with the Kelly's." Mike turned off his engine to help be heard as Austin came to stand in front of him.

"That's right...we bought it from old man Kelly." A smile tore across Austin's face as he remembered his father and Kelly had been sale barn buddies. His dad didn't always like Mr. Kelly, but he sure had loved haggling with him.

"Mr. Kelly died a few years back. His son has the property now. I went to college with Kitt. He's the one you bought the land from." Mike set the story straight for Austin.

"Mr. Kelly died? He couldn't have been that old." Austin stopped in mid-motion of getting back on the four-wheeler.

"Nah, he wasn't more than fifty-five, maybe younger. It was a heart attack. It wasn't that bad, but we're so far out. No one found him for a while and that's what killed him."

"That's too bad. He owned lots of land if I remember right. They were kind of the top dogs in the area." Austin secured his water bottle back in place.

"Yeah, they still are. Kitt's trying to restore things, bring in the new practices these old timers around here reject. It's been a struggle."

"And, I've been told that's why I pay you so much to bring these new practices in...to help streamline my ranch or some shit like that." Austin reached around for his helmet.

"Pretty much. Now, if you're rested enough let's get back on it. We're killin' daylight," Mike yelled louder as he started his engine.

"Lead the way!" Austin yelled, already loving the guy. Mike could no more care about his fame than his agent did.

The terrain leading to the pond was tricky and required Austin to navigate closely for fear of flipping his ride. As he drove and jerked over deep ruts, he failed to see how anyone thought this land was worth double the price of the normal acreage in the area. He actually got a little pissed off as he realized he'd been cheated. As the anger built, he tried to talk himself down. It was only money, and he had too much of that to even deal with. But damn, he hated to be taken advantage of. As they drove over the second hill, a half a mile or so from his house, he finally saw a crystal blue spring pond stretched over several acres, sitting in some of the greenest pastures he'd ever seen.

He'd been told it was a natural pond, not man-made, and it stretched through a small valley. It was more like a small hill surrounded three quarters of the pond, but for this flat land, it was considered a valley. His new fence reached across the water separating his part of the pond from the Kelly's. A log cabin sat just on the other side of the water.

Austin's men who worked the fence participated in a heated discussion with three other men on the opposite side of the fence. One being a muscular, shirtless cowboy who towered over two other men who stood behind him. It was the tall cowboy who caused Austin's eyebrows to rise in unexpected speculation.

The guy looked good. Real good.

All of a sudden this land purchase seemed to have turned out to be a far better deal than he'd ever expected. If *that* was what lived on the other side of the fence, life was getting better by the second.

A cowboy hat angled back on the shirtless guy's head, and his hands gripped the sides of his hips as he listened to Austin's security team. Austin watched his facial expressions and body language and finally clued into the conversation. It didn't seem to be going too well.

"Does the fence separate the property?" Austin asked, bringing the four-wheeler to a stop at Mike's side. Mike turned off the engine and unbuckled his helmet before speaking.

"Yep. And I think your men have just met the immoveable object named Kitt Kelly."

"Mr. Kelly's son?" Austin followed Mike's move as he stood.

Normally, he'd sit back, stay hidden behind the helmet, but the show going on in front of him was just too good. The hard body across the fence from him needed to be fully surveyed. Austin had been pretty certain he'd given up regular sex by moving out here, but one thing he'd learned over the last few years, you just never knew who was who until you tested the waters.

"Yep. Most people think Mr. Kelly was a hard, unmoving man, but they hadn't met Kitt. He gets something in his head and that's how it's gonna be." Mike swung his leg off the four-wheeler.

"Huh. So what's this about?" Austin followed Mike as they walked the distance between them and the men still in battle. All of them completely ignored their arrival.

"Don't know, but we should probably intervene if you wanna maintain a friendly neighbor relationship. And trust me, you want that. We need him. Shit, Kitt's brow just lowered, he's pissed. They're about to see..." Mike jogged the last few steps to the men, drawing their attention toward him.

Austin followed keeping his set pace as he monitored the situation. His men looked relieved to see him. Forced into the role of an Alpha for too many years, he was known for being a hard-ass himself. Funny how that man inside him had already begun to fade away since he moved back here.

"Hey, brother, what's goin' on?" Mike called out speaking directly to Kitt.

"These your men?" Kitt's tone held a hint of threat as he asked the question he already knew the answer to. The words emerged more an accusation than a question, and in that moment, something happened to Austin. His heart picked up a beat, his body hardened and his eyes focused fully on Kitt's face. He remembered Kitt from high school. Kitt played on the Varsity baseball team during Austin's senior year. His dick stirred to life as Kitt turned his angry gaze toward Mike. No one but his security men paid Austin any attention, and he clearly saw they waited for him to take control of the situation. An arrogant assumption on their part, and after being treated like an elitist for so many years, Austin liked being ignored.

"They are. What's goin' on, man?" Mike repeated calmly as he came to the fence line separating them.

"This pond feeds all my animals. I can't have it destroyed with a fence built from the bottom up. That's just fuckin' ridiculous! And, absolutely no electrical wirin's gonna run across it. I'm not takin' the chance of any of my herd gettin' electrocuted after the first fuckin' storm exposes a live wire to that damn water. Mike, you need to get a hold of these people and teach them right from wrong. Some dumbass citified pretend cowboy's not gonna fuck up everything I own because they're a stupid motherfucker!" Kitt sneered the last sentence, aiming his furious gaze toward the group of men who pissed him off. It issued a challenge and Kitt's shoulders involuntarily rolled as his fist clenched. He appeared ready to take them all on, no questions asked. He was fuming mad, no mistaking it. Mike held up his hands, trying for calm, and began to walk a little more cautiously as he moved forward to the water's edge.

"Kitt, buddy, I'd like you and Jose to meet the new owner." Mike turned his eyes back to Austin who finally made his presence known, stepping out from behind Mike.

Kitt, the cowboy, was sweaty, covered in dust, and hot as freaking hell. His chest was bare, showing broad sculpted shoulders leading down to a thin waist and a tight six-pack. The dusty blue jeans he wore rode low on his hips, revealing a hint of the waist band of his underwear. *Andrew Christian underwear!* Austin immediately lifted his gaze while trying to hide his smile.

The brand was greatly favored by gay men; they proudly wore their Andrew Christian's. Of course, straight men wore them too, but Austin's gut told him the man standing fuming in front of him was gay, thereby automatically making him the perfect neighbor. Austin's day skyrocketed to fan-fucking-tastic.

Recognition hit the two men standing beside Kitt, but he didn't see any change of expression in Kitt's face. Those red hot angry eyes focused on him, and he seemed to be prepared to do whatever necessary to stop such a clearly ludicrous act. At least, it was ludicrous to Kitt.

"I'm Austin Grainger, nice to —"

He was cut off as Kitt raged at him, all control on his temper gone. "I don't give a fuck who you are! You aren't gonna put my herd in danger for any reason. Our contract was very clear. You aren't to mess with the integrity of this pond for any reason. *Period!*" Kitt bellowed as he stalked toward both Austin and Mike with just the current barbed wire fence separating the three of them. Kitt's hand moved in Austin's face, a finger pointing directly at him. Kitt stated very clearly in both word and action as to what would happen to this piece of land and how he planned to back it up. Austin held up a hand to his men who were paid to protect him.

"You know, your dad got me in some serious trouble when he found me and Wanda-Sue Atkinson parked somewhere back here smoking pot and having se...fun. If I remember correctly, it was probably right here at this pond. She brought me out here, and I didn't know where we were until your dad showed up. You sound just like him. I appreciate that memory..." Austin said, looking down for a minute with a small smile spreading on his face. Unlike everyone else around, he wasn't intimidated by Kitt's outburst at all. His wet dream in a pair of Wranglers had his dick rigid, almost dripping with anticipation. Austin needed to diffuse the situation.

"He told my dad about it, but honestly, I still think I was more scared of your dad than mine. I knew my dad wouldn't physically kill me, but your dad...yeah, I wasn't quite so sure about him." Austin said it still smiling with his real grin, not the fake one he usually plastered on his face. He hadn't thought about that memory in years and years. He'd been fifteen to Wanda's eighteen, and she'd taught him well...well enough for him to know he didn't like girls at all.

"You know what? I'm real fuckin' glad for your trip down memory lane, but your men have me good and pissed off. This barb wire fence is the only thing I'm allowin' over this water and I'm only allowin' it because I live right there. I can monitor it and fix it before anything bad happens to any of our animals." Kitt stepped up closer to Mike and Austin, hooking his thumb toward the log cabin while he spoke. The barb wire had to be cutting into his jeans, but Kitt didn't even seem to notice it. Once he was done speaking, Kitt turned back to glare at Austin's security men. Austin got the distinct impression Kitt was ready to throw down with them all right now. End all discussion and duke it out. The idea of this sexy ass man going to blows to protect his animals turned Austin on like nothing ever had before.

"There's no problem with that. We can work within those guidelines," Austin said easily. He lifted his hand as Sam, his head security guard, started to speak. "I think we need to get together though. Go over things. See what we can work out. I have a high-end security system designed to keep—"

"To keep my cows from crossin' this pond? It's about fifteen feet deep and an acre wide. The barb wire's enough." Kitt said as if Austin was stupid, but his focus returned to Austin. Exactly where Austin wanted it to be.

"As I was saying, it's designed to keep trespassers off my land, and as a result, off yours too." Austin never took his eyes off Kitt as he spoke.

"I've never had a problem with that this far back," Kitt shot back. The look on his face was clear; he thought Austin was a first rate nut job.

"You haven't lived next door to me before now, have you? They're just here trying to keep us both private. For now, no one knows I'm here. If that changes, they need to be ready. Why don't you come over, tonight, tomorrow or whenever, and we can talk through it all. See what we can do to keep anyone off your land. What do you say?"

"There has never been a problem with anyone gettin' back here. We butt up against Hunt's twenty thousand acres and the National Forest after that. I can't see where it's a problem or why it needs any further discussion. If you weren't set with the terms, you shouldn't have signed the damn contract." Kitt refused to back down, his anger clearly fueled him.

"Really, Kitt, Austin's on the up and up. Come listen to what he has to say. He's extending the olive branch, man, and just told you the barb wire was enough," Mike reiterated Austin's words.

Kitt turned his heated gaze to Mike, and then cocked his head to the security men who looked disgruntled as hell. Lastly, he looked back at his own men who stood a little further back behind him. One of them nodded at him, and Kitt looked as if he visibly forced himself to calm down. Then, he did something no one had ever done to Austin before: he turned around, not saying another word, and walked away. Kitt just dismissed him.

Austin's eyes riveted to the Wranglers. He watched Kitt's ass swing with each step he took as he let the moment settle inside him. He appreciated being treated normal, he liked to not always be the center of attention, but dismissed? He wasn't so sure about that one. Kitt's men followed him. They all made their way to the log cabin sitting a few hundred feet away.

"He's a good guy, I promise. It's been a while since I've seen him like this. Really not since college, but he came over and helped me set up your barn. He's also the insemination specialist I told you about." Mike was clearly trying to sell Austin on Kitt's finer points.

Austin's gaze stayed glue to Kitt's ass until he stepped up on the porch. He let everything go and focused on his choice of underwear.

31

The brand was more pronounced as he walked up each step. Austin realized his heart was pounding and his dick jerked, begging him to go after Kitt. It had been a while since he'd had sex and he desperately wanted some of that hot, angry cowboy, to work him over in all the right ways.

"It's fine, I get it. He's protecting what's his. Can't blame him for that. I'll give it a day or two and try to talk to him again. Mike, if he'll listen to you, please ask him not to tell anyone that I'm here. It's in the contract we signed. I just want to make sure he remembers the clause." Austin didn't wait for Mike's reply, but turned back to his four-wheeler and rode back to the barn. His mind stayed on Kitt the entire way back.

Chapter 4

"Damn it!" Kitt growled and tossed his pillow across the bedroom. The clock read four-thirty in the morning, and he hadn't slept a wink all night. The television in his bedroom played an all-night marathon of *Gun Smoke*. He'd watched all five shows, wishing his brain would turn off so he could actually get at least a minute of sleep. It never happened.

Kitt's hard-on stayed unyielding no matter what he did to relieve the tension. He'd jacked off twice and tried a third time, but nothing helped. Kitt even went to his last resort; the thing sure to bore his brain into sleep. He got up to do his accounting. The farm's bookkeeping should have done the trick and firmly knocked him out, but it didn't work because about every thirty seconds, no matter what he did, his mind strayed back to Austin Grainger.

Hands down, Austin was the hottest man on the planet. He'd been Kitt's crush since high school. It was Austin's yearbook photo and newspaper sports page snapshots, Kitt used to stroke himself off when he was just a typical hormonal adolescent boy.

Austin left town straight after high school to begin a modeling career. Those photos carried Kitt all the way through high school and into college, jacking off about every other day. He'd even learned that if he whispered Austin's name softly when he came, it made the orgasm just a little bit better in the end.

It took a couple of years, but it was Austin's first movie role that finally made Kitt admit to himself that straight dudes didn't fantasize over being with men. Well not men. *A man.*

Only one man, but it was the image of Austin Grainger in Kitt's mind that helped get him through those dark days when he first admitted to himself he truly was gay. Back then, Austin stayed etched in his brain all the time to help fight the depression, giving him hope like only a high school crush could do. Seeing him in person, he understood he'd never lost the intensity of those feelings, not even after all these years. That was probably the single greatest thought fueling his anger while they stood outside this afternoon.

Stunned beyond words, Kitt's heart seized in his chest when he saw Austin standing in front of him. Almost struck dumb by the guy's presence, he fumed when his body betrayed him. It hardened and responded to just the air Austin breathed.

How could Austin still be so good looking after all these years? He wasn't that same youthful, sunny, blond boy running around town who charmed everyone in his path. Instead, he'd grown into a gorgeous man with thick, sandy colored hair, and strong, alluring facial features. His cheekbones were high and accented a long straight nose that flared just slightly at the end. His mouth was wide and his lips – Dear God, those thick, full lips! – spread into a glorious, easy going smile.

Kitt always imagined his cock would fit perfectly inside Austin's mouth, and a groan resonated in his chest just from the thought of Austin giving him a blow job. God, he wanted that so badly! He could see Austin on his knees in front of him. His fingertips running along Austin's strong, chiseled jaw and chin, Austin's deep cobalt eyes lifting up to lock on Kitt's as he sucked him deeper inside his mouth. Austin's hair was just long enough to thread his fingers through, to grip on to and guide himself deeper down Austin's throat. Man did he want to fuck Austin's mouth…

Refusing to allow another image to conjure in his overactive brain, Kitt forced himself to think of anything else, and his eyes landed on the pile of dirty clothes. He needed to do his laundry. He rose from bed, gathered the clothes and tossed them into the washing machine. Kitt started the machine with a push of a button and leaned a hip on its side. He may not have wanted to think about Austin anymore, but he didn't seem to have a choice. His brow furrowed as he thought about Austin's movie career.

Kitt owned every single one of Austin's movies, all the magazines from his modeling days up until now and regularly jacked off to every one of them during the long, lonely spells between visits with Sean. He'd heard Austin planned to retire. How had it never occurred to him that Austin Grainger could be the person buying his land? And what the fuck would happen now?

Kitt took a chance and grabbed his phone as the time ticked closer to five in the morning. He sat with a thump on his small sofa in the living room. He began a text to Mike. They'd been friends since college. Kitt had been in the graduate program. He'd just finished his Master's degree, working on his PhD, when he first met Mike who was just starting school. Mike came up and helped him when his dad died and when Kitt fired his dad's foreman. Those were dark days. The foreman didn't go easily, but Mike stood by him the entire time. Now, Kitt stumbled on his words, typing, erasing, and typing again.

'Hey man, sorry about yesterday. I was pissed off.' Kitt finally hit send and cringed at the time.

Mike's text came back immediately. *'No worries. I knew you were and you had every right. They didn't talk it over with me first. Sorry man.'*

'No sorry necessary. I don't normally let myself get that upset anymore. I need to apologize to your ranch owner. Was I just pissed off or was that really Austin Grainger in front of me?'

'It's him. I couldn't say anything, part of my agreement. It's grounds for termination and a lawsuit. He said he grew up around here.'

Kitt laid back, propped against the back of the sofa thinking that over.

'Yeah, I went to high school with him.' Kitt didn't say anything more. It would be utter humiliation if anyone ever found his stash of photos.

'He asked me to ask you not to say anything. He doesn't want people to know he's here. Did you know him back in school?'

Kitt barked with laughter at the thought of knowing Austin. *'Not really, he's a few years older. He was out the door as I was coming in. Are we still set for the cattle coming in tomorrow?'*

'So far we are. I need to check their schedule, but the first load should be here tomorrow. If you're still willing to come? Micah's coming, he signed an agreement, but it flows better with you here.'

'Of course I'm coming! Text me and let me know the time, I'll meet the trucks there.' Kitt had offered to help unload and register three semi's full of cattle. His only saving grace, it would be true manual labor, something he couldn't see a famous movie star signing up to do.

'Thanks, man. And seriously, Grainger seemed fine. He said he understood and agreed. He remembered the Kelly temper.' Mike replied.

'I hate that. I try not to be my dad.' Kitt typed in a rare moment of honesty about his father's reputation.

'Don't worry, you aren't. I gotta go. I have a ranch hand meeting this morning at five. I need to lay down the law about your pond. Take care. I'll text you later about tomorrow.'

And, with that, Kitt technically knew nothing more than before he'd sent the first text. As he sat back resting his head on the back of the sofa, he pulled up the message he'd received around midnight from Sean and re-read it.

'Kitt, I turned away a hot little number tonight. It's a first for me, but I'm texting you to let you know how serious I am about my offer. I'm planning to head down there tomorrow night. Don't stop me. Just send me directions. As time goes on, we can plan it better. I'll rent a truck, isn't that what all you cowboys drive? Now, think about the positive side. Sex, twice in one week. How long has it been since that last happened for you?'

Kitt planned to again ignore the text, just like he had when he first read it, until he looked down at his still partially erect cock sticking up in his underwear. The underwear was Sean's gift to him last Christmas. Kitt should have been set for a few weeks after last night, but then Mr. Hollywood made his presence known this afternoon effectively ruining the sex buzz from the morning. Kitt finally texted Sean back, *'I'll send directions through email.'* It was all the enthusiasm he could muster.

Frustrated beyond words, Kitt took a too cold shower, standing under the spray until his cock finally settled down. He dressed quickly with his lips chattering and his fingertips blue, but the icy shower did the trick. Until his body warmed up again, causing his cock to spring back to life.

~~~~~~

After three of the quietest days he could remember, Austin lounged on the back porch. He'd loved every minute of the peace. He refused to check email, and only answered text messages from Cara and his agent if truly necessary. Except, he rarely found them necessary. The nights were perfect in his little slice of heaven, and even though it was early fall, the days were as hot as he remembered. The nights came on earlier every single day, and by seven in the evening, the air turned cool. The only thing that vied for his attention were the crickets and shooting stars, shining brightly in the sky. God, he loved this life.

So far, Austin hadn't found a need to turn on the brand new plasma HD television installed the day before, nor a desire to sit on any of the expensive leather furniture delivered that morning. The back porch worked perfectly for him and represented all he seemed to really need in the world. He kicked back in a lawn chair. The light breeze blew, an AM/FM radio played old country classics and he held an ice cold Corona in his hand with a small cooler sitting at his feet. If he stayed true to his most current goal, the cooler would be empty before he went back inside for the night.

From the best he could tell, Mike appeared to still be working in the barn. The guy easily worked from before sunup to way past sundown. Austin spent most of the day lending a hand to get ready for their cattle to arrive the following morning. He found he'd turned soft over the years, no matter how many hours he'd logged in the gym, or how muscularly sculpted his body looked. Apparently, all that amounted to was looking good on the screen. His body wasn't suited for any true manual labor. He already ached in places he hadn't even known could ache, and for whatever reason, he loved that too. This whole place gave him a sense of belonging. One, he found he'd completely lost along the way. Austin felt like he'd really pulled his own weight today which might be the best feeling of all.

A grin spread across Austin's lips at the thought that he might actually get a real suntan again, not one of the spray ones he'd grown accustomed to living the Hollywood lifestyle. Maybe, he'd look as hot in his real tan as his next door neighbor did in his. And just like that, much like he'd done about five hundred times over the last twenty-four hours, Austin looked out over his pasture in the direction of Kitt Kelly's house. Just like every other time, the ridge obscuring his view refused to move, but if it had, Austin would have been able to see the little log cabin out in the distance.

Kitt Kelly was a problem. He stayed firmly under Austin's skin, having never strayed too far from his mind since the moment he stormed off, refusing to look back. But, it was okay Kitt didn't turn back. Austin did enough looking and lusting for both of them. After watching Kitt swagger away, Austin came straight back to the house to text Cara one simple question. Nine simple words, *'What kind of a man wears Andrew Christian underwear?'*

He knew the answer, but wanted reassurance from a professional shopper, and his fake fiancée fit that bill. And just like he'd known it would be, the answer he got back was clear, *'Gay men with money or husbands whose wives buy them.'*

The information didn't come free. He'd then spent the rest of the night trying to convince Cara he wasn't already hooking up down here and possibly blowing their cover. Which technically was completely true, he didn't lie at all. But, he planned on changing it very soon.

Based on Cara's assumption, Kitt would be a gay man with money. If run properly, these farms could bank, but he wasn't so sure Kitt fit the mold of a prosperous rancher. If Kitt had money, he wouldn't have sold such a prime piece of land. So the next question might be, who was it that bought Kitt that expensive underwear? Perhaps a boyfriend...jealousy Austin couldn't comprehend kicked up in his heart before his competitive side kicked in. Both feelings were odd and unexplainable considering he didn't even know his new neighbor.

With one leg propped on the porch rail, Austin leaned back in his chair and thought about the past. He remembered Kitt from their school days. Not real well, but he did remember one particular time in the locker room shower. Kitt was at the end of his freshman year and Austin was about to graduate. Even remembering the scene he'd walked into had Austin feeling a little like pervert, but he remembered it clearly: Kitt Kelly was hung. Something happened to the boy during his freshman year. He transformed from skinny kid to grown ass man in a matter of months.

It was funny how some things stuck with you. That one glimpse of Kitt standing all alone under the hot spray...oh yeah, Austin looked. He wasn't going lie to himself even as wrong as it felt. He'd fantasized about Kitt for months. In his visions, Austin had him on his knees, both from the front and back. Kitt regularly starred in every possible position Austin could dream to put him in and turned out to be perfect for any gay man's wettest of wet dreams. Now, as Austin sat there on his porch, he wondered if Kitt had gotten any bigger.

His eyes darted back in the direction of Kitt's house willing the man to appear before him. He lost track of everything as he thought about how Kitt might look walking toward him right now, completely naked, that huge cock hard as steel. The thought dried his mouth and had him taking a long draw from his cold beer in an attempt to cool off his now hot and bothered body. Completely caught up in his daydreams, he didn't catch Mike's approach until he was already walking up the porch steps. The inattention was incredibly unusual for Austin. Over the last few years, he'd gotten almost paranoid about sensing when anyone tried to sneak up on him.

"Hey boss man. I just got word, all three truckloads of your cattle are arrivin' tomorrow, for sure. They're close now and gonna book it through the night. I'm guessin' the first one'll be here around eightish tomorrow mornin'," Mike said, anchoring a hip on the porch rail in front of Austin.

"Want a beer?" Austin asked, his mind solidly on Kitt. He wondered if he could lure his foreman into conversation so he could learn more about the cowboy.

"Sure," Mike said and reached for the cooler. Austin cocked his head toward the empty lawn chair next to his for Mike to sit down. "I've got the crew comin' in tomorrow. I trust everyone comin' to keep your secret. The only one who doesn't already know is Micah, but like I said, I trust him."

"That's fine. Let me know what I need to pay everyone." Austin absently stared out in the night. He finished one beer while reaching for another.

"Nah, that's not how it works around here. We all pitch in and help each other out." Mike twisted the cap off his beer as he kicked his boot up next to Austin's on the rail. He took a long drink before removing his ball cap and rubbing a hand threw his sweaty hair.

"Yeah, I remember some of that. I just haven't given anything back," Austin said just as casually as Mike did.

"But I have. They're helpin' me. I've helped them enough, now they're givin' back to me. I've got Micah, his oldest two boys, Kitt, and all your ranch hands slash security who'll be here. They're all pretty worthless though. You do know that right? We're gonna have to hire more hands now the animals are comin', but I think we got enough people for tomorrow. I can get kids from the FFA program at the high school. They'll need volunteer hours for the class. You'd have to stay hidden if they came." Mike took another long drink.

"I'll be here to help, too. You'll have to tell me what you need me to do." Austin cast a sideways glance toward Mike.

"Tomorrow won't be too hard. It's just runnin' them through. It'll be taggin' and vaccinations that'll be what takes the time. They'll be quarantined and separated for a while. Micah and Kitt can handle all that. They're bringin' their horses, a couple extra too. They'll do their part on horseback. I'm thinkin' we'll start breedin' right away. I think I told you Kitt started an artificial insemination program a few years back. I know we agreed to run the bulls and cows together for now, but we could look at something like that, too. I know Kitt's cattle is gonna sell big this year," Mike said. His hat sat crooked on his head, and he seemed just as lost to the lure of the night as Austin.

"I need to apologize to him. I still feel bad about all that over the fence. Does he run the farm by himself?" Austin didn't hesitate to take his opportunity.

"Pretty much. His step-mom and sisters live in the main house. She does all the cookin' for everybody. Has a badass garden out there she maintains just about year round. Kitt's got about ten full time hands. He's really got it goin' on over there. It's just taken a lot to get the ranch back up and movin' forward again. His dad didn't modernize."

"Yeah, I can't see old man Kelly being too modern." Austin winced remembering the hardened John Wayne kind of a guy Kitt's father had represented.

"They butted heads pretty hard, but it turned out good for Kitt, though. He tried to come home after his Bachelor's degree. It didn't last. So he went back to school," Mike said finishing off his beer. Austin quickly handed him another hoping to keep the conversation going. Hell, Austin would get Mike drunk if he had to, he was already getting way more information than he thought he would.

"You met Kitt in college?"

"Yeah, he was in the graduate program. He got a full ride, he's freakishly smart. I met him when he was a teacher's aide in one of my classes. I think he might've become a professor if his dad hadn't up and died. I was on financial aid, and Kitt found me work pretty regular during the summers. He's a good guy. You shouldn't judge him by what you saw," Mike said, and this time it was him giving a sideways glance at Austin. It seemed Mike might be trying to smooth the path between him and Kitt. Funny, it was about the same thing Austin wanted, but for far different reasons.

Austin nodded as Mike kept his eyes on him. He thought that might be better than letting Mike know his overall plan was to fuck Kitt.

"Did he marry someone down here?" Did that sound casual enough?

"Nah, he says he doesn't have time for that even though the ladies in town try real hard to change his mind. He's real focused on that ranch." Without realizing it, Mike gave Austin exactly the information he wanted.

They both stared out at the night as Kitt's choice of underwear again entered Austin's thoughts. "Do you have his number? I can't get it out of my mind that I need to apologize."

"Yeah, sure. Here." Austin typed the number Mike spouted off. "He goes to bed early, but honestly, Mr. Grainger, Kitt doesn't get mad like that often, and he doesn't hang on to it like his dad did, either. He's fine." Mike turned his full body toward Austin, hooking an arm over the back of the chair and looked directly at him.

"Good. I'd hate to have already pissed off my neighbors." Austin chuckled.

"So what're you thinkin' about all this so far?" Mike's eyes never wavered. Austin was finding Mike had a way about him of just cutting to the root of a situation, finding out what he wanted to know.

"I love it. All the silence out here rocks! I love how y'all don't treat me any different. I regret ever leaving," Austin said honestly.

"Okay, I guess I can see that. What're you gonna do when you get found out? It has to happen eventually." Mike drained his beer and shook his head when Austin offered another.

"I'm hoping enough time passes that no one really cares anymore."

"Is your wife gonna come out and live here, or is she stayin' in California? You know what? Don't answer that. It's none of my business. Mr. Grainger, I gotta roll. Tomorrow'll be here pretty quick. Good night, sir." Mike stood from his chair. Just like that the conversation was over.

"Good night, Mike, and you can call me Austin." Austin stayed seated, but gave Mike's outstretched hand a shake.

"No, I already told you, all owners go by their last name." Mike called over his shoulder already down the steps walking out to his truck.

"Then lose the Mister. Wait, I don't remember that rule!" Austin yelled out after Mike.

"It's one we're definitely enforcin' around here," Mike called without looking back before getting in his car and driving off. Austin raised his beer in answer before looking down at the phone he still held in his hand. *He had Kitt's number!* Now, all he needed was the guts to call the guy. How long had it been since Austin called someone he was interested in? He couldn't even remember, and the thought made him more nervous. What would he say when he called? A simple 'I'm sorry' wouldn't have the conversation going much longer than a few minutes.

Austin needed a second reason. He could call Kitt and ask about artificial insemination. Mike made several references to Kitt's expertise in that area, but hell, Austin seriously couldn't remember jack about that shit. He'd been out of this world for way too long, and his own dad wasn't a modern kind of a guy himself. He could ask about pasture management, but again, he knew dick about it, not even enough to form an intelligent question. He could ask Kitt to come over and lick his balls. A smile spread across his lips as he took another drink. That topic he definitely knew plenty about. After a couple of swipes of his finger across the smartphone, he got enough of a signal to pull up the key facts about artificial insemination and began to read.

Austin sat on the porch for at least an hour forming his questions in his mind. He drank his beer and listened to the oldies play on the radio. When he felt reasonably comfortable at being able to ask a couple of legit questions, he started to dial Kitt's number, but Sam rang through first.

"Yeah?" Austin said a little too gruffly. His security team was to only call with problems. So far, no reason presented itself. Of course, the exact moment he planned to make his move, the phone rang. It kind of spoiled his good mood to even be reminded they were out there.

"Sir, we have a Fisker pulling along the property line. Along the east side of the Circle K. We've been tracking it since it left the highway. It's going slow, clearly the driver's concerned about the car, but it's headed south, coming your way."

"How far down?" Austin asked dropping his feet to the stone porch as he sat up a little straighter.

"Half way down, already."

"Who's inside? Anyone we know?" Austin asked, finally standing. *Shit, how the fuck did Rich & Mercedes find this place already?*

"One person, male. We can't see anyone else in the car. He's dark headed, no one I've seen before following you, but his windows are tinted. I could be wrong."

"Okay, stay on him, and keep me posted. Stop him before he crosses the fence line. Stay with the car. Maybe we can head 'em off." Austin bent down to turn off his radio and grab his cooler.

"We are, sir. We just wanted to notify you since you're sitting outside in the open."

Just like that, he reminded Austin that he wasn't truly as alone as he thought, and didn't that just completely suck.

He disconnected the call without responding and decided not to follow through with calling Kitt. Instead, he stood in place. He stared off toward the guy's house. Did Kitt let the world know he'd relocated here? How often did a hundred thousand dollar sports car drive down a rugged path to get to Kitt's cabin?

The underwear came back to Austin's mind.

He sprang off the porch in a matter of seconds, sprinting toward the barn. He never broke stride as he entered from the side. He grabbed a pair of binoculars from the tack room and the keys to his four-wheeler and took off toward Kitt's house. He rode full throttle, eating up the distance between their houses. As he got closer, he slowed the engine, bringing it to a crawl and turned off the lights. The moonlight guided him.

Austin spied a line of fresh new trees planted along the fence. By spring, they would grow big enough to hide the fence and all of Austin's land from Kitt's sight. For some reason, the move seemed intentional and it hurt his heart. He'd been so focused on seeing Kitt again while Kitt obviously spent his time trying to block Austin from his view.

He drove the rest of the way in the dark, still worried they could hear the motor. Austin stopped at least a hundred feet out and parked the four-wheeler in the middle of the pasture. He jogged the rest of the way, staying low as he bridged the small hill before the pond. He lay down on the grassy slope, edging forward until he got a clear shot of the car parked in front of Kitt's house. The curtains were drawn, closed up tight and most of the lights were out. Only a small glow peaked through the curtains from somewhere in the back of the house.

Austin moved forward and hid behind one of the trees. He stayed there watching the house. Beside the Fisker was a truck, he supposed Kitt's, but there was no sign of anyone. He palmed his phone and texted Sam on a very weak signal.

'Are they in the cabin or did they leave?' Simple, clear and to the point.

'They're still inside.' Equally clear.

'Did you see who arrived?' Austin asked.

'One man. Kelly opened the door, let him in. That's all we got.'

'Any visual on what's going on inside the house?' It was all Austin asked when he really wanted to know how the guy was greeted, what he looked like, and did anything personal happen in the way Kitt answered the door.

'No, not from any angle.'

'Me either, sir.' Good, more than one set of eyes locked on the house.

'Can you run the plates?' The binoculars returned to Austin's eyes before the message was sent. The car was new, nice, specially made. It had to have come from Dallas, maybe Houston, but probably Dallas. They were flashy kind of people up there.

'Already on it.'

'Let me know when you find out anything.' Austin's message ended the texting session.

Surprisingly, two hours passed as Austin stayed there, binoculars trained on the house. No real movement, nothing changed inside, but he planted himself there until he got word on the driver. His gut told him Kitt wouldn't sell him out. If for no other reason than the sheer fact Austin would bury him in legal trouble deeper than anything he could dig his way out of if he so much as breathed one word to the wrong person. Their contract was iron clad tight. Certainly, the educated hot cowboy wasn't that dumb.

Austin's phone beeped, alerting him of an incoming text message. It simply read: *'The car is registered to Sean Romero. Address 211 Cedar Springs Rd, Dallas Texas. Age 35. Senior Vice President of Global Market Share, a brokerage firm. Positive ID.'* Sean's picture came through and damn it if Fisker wasn't a good looking guy. The photo looked to be from some sort of a badge, a professional shot. The guy wore a cocky grin and tailored looking suit. Austin conceded he'd be attracted to Fisker himself if they crossed paths. Could this be Kitt's boyfriend?

The next text broke his train of thought. *'The background report isn't complete, but so far we aren't tying him to surveillance or the press.'*

'No connection to those two motherfuckers who follow me everywhere?'

'Not so far.'

'Alright, nothing's going on here. I'm going back to the house. Call me if anything happens. Anything! Send whatever pictures you have in the morning. I want him recorded leaving that house.' Austin stood, but stayed low as he ran back to the four-wheeler. He drove slowly back to the barn, turning on the lights only once he'd made it about half way back. Too many years had passed since he'd been to Dallas, and he'd only lived there for a few months before moving to New York. The name Cedar Springs rang familiar with him, but he couldn't place it no matter how hard he racked his brain.

Austin parked and silently made his way back inside his house. He flipped on the lights as he went. Did he seriously have the good fortune of living next door to a hot, young gay man? It was one thing to fantasize that a pair of underwear gave some sort of clue, but did Kitt's lover really just come to his house? Austin grabbed his phone and laptop and kicked back on his brand new leather sofa and waited to hear from security.

Chapter 5

Kitt Kelly nestled between his parted thighs was a glorious sight. That golden dark head of hair bobbed up and down…damn it, but he couldn't keep his eyes off Kitt's lips. A moan escaped Austin's throat in a primal sound. He felt wild and free as Kitt sucked him. Austin finally leaned back on the sofa, all the while keeping his eyes trained on Kitt's mouth.

He ran his fingers through the silken strand of Kitt's hair and watched the gold and blond filter through his hand. Austin groaned, frantically guiding Kitt back and forth as he thrust his hips deeper into the furthest depths of Kitt's mouth and throat. Kitt couldn't seem to get enough of him. He begged for Austin's taste, deep throating him every single time.

The shrill ring of his phone jerked Austin awake. He looked down at his hands and around his living room. Kitt was nowhere around. His cock throbbed as he realized how close he'd been to coming all over himself. "Damn it!"

SportCenter still played on the television; the volume turned down low. The phone sounded off again, alerting him of an incoming text. Ignoring his dick, he picked up the phone, and with a slide of his finger, pulled up the message. It was four o'clock in the morning, and his team had just sent the surveillance information to his personal email.

His hard-on stayed firm, irritatingly jutting straight out of the athletic shorts, begging him to finish the job. Instead, he pulled the laptop off the coffee table as he rose back to a sitting position on the sofa. It only took a minute to bring up his private email and open the message Sam sent. Nothing but a slideshow of photos filled the message. There was a total of five photos. Austin didn't hesitate to open them. His body's instant reaction to the first image caused him to involuntarily thrust his hips forward. His heart lurched in his chest and his breath hitched. His cock already throbbed painfully. He grabbed it and squeezed tightly as he felt the deep need to climax right then and there.

The very first picture showed Kitt coming through the front door of his log cabin wrapping a robe around his body. The camera angled perfectly in this one shot, making it obvious Kitt wore nothing underneath the robe. Austin got a full frontal view of his perfect body, and dear Lord, the guy didn't disappoint. Kitt was hung, actually even bigger than Austin remembered.

Austin kept the photo open and moved on to the other images. In the next one, the robe wrapped fully around Kitt, with no belt, only his hand held it closed. Kitt looked to be hurrying. He carried something small in his hand. The shot was too far out to see exactly what he held. Austin opened the third photo with Kitt jogging barefoot out to the Fisker where a man was just sliding inside the car. Kitt handed the object over as the guy sat inside the car. In the next picture, the man looked to be trying to pull Kitt down by the arm. His lips puckered for a kiss, but Kitt's eyes were up and looking out. The last photo captured Kitt's lips on Fisker's. It was dark outside, and based on the time in the message, the entire scene had literally just played out only minutes ago.

An odd mix of emotion poured through Austin. It was obvious Kitt was gay. At the very least, he was bi-sexual, but for some reason Austin doubted that theory and went straight for gay. Which meant, Austin was the luckiest guy on the planet. He could eventually work Kitt into his bed. Relief hit him hard. He looked up saying a quick prayer of thanks to the big man upstairs for letting his hideaway include such a sexy, hot gay man. His eyes returned to the photo, immediately zeroing in on Fisker. Who was he? He certainly didn't look like the farmer type. The car alone didn't fit down here. He was handsome, and he and Kitt looked good together. Jealousy snaked through Austin's heart, and wasn't that just the oddest emotion ever?

Moving the photo and whatever crazy emotions went with it aside, Austin flipped back to the first image and made it full size on the screen. The image captivated him completely. It took several minutes for Austin to realize how badly he'd broken Kitt's privacy by having the photos taken. Based on Mike's conversation earlier, Kitt must clearly be hiding his sexuality. A life choice Austin knew only too well. It struck him as he stared at the screen that perhaps he and his sexy as hell neighbor were more alike than either realized. Kitt would hate to know Austin had these pictures, but at the same time, for the first time in his celebrity life, Austin understood why the paparazzi had their jobs. He finally got the draw of taking candid shots of people who interested him. For the life of him, he couldn't turn away from this photo of his neighbor in the nude.

He had no idea how much time passed before he saved the photo to his computer. Leaving it open on the screen, he picked his phone up and dialed Sam. His eyes never left the picture as his head of security answered on the first ring. "I want these pictures destroyed, ASAP. Please tell me I'm the only one who got them."

"You are, sir. They'll be destroyed now. I have all the media cards, myself."

"Good. Do you have anything more on Fisker?"

"A full background report's coming our way right now."

"Good. Text me when it comes in." Austin didn't say goodbye. Instead, he just disconnected the call, his eyes still glued to the screen. Kitt was a beautifully made man. Austin witnessed it firsthand the first day they met when he and Mike drove up on Kitt with his shirt off. But staring at the picture, he could tell the thick cord of his muscle ran from head to toe. Kitt had solid, heavily muscled thighs that led to what could very possibly be one of the best bubble butts Austin had ever seen. Kitt sported manbliques; those perfect muscles forming a V from his hips to his pelvis, pointing straight down to that mouth watering dick. And dear God, Austin wanted to track those abdominal muscles with his tongue.

Austin tugged the t-shirt over his head. While it was wrong of him to keep the photos, especially with how badly he hated having his picture secretly taken, he cast the thought aside and pushed his pants all the way down and gripped his cock. His release wouldn't take long with the images of his dream still within easy reach in his mind. Austin leaned back on the sofa and exhaled a deep breath. Already stroking himself from tip to base, his hips rolled. His heart began to pound, his breathing turned into panting and his lips parted. He never lost focus of the image on his screen. Kitt's lips were thick and full. They would fit so easily around his cock. Austin wondered if Kitt gave good head. A smile tore from his lips with the anticipation of finding out the answer. On a huff, he thrust his hips forward, driving his cock harder in his hand and dropped his head back. The t-shirt barely made it in place to capture the hot jets of his come as the orgasm exploded from him.

The sensation was perfect, and even as his head rested back on the sofa, Austin never took his eyes from Kitt's image on the laptop. He planned to have a similar moment with the man very soon. Austin was determined. And, as if to prove he could, he left the picture open, but lowered the screen and walked back to his bedroom dropping his shorts on the floor as he went. He needed to sleep, and then formulate his plan.

~~~~~~~

Without turning on the overhead lights, Kitt saddled Bullet, his six year old chestnut mustang, in the dark barn. It couldn't have been much past four-thirty in the morning, and the sun would be rising soon. In about an hour, the barn would come alive, but for now Kitt needed the aloneness of wide open spaces. He needed fresh air, and Bullet was always up for a good run. If Kitt hurried, they could make it to the furthest ridge to watch the sunrise, and he might be able to settle some of this anxiety coursing through his body.

He tugged the brow of his cowboy hat down low on his forehead as he guided Bullet out of the barn, and then out of the corral. Kitt couldn't quite put a finger on what got him so worked up. He'd had good, fulfilling sex all night long, and twice in a matter of a few days. He searched his memory, but couldn't even remember the last time that happened. He should be relaxed, sated and sleeping heavily right now. But instead, for some unexplainable reason, he was all wound up like a bow. He mounted Bullet and kicked him into a trot.

The warm up passed quickly, and soon, they were in a full out run. Both knew the way. Bullet needed no guidance from Kitt on the direction. It meant something to Kitt to have a mount who knew him so well. They rode in perfect fluid motion as the first rays of morning made their presence known.

Kitt couldn't stay gone long, but he had a full thermos of gourmet coffee with him and a ripe green apple for Bullet. He'd volunteered to help Mike out for the next couple of days as the new cattle arrived over at the Grainger Farm. Bullet, who instinctively knew how to work cattle, would be needed and the best option for the job. It wouldn't take much to keep them in line as they were run through the registration process. If Kitt timed everything right, they would leave from here and head over to the Grainger farm around six. But, for the next hour, he was free. He prayed that it was enough time to clear his mind and purge himself of all the unwanted stress coursing through him.

Kitt rode Bullet hard, pushing him into a faster run. The stallion jerked forward, running easily without pause. The rush of their breakneck speed sent a string of goose bumps up and down Kitt's arms, and his heart picked up a beat. Kitt hunkered down low talking softly to Bullet, and slowly, the anxiety from last night washed away. Kitt could ride Bullet forever. He loved this horse.

The crest of the ridge came into view as the sun broke over the horizon. Kitt eased up on the reins, cooling Bullet down for the last few hundred feet. The sky opened up, inviting the day in with deep orange and yellow glows. The first moments of the morning began the slow heal of his soul, if only for the few minutes he stayed on the small hill. Bullet came to a stop, and Kitt slid down, landing on his feet. He pulled the thermos free of the saddle bag and stroked Bullet as he let the reins go. He knew Bullet wouldn't wander far. He would be here within a minute if Kitt gave their chosen whistle. Kitt let the animal go and walked the distance to a small cluster of rocks sitting right on the edge. He took a seat and poured his coffee letting the sun soak into his skin.

For the first time since seeing Austin Grainger, Kitt's dick lay limp. He'd used Sean hard last night, fucking him until neither of them was able to stand on their feet a minute longer. His thighs ached from the exertion he'd put both of them through. Once they fell on the bed, Kitt started over again. He fucked Sean for so long it made him question Kitt, jumping to so many conclusions. And, of course, Sean had gotten it completely wrong. He assumed it meant Kitt finally committed to him. Sean dubbed their sex as lovemaking which couldn't have been any further from the truth.

The honest reality and a fact he would never tell another living soul, he maintained in his head a rolling mental image of his new neighbor all night long. He used Sean's body to fuck Austin Grainger senseless. Sean told Kitt he'd been different last night, more fierce and aggressive, and he had. The sex had been dominating and possessive. He'd topped every single time, never giving Sean's ass a break. Kitt claimed Sean, but he never had Sean in mind at any point. In his mind, he fucked Austin, every thrust, every grip, the entire night of pounding Austin consumed Kitt's every thought.

Kitt tried to set Sean straight before he left. He explained to Sean that he didn't want what they had to end, but he also didn't want the obligation of a regular thing between them. Sean refused to hear any of it. Instead, he remained convinced they'd turned a corner last night and Kitt just had cold feet. When Sean left this morning, he left his wallet on the kitchen counter. When Kitt ran it out to him, Sean uttered those three little words to Kitt before the small kiss they shared at his car. It baffled Kitt. How in the world did things go from a random monthly fuck to a declared 'I love you' relationship in just seventy-two hours?

The thought caused Kitt to grimace and he rubbed a hand roughly across his face. He'd have to break it off with Sean. It needed to end, but God, Kitt hated the thought of losing Sean right now. They were past the getting to know one another's preferences phase. He'd broken Sean in to what he liked and vice versa. He couldn't understand how love had made its way into their deal? Kitt didn't love Sean, Sean didn't love Kitt. They fucked, nothing more. Why couldn't they just keep going like they were for the next thirty years without putting all the emotion and labels on it?

"Damn it!" Kitt muttered as he did the math in his mind. Sean represented the last remnants of his carefree college days. Pushing up the brim of his cowboy hat, Kitt leaned back and took a long drink of the hot coffee, letting it burn its way down his throat. None of it really mattered. Sean would have to go. At least until he got some perspective. And, Kitt needed to focus on finding another fuck buddy, soon.

It sure looked like Austin Grainger planned to put down roots which meant his future wife would be here at some point. If Kitt didn't find someone to fuck, he'd be walking around town with a rock hard cock targeted at a straight, married man. "Damn it!"

Bullet snuck up on him and nudged Kitt in the shoulder, startling him. It said something that Kitt was so lost in thought the horse was able to do that to him. The sun hovered in full view over the ridge. Kitt had missed that happening too. "What? Want your apple?"

Kitt dug in his pack, and grabbed the apple. Bullet greedily ate it while staying close to Kitt. He nudged Kitt again wanting to be petted. Kitt obliged running his hands down the stallion's silky coat. "What am I gonna do, Bullet? Where do I even start to find someone new?"

Bullet gave a snort shaking his head, moving further down in the touch. "I think that was a very distinctive 'Buck the fuck up. Get out of your own head, and take care of business.' Got it! And I agree. As usual, you're right, boy."

Kitt gathered his coffee and tucked it back in the saddle bag before mounting Bullet again to make their way to the Grainger farm. It was simple. He needed to work hard. Work so hard he couldn't think of anything else, and deal with Sean before the weekend because there would be no more use of the "L" word anywhere in his near future. After that, he'd start looking for someone else to fuck. Okay. Kitt admitted it wasn't a brilliant plan, but it would work. And, that's all he needed. Well, that, and maybe a haircut.

Chapter 6

Austin woke with a smile on his face, his body relaxed and his dreams the sweetest he could remember in a while. They all starred his sexy next door neighbor. How in the world did Austin get lucky enough to find his hiding place right next door to a beautiful gay man? Life was so looking up! When he'd made the final decision to move here, he knew his sex life would take a hit. He wasn't quite sure what he might do to work it out other than long dry spells and lots of jacking off while he tried to find someone to screw.

Now, all that was taken care of. He just needed a solid game plan to woo said hot neighbor to his bed. The thought caused him to stir fully awake with the image from last night's email at the top of his mind. He played out different scenarios, over and over, to fit that exact image, but they all included him and not the Fisker guy on the receiving end.

He naturally saw himself as the bottom in his and Kitt's relationship. Austin viewed himself that way, and any time he found a more than one-time sex partner, he chose to bottom. Austin wasn't really the hard, angry man most of the world saw. That image was the result of the extreme celebrity world he'd lived in. When he found a regular sex partner, Austin turned more pleasing, and he often wondered if that was what might happen in a true relationship. He wanted his sex partner happy. He found he gifted a lot. He had fun in their time together. He laughed, even became giddy and talkative. Austin encouraged his partner to always be the dominant one, letting him take a step back and be cared for. It was such a role reversal for him it took most guys a minute to catch up.

He hoped Kitt liked to top, to take charge, but Austin didn't even try to lie to himself. He found he desperately wanted to be buried deep inside Kitt's tight ass on the first go of things. To make that happen, he knew he'd have to work for it. It wouldn't come easy, and everything always came easy for Austin.

Austin flipped on the shower, brushed his teeth and stepped under the spray. He closed his eyes still fantasizing about Kitt seductively peeling off that robe of his in his bedroom. Austin imagined it floating to the floor as Kitt climbed on top of him, sliding straight down on top of his hard swollen cock. Kitt would ride him using those powerful thighs to fuck Austin. The image so perfect in his mind, he could envision Kitt's oversized rigid cock bouncing and slapping against Austin's stomach as he moved up and down on him, faster and harder.

Again, for a second time in only a matter of a few hours, Austin reached low and stroked himself to the same rhythm he imagined Kitt to so boldly perform on his body. God, the image was incredible, and made Austin buck his hips. He envisioned taking Kitt's cock in his hand, stroking him as Kitt continued the bareback assault on his hardened arousal. Austin slapped a hand against the wet tile to brace himself. He aimed for the drain as he came. The warm water ran freely down his head, pooling at his chin as he watched wave after wave of his release wash away. He closed his eyes for several minutes etching this particular fantasy deep inside his brain, wanting to be able to pull it up again when needed. Damn, if Kitt proved half as hot as his fantasies and dreams made him, Austin would never get bored with him.

The prospect of a condomless fuck intrigued Austin. He couldn't remember the last time he'd had sex without a condom and doubted it would happen anytime soon. Maybe if he could pursue Kitt and get some sort of exclusive agreement out of him, possibly a few months from now, it could become a reality. Austin shook his head and forced himself to take a mental step back at the thought of Mr. Tall, Dark and Fisker kissing Kitt before he drove away. The wooing process might take Austin longer than he liked. But whatever, the fantasy could hold him over until he got what he wanted.

'Slow it down, buddy. You have to get him away from Casanova and in your bed before you ever get to exclusive years of fucking together.' Austin's alarm went off at the same time he stepped from the shower, telling him it was seven in the morning. The cattle were due to arrive anywhere from eight to nine, and he wanted to be out there ready to experience it all. He knew Mike wouldn't come get him, even though Austin had made it clear he wanted in. He was still considered the citified boss. He hoped to change their opinion about

his ranching potential. He certainly owned the aching muscles to prove he'd worked hard over the last few days.

Austin quickly shaved and dressed in the standard for the area - boots, jeans and an old T-shirt – before he made his way through the house. Whooping and hollering sounded from outside. Austin ducked his head through the curtain to see a large semi-truck with a double-decker cattle trailer being unloaded in one of the temporary corrals they'd built the day before. Mike, all his security guys, Kitt, and a few others on horseback worked the cattle off the back of the trailer and toward the barn.

"Damn it!" The cattle trucks got in early, and he hadn't heard them arrive. Frustrated with himself for not having judged the situation better, he stalked through the house, out the back door, down the porch steps, and never broke stride until he got to the barn.

"When did they get here?" Austin aggressively called out to one his security guys.

"About an hour ago. The other two trucks are close by," the guard called back while waving his arms over his head, but the heifer he tried to corral zipped past him completely unconcerned with the crazy man in front of her.

"Damn it! I wanted to be out here," Austin muttered grabbing his leather work gloves from the tack room inside the barn. He judged the situation trying to decide where best he should jump in. His security team seemed completely useless. None of them had ever been in this kind of environment. As much as they rocked at keeping him safe, they sucked as cow hands. They did as much standing around as helping out. A guy on horseback rode up beside him.

"They got here earlier than we thought. Kitt and Mike were workin' them off when I pulled up forty-five minutes ago. I'm Micah, from the farm on the other side of the highway." The rider extended his hand, never batting an eye as he introduced himself to Austin. Micah looked to be in his mid-thirties, healthy, tanned and already sweaty. A red bandana hung around his neck, his ball cap was pulled down on his head, and his shirt was hanging wet on his back. He didn't look like anyone Austin remembered from his school days.

"I'm Austin." He took the offered hand and shook it.

"Nice to finally meet you. My two boys are here, too. Rusty's over there on the horse, and Brent's workin' with Kitt. They're fifteen and sixteen. We all signed that paper Mike asked us to. Your secret's safe with us. Let any of us know if you need anything."

"Where do you need me right now?" Austin called out.

"Mike's movin' them into the barn. They're gonna start processin' and taggin' 'em now. You can come with me. I'm gonna take over the unloadin'. The second truck just pulled on the property from the highway. It'll be here in ten minutes. You any good on horseback yet?" Micah asked, giving Austin an appraising look.

"It's been a while, but I've been picking it back up."

"Good. Mike has a mount ready for you. She's tied up over there. Come on." Micah pointed to a horse loosely tied to a fence post and rode off toward the gate to wait for the truck.

A hard day filled with backbreaking manual labor kicked off. They unloaded both trailers, and Austin managed to do his job reasonably well. Only a couple of head of cattle got past him, but he was able to draw them back to the herd without any help. Rusty kept them rounded up, pushing them to the different corrals Mike designated. Austin was hot, sweaty, and his ass hurt from the saddle, but he kept going all day long.

Mike and Kitt worked the cattle through the stalls like a well-oiled machine. They didn't mess around with any of it. They moved hundreds of heads through, tagging, indexing and vaccinating each of them. They kept them separated, but together, based on Mike's overall plan. If Austin remembered correctly, the herd needed to be quarantined per State of Texas' regulations before they could be put out to pasture.

They worked solidly from sunup to sundown. By nightfall, two thirds of the cattle were processed, fed and grazing in a front pasture. Austin's security guards gave out hours ago, but Mike, Kitt, Micah and his boys worked the entire time. They never stopped for anything, and didn't even seem overly tired at the end of the day. Austin used every acting skill he possessed to pull himself off his horse without wincing as every muscle screamed under the strain of just getting off the animal.

"Boys, it's gettin' dark out here. I have dinner ready at the house," Kitt's stepmom said stepping inside the barn. Occupied with his chores, Austin never heard her until she spoke. Mrs. Kelly was young, not much older than Austin, and strikingly pretty with her long dark hair, deep brown eyes and olive complexion.

"Good evenin', Mrs. Kelly. Heather's got dinner waitin'," Micah called out.

"Mrs. Kelly, I'm in." One of the security guards said from his spot on a hay bale where he'd been most of the evening.

"Me, too!" Another yelled.

"Kitt, any of these guys staying with us tonight? Do I need to get some rooms ready?" Mrs. Kelly asked her stepson.

"No ma'am. Mike's got it all taken care of." Kitt quickly pulled his work gloves free of his hands. He used the short arm of his t-shirt to wipe the sweat from his brow.

"You sure, Mike, they can stay at the house if you need."

"Nah, we got it," Mike said with a grin on his face. It was clear the whole team knew each other well, and Austin stood back watching the familiar camaraderie they shared. They were all good friends. He missed having real friends.

"And I suppose this is our new neighbor." Mrs. Kelly finally turned her attention over to Austin.

"I'm Austin." He nodded, walking up to her with his hand stuck out. It felt wrong to try and dodge her, and since she was a Kelly, he figured it was possible she might be bound by the terms of the land sale contract.

"I know who you are. Surely, the old biddies of this town haven't missed this." She grinned at Austin.

"It's on the DL, Lily. No one knows. It's that part in the contract we all thought was so dumb. You can't tell anyone," Kitt said. It was the first time he made any sort of reference to Austin being anywhere on the property all day long. Up until that moment, Kitt never acknowledged him. Hell, Kitt never even looked Austin's way, not one single time. Still hadn't. He spoke as he wrote on the clipboard in his hands.

"So, I can't say anything either. Well dang! I never get to have the news first at church on Sunday!" Mrs. Kelly said, and they all chuckled at her fake chagrin.

"Are you comin' to dinner, Mr. Grainger?" she asked over her shoulder while turning back to the barn's front doors.

"Please call me Austin, and I don't want to intrude. I can get something here."

"You aren't. I'll see you all in fifteen minutes."

With that, she was gone.

"I can get something to eat here, I don't want to put her out." Austin turned to Mike, and then Kitt. His muscles ached and throbbed; the idea of doing anything more than having a long hot soak and hours of sleep didn't appeal to him at all.

"Nah, she cooks for us all the time. She likes to feed us. It's really okay. You should come," Mike said. Kitt resumed ignoring him as he worked something on his clipboard.

A few minutes later, Micah and his boys took off. Mike and Austin checked all the gates, and shut everything down, making sure they were locked up tight. By the time they were done, Kitt was already riding off toward his house. Austin watched him and realized the only benefit of going to dinner at the Kelly ranch just rode off in the opposite direction without a backward glance.

"You wanna ride?" Austin asked Mike, finally giving in to the catch he felt in his leg. He moved with a distinct limp as the cramp took hold.

"Sure. You did real good today." Mike switched direction from his pick-up to Austin's brand new Silverado. It arrived today, driven by one of his hidden security guards who sure didn't stick around to lend a hand.

"I don't know. I let a couple get through. You guys have it all down, nothing gets past you," Austin said, climbing in the driver's side. He gave a solid wince as he sat in the seat. His back muscles spasmed, and he felt like such a pansy about it all.

"It's not the first time we've done somethin' like this." Mike easily climbed in and slammed the door closed several seconds before Austin even reached out to close his. It amazed him how hard these guys worked every single day.

"I guess not, but Rusty and Brent...wow. Micah has to be proud."

"Yeah, they're a good family, great kids. They have seven of them. Four girls, three boys. Those girls give Micah a run." Mike explained before letting out a yawn. "I'm tired."

"Tired? Thank God! I was beginning to think I must seriously be a lightweight. Every muscle in my body's on fire." Austin grimaced and tried to position himself so that all his body weight didn't lie on the parts that ached the most. He winced, not succeeding in his attempts, and Mike chuckled.

"Yeah, you never get used to it. My body's sore too. It's just a part of it. Besides, it's what you pay me to do. I never expected you out there all day today." Mike gave Austin a sideway glance.

"I loved it. It's been forever since I put in a hard day's work. It grounds you. Everyone should have to do this kind of thing in their life." Austin let his own yawn free.

It took them about ten minutes to get to Kitt's stepmom's house. It was called the main house, and it sat right off the road. The driveway was already full of cars, and as Austin pulled to the back of the drive, he saw a large patio filled with picnic tables. His men were already there, helping themselves to food, and Mrs. Kelly hovered over everyone, making sure they had everything they needed. Austin followed Mike up to the house.

"Kitt's got two sisters. One's away at college, the other's seventeen. Let me make sure she isn't here," Mike said at the bottom of the step before heading up to the porch. He was back a minute later. "Mrs. Kelly sent her to her room, come in."

"I don't want her to have to stay in her room." Austin immediately tried to retreat.

"No, trust me, she wants to stay in her room. I make her come out and socialize, but she absolutely doesn't want to," Mrs. Kelly said from behind Mike. "Come on in and fix your plate."

It took him a minute to comply. He hated the idea of the girl being sent to her room, but abandoned all thought of it as he spotted the large pot of homemade spaghetti, green beans and garlic Texas toast. The food looked delicious and smelled exquisite. She'd made enough to feed a small army.

"Thank you for all this. I need to pay you for feeding all my men," Austin said, standing at the back door taking it all in.

"No, absolutely not! I know what it's like to get to a new place, get everything set up. Mike and I planned this." She shook her head at him as she began to dish out loads of pasta and sauce.

"It looks incredible." Austin watched as she piled on the green beans and several pieces of thick, buttered toast. Austin took his full plate from her and followed Mike back out on the porch. They took seats out of the direct light on the porch. A nice breeze blew and electric bug zappers hung in every corner. He was given a beer, but wasn't treated any differently than anyone else. Mrs. Kelly monitored everyone, making sure plates and glasses stayed full. This whole world of blending in, just being another hand, was extraordinary. It allowed

Austin the opportunity to sit back and relax. He ate a quiet meal without being the center of attention and on all the time.

A four-wheeler appeared from the dark, its headlights getting brighter the closer it came to the main house. Austin made out Kitt when it was a few hundred feet away. He watched Kitt drive all the way up, and kept on watching even as he parked and walked up the porch. Kitt had showered and wore cargo walking shorts, flip flops and a t-shirt. His hair was windblown dry and slightly disarrayed, and for the first time since Austin laid eyes on Kitt, he looked young and easy going, not the hardened cowboy Austin had grown accustomed to. He liked this side of Kitt. Hell, he liked *all sides* of Kitt.

"Kitt! Mom won't let me get my belly button pierced!" A voice bellowed from above their heads. "Talk to her! Tell her everyone's doin' it."

Kitt took a couple of steps back down off the porch and looked up. "Bryanne, you know I'm not gonna do that. Get your head back in that window and do your homework."

"Gawd, Kitt! You act like you're ninety!" The window slammed shut and it took a second, but everyone chuckled at the exchange.

Kitt resumed walking up the steps, brought his head back down and his gaze landed on Austin as a smile spread across his lips. The sight caused Austin to stop his fork midway to his mouth and just stare. Kitt's firm square jaw and strong chin all eased when those full lips smiled, and that was definitely another first.

"Smells good," Kitt muttered coming to stand in front of his stepmother. He gave her a light kiss on the cheek as she met him at the back door with a plate full of food.

"I made you a plate, but don't get used to it, young man!" She teased with a wink.

"Never! And you didn't have to do that, but thank you." He took the plate and utensils she offered. Kitt pivoted on his heel looking around. He spotted Mike and began to walk toward their table. His eyes collided again with Austin's, and at the last minute, he took a seat at another table with his back to Austin.

"Mike, you want seconds?" Mrs. Kelly asked with the pot in her hand, already scooping seconds on his plate before he could answer.

"Yes ma'am! I love your homemade spaghetti." He smiled and dug straight in.

"Mr. Grainger?" She didn't just automatically fill his plate but paused, waiting for him to answer.

"Please call me Austin, and I think I'm done. I haven't worked this hard in years." Austin patted his belly. Funny, since Kitt walked up, all the aches and pains in his body seemed to have magically disappeared.

"How about another beer?" She offered.

"I'll get it." He rose from his seat, and just like that, the magic disappeared. A pain filled groan escaped his lips, and they all laughed. He even got a sideways glance from Kitt, showing him that beautiful smile again.

Austin sidestepped Mrs. Kelly, determined to get another look at Kitt. He grabbed a beer for himself, one for Mike, and then one for Kitt. He walked the long way around the tables to stand right in front of Kitt as he walked by, and handed him the beer. He could tell the offering caught Kitt off guard. He looked up startled, taking the can. There was a pause when their eyes connected. Kitt finally gave him a nod seemingly unable to break the eye contact. Austin held it as long as he could; until he was forced to avert his gaze when the image of Kitt nude popped into his head. Austin got warm all over and his dick stirred a little, hardening as he walked back to his side of the table.

"Mr. Grainger, how is it that no one knows you're here?" Mrs. Kelly asked. Most of the guys were done eating, and she doled out pieces of homemade chocolate pie. No one turned it away.

"I honestly don't know how I pulled it off. I bought land in Montana in my name and bought this place in the name of a company I own together with my family. I'm guessing they just haven't figured it out yet," Austin said, taking a big bite of his pie, moaning as the delicious dessert hit his taste buds.

"You're still a hot topic on the news. Everyone wants to know where you went," Mrs. Kelly said easily, finally taking a seat at Kitt's empty table.

"Still?" Austin asked between bites.

"Oh yeah," Mike confirmed before Mrs. Kelly could.

"Huh. I'm not that interesting. They think I'm something I'm not. They just don't know me."

"Is Cara comin' here?" Mrs. Kelly's next question came out of the blue, and it took Austin a minute. He weighed his answer as he feigned he had his mouth full. He was so sick of lying. These people were

61

good to him. On a whim, he decided honesty might be the best bet, at least there would be less to apologize for later.

"Probably not." He left it right there, not acknowledging the silence the answer brought.

"How're you likin' it here?" Austin could have told Lily he loved her for how graciously she changed the subject.

"Ah, now *that* I have a ready answer for. I love it here. It's great! I love the solitude, the quiet. Everyone I've met has been great. Mike's got all my muscles sore, working me hard, getting me back in shape. I really like it," Austin said easily, taking the last bite of pie.

"Mike, you shouldn't work him so hard." Mrs. Kelly scolded his foreman.

"Mrs. Kelly, poor people gotta work for a livin'," Mike replied with his mouth full of pie, making everyone laugh. All of Austin's crew on the back porch turned toward them, listening to the conversation. After Kitt polished off his plate, he got up and grabbed all the pie plates around him as he walked back into the kitchen.

"Kitt, I'll get 'em."

"No, sit. I need to wash my hands anyway. I'll just put them on the counter," Kitt said, and she let him do it. He grabbed a couple more plates as he made his way inside. Austin didn't hesitate. He grabbed his and Mike's plates. Mrs. Kelly tried to stop him.

"No Ma'am, I need to go to the bathroom." Could he have sounded more lame had he tried? But, there was no way he wanted to miss this moment alone with Kitt. The way things had worked today, it might not ever happen again.

Austin pulled open the screen door and walked inside, shutting the sliding glass door behind him. He saw Kitt at the sink, rinsing the food off the plates as he stacked them to the side.

"Don't tell me to stop. I see your leg's hurtin' you. It won't take me but a minute," Kitt said never looking back at Austin.

"I thought I was doing a better job at hiding all these aches and pains, but trust me, it's more than just my legs that hurt." Austin laughed softly and Kitt jerked around. The plate slid from his hands and hit the sink with a soapy thump.

"Kitt, I just wanted to apologize for the other day. I haven't had a chance, yet." Austin walked up to him. Kitt turned back to the sink and picked the plate back up, rinsed it and turned back to Austin almost immediately. The look on Kitt's face was clear: he had no idea what Austin was talking about.

"With my men at the pond," Austin explained. The nice view of Kitt's ass ensured Austin stayed behind him as he spoke. Something about this man doing the dishes for his stepmom seemed incredibly sweet and still totally hot at the same time.

"I should be apologizin' to you. I don't usually lose it like that. They just weren't takin' no for an answer," Kitt said, finishing the plate. He grabbed a hand towel, but didn't turn around. He just kept looking down at the sink.

Austin took the chance to slide in behind Kitt, placing the dirty plates he carried in the sink. Kitt jerked forward, but the sink was in his way. He sidestepped Austin, immediately moving away from him as quickly as possible. His movements were jerky and rushed, making Austin smile. Maybe, Kitt wasn't quite as unaffected as he pretended to be.

"Should I wash these?" Austin very casually asked, keeping his eyes on Kitt.

"No, I'll do it," Kitt said and clearly waited for Austin to move.

"I can do it," Austin said finally looking down at the sink. He couldn't remember the last time he'd washed a dish. Even now, a cleaning lady came in every morning to go over his house. Regardless, it didn't seem too complicated. Soapy water on one side, clean water on the other. He began to wash his and Mike's plates. "My men are paid to be protective of me, and I'm sorry it got out of hand. I talked to them, told them to stay off your property. I've been known to be a bit of a hard ass in my former life, they thought they were just following my orders."

Kitt stayed silent. Austin glanced at him from the corner of his eye and drew out washing the second plate.

"Thanks for all the help today. You pretty much run the show whenever you're around. The men here really respect you," Austin said, putting the second plate in the drying rack. He looked around for a hand towel, and Kitt handed him the one he folded and unfolded in his hands.

"We all respect one another. It's the way things work around here," Kitt finally replied after a moment's silence. Austin looked up to see his cheeks were stained with a blush, the sight catching him off guard. It took a second, but Austin realized he had to be responsible for the blush. His heart warmed with the knowledge he unnerved Kitt just as much as Kitt unnerved him. Everything inside Austin softened just a bit. He liked Kitt. This whole time he'd only thought of him as a sex toy, but in this moment, he knew there was more to it than he'd realized.

"You two! Kitt Kelly! I knew you were in here doin' the dishes. And, Austin Grainger doin' dishes in my house, no, absolutely not! You two, go. Everyone's tryin' to leave anyway. Early day tomorrow." Mrs. Kelly grabbed the towel from Austin's hand and shooed them toward the door.

"Thank you for dinner, Mrs. Kelly." Austin chuckled at the look on her face.

"I'm Lily and you're Austin and you're welcome," she said with a smile, standing in the door once they were back outside. "You're welcome here for dinner anytime."

"Thanks, Mom." Kitt said. He was back to himself and again completely ignoring Austin as if none of their conversation had just happened. Kitt turned back, but only to give Lily a wink before he took the first step down. Austin wasn't sure Lily was all that much older than Kitt. But, they seemed to like each other and it was clear Lily mothered Kitt.

Austin found Mike standing at the railing of the porch waiting for him. Kitt got a knuckle bump from him as he went by.

"Good night, everyone. Kitt, stop by for coffee in the mornin', it'll be ready." Lily waved at them all before shutting the door.

"She's lonely," Mike said following Kitt down the stairs.

Kitt turned toward his four-wheeler and climbed on. "I know. Good night, see you in the mornin'." He started the machine giving it gas as the engine fired to life.

"Good night," Austin said quietly as he took the steps down a little slower. He watched as Kitt never looked back at him. His heart lingered in that moment with the bright red cheeks. Kitt certainly couldn't hear Austin. He was already backed out and barreling away. "See you in the morning."

Chapter 7

How many sheep did a guy need to count to get his brain to stop and allow him to get some shut eye? Kitt never had a problem sleeping. He never struggled. He fell into bed every night, closed his eyes and sleep came. But, in the last three nights, he'd only logged a handful of hours in. The problem stemmed from the fact most of his thoughts stayed fully focused on Austin which apparently translated to a stout case of insomnia.

After three full days of seeing Austin every single day, it wasn't even so much a sexual thing anymore. Okay, completely not true, and Kitt rolled his eyes at the thought. It totally was a sexual thing, but that's not what kept him up night after night.

Tonight, his mind stayed focused on how hard Austin Grainger actually worked. It was hard work, and they kept a grueling, back breaking pace. They let nothing get in their way. Kitt, Mike and Micah had worked like this together for years. They had it all down to a routine and knew each other well, but still Austin managed to fit in working side by side with them without problem. He instinctively fell in sync with their team.

Kitt knew the guy's muscles had to ache. No way could Austin be used to putting in this much physical labor, but he never complained. Nor did he stop, and he never showed any sign of fatigue. Instead, Austin worked hard. On that first day, he'd been pretty rusty, but picked it all back up quickly. He'd even jumped on a stallion, handling him like a pro. Kitt finally let himself admit Austin looked hot as hell as he rode that horse. Austin had never done a Western in any of the movies he starred in. In Kitt's mind, he'd missed his calling. Austin looked like a natural up on a horse. Rugged, manly, strong…

After the day's work was done, Austin sat on his stepmom's back porch like he truly was one of the guys. He acted like it was the most natural thing in the world to have a three time Academy Award winner eating homemade spaghetti at his parent's house.

The only repeat Kitt ensured didn't happen was getting stuck together with Austin in his stepmom's kitchen. Kitt's body had hardened to painful degrees when Austin slipped in behind him at the sink. It was a natural move, normal, and one he himself had done a hundred times. Just sliding your plate in the sink to help the washer out, but his body freaked. His heart plunged, his breathing turned into a pant and he had to get away. And then, Austin turned into a normal decent guy, apologizing and even complimenting him in the process.

What person in this world was on Austin's level in life, yet kind enough to make sure the two of them were on good standing after the brawl over the fence? All those kind words about respect made Kitt blush like a little girl.

Kitt hadn't been able to get out of that kitchen fast enough. He tried to stay the cool guy, feigning easy going and unaffected, but when his stepmother opened that door, he'd wanted to holler 'Hallelujah!' and kiss her right on the lips in appreciation for giving him an out. After that incident, Kitt made absolute certain he was never left alone with Austin again. If there was even the slightest hint of that happening, Kitt bailed on whatever task he worked and assigned it to another.

It wasn't easy. No matter how much distance he put between them, the connection between them sizzled, at least for Kitt. He needed to stay away from the Grainger farm. Mike would just have to understand. Damn! Mike complicated the whole deal. He'd been so pumped when he landed that job. Kitt had promised Mike he'd help in whatever he needed, and he knew Mike wanted the Grainger farm to get involved in the investment group Kitt started to fund his new ponies about to birth. Breeding quality race horses was too exciting an opportunity not to pass on to the few of them interested. Kitt didn't see how he could let Austin Grainger in. He'd have to figure something out for Mike. Figure out a way to explain it to him, get him to understand. But what could he really say? Nothing would make sense and the investment group needed the capital to keep breeding their horses.

"Damn it," Kitt muttered in frustration and finally rose from bed. It was way too early to get up, only three in the morning. But, he got up anyway and started on his day. He wasn't scheduled to go back over to the Grainger farm until later and that was to check a couple of head of cattle for some possible respiratory issues. If anything else came up, he'd send Jose, his foreman over in his place. Kitt desperately needed distance. To help him find perspective, he decided to take Sean up on his offer. Even thinking it caused his heart to drop, but his head knew it was the right decision. Kitt had to use his head. He needed time to get comfortable with Austin living next door. Surely, something regular and faithful would help Kitt get past this unhealthy consumption.

For God's sake, Austin was a straight man engaged to be married! Jealousy spiked up in Kitt at the thought even though he knew possessiveness had no place searing through him. So yeah, Sean as his boyfriend, sex twice a week…it wasn't the hell he'd thought just two days ago. It's what he needed to get his mind back focused right, but he'd have conditions. Sean would have to stop with the 'I love yous'. That was the deal breaker. Maybe.

Besides, being away from here once a week could help get Austin out of his system. And, the other night, Sean offered to invest in his breeding program as a silent partner. He needed the money. If the hay baling didn't pan out like Kitt hoped, the extra cash would help and buyers weren't jumping in to buy his hay as easily as he thought they might. Maybe, Sean had a point. Now that they were a couple, weren't they supposed to do things like share with one another? The bigger question though, why did the weight of thinking they were a couple settle so heavily on his shoulders?

~~~~~~~

Sweat trickled down the side of Austin's face as he loaded the last heifer in the chute. Tugging his t-shirt up and over his head, he wiped the wet cotton over his dust streaked face. Austin, Mike and a few of his security guards were the only ones on the job today, and they'd done it. Job complete. All the animals were tagged, vaccinated, fed, sectioned off and quarantined. He didn't know what anyone else thought, but he considered this a job well fucking done.

"Good job, boss man." Mike came to stand on the other side of the stall. He took off his work gloves and anchored an arm on the rail.

"Fuck I'm tired." Austin slapped the heifer out of the rack. She took off, not needing to be urged twice.

"Yeah, it's a hard day's work out here," Mike said. He didn't seem to be in a hurry now that they'd finally gotten everything done. Austin longed for a shower and some food, but he mimicked Mike's stance and leaned on the rail. If the guy wanted to talk a minute, he guessed he could do likewise.

"Thanks for arranging the meals. I'll do better next time."

"Nah, it's my job to arrange all that. As we grow, I'll start lookin' for a regular cook, but until then, the place in town caters the meals. Mrs. Kelly likes to do it, too. I gave her some money," Mike explained.

"Good. Is it still called the Horseshoe Café?" Austin asked.

"Yeah, they did this meal for us today," Mike said.

"Everybody still go there on Friday night for supper?" Austin asked, searching for conversation now. He wasn't completely sure why Mike still stood there so he straightened, working his aching muscle out.

"Yeah, but it's got a pool hall and dance joint added on to it. The Baptist church doesn't like it at all, but it gives everyone a place to gather and somethin' for the church folk to talk about," Mike said grinning.

If Mike planned to continue the conversation, it would have to be while heading out the door. Austin was done for the day. "Maybe someday I'll check that out."

"You need to. The local girls'll go crazy." Mike followed him out.

"Yeah, that's what I'm afraid of. I'm digging this quiet thing. Your buddies didn't treat me any different," Austin said, pushing open the barn door. The bright sun hit him, and he squinted under its glare.

"Nah, they're salt of the earth kind of people. Work too hard to get lost in the glitz. Listen, I've got plans in town tonight. Your hands are gonna be on the watch for the cattle, but it should all be fine. We'll stay like this for a few days, make sure the herds healthy, give the State time to come out if they want."

"You handle that part," Austin said, and again stretched his body out. "Have fun tonight. I'm going in."

"Will do. Good job, again," Mike said.

"You too. Thanks Mike," Austin tossed the words kind of over his shoulder never fully looking back. He feared that if he didn't concentrate on moving each sore leg in front of the other, he might not make it all the way to his house. How embarrassing would it be to collapse in the middle of the yard in front of Mike and have to have him carry him inside?

Once he made it up to his back porch, Austin felt like congratulating himself. If anyone knew how sore he really was, he'd die. The back porch entry led him straight into his living room and kitchen area. The big windows spread all along the back part of the house were outfitted with remote controlled planter blinds. Just a touch of a button closed them all quickly, but since they had been installed, Austin kept them pulled up, leaving the windows completely open. It gave him such a sense of peace and normalcy to be able to look out and see nothing but wide open flat lands.

Austin couldn't wait to get out of the sweaty, dirty clothes he'd worn all day. He tracked a small trail of dirt across his marble floor as he made his way to his bathroom. He peeled off his jeans and dropped his underwear, kicking both aside once he hit his bedroom door. The t-shirt made it close to the hamper in the bathroom.

Austin had let the decorators come in and finish the house over the last two days. He'd stayed discreetly hidden, tucked away in the barn. He'd also scheduled the local grocery store to deliver once a week. They left his order at Mike's trailer every Friday. His Spanish, non-English speaking, senior citizen housekeeper apparently had one of his hands bring it down to the house. Mike hired the housekeeper before Austin ever arrived, swearing she had no clue as to his identity and would absolutely keep things quiet. She turned out to be one of Mike's aunts and did a fantastic job. She even cooked for him a little. Spicy hot, jalapeno filled foods, but extremely delicious nonetheless, He was grateful for it.

Austin padded across the floor of his bathroom in nothing more than an exhausted smile. He didn't touch anything, knowing a fine layer of dirt coated his skin. The shower was hot and he let the pounding of the water spray down across shoulders and back. He rolled his thick muscles under the spray trying to loosen them. By tomorrow, the aches would be at an all-time high. He ran his hand over his stomach, feeling each defined abdominal muscle and could tell he'd already slimmed up. For years, he'd worked out daily to maintain the bulk and sixpack stomach. Closer to his retirement, he'd let the strict workout regime go a bit and had put on a few pounds. But, the real work he now performed would slim him right back up quick, trim him out, and it looked to already be happening.

Austin stepped out of the shower and took a minute to shave, brush his teeth and pluck a stray hair or two. As he stood there looking in the mirror, combing his sandy blond hair in place, he again thought about Kitt. Austin had watched the sway of his ass as he came by the barn today to check his cattle for infection. Kitt never came inside the barn, staying outside the whole time, but it was a perfect angle for Austin to watch him out of a window. Kitt bent over checking the animals, as if inviting Austin to take a good long look at his ass. And, he did. Kitt so had that perfect cowboy swagger thing going on. He wore it well and pulled it off so naturally it was like he invented it himself.

Even when Kitt had worn those casual khaki cargo shorts, a loose fitting t-shirt and flip flops, he couldn't hide that cowboy strut. He carried his long, lean body with confidence and ease. Austin had witnessed his temper first hand, but he also knew it wasn't who Kitt was as a man. As a man, he was smart, articulate when necessary, and other times he was quiet. He never forced himself on anyone. He was a natural born leader. Austin wasn't sure Kitt knew that about himself based on the blush that rose on his face when Austin had mentioned it in the kitchen.

From spending time with Kitt and the others Austin learned Kitt usually came to the answer first in the group, but he always let the others settle into it before pushing forward with the plan. There was no doubt Kitt was the boss out there. The one the others looked up to, and the one Austin desperately wanted be buried deep inside.

That thought lead Austin to another: he prayed again Kitt would bottom at least on occasion. Natural born leaders like Kitt were rarely bottoms, but the more Austin waited, the more he wanted in Kitt's tight ass. He wanted it real bad. It was absolutely the most prominent thought in his head.

Austin opted for a pair of blue jeans and a polo going commando in the process. His big plan for the evening was to cook dinner, maybe grill a steak and watch some television before turning in. It might seem a boring night to many, but for him it sounded perfect. As he walked through the house, a stray thought slammed into his head and a smile hit his lips. The only question, would he be able to pull it off?

The warm water of the pond soaked into Kitt's skin as he floated on his back. The evening was coming on quick. A cool breeze blew across his skin in contrast to the warm water, sending goose bump springing up along his arms and legs. They were in the midst of a true Indian summer. It was quickly becoming one of the hottest October's on record with a heat wave breaking century old temperature highs during the day, but the nights were still cooling down nicely. Kitt fought back a yawn, hoping he'd be so badly worn out from the day's work, he'd have no choice but to get some sleep tonight.

Thank God, Mike didn't need his help anymore today. This morning, Kitt made the official announcement to his staff at the barn, that he'd be sending Jose over in his place for anything Mike needed in the foreseeable future. He figured Mike would need some help in breaking the herd up and sending them out to pasture. Jose should have no problem filling in for Kitt.

After their impromptu meeting, Kitt worked himself into the ground. Anything requiring manual labor, he did himself. He still hadn't called Sean to let him know of his decision and decided to put it off another day. He needed to talk to Jose and Lily first, check their schedules to find the best time to go up to Dallas this weekend.

A bonus, as if to reiterate Kitt's need to exhaust himself, one mishap after another happened all the way up until dinner. Once he got done over at Mike's place where he successfully managed to dodge Austin, he got a call about a fence break on his property. The repair only took a minute, but corralling the herd back inside took some time.

As they broke for dinner, Kitt's stepmom met him at the barn, panicked. Some four legged something got into her prized garden and apparently ate quite a bit. She'd found enough to know that whatever the culprit, it dug under the fence this time instead of going over it. While she finished preparing everyone's dinner, Kitt repaired the damage to the garden's fence and anchored it better into the ground, making this long day even longer. This time when the yawn threatened to come out, he didn't stop it. Thank God, tonight, he would finally sleep!

He'd opted to skip having dinner at the house. Instead, he'd fixed a plate to eat later and took it back to his cabin. He'd driven the four-wheeler to the pond, parked it and jumped off, stripping as he stalked over to the water and dove in. He had spent almost every night of his youth in this pond, and it felt just as good now as it did then. As Kitt gently kicked his way in a circle, he dove under the water head first and came back up again, flipping on to his back as two blue jean clad horizontal legs caught his eye. Kitt flipped back around again lifting his head, slinging water with his wet hair. Austin stood before him.

"I didn't think you heard me, even though I wasn't being quiet," Austin said smiling while resting an arm on the fence. He stood on his side of the divide. His four-wheeler sat parked a few feet away, and it looked like he'd been there for a while.

"No, I didn't." It sounded lame even to Kitt, and he checked the urge to roll his eyes at the obvious.

"I didn't think so." That crooked, charming as hell smile still graced Austin's face. Neither of them spoke for what felt like a long time, but in reality, it couldn't have been more than a minute.

"Did you need somethin'?" Kitt finally asked ending the silence.

"Mike and I were talking about artificial insemination, and I was wondering if maybe we could talk about it tonight. If you're not busy. I got three big, thick steaks ready to go on the grill. It won't take long," Austin added, still perched in the same position.

"Umm… Sure…" Kitt begged his brain to find a way out.

"So, you'll come?"

"Yeah, I guess so," Kitt said, still treading water to keep his head above the surface.

"Alright. So I'll see you in like thirty minutes?" Austin's eyes seemed to be glued to his. Why was he staring at him like that?

"Sure." *No!* His brain rejected this so solidly he worried he'd said the word out loud.

"Alright then, I'll just go get the grill started." Austin slowly sauntered off back to his four-wheeler. Kitt watched him the entire time, never moving just keeping his body underwater until the four-wheeler drove out of sight.

"Fuck! What the fuck?" Kitt yelled out into the night slapping at the water with his fist. He swam hard to the side, almost running to his clothes. His giant hard-on stuck out like the pain in the ass it had become.

What the fuck was Mike thinking? He knew Kitt would be more than happy to do anything his buddy needed, but why were they discussing artificial insemination with the ranch owner right now? No way the Grainger farm was even remotely ready to begin anything like an insemination program.

Kitt dug a hand in the pocket of his jeans, palming his phone. He was all set to send Mike a straight up, go to hell message, when he stopped in mid type. Mike would never get why he was so upset. And, what could he say? *Your boss's about the best looking thing I've ever seen, and I can't think of much else than fucking his brains out, so why did you invite me over you fuckin' idiot!?!* Yeah, no, he definitely couldn't say that.

"*Fuck!*" Kitt growled out into the night.

Feeling much like a fool and completely out of his element, he forced the phone back down in his pocket and stalked to his cabin carrying his bundled up clothes under his arm. He dumped them in the general direction of the laundry room area. He didn't stop, but went straight into the bathroom and turned the faucet on for the shower. He stepped under the cold stream and prayed his cock would calm before he got to Austin's house.

~~~~~~

The grin never left Austin's face as he drove back to the house. And, he certainly didn't jump right in to making dinner. Instead, he detoured to the bathroom to jack off before Kitt's arrival. It didn't take much for him to come. Seeing Kitt in the pond, easily making out it was him from at least fifty yards away, had him pulling the four-wheeler straight up to the fence line. He'd watched Kitt swim and float around in the water, his long legs kicking up, his ass sliding under water, and that long thick dick floating freely. Austin walked to the fence line never trying to hide he was there.

He anchored a foot up on the first post, and lifted his Ray-Ban's and just watched Kitt as he relaxed. Kitt was completely lost in thought as several minutes passed with Austin just watching that perfect body arch and twist in the water. When Kitt realized he stood there, everything changed. The air between them crackled and intensified. Kitt's relaxed mood vanished and all he gave were clipped, one word answers. Austin wasn't sure where the brilliance of three steaks came from, knowing Kitt would think Mike planned to come, but he said it and Kitt bought it.

Now, as Austin stood in the hall bathroom stroking his dick, he closed his eyes with the grin on his face broadening. He let the thoughts of sliding Kitt's thick cock between his lips take over, and that was all it took. Austin's orgasm came fast, pumping out into the sink.

He stayed leaning against the sink even after he finished, etching the image of Kitt floating in the pond deep into his memory. Very much like he'd done fifteen years ago in the locker room of the high school when he'd caught Kitt in the shower. Austin was beginning to realize everything about Kitt Kelly had always called out to him.

Austin let himself feel the romance of his thoughts as he slowly opened his eyes to look at himself in the mirror. He couldn't stop grinning. As crazy as it sounded, he felt like that boy in high school, all those years ago, with his first crush finally paying attention to him.

Whatever caused the feeling, Austin wasn't ready to let it go. It fit perfectly into his new solitary life. Hell, maybe it was just the glorious feeling of finally being left alone. But whatever, he wasn't in a mind set to let it go, and oddly, he wanted to dress up for Kitt tonight. He wanted to impress Kitt, to look his best for him. He decided to give into the urge.

Austin changed up his sun streaked hair, adding mousse. He styled it in the slightly disarrayed look so popular these days. He chose his Armani slacks with a matching light weight cashmere sweater, both in colors to compliment his complexion. The Italian leather loafers came from the shoe collection he started fifteen years earlier after getting his first real movie contract. The shoes cost a pretty penny back then. Made of the softest leather on the market, they felt incredible on his feet, giving him confidence. They also matched his clothing perfectly.

He chose to wear his Rolex on his wrist and checked his reflection in the mirror before spraying himself with cologne. With one last glance, Austin checked his teeth as the knock on the back door sounded. Judging by the time on his watch, Kitt was punctual.

As he made his way down the hall, the wide open window showed Kitt finger combing his hair. The windblown look did wonders for the guy who stood in his starched Wranglers, polished boots and a pearl button, solid white button down. Standard dress-up cowboy attire. The thought that Kitt had dressed up for him made Austin grin. He went straight to the back door and opened it.

"Thank you for coming over." Austin used the grin most people said was his most charming. He looked Kitt over as he stepped back to let him in. During the time they'd spent working together, Austin had studied Kitt enough to know his hair wasn't copper like he'd convinced himself in the beginning, but a natural darker brown. The sun had just worked its magic on it, bringing out the natural blond, gold and auburn highlights, giving it a rich depth. Kitt's eyes, hair and skin tone all matched, and as far as Austin was concerned, Kitt was an embodiment of a tanned chiseled Greek god standing before him.

"Sure, thanks for invitin' me over." Kitt stepped inside, tucking his fingers in his front pockets. He didn't move more than a step inside the house. "I didn't see Mike's truck out there."

Austin assumed it was manners more than nerves that kept Kitt right at the door. He needed to invite Kitt in.

"Make yourself at home. Would you like something to drink? Beer, wine, mixed drink?" Austin asked shutting the door behind Kitt. He resisted the overwhelming urge to lean in closer and take a deeper breath of Kitt's scent, because from where he stood, Kitt smelled fabulous.

"Beer's fine," Kitt said, and now, Austin realized it was nerves rather than manners keeping Kitt back.

"You drink Bud Light, right? I had some delivered today." Austin walked in the kitchen to the refrigerator. The living room led into the kitchen with a large granite bar separating the two rooms.

"Yeah, but whatever you have that's cold is fine."

"I was just heading outside to start the grill. I'm a little behind on the steaks, but the baked potatoes should be done and warming, and the salad's ready. You do eat salad, right?" Austin asked handing Kitt the beer as he placed the steaks on the kitchen island.

"Sure. I guess," Kitt said, his eyes constantly tracking Austin, but he didn't move from his spot.

"Good, I've got an excellent spinach and feta deal in there. I think you'll like it. Just a sec, I'll be right back." Austin stepped out and made quick work of starting the grill that sat on the porch close to the back door. It didn't take long and he was back inside. Austin noticed Kitt had taken a seat on the bar stool that he'd stood behind just minutes ago. As Austin watched him, Kitt took a long, long, swig of the beer in his hand. Austin was suddenly struck by how good Kitt looked in his house. He was a cozy kind of guy, just like Austin's house had turned out to be. Okay, well, Kitt was a cozy kind of guy when he wasn't bowed up tight like right now.

"You look nice tonight," Austin said.

"So do you." The words came automatically before Kitt narrowed his eyes and looked down. His face reddened and he turned away.

"Thank you, I did a quick change. I'm glad you decided to come tonight. How do you like your steak?" Austin asked as he reached for the plate of steaks.

"Medium rare." It wasn't quite the one word answer Austin had come to expect from Kitt, but close.

"Me too." Austin looked up at Kitt with a grin. "I thought we'd eat inside, but if you'd rather eat outside, I can move everything out."

"No, it's fine. Where's Mike?" Kitt asked. He was up to five words now.

"I'm guessing in town, but I don't know for sure. I think he's got the hots for the young woman who brings the groceries. He may be heading somewhere else."

"Laura?" Kitt asked, draining his beer. Austin wound his way back into the kitchen and reached in the refrigerator to get him another. He slid it across the bar before dumping the empty bottle in the trash.

"I guess. Short, Hispanic, pretty...he might have said something about a date, I'm not sure. Let me go put these on, I'll be back."

The night was full on now and Austin didn't turn on the porch light. He didn't want to draw bugs to the food. He worked from the light shining through the window to lay the steaks on the sizzling hot grill.

"I thought you and Mike were needin' insemination information," Kitt said from behind Austin startling him a bit. He stood a few feet away and held Austin's beer out to him. He took it and took a drink as he weighed his answer. He extended a hand to the table on the patio for Kitt to take a seat. Nothing brilliant came to his mind so he decided on the truth.

"I must confess. I'd love to listen to you talk about artificial insemination, if you're so inclined, but this was more of a get to know my neighbor kind of invitation."

Kitt stayed quiet for several long moments, just staring at Austin under the weight of the moonlight climbing high in the night sky.

"Okay. So no Mike?"

"I didn't ask him to come. I can call him up if it makes you more comfortable," Austin offered taking a seat at the table.

"No, it's fine." Kitt took another long drink of his beer.

"You were a great help to us the last few days. You and I got off on the wrong foot, I just wanted to make sure we were good," Austin said.

"I'm good." And he was back to two word sentences.

"I can see you are." That got Austin nothing but silence. "Good with everything."

Kitt nodded. There was more silence and both men sat staring at the other. Finally, Austin rose to turn the steaks and shut the lid before coming back to the small table.

"Would you like another beer?"

"Sure." Not that the one word didn't answer his question, but Austin hoped for a little more.

Awkwardness surrounded them again, and much to Austin's frustration, Kitt offered nothing for him to grab on to keep them talking, nor did he seem to want to instigate conversation himself. Austin schooled his features, keeping his face pleasant as he excused himself and went back inside. Silently, he berated himself. He'd completely failed to make Kitt comfortable, and he was rushing this dinner. He should have never started cooking so quickly. What was he thinking? Well, he knew exactly what he thought: if they got dinner done and out of the way, nothing would stop them from filling the rest of the night with hot sex.

Austin struggled within himself. He didn't know how to recover, how to make Kitt feel more comfortable. He worked quickly placing the salad and baked potato condiments on the table. The steaks were close to being done, and he grabbed two more beers before going back outside.

Austin took it as a good sign Kitt hadn't left. He handed one to Kitt before walking over to check the grill.

Austin forced himself to take a deep breath and calm down. They'd have dinner together. They'd sit and talk during dinner. He would bring the conversation to their sexuality and let Kitt know he was gay. Certainly, it would be all it took. Things weren't as bad as they seemed, he just needed to get them inside over the intimacy of dinner. The steaks looked done, and he put them on a plate before looking up at Kitt who stared out into the night.

"Let's eat."

Chapter 8

Well, if Austin were being honest, he'd rate this dinner experience somewhere around a three. A three out of about a thousand, and that measure only applied if a thousand meant things were just barely fair.

They ate together at the kitchen table. Austin sat directly to Kitt's right, close enough so that they kept bumping knees together under the table. The bumping was intentional, of course. Austin made it a slight caress, falling just short of running his foot up Kitt's leg. The whole thing totally turned him on except Kitt seemed to want nothing to do with it. So much so, he angled himself until he sat awkwardly at the table. Completely out of Austin's reach.

Austin switched them to wine. It was a great bottle, something many years old that he'd brought with him from California. Kitt drank it like it was water, pretty much finishing the whole bottle himself. About two minutes after sitting down, Kitt started talking about artificial insemination and kept going on and on through the salad, steaks and baked potatoes.

Now, had Austin paid attention, he would know for sure. But since he really hadn't, he could only guess Kitt started at the conception of the idea of artificial insemination and moved through each year's struggles and highlights until they reached using it in the day to day life of a farmer...yeah, Austin was done hearing about artificial insemination.

Austin picked at his food. He never took full bites and drank quite a bit of the second bottle of wine he opened. The original plan was to slow dinner down to keep Kitt at the table drinking more wine, but now, he couldn't eat because all hope of turning this dinner around to anything positive faded fast. Kitt, on the other hand, ate quickly. It was amazing how Kitt could eat so fast, yet never break his lecture of agriculture management. Kitt couldn't have been in his house for more than an hour, but he could see the other man physically trying to find his way out of the situation and right out the door.

What Austin couldn't tell was whether the bulge in Kitt's Wranglers was due to his interest in Austin, or whether Fisker might be waiting for him. Maybe, Austin got in the way of their plans tonight. That caused a scowl to form and determination to set in. He wasn't going to let Kitt slip away so easily. If Kitt refused to give him the chance to romance him, then Austin would change tactics. Kitt was a hardworking, straight forward kind of a guy, and that's how Austin would play it. Should've done it like that from the beginning.

"So talk to Mike and let me know when you're interested in movin' forward with any of it. I have no problem helpin' you out. I've got the equipment, even the storage devices. I do it for everyone around here, and I won't charge you anything to help make up for that first day we met. Thank you for the dinner. I should get goin'. Want me to help with the dishes?" Kitt rattled on like a machine gun and started to rise from his seat.

"How long have you hidden?" Austin asked as straight forward as he could.

Kitt's nervous energy faltered. The question clearly confused him. Austin pushed his chair away from the table, sat back in his seat, crossing his right leg over his left knee and picked up his glass of wine to take a sip, all the while looking Kitt directly in the eyes.

"I don't hide it. Everyone around here has the same offer I gave you. Well, not the no charge part, but everything else."

Austin reached forward, placing a hand on Kitt's hand as he started to pick his plate up.

"Kitt, hold up. Give me a minute," Austin said purposefully directing his gaze to Kitt's chair. He waited until Kitt sat back down, and then nodded his head to Kitt's glass of wine. "Don't run off so quickly. I have a couple of questions for you and I think you misunderstood the first one. Do you hide from everyone, or just from the people around here?"

Kitt didn't answer. He just gnawed on his bottom lip with his eyes trained on Austin. The nervous energy turned into a shell shocked look.

"Kitt, it's the biggest reason I'm here. Please understand, I'm not calling you out, I'm just tired of always hiding, and I've never been any good at guessing who's what. I am the master of hiding though, so

I can spot it in someone from a mile away. I'm gay, Kitt. And I think you are too." They never broke eye contact as Austin revealed his biggest secret to Kitt.

"You're gay?" Kitt asked.

"Yes." Austin said it with more confidence than he felt. It was only the third time ever in his entire life he'd said it out loud.

"But you're gettin' married." It wasn't really a question, but a statement of fact, and it clearly confused Kitt by the look on his face.

"If I was getting married would I be here without her? Cara's paid and paid very well indeed. I'm trusting you with my secret. Only a handful of other people know about me, and honestly, I've had the hots for you since I first laid eyes on you." Austin let that sit there between them, never breaking their eye contact. A blush slowly crept onto Kitt's cheeks.

"Do you date?" Austin asked after a moment of silence. It was really more of a *'Do you randomly fuck?'*, but he changed it at the last second.

"No." Kitt's response came immediately. He still hadn't admitted anything to Austin, but at this point, Austin assumed the yes had been given.

"What about Fisker?" Austin wasn't going to leave anything out.

"How do you know that?" Kitt asked, the blush crossed with a little bit of alarm on his face.

"My security watches the place from every angle. I'm hiding here until people stop caring about me. I'm seriously done with that other world. I'm done living that kind of lifestyle. They caught the car out on the highway. It doesn't fit the area, they tailed it." Austin kept it simple, not explaining anything more.

"You saw a Fisker and decided I was gay?" Kitt asked incredulously.

"No. Seeing the driver helped me come to that conclusion, but it was the Andrew Christian underwear you wore on the first day I saw you that gave me the true hint."

"Damn, I *knew* I should've ditched those." Kitt muttered breaking eye contact with Austin for the first time since he sat down. His brow narrowed and his lips pursed, but his eyes came back up to meet Austin's as he heard the next question.

"Hmm… I guess that's as close to a yes as I'll get from you. It feels good to say it out loud though, you should try it. I've hidden for eighteen long years. Is Fisker your boyfriend?" Austin asked.

"No," Kitt said quickly, shaking his head, but stopped. "Shit! Okay, maybe. I don't know."

"You don't know?" Austin asked, still sitting in his casual stance. He took a sip of the wine to hide the fierce jealousy Kitt's simple '*I don't know*' provoked within him.

"No, he's not my boyfriend. But all of the sudden he's pushin' for it," Kitt explained.

"You don't want it?" Austin asked and reached over to fill Kitt's glass of wine for nothing more than something to help hide the aggression.

"No, it was good the way it was. He made time for me, and I drove to Dallas when I could."

"How often?" Austin asked, somewhat relieved, but still possessive.

"Once a month, give or take a week or two," Kitt said, before draining his newly filled glass of wine in one long swallow.

"Hmm. And now he wants more. So he's planning on coming down here regularly?" Austin kept asking questions trying to get a clear image of what exactly Kitt's relationship with the Fisker guy was and if there really was a chance for him in Kitt's life.

"He wants to. I don't know," Kitt replied shrugging.

"Well, to come to the real reason I asked you to dinner. I definitely want more." Austin finally got to the point of this whole evening.

His revelation seemed to confuse Kitt. Austin leaned forward and took Kitt's hand, threading their fingers together. Kitt's eyes stayed glued on Austin. He didn't necessarily participate in the handholding, but didn't pull away either. Austin was forced to continue with his speech with no real encouragement whatsoever.

"I want more. I'm hiding here for an indefinite amount of time. The frenzy it would cause if I came out would hurt everyone involved in my life. I need to get them settled before I make any further moves. In saying that, I think I'd like to pass this time here with you."

"Just sex?" Kitt asked immediately. He finally showed some signs of interest when his fingers tightened around Austin's.

"It's a good place to start…" Austin didn't move a muscle. He just stayed leaning forward with Kitt's hand in his, and waited for him to answer.

"Keep it under wraps?" Kitt nodded as he spoke.

"Yes, absolutely," Austin said, and Kitt nodded again. It seemed they struck an agreement. The tone of the entire conversation stayed very matter of fact which completely contradicted what was actually going on inside of Austin. He forced himself to stay easy and rejected the notion to jump up right way, push Kitt down on the table and shove his dick straight inside Kitt's ass. "Tell me, how do you like it?"

"Sex?" Kitt asked.

"Yes." They never broke eye contact.

"I usually give, but I like to receive. I just don't get it very much. How do you like it?" Kitt increased his hold on Austin's hand. They were talking so casually about things. Getting all the ground work laid out seemed just like something Kitt would do. Austin could see how he made such a great student and excellent business man. Kitt wasn't the rush in kind of guy at all.

"Every way's the right way for me, but I'm going be honest. I've fantasized about you pretty much nonstop since I first saw you," Austin said. He leaned his body a little bit closer to Kitt. He wanted to kiss him so badly. Kiss him, stroke him, make love to him, do everything he'd dreamed of, but instead, he forced himself to stay seated and talking.

"Really?" That seemed to surprise Kitt.

"Absolutely!" Austin nodded as he said the simple word.

"Me too." Kitt finally gave a small smile and Austin's heart began to pick up a beat.

"Good. You hid it well, I couldn't tell at all."

Their hands stayed linked together, a little tighter now since their admissions. Austin saw the hints of insecurity lingering in Kitt's eyes. He got it. Hell, he felt exactly the same way. The only way he knew how to lose it was to lean in slowly and place a simple kiss on Kitt's perfect lips. From the moment their lips touched, Austin felt the connection in his heart, but he schooled his facial features, not letting that thought show. He'd gone without sex for a while, of course it might get emotional.

Austin reluctantly broke the contact, sitting back just staring at Kitt before he rose and pulled Kitt up with him.

"I've thought so much about you…fantasized of being buried deep inside you. Will you let me?" Austin asked while pulling Kitt's shirt free of his jeans. He unbuttoned each pearl button from the bottom up. He kept his eyes moving back to Kitt's face to gauge his reaction. All he got was a nod, and Kitt took over the buttons on his shirt, then at his wrist.

"Do you know how badly I want to lick my way up these?" Austin said in almost a whisper. His rigid cock strained against the binding material of his slacks, begging to be released. He forced himself to keep it casual and trailed his fingertips up Kitt's stomach, smiling as the abdominal muscles rippled and flexed under his slight touch. The moon caught his attention, and he remembered his back windows were open; his security team could see in. It physically cost him to move away, but Austin took a step back and turned as Kitt began to unbutton his blue jeans and toe off his boots.

"I have condoms." Austin kept his calm facade in place as deep seeded need coursed through his body. He walked around the bar into the kitchen. He took off his watch and opened a drawer, keeping his eyes on the man undressing in his living room. Kitt did participate, but that shell shocked look stayed planted on his face. Austin reached inside the drawer and pressed the remote to darken the windows, instantly shutting the blinds. The night had gone from a zero to a ten in a matter of minutes, and he wanted to savor every second of it. Yet, with the pounding in his heart, he wasn't sure if it was possible. He planned to fuck Kitt Kelly until he came, and then do it all over again. Austin tugged his sweater up and over his head, tossing it carelessly across the bar as he rounded the corner back toward Kitt.

Kitt was just dropping his underwear in the pile with the rest of his other clothes. His eyes never left Austin and his hard rigid length jutted straight out, ready for Austin's touch. Austin came to a stop about a foot away from Kitt and toed off his shoes before stepping forward to grip Kitt's cock with his hand. A hiss tore from Kitt's lips, and his eyes closed into slits as he threw his head back when Austin dropped to his knees.

The condom and lubricant fell to floor as he stroked Kitt. With a quick swipe of his tongue, Austin wet his lips and opened wide, taking all of Kitt into his mouth. He slid Kitt's cock in deep, swirling his tongue as he licked and opened his throat, deep throating Kitt on the first try. The feel of Kitt's cock in his mouth caused Austin's eyes to roll into the back of his head. This was it and so much better than his dreams! Kitt responded immediately as Austin sucked him; his legs buckled and his hands reached forward to grip Austin's hair as he pulled himself slowly out of Austin's mouth.

"Jesus Christ, that feels so good," Kitt moaned and Austin's eyes lifted to look into Kitt's, with a smile tugging at his lips. Kitt's face showed every bit of the same deep passion Austin felt. Kitt's eyes focused on his with such intensity that took his breath away. All Austin could do was open wider and take the fucking Kitt began to give him.

Kitt tightly gripped Austin's hair in his hands and slammed his hips forward going deep, touching the back of his throat before sliding out to do it over and over again. Austin reached his hands around to grip Kitt's tight, firm ass, massaging the globes until he worked his way to the tight rim. He didn't hesitate, but shoved his finger inside. He instantly found the spot and began to massage, making Kitt's hips go into piston mode; his cock a jack hammer ramming further down his throat. The rhythm sent Austin's dick slamming against his slacks, begging to be inside Kitt, as he inserted a second finger continuing to work Kitt from behind.

Austin felt the tensing begin in Kitt. He reached lower with his free hand and massaged his retracting sac. He never lost the rhythm he'd created from behind and added a third finger to the tight ring of muscle. He knew Kitt was close. With every forward push of his hips, the taste of Kitt's essence intensified in Austin's mouth. He pulled the fingers free of Kitt's rim and gripped his dick hard in his fist, jerking his head back. He smiled as Kitt fought to pull him back.

"No! I'm close... Nooo..." Kitt moaned.

"I want us to come together." Austin squeezed Kitt's dick hard stopping his orgasm before he dropped both hands down to his slacks, freeing his cock. He reached for the condom and lube and worked quickly, sliding the thin plastic down his already leaking cock. With his thumb, Austin flipped open the top of the bottle. He squirted some lube directly on both his cock and his hand as he rose. His slacks fell to the ground, and he kicked them away. His eyes focused on Kitt.

"See this? It's been like this for days. You aren't super tight. I guess I have Fisker to thank for that, but somehow I can't find it in me." Austin stalked toward Kitt who took a step back. In one fluid motion, Austin flipped Kitt around and pushed him over the side of his sofa. He lowered his oil coated fingers and rubbed them across Kitt's crease seconds before plunging his cock deep inside. All thoughts of savoring Kitt fled as he pushed forward, forcing himself fully inside. Kitt gripped Austin, milked him like a fantasy come true, except Kitt felt far better than Austin ever dreamed he could.

The bottle of lube was still in his hand. He poured drops directly onto his cock as he slid out and pushed back in. It was just enough to work himself easily inside. He slid out again, dropping the oil to the floor and gripping onto Kitt's hips as he plunged forward. Austin picked up the tempo, biting his lip, and this time, his balls slapped against Kitt's ass as he pounded from behind. He realized only a minute could have passed by as he reared back preparing to slam forward, this time he released the breath he'd held since he started.

Austin centered into himself and opened his eyes as he slammed forward again. The long line of Kitt's spine splayed out in front of him. He ran one hand up the man's back, gripping his shoulder, pulling Kitt back toward him, and smiling as his balls slapped Kitt's ass again. He tried to remember to grab Kitt's cock and stroke him off at the same time. But, he couldn't maintain any sort of rhythm as he fucked Kitt Kelly's ass. Kitt's back bowed and Austin's head jerked up. He could see the man clearly in his darkened television screen. Kitt's hands gripped the soft leather of the sofa, and his eyes clenched shut. His lush lips were slightly parted. A deeply erotic feeling snaked its way through Austin's body, making him slow his movements. The mirrored image of Kitt in that dark screen turned the pounding meaningful.

Austin's heart kicked up a beat, stuttered over itself, and his hips began to move more sensuously. He focused on Kitt's pleasure, not just his own. He worked the gland with every thrust, and his eyes stayed on the screen as he used the palms of his hands to lift Kitt's chest up, bringing him to a standing position in front of him. They were about the same height, maybe Kitt was an inch or so shorter, but their builds were similar. Austin watched the entire movement. He couldn't tell if he'd hurt Kitt or not, but he reached up Kitt's chest and turned his chin back to meet Austin for their first heated kiss.

As Kitt's tongue slid across his own, the moment turned magical. Tingles rippled across his body. He wrapped Kitt tighter in his arms and softened the kiss. Austin slipped completely out of Kitt and turned him in his arms, never breaking from the hold, or the sweet swirl of their tongues. With Kitt wrapped tightly against his chest, the kiss deepened as Kitt plunged his tongue forward making love to Austin with his mouth. The pesky need to breathe finally tore him free, and he latched onto Kitt's neck. He worked his way up until he could whisper in Kitt's ear.

"I want to do this right. I want to watch you when we come," Austin whispered and slowly lowered them to the rug of his living room floor. The bed just seemed too far away to wait to be back inside this lovely man in his arms. Austin laid Kitt out in front of him and climbed in between his parted thighs. Reaching up, he kissed Kitt again. Austin knew he could kiss this one man over and over for the rest of his life. Kitt was an expert kisser, made just to kiss him.

Kitt anchored his legs around Austin's waist and tugged free of the kiss, keeping a tight hold around Austin who lay on his chest.

"Finish us off," he whispered quietly into Austin's hair.

He didn't need to be told twice. Austin rose and reached for the lube, not wanting to hurt Kitt, but Kitt stopped him.

"I'm good, just really close." Their eyes connected, and Austin positioned himself, and slid straight back inside. Kitt rolled his head back and threw his muscular arms up over his head, gripping his fingers into the plush rug. Austin grabbed Kitt's twitching cock matching the strokes to each drive of his hips.

This was different. There was meaning in this, more so than any other time in his life. His eyes never strayed from the sexy body splayed out in front of him. He watched every muscle in Kitt's body strain and flex under his assault. Kitt's sac retracted again as his cock grew more swollen, hardening tighter in his hand. Austin made love to Kitt.

"I'm coming," Kitt groaned; his eyes still closed tight.

"Me too," Austin whispered, giving in to the moment. His hips bucked in erratic clumsy strokes as his orgasm exploded in wave after wave of ecstasy. Austin couldn't seem to stop the movement of his hips and couldn't be sure that Kitt actually came. Everything closed in on him until there was nothing else but him and this man under him. For the first time ever, Austin was at one with another human being. Kitt was an extension of himself, and it felt so right to connect on this level. Austin dropped forward on top of Kitt, falling face first, but Kitt was ready for him.

~~~~~~

"I need to go," Kitt said looking over the kitchen bar at the clock on the oven.

"No, don't leave until morning! I'm not done with you yet," Austin said pulling Kitt back into his arms as a yawn escaped him.

"It's already mornin'. It's five. I need to get goin' before Mike shows up," Kitt said. Still, he didn't move from the embrace Austin held him in. They'd never made it to the bedroom. They'd made it to the living room floor, the kitchen counter, the bathroom, but never to the bedroom.

"I don't want him to see me leave." Kitt lifted enough to kiss Austin's right nipple.

They'd made love, but they'd also watched television, eaten again, talked a little, and laughed over Kitt's nervous lecture at dinner. Right then, Kitt stopped his over active brain from making too much about how well they connected. It wasn't 'making love', it was sex. They'd had sex. Really, really great sex several times over the last six or seven hours. It didn't take them long to find their fit, and boy did they fit well. But, it was still just sex.

"When can I see you again?" Austin asked, threading his hand into the back of Kitt's hair, tugging him up from the nipple to look him in the eyes.

"When do you want to?" Kitt leaned forward as Austin lifted for a small, light kiss.

"I love kissing you and today," Austin said, laying his head on the rug. Another yawn formed, and he finally let it out, not able to push it back down.

"You need sleep, and I'm not sure that's wise," Kitt answered, pushing up from the sofa. His body was sore, his ass very sore, and he stood stretching up to touch the ceiling.

"Tonight, then. After dark," Austin said. His eyes stayed on Kitt.

"I could cook." Kitt threw over his shoulder, looking around for his clothes, before he spotted them on the floor on the other side of the sofa where he took them off hours ago. Never did he expect anything like this when he walked into this house last night.

"Should I bring anything?" Austin rose to a sitting position, raking his fingers through his hair.

"No, I can get what I need from the main house," Kitt said, pulling on his clothes. His eyes kept darting over to Austin as he finally stood and walked over to Kitt.

"Okay. If that changes, text me. I put my cell phone number in your phone last night. I wanted you to have it," Austin said, not letting Kitt button his shirt. Instead Austin slid his hands in the open shirt, wrapping his arms around Kitt. "I thoroughly enjoyed myself. I'm a happy man to learn the real thing was far better than the fantasy, because boy, did I have you doing some good stuff in my dreams." He grinned at Kitt.

Kitt wrapped his arms around Austin and stared at him for several long moments, not saying a word. He felt exactly the same way, except he had ten plus years of fantasizing about Austin to compare with.

"I need to go. Mike'll be here soon." Kitt pulled free of Austin's hold.

"Hold up, kiss me goodbye." Kitt couldn't resist the sexy man leaning against him. He bent in thoroughly kissing Austin again. It was only under protest that Kitt moved away.

"I gotta go," Kitt said purposefully moving to the back door.

"Be careful going home." Austin followed him to the back door, still completely nude. Kitt opened the door and looked out making sure the barn and surrounding area were quiet before he turned back to Austin.

"Bye," Kitt muttered and reached out for a quick sweet kiss.

"Think about me," Austin said.

"I don't think that's gonna be a problem." Kitt finally pulled the door open and stepped out on the porch. It was still completely dark outside, the moon was gone and the sun nowhere ready to rise. Nothing guided his path.

"That's the right answer," Austin said quietly as he watched Kitt make his way to the four-wheeler.

Chapter 9

Kitt sat on his front porch, looking out over the pond. The moon cast a perfect glow on his little log cabin. His place was small, nothing more than a bedroom, bathroom, kitchen and living room, but he loved it out here. It couldn't have been any more perfect for him. Kitt built the cabin almost completely on his own, way before his father died.

He was eight miles from the main house, and about nine miles from the highway. He'd worn a pretty decent trail leading from the main road up to the cabin, but the idea of Sean driving his Fisker, navigating it over the rugged terrain, made Kitt chuckle. Too bad it hadn't been full daylight outside so he could have watched that little ride pop and bounce off the ruts and holes along the way.

Both the horse barn and cattle barn sat between his cabin and the main house. His front porch looked out over the pond, and on clear evenings like this, he could see the moon's glow perfectly on the water. It acted as a beacon to his animals. On a recent aggravated whim, Kitt planted trees along the new fence line in order to help block anything to do with his new neighbor. After the last few days, he knew the attempt was futile; nothing would ever rid him of the memory of the super hot Austin Grainger.

Kitt twirled the empty long neck with his finger against the arm of his chair. He needed another beer, but instead of making the trek to his refrigerator in the house, he kicked back in the recliner lawn chair. He wasn't inclined to move at all. After a solid week of no sleep and long hard days, Kitt broke free this afternoon a few hours early. He came home, napped for about three hours, showered, and then he cheated. He went back to the main house, fixed an oversized plate of food and gave a random excuse as to why he couldn't stay. Now, he just sat outside waiting for Austin who seemed to be running a little late from the schedule they'd been on.

His cattle were on the move, coming to the pond. They surrounded the house while moving forward. Kitt watched them closely. He couldn't help but do it. His herd sizes were growing fast. His cattle were breeding and multiplying well. Against the advice of just about every old timer in the area, he hadn't sold a female for the last two years. He was also making sure his females stayed healthy and strong, carrying their young through full term. His herd count was close to double already.

Kitt would have to sell some in the spring. Financially, he had no choice, but only a few hundred head would go to sale. The organic way Kitt fed them would fetch a pretty high price, and he'd already signed the contracts to move them out come selling season. Surely, the hay and cattle sales would sustain their cash flow through next year's long hot summer.

He told people he placed the log cabin out here to help keep an eye on things, but it was the solitude that drew him out this far. He'd hidden for so long, he'd become accustomed to keeping to himself. But since he and Austin started their deal a few days ago, every night Austin had been over or vice versa. Kitt found he enjoyed the camaraderie and companionship they shared. They were becoming buddies, and it was all completely new to him.

When Kitt was in college, things were easier, but even then, no one in the agriculture program knew about his sexual preference. He had never fully shared his day to day life with anyone. Off campus access to so many gay men was great. Houston wasn't that many miles from Texas A&M, and gay bars populated the area by the hundreds. Kitt never got lonely, but to find someone in the same world he lived, changed everything.

He and Austin shared more than just sex. Austin lived a life even more hidden than Kitt's. Neither wanted to breech those walls, so in return they were becoming fast friends. Austin easily talked to Kitt about his day. Kitt did the same, and they shared the same sense of humor and political views. They argued over religion, both supporting their view points, but neither got offended when the other rolled their eyes scoffing off a thought. Most of their talking came after making love. Kitt liked that part the most.

"Whoa, Kitt Kelly, hold your horses. It's sex, not making love. It's sex. Just sex. Only sex," Kitt said out loud to himself.

So many memories of his past crept into his thoughts tonight. It would be natural to think about his father. It was a buried hurt for Kitt to know his dad never really forgave him for not coming back and working this land. He'd needed Kitt here, apparently worse than Kitt knew. The ranch was failing badly, but it failed because his dad was an old man set in the old school ways of farming. He needed Kitt's brawn, but hadn't wanted his brain, which in Kitt's estimation was what he truly had needed the most.

Even if Kitt had come home and stayed, it wouldn't have helped anything. He and his dad always butted heads. His dad had no problem maintaining the role of strict disciplinarian even after Kitt became an educated, full grown man. His father demanded Kitt use his fists when they were at odds, and Kitt took the beating. He never doubled his fist up at his father. Even during the times he grew stronger and knew he could take him, Kitt never fought back. His father considered that a weakness in him.

They'd been in a big fight the day his dad died. The hard headed fool of an old man refused to listen to him even in the days leading up to his death when his left arm was hurting so badly for no reason. His dad just wasn't going to be told what to do by his brainiac, worthless son.

The longer Kitt sat out on the porch, the more the memories flooded. Stuff he'd pushed away and refused to deal with for so long. His dad's foreman, Verne, sabotaged him in so many ways after he took over the farm. Hell, he even suspected Verne was responsible for some of his recent broken contracts, but there was no way to prove it. Verne was an old drunk. He'd been with the farm since Kitt's birth, and he blamed Kitt for his father's death. Verne forced his hand one too many times, and Kitt had to fire him within the first month of being back. He hadn't taken that well at all.

His stepmom and sisters were completely clueless to the true state of the farm. He'd had to stop all their spending. The last few years had been tough on them. Changing this rundown place into a productive, progressive working ranch took everything Kitt had and it was still iffy. One bad move, one extended drought would wreck everything they worked for.

As Kitt's attitude began to take a full nose dive, the lights of Austin's four-wheeler appeared over the ridge. Funny how just seeing Austin in the distance made Kitt's mood pick up. He watched the headlights get closer and closer as Austin took form in the night.

Kitt's smile turned into a chuckle as he remembered the first night Austin approached him. He'd been stunned stupid over Austin's admission he was gay. He'd half expected the producers of candid camera to pop out and laugh at the big practical joke Austin just played on him, but the pounding his ass took a few minutes later propelled his brain forward, catching him quickly up to speed.

Without question, Kitt knew Austin wouldn't stick it out here in Texas for long term. Once Austin remembered what drove him away in the first place, it was sure to have him take off again. No matter how much Austin tried to deny it, he was still *the Austin Grainger*, for God's sake. And *the Austin Grainger* was worldly, elegant and just on a higher plane than the little people in the world. Everyone either wanted to be Austin, or get a piece of him, but for right now, Kitt was fully invested in this fantastic fuck fest. He wanted to capture every memory of their shared time together. He cherished each night and spent his days reveling in the fact that sometimes dreams did come true. As long as he could keep his heart somewhat separated from it all, he'd be okay when Austin eventually left.

Kitt watched Austin park the four-wheeler and climb over the fence, weaving through the cows as he made it to the front porch steps. Kitt stayed seated with his feet kicked up.

"Sorry I'm late. I had to take a call," Austin said coming to stand in front of Kitt. He extended his hand to Kitt, pulling him up from his seat.

"Everything okay?" Kitt asked looking closely at the worry in Austin's eyes.

"I don't know, I've got to fly back to LA. Cara's having some problems," Austin said. He was usually so forthcoming, he told Kitt everything. Actually, Austin talked a lot, but this time he didn't elaborate and his expression made it clear things weren't good.

"While I was on the phone, all I could think about was being here with you," Austin added, leaning in for a kiss. "You're already making my life better."

Both of Kitt's hands entwined with Austin's. Normally, Kitt didn't do these kinds of public displays, not even being out here so completely alone. But, Austin was a touchy, feely kind of guy, and the obvious concern he felt for Cara worried Kitt.

It took a second for it to even register on Kitt's brain Austin said something about already flying back to LA, and then he was hurting. He'd thought he might have as much as six months with Austin here, maybe even a year, before he got bored and left. Now, just a few days after they got started, Austin was already making plans to leave.

"How long will you be gone?" Kitt asked trying to school his facial features so that none of his feelings showed on his face. Unfortunately, Austin had a knack at reading him, an uncanny way of seeing through him.

"It should only be for a day or two. Are you gonna miss me?" Austin teased as he stepped forward, closing the little bit of distance between them.

"Hmm... Have you eaten, yet? I got chili from Lily, enough for both of us." Kitt ignored the question pulling free of Austin's hold. He turned toward the front door to his cabin only to have Austin grab his hand back in his own and tug him back to look him in the eyes.

"I'm gonna miss you. I've enjoyed these last few days," Austin said, wrapping Kitt in his arms.

"Me, too. Come inside." Kitt's eyes darted out across the pasture. Only the cows were out, but it was an involuntary scan he couldn't help. Maybe, it was because for the first time ever he'd brought all this to his home, but lately, he hadn't been able shake the feeling that someone was out there watching. He'd never found a soul, but he couldn't lose the feeling. He tugged free of Austin's hold and stepped into the house with Austin following close on his heels.

"Did you call Fisker yet to tell him you weren't seeing him anymore?" Austin's question caught Kitt off guard and he stopped, turning quickly around, confusion clear on his face. They'd never discussed Sean after the first mention of him.

Austin stood right behind him, ready to step up for a soft, sweet, light kiss and a tight embrace. He pressed Kitt against the length of his body. The front door still stood wide open. "You look surprised that I remembered my competition. Have you called him?"

"I sent him a text. Pretty lame, huh?" Kitt would have to talk to Sean, but he decided to give it a few days, see what was really going on between Austin and himself. A regular fuck buddy didn't just fall from the sky. Replacing Sean could be a challenge, and if Austin already planned to go back, he'd need Sean. On so many levels, Austin had dug himself firmly under Kitt's skin. The fact that it had been only three days didn't matter. Kitt chided himself even while standing in the circle of Austin's arms. *Sex! This is convenient sex between two grown men due to proximity, nothing more!*

"What did you say to him?" Austin persisted. Where was this coming from? Kitt extended his leg and kicked the front door closed with his foot when Austin refused to break free of their hold.

Kitt didn't answer right away. He tugged free of Austin's hold on him and started toward to the small kitchen. Austin stayed on him, stopping him with the slide of his hand down the front of Kitt's shorts, pulling him back against Austin's chest.

Kitt was hard and ready, but he was always ready for Austin. Austin massaged his cock and placed his lips on Kitt's neck, sliding his tongue up until he whispered in Kitt's ear. "I love to see you out there waiting for me. Tell me babe, it's important to me, what did you say to Fisker?"

"Not a lot. That feels good," Kitt said, closing his eyes, letting the moment consume him. He dropped his head back on Austin's shoulder and rolled his hips forward. He loved Austin's hands on his skin. It was such a turn on. The best foreplay ever.

"Mmm you like this? It feels good to me too…listen, handsome. I've been thinking. If you can break free early tomorrow, maybe we could go camping. Spend the night out somewhere remote," Austin suggested and finally slid his hands inside Kitt's shorts pushing him forward through the house to the bedroom.

"I could probably do that," Kitt answered, stumbling a bit, grinning at their awkward moves because he was completely unwilling to walk normally and lose Austin's hands working his cock.

"Tell your foreman you're going to Dallas and sleep in with me in the morning. Can you do that for me?" Austin said, reaching lower to grip and massage Kitt's sac. He nipped at Kitt's earlobe before plunging his tongue into its far depths, exploring his entire ear. Austin knew Kitt liked it a little rough and gently pinched his sac. The move set off an explosion of sensation throughout Kitt's body. He couldn't respond or take another step. Pre-come wet the tip of his cock. Austin used his thumb to spread the liquid all over his broad head as he shoved Kitt's shorts down. Austin kept the massage going even as Kitt arched his hips forward, pushing his cock harder in Austin's hand.

And then, Austin made the move Kitt loved. He leaned down to lick his tip before placing a kiss on his slit, working it gently with his tongue. Kitt slid a hand up Austin's neck to pull him back up for kiss. He thrust his tongue forward, lapping at the depths of Austin's mouth. They were somewhere close to the bed, but Kitt was too lost to know for sure. Right here on the floor would do just fine. It wouldn't take Kitt long with Austin on his knees.

"Answer me, Kitt. Say yes, please," Austin whispered.

"I think you make it too hard for me to think straight." Out of nothing more than self-preservation, Kitt pushed free of Austin's hold stepping back a step or two until his knees hit the bed. His eyes stayed on Austin and Kitt watched as that sexy grin of his spread across the male's stunningly beautiful face. Even after so many days of deeply gratifying sex with Austin freaking Grainger, it still took only one look from the man to make Kitt breathless.

Kitt kicked off his shoes as he yanked his t-shirt over his head.

"You have no shame. I swear to God you do it on purpose," Kitt said, releasing the button on his shorts.

"It's because I see clearly what I want, and what I want is standing so enticingly in front of me." Austin waggled his eyebrows dropping his clothing on the floor as he stepped closer to Kitt.

Kitt was undressed first and lifted his hands to Austin's face turning him in the perfect angle to claim those wonderful lips.

Chapter 10

Packing his toiletries, Austin lifted his gaze to look in the bathroom mirror. He ran his fingers through his hair, setting it just right. He'd packed dinner with a couple of bottles of wine and used a small backpack for a change of clothing. Kitt was bringing a sleeping bag and the little bit of gear they needed to camp out tonight. As far as Austin knew, they were taking Kitt's truck and going a few miles farther back on the Kelly's property to a tucked away section of land Kitt always went to watch the sunrise.

A grin spread across Austin's face when he thought about lying in Kitt's arms last night after a particularly gentle session of their love making. Austin persisted on the idea of their camp out until Kitt whispered quietly into his hair he wanted to share a place with him. For some reason, those were some of the sweetest words ever said to him. Especially, since he knew Kitt had never taken another out there before.

It surprised Austin how much he looked forward to tonight. Kitt always got up and left in the middle of the night, refusing to stay until the morning. And, he wouldn't let Austin stay either. Kitt remained vigilantly conscious over where they were and who might be around to see them. Austin slung his backpack over his shoulder at the same time his phone sounded from the dresser. A groan erupted and he warred within himself on answering. If he hadn't stopped to check his appearance, he never would have heard it. It was always his plan to leave the phone here when he left to go to Kitt tonight. He almost didn't check it.

But things were too rocky with Cara right now, and the press was still all over his ass so he couldn't ignore whoever it was contacting him. More importantly, why were they contacting him? Frustrated, Austin stalked across the room to his dresser.

He palmed the phone and read the message. A frown tugged across his brow. His manager, Phillip Philips, sent their designated emergency code through text message. It was the one not to be ignored. He dialed the number quickly, and his call was answered on the first ring.

"Grainger, I think you're gonna be done with this seclusion thing when you hear this. Scorsese has a new movie. It's big and he wants you. Sandy Bullock has already signed on. You need to do this, Austin."

"Please tell me that wasn't the emergency," Austin said, a little relieved this was all there was going on. He pivoted and walked down the hall to the living room.

"It's not, but it's in my hand. You need to take it," he said.

"No. I've told you I'm done. Now what's the real reason you're bothering me?" Austin adjusted his pack across his shoulder and headed for the back door where the cooler was waiting.

"The security reports show you're spending regular time with some cowboy." Phillip didn't even try sugar coating it.

"So?"

"Who is he?"

"Why?" It came out defensive as hell.

"Cara's concerned." Phillip's tone changed from aggressive to worried.

"Why?" Austin repeated his earlier question giving nothing back in way of an explanation.

"She isn't doing too good, Austin. She's drinking too much. The pills are stronger and more frequent."

"I spoke with Seth last night and I'm heading back to LA tomorrow. I'll take care of it," Austin said, deciding his manager might not have to be fired by the end of the phone call after all.

"She thought you'd already be back by now."

"I know, she's told me, but I couldn't have been anymore clear to everyone. I'm done. I'm actually happy again. You should give it a try," Austin said, grinning at his last little dig.

"Austin, just be careful. We don't know anything about this guy. Let me run him."

"No! Besides, that would be a waste of time. I've known him all my life. Listen, keep the cameras and media focused elsewhere. He already doesn't know we're being so recorded. I'll meet up with you tomorrow, I'm late now," Austin said, reaching his thumb out to hit end to this call.

"Late for what? Cow chipping?"

The question made Austin smile as he disconnected the call.

A knock sounded on the back door. He looked down at his phone to check the time. How was he again late to meet Kitt? He opened the door a little more aggressively than he planned to before seeing Mike on the back porch.

"Hey boss man, you wanted to see me? You haven't been around much today," Mike said in his generally good natured way.

"Something's come up. Come in for a minute." Austin held the door open, antsy as hell. His right leg bounced as he tried to slow down and not be rude to Mike.

"You goin' somewhere?" Mike asked, stepping in only a step or two like he normally did, just enough to shut the door behind him.

"No...well, yeah, I am. I'm packing for a trip. I have to head back to LA tomorrow for a day or two," Austin said, keeping a hand on the door knob.

"Alright. Well, I've got things covered here." Mike nodded. "I was just headin' into town. Need me to pick up anything?" Mike asked, his fingers shoved in his front pockets.

"No, I'm good," Austin said, and opened the back door again. He prayed he didn't offend Mike, but the sooner he left, the sooner Austin could get out the door. He still needed to walk over to Kitt's which would make the whole night even later in getting started.

Mike took the hint. Halfway down the porch steps, he looked back at Austin over his shoulder. "Take care."

"Yep, you too," Austin responded, and he shut the door, watching until Mike drove off.

Both back to back conversations totally stressed him out. How had he shut down his entire life to move back to Podunk, Texas in the hopes of finding some freedom only to still be hiding so completely? He'd loved these last few days more than any other time in his life. Having Kitt around, changed everything for him.

Austin was happy again, and his heart actually had a feeling other than negative cynical energy coursing through it. His tattered soul began to heal by leaps and bounds, and it was all due to the sexy cowboy next door who paid him only a little bit of attention.

Kitt didn't give Austin an inch. He made Austin work for every smile, every conversation they shared, and Austin loved every minute of it all. Even with Cara clearly flipping out, calling him all day and all hours of the night, drunk and stoned, talking smack to everyone; a smile still came to his lips when he thought of Kitt.

Their only problem, if it were even possible, Kitt hid more than he did. And, Austin was beginning to realize that the five or six hours a day he spent with Kitt wasn't nearly long enough.

For the first couple of nights, it wasn't much more than non-stop, fantastic sex. Way more sex than Austin had experienced in years. Neither of them seemed to get enough of each other. But, during those marathon hours spent together, Austin realized he actually enjoyed Kitt's company. The guy was funny, smart and sexy as hell. After two days and tons of ridiculous debating, Austin managed to talk Kitt into agreeing that once they were inside his house, it should be considered nudist territory. Everything they did must be done naked for the sole reason Austin loved to look at Kitt's rocking body.

By day four, Austin seemed to eat, drink, and sleep Kitt Kelly. He craved everything about him, thinking of little else for most of each day. Without question, Austin was totally taken with his super-hot cowboy, and he felt like Kitt shared his feelings. It seemed like a win-win situation for them both.

Yet, something changed last night. He'd watched Kitt sitting outside on his porch, relaxing and waiting for him. The moonlight hit Kitt just right, and Austin lost his mind for a moment. Kitt looked stunningly handsome. His strong jaw and chiseled hard features were softened by the long sweep of hair falling down across his forehead. The moonlight shone right down on him. In that moment, Kitt literally took his breath away. Austin took the steps separating them, and the strong emotion he felt for Kitt grew with each step.

In every way, Kitt was perfect for Austin. He didn't make a big deal about Austin's celebrity status or fame. He never wanted anything from Austin. If Austin made a meal for Kitt, Kitt insisted on returning the favor. They spent as much time at Kitt's house as they did at Austin's. Kitt seemed to just be happy with his company, and he seemed to like their sex just as much as Austin did. Those were both such foreign concepts to Austin that they helped seal the deal for him. But, as he took the porch steps up to Kitt, jealousy racked through him like nothing he'd ever experienced before.

Austin hadn't asked about Fisker since the first day, and Kitt hadn't volunteered a word. But, if he was going out of town, it gave Kitt the opportunity to see the guy. That would never do. Austin might have to order one of his security guards to shoot Fisker on sight for daring to touch what Austin claimed as his....and then, having Fisker killed would create all sorts of complications for him, because surely, there was someone who might miss him. However satisfying the idea of killing Fisker was, he quickly decided it also would be a very bad idea. Besides, Austin didn't truly have a killing bone in his body. So, instead of having the guy offed and buried six feet under, he needed to ask Kitt about him.

Kitt owned the title of Expert Dodger. He excelled at avoiding direct questions. But, Austin had learned; the best way to get answers from Kitt was through sex. Kitt couldn't lie during pleasure, and it was the coolest thing in the world to know he could have that effect on another. So, as any normal person might do, Austin manipulated the situation, moved them past dinner and straight into bed. In return, Austin promptly forgot the questions he wanted to ask and lost track of what he tried to accomplish when Kitt put his lips on Austin's ass.

Armed with new-found determination, Austin decided he'd find those answers tonight. If everything went the way he hoped, by tomorrow night he'd have an exclusive commitment from Kitt, Fisker no longer in the picture – without bodily harming the man – and Cara in rehab. Please God, let it end like he wanted it to!

~~~~~~

Austin got a good look at Kitt as he climbed over the fence, and realized Kitt had dressed up for him. His sexy almost boyfriend could easily be a male model for Wrangler. The thought tugged a smile on his lips.

Kitt wore starched jeans, a pearl button, button down, shiny belt buckle and equally shiny boots. His cowboy hat, that Austin had grown to love, rested on the hood of his truck as he worked to load their gear in the back of his Silverado. Kitt wore that hat regularly, and it fit him and his style perfectly.

Austin didn't say a word on his approach. He carefully positioned his backpack with their dinner in the bed of the truck. Kitt kept it casual as the air between them intensified. It crackled as Kitt started to walk past Austin back to the cabin, never willingly doing a PDA even out here so isolated from everyone. They were clearly the only two around. Austin grabbed Kitt by the waist, easily gathering him in his arms. He leaned in to give a tender kiss, adding only a small swipe of his tongue in the chaste kiss. He loved kissing Kitt. His reward was the slight tremble of Kitt's lips. God, he loved that tremble!

"I'm sorry I'm late again. I missed you." Austin's voice emerged low as he looked down between their bodies, letting his eyes freely roam over Kitt. "You look seriously hot all cowboyed up like this..." He let his palms push down over Kitt's ass to grab each cheek.

"Are you sure it's safe for some of your security to know about us?" Kitt's body stayed tense in the embrace, causing Austin to narrow his brow. No simple *hello* or *I missed you too*, just straight to the point.

This morning Kitt finally noticed the security lurking around when Austin left. He'd only spotted one of them, and Austin tried to play it off as the man being his bodyguard. He should have known better than to think Kitt bought it. He was too smart. The look Kitt gave him just now made it clear he'd figured it all out in his head.

"They're keeping everyone else away, I promise. They keep me hidden, and the cameras away. They keep Mike, or Jose, or anyone else from finding my four-wheeler out here or yours at my house. I've never had a problem with any of my security staff. They sign all sorts of confidentiality agreements. And, I asked them to stay away tonight, so it'll be just us," Austin said. Kitt listened, but tugged free of him to finish loading the last few things from the cabin into the back of the truck.

"It worries me," Kitt said on a pass by he made a minute or two later.

"I know it does and I'm sorry for that, but it can't be helped." Austin didn't let Kitt pass by again without taking his hand. Austin walked beside him up to the house. "What else do we need?"

"Just the sleepin' bags, they're by the door. Everything else's loaded." Kitt stepped in to grab the two sleeping bags. Austin took one from him, tossing it on the sofa.

"This will be more than fine," Austin said.

The move erased the worry from Kitt's brow. He laughed and let Austin circle him in his arms as he pulled Kitt back out the front door. Kitt tossed the one sleeping bag in the back seat of the truck while Austin made his way around and got in on the passenger side. He watched Kitt grab his cowboy hat, and place it on the center console as he slid inside the truck.

"We dub this place Kelly Ridge," Kitt said, as he started the truck and backed away from the house.

"I used to hear about that place. What's the story?" Austin asked, content with just listening to the sound of Kitt's voice.

"It sits overlookin' the back pasture on a slight hill. There used to be a pond down there, but it dried up years ago, before I was ever born. My dad used to take me down there to camp when I was little. You can see for miles and miles..." Kitt said, sounding a little distracted. He didn't finish the thought, but turned on the radio to the local country station he liked. He turned the volume down low.

"Lots of memories then," Austin said, taking the cowboy hat and carefully placing it in the back seat. He lifted the console before sliding in the middle of the seat, closer to Kitt. He couldn't decide if it were a good thing or bad thing to be going somewhere Kitt's father use to take him.

There wasn't a trail and Kitt drove slowly. The headlights of the truck bounced around with every rut they hit. Austin watched Kitt as closely as Kitt watched the pasture in front of the truck. He lifted a hand and brushed Kitt's hair back from his forehead. Austin got a sideways glance and a small grin as he ran his hand down Kitt's thigh, scooting in as close as he could.

"I used to do this in high school. The girls sat right next to me. I think about that when I see you in this truck. Me sitting right here next to you," Austin said, tucking his hand between Kitt's parted thighs, and sliding his fingers under Kitt's leg.

"My friends always did it too. Their wives still do it," Kitt said. His eyes returned to watching the field in front of them.

"You never did?" Austin asked. His only real care in the world seemed to be the man sitting next to him.

"Nah, I never dated any girls. I haven't ever really dated anybody. I've always known I was gay from the time I was little." Kitt said it all so matter of fact, keeping his hands on the wheel, navigating all the ruts in the pasture. He only tossed them around a little as he drove.

Austin kept his eyes on Kitt, watching him closely for any sign of emotion about what he just said. He wasn't at all sure he liked that statement. Kitt deserved someone to be nice to him. Take him out on a date or vice versa. He was sure Kitt would be an excellent date. Someone you'd be glad to have on your arm. The thought brought a smile to Austin's face before his heart ached painfully. He wouldn't ever be the man to take Kitt anywhere. He closed his eyes, turning his head back straight.

"What?" Kitt asked, looking over at Austin.

"Nothing," Austin said absently.

"What?"

"I just wish I could take you out on a real date, and I realized that it will never happen," Austin finally said.

"No, it can't. I've got too much ridin' on things right now. I've learned to live with it. And so have you." Kitt bumped Austin in the shoulder; giving him another sideways glance. The truck hit a good, deep rut and bounced them around, making Kitt quickly cut his eyes back to the pasture.

"It's not bad, Austin. It's actually the only life I know, so I'm good. We should probably slow this down some between us. If we keep goin' every night, someone's gonna catch us." The words came so easily, like it truly was an option for them. "Maybe this trip you're takin' would be a good time to start makin' this a weekly deal or something like that."

"Ah, well, Kitt Kelly, you just managed to take the small ache in my heart and balloon it into a major throb. I'd hate to slow this down," Austin said, his brow narrowed. His eyes focused on Kitt's face. It took a minute, but Kitt looked over at him, slowly giving him that grin of his until another damn rut lurched the truck, making Kitt turn his eyes back to the pasture.

"I'd hate it too, but it's risky what we're doing."

Austin didn't reply. Instead, he lifted his hand between Kitt's parted thighs and slid it up his dick. The bulge under his hand hardened inside the Wranglers.

"So…you've never had sex with a girl?" Austin asked, keeping his hand massaging Kitt's cock. One thing was for certain, Kitt's cock seemed to really like Austin being around.

"Nope, not once," Kitt said, his voice a little deeper since Austin began the intimate massage.

"Huh."

"What's that mean?"

"Just huh, nothing more," Austin said casually. He'd had more sex with women in his life than with men. As he got older, he needed to be drunker, and even stoned. But honestly, he'd learned to take sex however it was offered. A girl's ass wasn't much different than a guy's, and if he closed his eyes and imagined, he seemed to get through it alright.

"I couldn't even get it up with a girl. You probably go both ways, right?" Kitt asked.

"I'm all of a sudden a little ashamed to say yes to you. I prefer men. I need to drink quite a bit to be with a woman, but I do it," Austin said.

"Have you been with Cara?" Kitt asked, now looking directly at Austin. The truck slowed almost to a stop.

"I'm not sure I wanna answer that," Austin said, looking out the front window.

"So it's a yes," Kitt said, their gazes switching places. He looked out the front window as Austin looked at him.

"Not recently. Once I decided I was really done with that world, I sobered up, put the drugs down and cleaned myself up. I've only been with men since then," Austin said.

"How did you work that and keep it quiet?"

"I wasn't always discreet. There're lots of rumors out there. Cara's good at lying about where I was, on and on."

"But she isn't here if we get caught."

"No. But for me, I've decided it can't really affect me anymore. I left that world behind although no one seems to believe me. It's just the cameras are such a pain in the ass. I need a few years to be out of the picture, prove I'm really retired before I let anyone know. If I ever let anyone know. I want my privacy. I *miss* my privacy." Austin said it all again for what felt like the hundredth time in the span of just a few days. He moved his hand back and forth across Kitt's thigh, finally tucking it back under his leg.

"I can't ever come out, Austin. No way this ranchin' world would ever accept it. It's like the 1950's around here. It would ruin everything, and I just can't have that. I have Lily and my sisters to think about."

"No one questions you?" Austin asked.

"If they do, I never hear it. We're here." Kitt brought the truck to a stop at the base of a small ridge. He put it in park, resting one arm on the steering wheel while he hooked his other arm around Austin's shoulders. He used his thumb to lift Austin's chin as he leaned in to kiss him. When he pulled away, Kitt slowly opened his eyes.

"I don't wanna talk about this anymore. It depresses me. I like what we have right now, and the future doesn't look so good for either of us. Just know that when you're ready to go, it's okay, no hard feelings at all," Kitt said, looking straight at Austin. Austin leaned forward, kissing Kitt again, swiping his tongue forward this time before he brought his hand up around Kitt's neck. He pulled him back to deepen the kiss, and drove his tongue forward, dominating the kiss. Beneath his palm, he felt Kitt's heart pounding in his chest when they broke apart.

"We need to set up camp," Kitt whispered still in Austin's face, searching his eyes with his own.

"Kitt, I don't want this to end between us. I feel more alive now than I've felt in years. If we have to stay hidden, then so be it, but I want this between us." Austin realized he gave Kitt no choice but to stay close as he gripped Kitt's shirt. Kitt nodded, looking at him closely for several long moments before he pulled away and slid out of the truck. Damn how he hated it when Kitt went quiet on him!

Chapter 11

They set up camp right on the ridge overlooking the pasture. The night was clear, and the wind blew a mild breeze through the overgrown grass. Tall trees swayed in the distance. The two of them lay spread out on a blanket. A roaring fire flickered just a few feet away, keeping them and the food warm as a mild cool front pushed through the area from the north. Dinner was excellent. They ate small, bite size pieces of food Austin had cooked himself.

"Here, taste this last bite for me. It's hot like you like it. It's a shrimp, jalapeño, bacon something. I found the recipe online." Austin ran the bite over the peppered jelly before lifting it to Kitt's mouth. Kitt relaxed on the blanket, his body sprawled out with his head close to Austin's knee. His standard Bud Light sat close by while Austin opted for wine.

"I'm gettin' full," Kitt said, but still opened for the bite. No way he would refuse anything from Austin, especially something he cooked with his own two hands. Kitt chewed and swallowed as Austin leaned in.

"I got some jelly on the side of your lip," Austin murmured, leaning further in to swipe the sweet and spicy mix from the corner of his mouth. "Mmm…you taste delicious."

"That's your food you're tastin'," Kitt said and leaned up on an elbow to reach for another shrimp.

"It tastes better on you." Austin chuckled at the roll of Kitt's eyes.

"Whatever! Open up, have you tried it? They're delicious." Kitt rose further up to give Austin the bite he just picked out. Austin sucked his fingers in, licked them as Kitt pulled them out.

"Mmmm…you're delicious. I think you need to be on the menu." Austin waggled his eyebrows as the perfect follow up on the cheesy line.

"You're a mess, Austin," Kitt said, as he reached over to grab another bite. He popped it in his mouth before he lay back down on the blanket, looking up at the stars. "I'm glad no storms came with the front. I like us bein' out here together."

"Me, too." Austin brought another piece of shrimp up for Kitt who ate it easily.

"We eat too well. You're gonna get me fat." Kitt swallowed and lifted up to take a drink of his beer.

"Yeah, I don't think there's any fear of that. You work way too hard. But you know, it might not be such a bad idea for you to gain a hundred or so pounds. Maybe it'd help my insecure heart not worry about Fisker, or any others coming to steal you away from me," Austin said absently.

Kitt cut his eyes directly to Austin. There was a lot of meaning in the words just spoken. He laughed at the funniest thought. "If I gain a hundred pounds, I'm not sure you'll wanna keep your eye on me, but give me another bite! We can try it and see which theory proves true…" Kitt swiped the shrimp through the jelly before popping it in his mouth.

Austin just laughed at him. He'd slowly put things away as they were finishing. He moved the shrimp now, keeping it close to Kitt, but making room for himself to lie out beside him. Austin propped his head in his hand. He was at the right angle for Kitt to move in and kiss him softly. "Thank you for dinner."

"So this is your favorite place on the planet?" Austin asked.

"Mm-hmm." Kitt managed to look out over the darkened pasture. "My dad and I came up here when I was a little boy, before things got so messed up between us. And, my oldest sister sometimes came out here with me when I'd come home to visit. I imagined if I ever got married it would be right here. I would have to plan it perfectly with the wind blowing gently, like this, but in the daylight." Kitt loved this part of his land. It was in the very back of the property, right along the property line, and he'd spent so much time here throughout his life it felt like his personal sanctuary. Tonight was no different. As he lay there looking out over the pasture, he watched the night. It took him a minute to realize what he'd just said, and he felt the heat creeping up in his cheeks. He tried to cover it as he pushed up on his feet to stoke the fire.

"I think I was just ensuring I'd never marry. What person in their right mind would agree to have a wedding out here?" Kitt chuckled. He tried to make light of the thought, adding logs to the fire. As he worked, Austin unrolled their sleeping bag.

"You know, we might be an absolute mess in the morning. I'm not sure it was one of our brightest ideas to try and feed each other in the dark," Kitt said, over his shoulder, looking at Austin who stood stretching his long body before he began to undress. Kitt turned back to the fire, tossing a couple more logs on it. All of the remnants of their dinner were gone, and the sleeping bag lay on the blanket for a little extra padding.

"It's cold over here by myself," Austin said, from inside the sleeping bag.

"We can't have that." Kitt grabbed a beer and a bottle of water from the small cooler. After grabbing a roll of paper towels, condoms and lubricant, he laid everything within easy reach. He stood between Austin and the fire undressing before he stretched out.

Austin didn't hesitate to move into Kitt's arms. The pillow was positioned so they could both lay on it, but Austin opted for Kitt's chest to lay his head on. He gave Kitt a small kiss, not letting him take it deeper like he tried to do.

"It's colder outside, winter's close," Austin murmured. With Kitt's urging, he lifted again for another kiss, but again denied him deepening the kiss. He kept it simple and sweet, which was not at all the direction Kitt had in mind.

"That's October in Texas for you, warm days and cool nights," Kitt said casually. He wondered why they were talking about the weather. Kitt took more initiative and rolled them both so they lay on their sides. Running his nose along Austin's jaw, Kitt wrapped him in his arms, caressing his fingertips down the bare skin of Austin's back to his ass.

Both their cocks were good and hard. Kitt pivoted his hips, rubbing them together as he snuck his finger down to massage the tight rim of Austin's ass.

"I was thinkin' maybe I'd lick you right here tonight. See if I can get you to come with just fuckin' you with my tongue. We haven't done that before, but I've wanted to. I used to be pretty good at it in college," Kitt whispered in the crook of Austin neck. He kissed and nipped the skin as he spoke. Austin again leaned in for a kiss, but kept it light and stopped his hand before he was able to slide his finger inside. That was a hard sign to get past and Kitt looked up confused. "What's wrong?"

"Nothing's wrong. I just like spending time with you. It doesn't always have to be just sex," Austin said, looking him in the eyes. It kind of threw Kitt off.

"Okay." He pushed back to match Austin's position. He lay with his head propped up on his hand, but the confusion was clear on his face.

They spent a lot of time talking and never about anything important or relevant to their lives, except maybe when Austin asked him questions about the ranch. Everything else was either the past, like what happened to kids from high school or safe topics like world events and what beer was the best on the planet. That answer never changed for Kitt no matter how Austin tried to persuade him Bud Light wasn't truly the king of beers.

"Stop with that look…and come closer. I didn't mean for you to move away. Scoot closer," Austin said.

After a minute of speculation, Kitt did move back closer to Austin meeting him half way. Austin pushed Kitt back down on his back and leaned up on his elbow. He looked down at Kitt who just watched him, trying to read his expression. Kitt couldn't get a vibe for what he might be thinking. Austin gave nothing away.

"I'm gonna miss you when I go back to California," Austin said, studying Kitt's face.

There was a pause as Kitt tried to figure out what the sentence really meant.

"You might decide you like it better there and stay. It's a pretty lonely kind of life around here. Or wait, is that what you're tryin' to say to me now?" Kitt asked, immediately schooling his features and forcing himself to stay casual. The pain of his unguarded words pierced his heart and ran rapidly throughout his body.

"Absolutely not! Babe, I like it here. I know I get in the way and slow things down, but I like working my body, learning all these new ways of things. It feels right to be here." Austin lifted his fingers to run across Kitt's lower lip as he spoke. "Besides, I've had everything, but solitude since I've been here. You all night, Mike and the guys all day…I need some alone time!" Austin leaned forward for another chaste kiss on his lips. "Remember what I told you in the truck. I want this between us, Kitt. I do."

Kitt let it settle between them; gave his heart the minute it needed to slow, to stop the instant jerk of panic and ache. His gaze still searched Austin's face. "How long are you gonna be gone?"

"I hope not more than a day, maybe two, max," Austin replied, now back to just staring down at him. He ran a stray finger across Kitt's cheek.

A day wasn't so bad. Kitt's heart begged his brain to listen to Austin's words. He didn't want to be the always too practical, negative and analytical one, constantly dissecting everything.

"When I was growin' up, I always thought I'd be outta here the first chance I got. I hated workin' with my dad. He took raisin' me so seriously. I'd get licks for goofin' off, and the whole time he was wallopin' me, he'd tell me it was for my own good, to make me strong. But, the first chance I got, I didn't bolt. I dug my own roots in. I wouldn't even know what to do if I wasn't ranchin' and runnin' cows on this farm."

"You're really good at what you do, Kitt. Mike talks about you all the time." Austin showed some anger when Kitt spoke of his father, but never mentioned it or said anything.

"We all help each other out. Mike just didn't come from that kind of life. It always surprised him when I'd show up to help, but he's always the first one anywhere to lend a hand. He's a good guy. I liked him from the beginning. Older than his years. He's only twenty-three, you know," Kitt said.

"There's more to it than that. Besides, you act older than your years, too. I think it's this farming lifestyle. Micah's kids are the same way."

"Mike's a good hire for you," Kitt replied, not saying anything more. He always shut down when Austin tried to compliment him.

"I can see that."

Silence fell between them. Austin kept his eyes on Kitt, searching his face. Kitt resisted the urge to run a hand over it to see if any stray food might be left behind.

"You're a very handsome man," Austin said a little louder than a whisper. Those eyes of his kept roaming his face, and Kitt couldn't stop his crooked grin from stretching across his lips.

"Not so much. Not like you. I'm pretty scarred up and broke my nose one too many times," Kitt said. That was his dad's doing.

"I've been trying to think of anyone I've ever seen who was or is as handsome as you," Austin said quietly. "But, I can't come up with anyone."

"You help my ego." Kitt grinned as he ran a hand through Austin's thick hair, and then down along his jaw until his fingertip ran the length of his face. Austin was so good with the compliments. He said them so matter-of-factly Kitt wanted to believe them, even the crazy, absurd ones like this one.

"I want this to continue between us. I don't wanna slow it down. Straight guys have friendships all the time with each other. It can just look like you're my buddy, but I don't want this to slow down at all. I like it. You're unexpected, but very good for me," Austin said, entwining their fingers together as he spoke.

"Okay. We can see how it goes," Kitt said cautiously.

"I wish things were different. You need to know I would date you. Take you out, show you a good time and feel privileged to be with you." Austin brought their joined fingers to his lips.

"I'm havin' a good time like this. I don't need to date." A mischievous smile came to Austin's lips at Kitt's words.

"A good enough time to ditch Fisker for good?" Austin lifted his brow in question, but kept his eyes trained on Kitt.

Kitt stared back, not answering. How were they back here again? This was like the third or fourth mention of Sean in the last twenty-four hours. Kitt didn't want to talk about this at all, and Austin wouldn't give it up.

He'd already texted Sean, told him he'd met someone unexpectedly. Sean hadn't taken it well. He'd called Kitt a fool for wasting away over someone who wouldn't be there in a few months. By the end of the text marathon, Sean made it clear he'd be there for Kitt when it was all over, but Kitt would have to work hard to get him back. Apparently, Sean looked forward to the moment. Kitt knew, without question, Sean was one hundred percent right, but none of that mattered right now because Austin already meant something to him. Even if it was only for a few months, or hell, even if it were only days they shared together, he didn't regret letting Sean go.

Austin tightened his grip on his fingers. "Don't avoid the question this time. Answer me."

"I've been with Sean for a long time." As soon as the words came out of his mouth, Kitt saw the hurt they caused Austin although he quickly masked it, hiding behind something Kitt wasn't sure about.

"I understand." Austin leaned in to kiss Kitt, deepening it quickly. He pulled his hand free to reach low and stroke Kitt. It brought his half aroused cock to a full rigid hard-on in seconds. Somehow the tables had turned. Now, it was Kitt who stopped Austin by placing a hand on his. He pulled from the massage and the kiss, linking their fingers back together.

"Hold up, Austin. You didn't let me finish. You need to know I don't play around. I've been with Sean a long time. He's the only person I've been with over the last five years. I can give him up with no problem. It's just, I don't know how long you're gonna be here or even want me. What if you go back tomorrow and decide to stay? And if it's not tomorrow, then the next time you get called back? What happens when you decide you've had enough of this life, of this town, or of me? You're an international superstar. You've experienced life on a level I'll never understand. This is all I've ever done, or will ever do." Kitt's voice was low, and he had a hard time keeping eye contact. It felt like he rambled, but he forged on through everything on his mind, hoping he answered whatever question Austin was truly asking him.

"It's so frustrating! I can't get anyone to believe me. I'm done with that world. That life isn't what it's cracked up to be. I would put this last week up against any other time in my life, and I would pick you every time. I'm done with that out there. I promise you, I'm done. This is where I want to be. Right here, right now. For me, I know if I stay off the radar, they'll eventually leave me alone. Someday, I'll be able to lead a normal life, but Kitt Kelly, I swear to God, if the last five days with you are any indication, I can promise you I'm gonna want you there with me." Austin faltered in his words as he looked Kitt directly in the eyes.

"Austin... You don't even know me."

"I know enough." Austin's reply was instant.

"Is this a commitment you're willin' to make in return?" Kitt asked, knowing in his heart Austin wouldn't be able to handle it long term no matter what he said.

"Absolutely I will. I have fierce jealousy going on inside me about Fisker. He was too smooth...too good looking. I think we could both easily give a commitment and follow it. Seriously, how much more could I need? I have you three, four, five times a night. I'm fucked good and happy, Kitt. Unless, I had you all day, too. I'd like that more," Austin said.

"How do you know that about Sean? When did you see him close enough to know that?" Kitt's question rang sharply.

"Shit...damn it, Kitt, don't be mad," Austin said, and dropped back on his back.

"What?" Kitt rose immediately, looking down at Austin.

"I told you we followed him in. When he got to your place, we tracked him. You were so pissed off at my men you could've easily blown it for me," Austin said, looking up at the stars now, avoiding Kitt who loomed over him. It was an effort on Austin's part to keep his eyes averted from Kitt who was right over his face.

"You told me you tracked him. It was dark. What did you do, watch me?"

"Kind of..." Austin said with a wince.

"So you knew without question before you ever asked me that night?" Kitt asked even though the answer was clear.

"Well, I didn't see what went on in your house." Finally, Austin's guilt stricken eyes came back to Kitt's. It looked like Austin was regretful, but still for a man who hid and went out of his way to be so careful.

"Damn, Austin," Kitt muttered and fell back, breaking their stare.

"I know! I know and I deleted all the pictures."

"You took pictures?" Kitt popped his eyes back in Austin's general direction.

"We had to know who Fisker was...head off anything trying to get in. If I needed to leave, I needed to know." Austin quickly defended his actions.

"He was there for me!" Kitt said and scrubbed his palms down over his eyes. Austin and his entire security team had known he was gay from the beginning. What if it got out?

"I know that now! And it made me crazy, insanely jealous, and I didn't even know you!"

"See? You don't know me like I've been telling you. If you did, you'd know I wouldn't ever tell anyone you're here. I don't spread a bunch of bullshit gossipy crap! Austin, you took pictures of me and Sean, shit!" Kitt sat up with his legs bent, and stared out in the night.

"Kitt...damn it, I was wrong to have those pictures taken. I knew the minute I got them it was wrong, and I do know you now. Do you remember when we were in high school? You played baseball on Varsity. I was a senior. Remember that?" Austin rose up next to Kitt, wrapping an arm around his back, trying to pull Kitt to look at him.

Kitt refused to answer.

"I watched you shower. I felt like such a perv, but I did watch you. You grew into this hot body that year. Everyone knew your dad sucked. He worked you hard, too hard. You stood in that shower with the water pouring down you. All these muscles flowing, and I watched and I remembered. I still remember."

Memories of that day came flooding back to Kitt. He'd thought he was the only one in the showers, but he'd caught sight of Austin leaving the showers from the corner of his eye. When he'd realized who had just turned away, his dick had grown instantly hard. It was a hard-on to end all hard-ons, and he'd been worried Austin might have seen him get hard. At the time, Kitt had thought Austin left because he didn't want to be there with him. And now...to think Austin stood there looking at him like he would look at Austin...damn!

Kitt shoved himself up off the sleeping bag. Austin reached for him, but he moved away. Kitt had all the same possessive emotions coursing through him as Austin seemed to have. He was jealous as hell of Austin going back to Cara and that life, especially now he knew Austin swung both ways.

Kitt knew what he and Austin shared wasn't love no matter how strong it felt. All this flowing through him was sexual tension and deep seeded lust, nothing more. It was his pin up poster come to life, materializing in front of him.

He bent down close to the fire, resting his arms on his knees and watched the flames flicker. Why was he being asked to give up Sean when Austin had a line of ready sex partners just about everywhere...doing both men and women sure made it easy for him to find someone to fuck. How pathetic would it look for him to have already broken it off with Sean? Except, Austin had thought about him over the years. Damn it! Kitt's runaway heart burst at the possibility of what that might mean.

"You're a frustrating man, Kitt Kelly. Come back to bed." Austin matched Kitt's position and wrapped an arm around his shoulders. He leaned in, but didn't pull Kitt to him. He just looked at him. "I'm sorry. I've asked too much, too soon. I need to prove myself to you.

This whole relationship thing is all new to me. Here's what I should have said. I'm not going to be with anyone else, you're enough for me. You can do what you want, I'm fine with it. Now come back to bed. It's getting late, and I want to make love to you at least a dozen times before morning." Austin grinned and kissed Kitt's shoulder.

Kitt gave him a sideways glance, but turned back to the fire not trusting himself. Austin rose and held out a hand. "Come on, I'm really sorry for bringing all this up. Come back to bed."

Kitt took the hand and stood, but wrapped his arm around Austin's waist, anchoring him tightly against his chest. Kitt's eyes trained on Austin's with an intensity he was sure he couldn't hide. Kitt was learning that although Austin was an accomplished actor, there were a few seconds after every word spoken that Austin was raw, showing his honest feeling before reminding himself to hide behind his skill.

"I already told Sean I couldn't see him anymore. I was clear that I'd met someone down here. He thinks I'm a fool to trust it." Kitt finally cut his eyes from Austin's, landing his gaze somewhere around his chin. "I'm not comfortable being photographed without knowin' it, but I get you need the protection. I want you safe. We're gonna have to work somethin' out, somethin' in the middle that's good for both of us, because I like the idea of the future you just drew out. But, you have to know I won't ever willingly come out. Not as long as I'm responsible for my stepmother and sisters and this farm. They need me to be at the top of my game, and this industry's too redneck. They're never gonna accept a gay ranch owner. They would never take me seriously; all they would ever see when they looked at me is whether I topped or bottomed, nothing else would matter. I can't have that, Austin."

Austin used his thumb of their joined hands to push Kitt's chin up, forcing his eyes to follow.

"What is it you need? Is it money? I have enough money to keep you and everyone in this town livin' in style—" Austin began, but Kitt cut him right off.

"No, I'm not takin' your money! I'm workin' my way out of a financial mess my father left behind. It's for me to deal with, no one else, but I can't risk anything right now. I don't have the luxury to gamble at anything," Kitt said firmly.

"Is that why you sold me the land?" Austin asked.

"I don't want to talk about it anymore. It's my responsibility, and I'll get through it on my own. I've got the hay baler now, cows about to go on sale and four quarter horses about to pop. I'll handle it myself." Kitt had already said more than he intended and refused to say another word.

"If this lasts between us we're going to have to talk about it because that's what couples do. Not that I'm jumping us ahead to couple status so get that look off your face. You frustrate me, Kitt. You never give. Ever. What would be so bad about being a couple? No, don't answer. I don't want to argue anymore tonight." Austin brought both his hands up to cup Kitt's face, holding him right there as he spoke.

"There are far more important things we should be concentrating on…I want to fuck you like crazy and then do it again! I'm celebrating. Fisker worried me…" Austin leaned in to capture Kitt's lips with his own. He thrust his tongue forward, swiping at the seam of Kitt's mouth until he gained entrance. He wasn't going for the sweet tender kiss Kitt planned. No matter what angle Kitt came in, he never got the upper hand in the kiss. Austin dominated him at every turn, and Kitt grinned when he found himself being pushed down to the sleeping bag.

"Lay down, Kitt, before I drop you to your knees on this hard ground. I'm feeling possessive as hell right now. You made me work too hard for that commitment. You make me work too hard for even your simplest smile. I need to fully fuck you until you get it through that thick skull of yours that you're mine." Austin meant every word said.

It was pitch black outside with only the stars and fire giving off any light. Kitt stumbled as Austin flipped him around. He landed on his knees on the sleeping bag. Austin was right there on him. His movements were forceful as Austin spread his legs, sliding two dry fingers in his rim, stretching him quickly.

"I can't see the lube," Austin grumbled still working Kitt, adding a third finger. Kitt felt around on the ground in the general direction of where he thought he laid it earlier and grinned when he found the lube and condoms. For a short moment, Kitt thought he might tease Austin, say he couldn't find them, but he gave the guy at his ass a break and tossed them over his shoulder.

Austin wasted no time. He condomed up and burrowed deep inside Kitt in the first mind blowing thrust of his eager hips. Austin easily conquered the tight rim, going straight for the spot, massaging there as he dove inside.

There was only a momentary hiss from both men before Austin pushed Kitt down between his shoulder blades. Austin kept his hand there to hold Kitt in place. Kitt's head was smashed on the sleeping bag, or it may have been the ground, who knew for sure.

Austin kept one had on Kitt's back and anchored the other hand against his hip. He rose up on his feet for a better angle and used the leverage from Kitt's body to help better pound into him. Those sweet moments of gentle caresses and loving words were long gone. Austin worked Kitt over like he had a right to be there. Austin's balls slapped Kitt's ass with every single fast thrust he made moving deeper and deeper inside him. He had no choice but to take it and open wider. Austin wasn't going to be done until he claimed Kitt in both body and soul. There was no formality to it, definitely no foreplay, just the hard fucking they both seemed to desperately need.

"It feels good...move a little to the left....*Yeah! Fuck, Austin!* That feels good."

"You're mine Kitt. Say it. Say you're mine." Austin jackhammered his hips, relentlessly pounding into Kitt. He pushed down harder with the hand holding Kitt's hips forcing his ass a little higher in the air.

"Say it Kitt. You've made me wait too long. Say it," Austin demanded, panting between deep breaths.

"I'm gonna come," Kitt said through deep, breathy moans.

His response caused Austin to drive harder into his ass. Austin said something as Kitt's body felt like it was ripping apart. The lines of pleasure and pain blurred. Kitt reached out fisting the sleeping bag, shoving his ass higher in the air to get his other hand around his own engorged cock.

"Say it," Austin growled, changing his position when he realized Kitt was stroking himself underneath. He pushed Kitt's hand away, and gripped Kitt's dick, squeezing it tightly, refusing to let him come. The pounding never stopped.

"Say it, and I'll get you off," Austin bellowed.

"...I'm yours..." It came out in a whimper.

"Yeah you are." It was all Austin needed to hear. He stroked Kitt erratically, with no skill whatsoever, making Kitt instantly come. Austin shouted his own release just seconds later as he fell forward on Kitt's back, pushing them both down on top of the sleeping bag.

Chapter 12

The sudden shake of his head startled Kitt awake. A smile came to his lips as he closed his eyes against the early morning sun. His mind fought the urge to fully wake. He ran his nose along the top of Austin's head breathing in his scent. This morning Austin's hair was mixed with a little bit of smoke from their fire, and a little bit a sweat from their all night sexual quest. Kitt's ass was sore. Deliciously sore, he'd heard said somewhere along the way, and now he understood completely what those words meant.

All night, Austin had stayed rough and eager, giving and taking before turning gentler, sweet and tender. The one thing he hadn't exaggerated about, they went at it all night long. Kitt's ass got a couple of solid poundings, the kind that would cause this ache to stick around for a few days. Austin told him he intended it to remind Kitt who his ass belonged to while he went away to Los Angeles.

Funny how the thought of commitment and exclusivity with Sean had freaked him out, but now with Austin, his heart felt light and breezy, ready to be Austin's for however long he wanted it and him. The romantic thought caused Kitt to smile again, and he kissed the top of Austin's head.

They lay zipped up tight in the sleeping bag. Austin sprawled across Kitt, and they held each other tight. It didn't look like they changed position much over the last couple of hours. In these early morning hours, Kitt still couldn't fully wrap his mind around the fact that Austin wanted a long term, exclusive relationship with him. Well, now, relationship was never actually mentioned, but exclusivity was made very clear. A long term fuck buddy with someone who was hiding from the world had to mean a relationship of some sort, right? Kitt felt shockingly great about it all. Maybe shocked better described it, but to know the person you wanted most in the world actually wanted you back...yeah, the word great fit right up there too.

Based on the sun, it had to be early. Kitt guessed it close to seven. A noise caused him to look to the side of their sleeping bag. He figured the cows were making their way down the pasture. It was where they came first thing in the morning. That was probably what woke him. Kitt looked to the left of them but saw nothing. He looked to the right and saw the fire was just embers now. He stroked his hand up Austin's back thinking if it were early enough, maybe they'd have time for one more round before Austin had to get going. After a minute more of lightly stroking his fingertips across Austin's back, Kitt ran his hand down to Austin's ass, sliding a finger into the crease. It was still a little oily from last night and his finger slid in easily. It made Austin finally lift his head. Sleepy, tired eyes met his with a big grin.

"Good morning, sexy....funny how my ass hurts, yet that feels so good. Can we go back to the licking thing you started with last night?" Austin leaned in for a kiss, but something caught his attention and he lifted his gaze. His eyes grew wider as Kitt watched. "Kitt, we aren't alone."

Kitt threw his head back, looking upside down at what Austin was staring at. His sister, Kylie, sat on top of her horse between them and the truck. Panic struck his heart. He immediately tried to separate from Austin, but they were zipped up tight. All he could do was jerk his hand from Austin's ass. "What are you doin' here?"

"You know what, Kitt? I was gonna quietly leave when I saw you, but then I got so *mad*! And for the record, I *knew*! But *you* should have told me!" Kylie yelled. She was a short fiery little red head, and she dismounted with only the flair and fight of a true Kelly. She didn't just let go of the reins, she tossed them. Just like with Kitt's horse, hers was well trained - he ignored her outburst as he sauntered off. He wouldn't travel far.

"Kylie! What're you doing here?" Kitt asked again, unzipping the zipper and dislodging from Austin. He pushed away, but there was little room in the sleeping bag. Kitt flipped the top open dumping Austin to the side. Austin tried in vain to cover himself, but he lay partially exposed when Kitt jumped up. Kitt dropped his hands down, covering his package. Kylie was purposefully trying to embarrass him now, standing with her arms crossed over her chest and feet spread apart, tapping her foot, her angry blue-eyed stare trained on him.

Kitt went straight for his underwear and jeans, shaking them out and turning from both Austin and Kylie as he pulled on his underwear first. From out of nowhere, Kylie snuck up behind him and jerked the jeans away from him. She ran away several feet, hiding them behind her back until the fire was between them.

"Give me my jeans!" Kitt growled, using one hand to cover himself. Austin tossed him their pillow, and he used it to hide behind. He darted around the fire, but she ran away from him. No matter which way he went, he couldn't trick her or get to his clothes.

"No! I tell you everything, Kitt. Everything! You're like my mom and my dad and my brother and my best friend all in one, and *you like boys* and you never tell me? What's that about? This is so not fair! And, for the record, I knew it! Or I suspected it, but you still should have told me!" Kylie finally came to a stop after her rant, and Kitt stalked to her. He was barefoot, toeing around rocks and grass spurs as he went toward her. Making a dramatic flair of pulling his jeans away from her, he turned around to see Austin sitting on the sleeping bag. Kitt pulled each leg of the jeans up, bouncing as he covered his ass with the denim and buttoned up his Wranglers.

"Kylie, go home. We'll talk about this later. And for God's sake, don't say one word to anyone about him. Or me!" Kitt said turning back toward her. He grabbed the rest of his clothes she now held in her hands. Kitt walked through their camp, picked up Austin's clothes, and tossed them in his general direction.

"No! I'm not leaving until you explain why you never told me. Kitt, you were my best friend growing up! I can't believe you didn't trust me enough to tell me!"

"Why aren't you in school?" Kitt asked, ignoring everything she said and scrubbed his hands over his face. His wonderfully blissful morning had turned to crap in a matter a seconds.

"Because I've been calling you, and you were avoiding me. So, I drove home. They said you were in Dallas, so I came out here, where you and I used to come because I miss my brother and needed to be in the one place we both love. Kitt, why didn't you tell me?" Kylie asked the last sentence in more of a whine, and for the first time since they started talking, Kylie looked over at the guy sitting on the sleeping bag.

"*And you're Austin Grainger! Oh my gawd!* Kitt, that's Austin Grainger!"

He stopped his hand in mid-scrub down his face and looked over at Austin who still sat there in nothing, covered from the waist down in his sleeping bag. The only words that came to mind were simply, "I'm sorry."

"Why're you sorry?" Austin asked at the same time Kylie did.

"Is he your boyfriend? Oh my God, is this why you left acting, to come here and be with my brother? Kitt, that's so romantic!" Kylie said it all, looking between them both. She had the most love struck look in her eyes, and all Kitt could do was groan and roll his eyes to the heavens, begging for the world to just swallow him up whole.

"Kylie, I need you to go back to my house and wait for me. And don't speak to anyone." Kitt stood between her and Austin now, but Austin rose, keeping himself wrapped in the sleeping bag and walked toward them. He slid in behind Kitt, wrapping one arm around Kitt's stomach, the sleeping bag anchored between them and stuck out his other hand toward Kylie.

"I'm guessing you're Kylie, the sister he's so proud of," Austin said, giving her his charming grin. It didn't matter his hair stood on end, or that he was draped in a sleeping bag. Austin was sexy and hot as hell, just sucking Kylie further in when Kitt tried to push her out.

"Yes...Oh my God, I can't believe you're here. Are you the one who bought our land?" Kitt watched it happen in front of him, and his heart began to slowly sink to his knees. Kylie was the only one who knew about this special place he brought Austin to. It had never occurred to him she might come home from school this weekend. Hell, Austin had him so tied up in knots he didn't even realize he missed her calls. He would have never dodged her on purpose, and he could feel his precious secret slipping out of his grasp as more people found out.

"I am. It's my pleasure to meet you. I'm going on the other side of the truck and dress. I brought gourmet coffee. Please ignore your brother." With that, Austin kept the sleeping bag around him and carried his jeans and t-shirt the few steps behind the truck like it was the most natural situation on earth. Kitt started shaking his head to tell Kylie to go home, but she was too excited, jumping right in on him.

"Kitt, you should have told me! And you're datin' Austin freakin' Grainger!" She beamed. "I'm really happy and really mad at you all at the same time!"

"No, I'm not datin' him. You need to go—" Kitt was cut off by Austin.

"*Yes, he is dating me!*" Austin yelled back. The outburst had both Kitt and Kylie, looking back at him as he pulled the t-shirt over his head. He tossed the sleeping bag into the bed of the truck and finger combed his hair, taking careful steps back to them.

"You're like all over the news. Everyone's lookin' for you. They think you're hidin' out in a villa in Italy. How're you down here? Is it cause of Kitt? Did you come back here for him? Kitt, is this why you never go out?" Kylie fired off the questions, staring at Austin with a big smile on her pretty upturned face.

"Kylie..." The last question horrified Kitt. Austin didn't seem to notice as he stood beside him, wrapping an arm around his waist. It was hard not to move out of the casual touch.

"So far, no one's thought to look here, and I need you to keep all this to yourself. Only a handful of people know I'm here. But honestly, your brother's the most important person to me in this deal. I know he's not comfortable with you, or anyone for that matter, knowing about this or him." Austin's words were so perfect. Kitt watched Kylie, trying to gauge her reaction, but the star struck wonder just stayed the most obvious part of her expression.

"Does Mom know you're here? She's safe. She hates all the gossip in town. She won't tell anyone, I promise."

"She knows, but your little sister doesn't," Austin said, and Kitt just let him do the talking. That numb feeling began to wear off with dread closing in fast.

"Okay, so I can keep it quiet. Have y'all been like in love since high school?"

"No! No, no, *no*! Kylie, enough with all the questions! Shit!" Kitt threw his hands up in the air. "Please, go home."

"I wish I'd been with your brother since high school," Austin said, looking over at Kitt who now paced until a sticker got him good in the foot and he was forced to stop and dig it out.

"Okay, let me ask this. Why aren't you tellin' people? You two are like, hot, together," she said.

"We're done. This is done. You're leavin'," Kitt said, tossing the sticker aside. He whistled for her horse, and at the same time, Austin's phone rang, startling him.

"I have to get going. My security team's on their way out here to drive me to the airport. I need my tennis shoes."

"Here! Are these yours?" Kylie said, all smiles and helpfulness bundled in an incredibly annoying little sister.

Austin's pickup truck came out of nowhere, slowly making its way through the pasture. Kitt could only watch it drive up. He'd thought they were all alone out here. Austin told him they were, but clearly his security knew where Austin was at all times. Had they watched them last night? The thought caused a deep heat of a blush to rise in his cheeks as his eyes riveted to Austin. They only stared at one another for a second or two, but he could see Austin knew his thoughts when he shook his head mouthing a very clear *'no'* in his direction.

For the first time this morning, Austin's brow lowered, frustration clear in his eyes. After a second of everyone looking at each other, Austin took matters in his own hands and pulled Kitt to the back of his pickup truck, ignoring the rest of them.

"I need to go. I'm sorry I can't stay and clean this up with you. I promise you they weren't around last night. They tracked me through my phone," Austin said. He took Kitt in his arms, coming to stand chest to chest at the tailgate of the truck. Kitt reluctantly followed the move. He cut his eyes up to see if the others were looking their way.

"This so wasn't how I wanted our morning to start. I'm sorry," Kitt said quietly.

"It was still good. Your sister's lovely. I think she'll keep it quiet," Austin said, pulling Kitt tighter against him. Kitt again cut his gaze over to see if anyone looked their way. "I'm right here, Kitt. We seriously have to work on you being so jumpy. These people already know. Now kiss me like you meant everything we discussed last night, and make me think you'll only think of me while I'm gone."

What if Kitt was right and Austin didn't come back? What if this was the last time he spent with Austin? Kitt lifted his hands, holding Austin's face in place and slanted his mouth over Austin's, kissing him thoroughly in a swirl of tongue and teeth. Kitt meant everything he said last night, and he threaded his fingers through Austin's hair, positioning him better to extend the kiss. If this was their kiss goodbye, Kitt wanted to remember it for the rest of his life.

When they finally came up for air, Austin grinned with his eyes closed. "Yep, that was exactly what I needed. I'll be back as soon as I can. I'm hoping about a day, no longer than two." Slowly, Austin opened his eyes, and Kitt stepped away, but kept his gaze intently focused on Austin, trying to memorize everything he could about the man.

"I hope your ass is as sore as mine. And don't call Fisker. Jack off until I get back!" Austin said as he walked over toward his truck. Kitt couldn't keep the smile from forming on his face. Austin was jealous of Sean, and as wrong as it was, it did great things to his heart.

Kitt watched Austin drive off only then remembering Kylie. He turned quickly, wondering if she'd heard the jack off remark, but both she and her horse were gone. She'd finally got a clue and gave them privacy. She'd also picked up their camp, leaving the site mostly clean. Kitt lifted the cooler into the back of his pickup and checked the fire pit one last time. He sat there alone a minute, tugging on his boots. He already missed Austin even before he got inside his truck and headed for his cabin.

Chapter 13

"You should've told me. We're a team! I always thought it was you and me against the world," Kylie said, following Kitt into his bedroom.

"You're supposed to concentrate on school, not come back here," Kitt said back just as confrontational. He slammed the bathroom door and locked it behind him so she wouldn't follow him in. The door didn't stop her from yelling at him through it.

"Just tell me why you never trusted me enough to tell me about yourself," Kylie yelled. It took a full minute of him standing on one side of the door, imagining her on the other side, both just staring at the closed door.

"Kylie, I couldn't tell you. You're a little girl…" Kitt said. His tone was soft, and he turned from the door to start the shower, not completely drowning her out, but close.

"I'm not a little girl, I'm eighteen years old. And, I guessed it. But, all those trips to Dallas threw me off. Everybody says you just have a thing for city girls," Kylie called out as Kitt stepped inside the shower. He stayed there longer than normal, hoping she'd get tired of waiting and leave.

He took his time grooming. He thoroughly brushed his teeth, brushed and dried his hair, even shaved and plucked a few unwanted hairs trying to drag it out. Kylie was impetuous, always moving. No way could she stay out there waiting for him for the forty minutes he took in the bathroom.

As a precaution, Kitt wrapped a towel around his waist before he stepped into his bedroom only to be faced with Kylie sitting on his bed, looking at his door. The bottom drawer to his nightstand was open with his latest *People* magazine in her lap. The issue featured Austin Grainger, *People's Sexiest Man Alive*.

"I guess it was more like city boys than girls," she said, flipping through the pages. "Sorry, couldn't resist. Now, I get why you have all these magazines around."

Kitt stalked over to her, frustration clear on his face, and jerked the magazine away from her.

"I'm sorry! Kitt, this is all fine to me. I'm glad to know. But, no one else knows? Not anyone?"

"No one! I haven't told anyone." He dropped the magazine back in the drawer, slamming it shut with his foot.

"That makes me feel bad for you. What a lonely life you must've led, I'm sorry for you. You're such a good man. I honestly don't think people will care. My campus is loaded with banners and petitions about equality for all. And, now that Dad's gone, he can't disown you or anything like that," she said, sorrow now securely in her eyes.

Kitt held the towel in place, pulling jeans and a t-shirt from his closet. He stopped by his dresser, grabbing underwear before he went back to the bathroom to dress.

"They'll care, and it will ruin everything so you can't tell. Period, end of story!"

Kylie didn't respond. Kitt dressed quickly and walked back out into his bedroom. He stopped and stared at his sister, with his socks and boots in hand, waiting to get her promise to keep quiet.

"I already promised you, Kitt, but how crazy is it that my brother's datin' Austin Grainger! You are datin' him, right?" She jumped off the bed, following him as he headed toward the living room.

"I think so. He wants to be together as best as we can. He needs time to get past all the media, but Kylie, I can't ever come out, and I don't see him stickin' around here for any real length of time. He's just burned out right now, that's all. He'll go back to California. So don't get all excited about it. I don't think we have any sort of future, but right now it's cool, I guess," Kitt said. He sat down on the sofa to pull on his boots, and Kylie sat down beside him.

"I thought he was engaged?" She sat still, her hands in her lap, watching him with his boots.

"Nah, she just works for him. People aren't as acceptin' as you think. He had to hide too." Kitt pushed down on both heels and stood, stomping a couple of times, making sure the boots were tightly on his feet. He made his way to the kitchen, Kylie back on his heels. He pulled sandwich stuff from the refrigerator and began to make them both a sandwich.

"You need to stay at school, not worry about things goin' on here. We talked about this already. Next year, after you get in the swing of things with balancin' class and studyin', but not now," he said, looking down as he worked.

"The cafeteria food sucks." Kylie came to stand with her hip propped on the kitchen counter.

"I can give you more money a week. You should've said somethin'. I know I talk about how bad things are around here, and it's still gonna take a few years to pull this place back up, but it's not as bad as it was. I still have money from sellin' the land, and I have seven insemination jobs lined up. Did I tell you I might've sold a colt to a racin' farm in Kentucky already? We just need him to get here and let them come see him. So we're doin' better, or at least the future's not so dark anymore," Kitt said, handing one sandwich to Kylie before taking a big bite of his.

"I shouldn't have gone to A&M," Kylie said, and took her sandwich, looking at it but not taking a bite. Kitt saw the concern in her eyes.

"Yes you should've and I don't wanna talk about it anymore. You're where you need to be. Plus, in eight years we're gonna need a vet around here."

"Let's go back to Austin Grainger. I like that conversation better! Kitt, he's seriously hot," Kylie said, finally taking a bite of her sandwich.

"I know, right?" They stood there together with their hips perched on the counter eating. This was how it was with them. They were always comfortable with one another. It was an unconditional kind of deal.

"They could legalize gay marriage, Kitt. It looks like it's comin'," she said with her mouth full.

"No way Texas will ever, unless it's forced on us. And, even if that happens, it's not gonna happen like that for Austin and I. Kylie, seriously, he's just here catchin' his breath. He's not gonna stick around for too long, or pick some country boy to be with for the rest of his life. It's just convenient for him for now." Saying it so candidly to his little sister made Kitt blush a little, but he took another bite, grabbing two Dr. Pepper's from the refrigerator and shoved one toward his sister.

"You're wrong about yourself. You're a catch. He'd be lucky to have you."

"Whatever! He could get some of those hot male models, not a scarred up, broken nosed, cowboy." Kitt said with a laugh. The thought was totally ludicrous. He laughed so hard he choked on the soda he drank from.

"Whatever back! Have you looked in the mirror? You're hot, and I know the ranch's failin', but you're workin' through it. And, if nothing else, we could sell the land and it would free you up." Kylie nodded, shoving the last bite of her sandwich in her mouth.

"No one wants this much land in the middle of the desert down here close to nothing. And, I don't want to have this conversation. Now, seriously, why're you here this weekend? It seems like I just dropped you off, and if I remember correctly, there was somethin' about never comin' back to this town again."

"I missed you guys…" Kylie smiled as she said it.

"Why?" Kitt cocked an eyebrow.

"Ha ha! I did miss you, and you must really be out of touch. It's Homecomin' and you weren't returnin' my phone calls. You should come to the game tonight with me," she said.

"It's Homecomin' already? Really? How did I miss that?"

"My guess is you aren't spendin' any time in town, just with Austin freakin' Grainger!" Kylie dumped her napkin in the trash laughing, and put everything back in the refrigerator while Kitt finished his sandwich.

"How're your grades?" Kitt asked in an attempt to change the subject as he took his last couple of bites. He refused to say another word about Austin.

"So far so good. I'm strugglin' in Chemistry, but I have a good tutor. I think I can pull a low A if nothing else."

"Promise to let me know if you need help before it's too late. I can get online, do that webcam thing and help you." He tossed his napkin in the trash and looked around for his phone and keys. It was already after nine, and he needed to get started on the day.

"I will. I'm goin' back to the house. Mama's gettin' ready for the parade, and Bryanne was gonna paint her fingernails leopard print to match her bow, just in case she wins Homecomin' Queen."

"Y'all have fun," Kitt said, and Kylie followed him out.

"Are you sure you don't wanna go with us tonight? Everyone'll be askin' about you," Kylie asked, mounting her horse.

"Nah, I gotta catch up on some stuff and check out the baler, get it ready for next week," Kitt said, getting in his truck and rolling the window down.

"Alright, brother, I love you. I'll come see you when we get home. Bring you dinner," she said, turning the horse around. "Kitt, I get that you don't wanna talk about Austin, but I can tell you like him. I'm happy for you."

She didn't wait for an answer, nor did he give one. He just watched her go in the rearview mirror. As she faded away, he stopped watching her and looked at himself.

He couldn't see why anyone would find him good looking. He had a deep scar in his eyebrow from one of the fights his dad had tried to pick with him. It started above the eye, threading through the brow and up into his forehead. He also had a scar across his bottom lip. Both were fine, thin lines now, but still there. And his nose had been broken at least three times that he remembered. Nothing about him classified as pretty at all.

He also didn't have those polished hard bodies you got from trainers and gym workouts. Those guys were sculpted from head to toe to have every muscle toned, fit and flowing together. Austin's body was like that – just hot from head to toe. Kitt sported muscle, but it was different. His muscle came from hard work. They were two completely different things. His thighs were too thick, his ass too round, and the sun had done its fair share of damage to his skin. At twenty-eight years old, the lines were already forming around his eyes and mouth. He was starting to agree with Sean, he should consider sunscreen.

Kitt switched his gaze to his too long hair. It had grown out past the point of whatever style the hairdresser last cut it in, and it was a strange color. Mostly auburn with gold and blond in it, but it was odd. It was all the sun's doing. The complete study of his overall physique helped settle some of the hope his runaway heart had let filter in last night. No way did he compare to the Seans and Austins of the world.

Kitt might be momentarily happy, but he couldn't lose sight of the fact that he was convenient and available. Austin had secluded himself here with no one else. After time faded and people stopped caring, Austin could come out and find someone better suited to him, and it was almost laughable how the thought hurt Kitt's heart. Kitt pushed the pain aside. He'd made the decision last night, committed to this thing between them until Austin decided to leave. Which Austin technically already did…but, if he came back, Kit would enjoy the regular sex and the friendship. He wasn't going to make anything more out of it. Looking back at the mirror, he nodded to himself to confirm the thought.

He finally reversed the truck and began to back away from the cabin. Focus on his future required he spend a full day at the barn. No more time for distractions. He pulled out on the trail and his phone vibrated. The message was from Austin.

'I loved waking up in your arms. It's something I want to repeat as soon and as often as possible. I enjoyed myself last night. I can never decide what's better, for you to be buried inside me, or me in you… It's a tough call, but my ass is sore in all the right ways. I shouldn't be gone more than a day or two. I'll call as I can. Think about me while I'm gone. Your sister's lovely. A'

Kitt read the message, and then he read it again. His heart gave a little flip in his chest as he brought the truck to a complete stop in the middle of the trail. After a minute, he began to scold himself. "Stop! It's not really anythin' more than sex, *so stop reading more into these words*! It's not real. It's not real. *It's. Not. Real!* He doesn't really want you, you're just fillin' time."

Kitt put the phone down without returning the message. He drove all the way to the barn with the phone sitting beside him. The big white elephant in the cab. Finally, when he came to a stop in front of the barn, he picked the phone back up, warring with himself until he sent a message back.

'I'm sorry about my sister. Be careful.' He barely had the phone clipped to his hip before another message came back.

'Tell me what happened to already have you back to the super quiet attitude. Never mind, don't answer that. I look forward to convincing you again that I'm for real. Have a good day playing sexy cowboy. I'll try to call you tonight if I'm not already home.'

Kitt didn't respond and refused to read the message more than once. He didn't have the time to be playing phone games when there was so much work to be done. First on the to-do list, the maintenance on the discounted, yet still expensive as hell hay baler he'd bought at auction. Second, see if any orders had come in for all this hay he was about to have up for sale.

Chapter 14

The plane touched down in the bright California sun. The breeze outside was mild, and the temperature perfectly warm, just like always in sunny California. Austin made his way through a private entrance of the small executive airport. He kept his head held low, a ball cap pushed down over his eyes, and his Ray-Ban Avatar's on, trying to hide himself as much as possible.

A private car waited for him at an exclusive side entrance, and Austin made it almost to the door before the stares started. Little side nudges caught his eye, and he knew he must hurry. He wasn't fast enough. The pointing started, a few fans approached him, and the paparazzi who hung outside spotted the commotion. Austin never stopped his stride as he scribbled his signature on a couple of open notebooks. He ducked into the backseat of the waiting car within sixty seconds of stepping outside. It didn't matter how his driver drove, they got surrounded almost immediately with the cameras snapping his picture, trying for any shot they could get. Austin had his phone programmed to alert him when his name was mentioned online, and before he got out of the parking lot, *TMZ* already posted their shots of him sitting in the car.

The mellow mood of the last few weeks evaporated completely. In its place, a deep disdain smoldered and slowly grated on his nerves. With all certainty, Austin never wanted back into this chaos. If Kitt had any real clue what this world was all about, he'd never again question Austin's decision to leave.

The drive to his house in the hills of Hollywood took longer than it ever should have. The police finally got involved and escorted him to his driveway, and even then, it was a slow drive. People jumped out in front of the car, risking their lives just to get a shot of him. He even spotted Rich and Mercedes already there, cameras snapping away. They were the two paparazzi who had constantly plagued him over the last ten years. They never gave him a break, and now flung questions at him through the car's side window, like he would ever answer any of them. Dozens of paparazzi blocked his way, even as the gate opened. A police officer stood on guard, keeping everyone at bay as they drove down the driveway.

Austin stayed tense and stone-faced the entire ride. He never looked at any of them. Instead, he kept his head slightly lowered making it harder to get a good shot. He resisted the urge to pull up Kitt's picture on his phone for fear someone with a great lens might catch it. But, dear God, Austin's dependent side needed to get a look at Kitt. Kitt represented peace, love and simplicity. Everything that was right in his world. In just a few days, Kitt helped to settle his soul and center him. Amazing, how a chance encounter allowed him to meet someone who so completely turned his world around in such a short time. The realization made Austin wish Kitt was with him now.

"We were quiet, no one knew, I swear. Just me, you, and the driver," Seth said, meeting him at the car door.

"I know. I watched it fucking happen at the airport."

They were in the back of the house with high fencing and security, but who knew who might get through. Austin kept his head low, hurrying into the open garage.

"Damn, this is going to complicate things." Seth kept up with Austin stride for stride.

"Exactly my thought during the entire fucking drive here. Goddamn, I hate those mother fuckers. And those two asswipe fuckers were right there in the middle of it all. They had their cameras pressed against the window. I hate Rich and Mercedes! Goddammit, those fuckers need a life." Austin raged as he stepped inside the garage and forced himself to calm down. After a minute, he shook his head, forcing the images out of his mind and concentrated on why he was here.

"How is she?" They slowed their pace, talking quietly like it was some big secret, that the people who worked here couldn't possibly notice the female spiraling out of control right in front of them.

"Not good at all. She's got herself locked up in the back room. She's strung out. She's missing tapings, and they're telling me today, if she doesn't get help, they're publically canning her from the film."

Seth didn't mince words, he was a straight shooter. It was one of the things Austin liked most about him.

"Damn it! How did it get this bad, this quick? Whatever. Did you call Arizona, get something ready for her?" Austin asked about the rehab center they'd discussed over the phone.

"Yes, they're waiting for us." Seth nodded while gnawing at his lip. Austin got the distinct impression he wanted to say more, but didn't. Austin eyed him closely, willing Seth to say whatever he held back. When nothing came, Austin let it go. He'd find out soon enough. He continued on as if he hadn't noticed the hesitation.

"Okay, let me go talk to her," Austin said, and walked through the house into the kitchen. The driver sat at the table, waiting for his directions. His housekeeper looked up. She didn't speak much English, but worry was clear on her face. Austin gave her a polite pat on the shoulder as he walked by. He prayed this would be an in-and-out kind of deal. The odds of it happening seemed against him with the worry on everyone's face.

Cara's history in this area wasn't good. Usually, when she let herself get this far out of control, she was a raving bitch of a nightmare to deal with. As he got closer to the bedroom, he heard loud music blaring from inside. The temperature in this part of the house was freezing. The air conditioning was turned way down.

Austin didn't knock and the door wasn't locked. He walked straight in to see Cara sitting with her robe open, her body nude underneath. Two young men were with her in the room. One sat perched on the floor between her spread thighs, rubbing one hand up the inside of her leg. His other hand massaged her clit where his head was headed. The second man sat behind her. She sat on his lap with her legs spread open, straddling his parted thighs. Clearly, his dick was inside her as he rolled his hips back and forth at a slightly awkward angle. In one hand, he held the crack pipe she smoked from while the other rolled her nipple between his fingers. Cara was so stoned, her eyes weren't much more than slits as they looked over at him. She sucked in a breath, held it and let it go never acknowledging he walked into the room.

"It's good, isn't it?" The man in front of her never heard Austin come in the room, but the one behind her had no problem seeing him. He panicked, trying to get her off him. But, she dropped the pipe and rolled her head back falling straight back on the man, making it harder for him to get out from under her. Cara's body lay completely bared to them all. She rocked her hips against the penis slipping in and out of her and wrapped her long legs around the man in front of her, ignoring the one behind her trying to get away.

"Fuck me...*He* won't fuck me anymore..." She moaned, reaching her hands up around the neck of the guy behind her, trying to hold him in place, trapping him there.

"Cara." Austin's only word came out in the despair he felt so deep in his soul. The sight was pathetic, crushing his heart. He couldn't believe they were here again. The guy between her legs whipped his head around, seeing Austin for the first time. She tightened her Pilates strengthened thighs around him, not letting him move. The guy underneath her finally broke free, rolling as quickly as he could away from her. Austin didn't pay him any attention as he moved across the room to turn the music off.

"Noooo, don't stop. Austin, come join us...where's Seth? Austin, make him come in here and fuck me! He won't fuck me anymore. Austin..." Tears sprang to her eyes, and she dropped her legs, letting the second panicked man free. He too darted up, making a wide dodge around Austin, and moved fast to get out of the room. Austin didn't care about either of them. His only concern was Cara, and he went straight to her.

"Baby, you have to stop this." He covered her with her robe before picking her up and moving her up on the bed.

"No! Austin, *no*! Don't make me stop it. I love it! It makes me feel alive." Cara jerked herself up from the bed, moving erratically. She slung her body around as she spoke until her robe fell to the floor. She grabbed her silicone filled breasts, crushing them together. "Take a hit like the old days and come fuck me, Austin."

Her step forward had her tripping, and she fell to the floor, splayed open before him, exposing everything to his view. "Make Seth come in here and make love to me. I miss him, Austin. He'll do it again if you make him."

"I'm not doing that, Cara," Austin said. He reached down to pick up her robe, before bringing her back up to her feet. She swayed, and he caught her easily before she fell again. "We've got help ready for—"

"I love him. I wanted to marry him, and have babies with him, and live a normal life, like normal people, and he won't because of you," Cara said, her eyes sliding closed. She opened them again after a few seconds. "I love him and he won't..."

"I'm going to get you help, Cara," Austin said, scooping her up again. She was no help, almost dead weight on his arms.

"I don't need help. I need Seth." Her eyes closed as she passed out.

~~~~~~

Tucked in bed, Cara finally slept it off. Austin sat beside her, watching her sleep as he weighed his options. He could load her up now and take her straight to rehab, which would get him back to Texas in the next few hours. Or, he could let her sober up and allow her to walk into the center on her own two feet. Damn it! He knew the decision he needed to make, but it meant longer than he ever expected before he could return back home. Even in all this chaos, a smile spread across his lips as he realized he already thought of Texas as his home.

Cara had definitely overdosed. Since the world knew Austin was home, they were all holed up in the house. He'd contemplated an emergency room, but Seth arranged for a physician to treat her at home to help keep things on the down low. Austin stayed by Cara's side the entire time. Seth stayed even closer to her. By the time the doctor left, Seth had stationed himself in a chair close to Cara's head. Worry was clear on his face. Austin grabbed a trash can. Going through everything she owned, he threw away all of the alcohol and anything else that could possibly be construed as a drug or drug paraphernalia.

Once he went through her room, he went through the rest of the house, looking for anything and everything she may have stashed. When he made his way back to Cara's bedroom, Seth still sat under constant vigilance, not having left her side.

"How long's it been going on?" Austin asked without malice, just concern in his voice.

"Not long. It was an accident. I should've told you," Seth said, never turning his gaze away from Cara.

"Was it serious? Because it was to her." Austin kept his tone quiet, standing at the end of the bed, running a hand over her leg covered by the bedspread.

Austin loved Cara. She'd been with him for the long haul, and it wasn't too many years ago that he'd been right there with her, drugging himself to keep the facade in place. If he hadn't cleaned himself up, there was no question he'd have been right in the middle of those boys, doing it all with her today. Being clean and happy was such a better way to live your life. He hated seeing her like this.

"I don't know. Everything here's so fragile. You were leaving, she was worried about you. She's a beautiful person, inside and out, and so alone. Yeah, it meant something. Too much, we knew it then. It still means something now." Seth finally turned away from Cara and looked Austin straight in the eyes.

"Obviously it does. I'm just glad you admitted it. If you care about her, when she wakes, we need to double team her and be ready to get her out the door. No hesitation. I'm going to put this place up for sale. Get her out of here. I want to call and pull her from the movie. I'll pay whatever the fines are, but she needs to heal from all this. I can bring her to Texas if she wants."

"You're already in a better emotional place, Austin," Seth said, and moved his eyes back to Cara.

"I feel normal again. After she gets out of rehab, maybe you two can come together to stay in Texas with me for a while. If she's strong by then, we can plan for the future. If she wants to keep acting, we'll get her something healthy to work on." Austin sat on the end of the large bed. They talked quietly, but nothing disturbed Cara as she slept off her high. Seth watched Austin for a couple of minutes and narrowed his eyes.

"He means something to you." It wasn't a question, but a statement of fact. Since Austin Grainger was more of a corporation than a person, he knew everyone got the security reports. Kitt had to be mentioned in them, and wouldn't his almost boyfriend just love knowing that little piece of information.

"Yeah, he does. I...he's...yeah, it's strong. He doesn't know that yet, but I do. You can meet him when you come out." Austin never faltered in his declaration, and that said a lot for a man who hid so much from everyone.

He was proud of Kitt, proud of the normal life he found. He'd only had a beer or two, maybe a glass of wine here or there since he'd left California. He didn't even have the need for anything more, and he knew that was due to Kitt being in his life. Kitt made him want to be a better man.

"Okay," Seth said after only a slight pause. He'd thrown Seth with what he said. Hell, it threw *him* off, but that didn't change the facts.

Austin wanted out of this crazy house, this crazy world, and back inside Kitt's sane, normal, everyday life as soon as humanly possible.

"Then go pack your bags. We need to be ready when she wakes. I'll call and find out what she needs and pack her up," Austin said, palming his phone.

"They said just clothing and minimal toiletries. Easy wear clothes like sweaters and yoga pants, things like that," Seth said, keeping his eyes locked on the sleeping Cara. It took a minute, but he finally rose, and did as Austin asked. He only left Cara's side long enough to pack before he came back to hover and stay by her side until she woke.

Austin went to Cara's closet and grabbed a tote to pack her a few things. As he went through the motion of loading her bag, he palmed his phone again. He ignored all the alerts from Google and Twitter that let him know his name was being posted about every twenty seconds, and instead, went straight to his text messages. Kitt wasn't responding to him. Austin had sent five or six messages in the last few hours and gotten nothing back. He figured Kitt was shutting him out. It seemed like Kitt's way of things when Austin wasn't right there, face to face, pushing at him to open up.

Frustrated, Austin tucked his cell back into his back pocket and packed for Cara in earnest. He chose several pairs of jeans, some random shirts and sweaters, trying not to let it bother him how easily Kitt could let him go, and keep him at a distance. Not more than twelve hours had passed since he'd seen Kitt, but technically, if he were home right now, they'd be together, having dinner, maybe making love. Okay, probably making love before they ate dinner. They never could seem to make it through the door without hitting the floor, clothes abandoned, and one of them on their knees sucking the other off.

The thought caused desperation to form and well up inside Austin's heart. Kitt had been very clear with Austin last night. He thought Austin would eventually bolt, but he'd be in the relationship for however long Austin wanted him. Distance had to be a self-preservation deal for Kitt. The problem was, Austin seemed to have a constant need for validation from Kitt who was clearly not in an emotional place to give it.

After another minute more of shoving a handful of panties and socks in the bag, Austin reached for his phone again. He typed out a quick message. He didn't monitor his words or play the game of "if-I-say-this,-hopefully-he'll-say-that" he just typed what he felt.

'I'm not sure if you're getting my messages, but Cara isn't good. I might be a day longer. I need her to sober up before I can get her to help. I'm not liking that I can't see you tonight. I need you to respond to this message. Please don't leave me here hanging without a word from you.' Austin didn't even give himself a read through he just sent the message.

'Are you okay?' Kitt texted immediately back. Austin guessed three words were better than no words.

'I'm worried.' Austin typed back.

"I'll call. It'll be late, after 10. Is that ok?'

'Call whenever, it doesn't matter the time.' Austin found himself wanting to ask why it would be so late. If he were home, they would be together. He never thought to ask Kitt if he'd made plans. Why did he just assume Kitt would be there waiting for him? Wait, Austin never assumed it. He *feared* Kitt wouldn't be waiting. How did he not know what Kitt had going on?

'Alright.' Kitt replied in his one word text. Austin felt better after texting him. It wasn't a huge conversation, but with Kitt they rarely were. Austin kept his phone close, making Kitt's photo his screen saver as he went to Cara's office and began the process of sending emails and messages to everyone, letting them know she was coming to spend time with him for indefinite amount of time.

Chapter 15

Kitt crawled down off the hay baler with a jaw cracking yawn tearing across his lips. It was three forty-five in the morning, and he couldn't sleep. He wiped the sweat from his brow, smearing oil and engine soot across his forehead, and shrugged his Carhartt jacket off his shoulders, tossing it aside. It didn't seem to matter how hard he worked, or what he did. Kitt's mind stayed completely wrapped around Austin, never giving him the slightest break, not even to get a couple of hours of sleep.

Night two of Austin being gone, and it amazed Kitt how much he missed the man. At the same time, it scared the crap out of him. He'd thought he had a better mental hold of himself. His arms seemed to miss holding Austin at night. When he closed his eyes, the only thing he saw was the image of Austin smiling his big, toothy, sexy grin. Austin's real smile. The one he wore any time he teased Kitt, or they laughed about something just between the two of them. Kitt missed that smile.

Kitt didn't call Austin the first night. Fear kept him from making the call. His heart was too closely connected, making him too involved. Kitt needed to find distance between them. Complications weren't his thing. Kitt lived his life as a total drama free zone, and it needed to stay that way. The movie star, Austin Grainger, had drama filled complication stamped right on his forehead. Austin needed to either move back to Hollywood, or move back to the place in Kitt's mind where they were fuck buddies. Fuck buddies didn't matter. They were tension relievers and nothing more. Kitt shouldn't care about how Austin coped in his crazy ass situation back in California. He had never thought about Sean's coping ability in any situation.

Kitt placed himself in straight up, pure protection mode. If Kitt could slip Austin back in the right spot inside his brain, it wouldn't hurt so badly to be without him, and Kitt definitely would be without Austin. If these last two days were any indication of the future, Kitt would be a big whiny ass mess when Austin finally left him for good. He couldn't let it happen.

To give Austin credit, he kept Kitt informed. He messaged every few hours both day and night. Austin told Kitt everything they were doing, and every text included sweet words of missing him. Austin also started calling. Kitt let the calls go to voice mail. Around midnight tonight, he finally responded to another text Austin sent asking if Kitt made it home yet to give him a call. He didn't lie when he said no, but he'd just left his house to come back to the barn once he figured out there would be no sleep tonight either.

The text he'd sent back was a moment of weakness laced with a small amount of compassion. Kitt got the impression Austin was a little desperate, or it could've just been his own emotion he read inside the typed words of the text. He probably shouldn't have asked how Austin held up; it invited conversation. But, he couldn't help it. Austin replied back immediately, he was just waiting for Cara to wake so they could board the flight. Kitt told himself it was nothing more than polite manners, not the deep connection he felt, that had him texting back a simple, '*Make sure you take care of yourself*'. Kitt didn't reply to anything else.

An old fold-up chair sat in the corner of the work barn housing the baler. Kitt sat down with a thump and dropped his head in his hands. There were so many other things he should be thinking about besides Austin. He had two long days in front of him to get ready for a longer month of hay cutting and baling. His entire farm would work from sunup to sundown, seven days a week. They needed to cut and bale thousands and thousands of acres of hay, and in return, Kitt would be getting half of every field they worked as payment.

On top of all that, he'd only gotten two firm contracts to sell the hay. He'd had some verbal promises, but they were falling through. As it stood right now, if he didn't get on the phone and start making some calls, he'd be stuck with about twenty thousand bales with nowhere to put them.

Kitt shook his head hard. Okay, so thinking about the farm caused as much tension and worry as thinking about Austin. So what else could divert his sleep deprived brain? Kitt rose, grabbing a stray wash rag as he strode from one barn to the next, making his way to Lady. She was the current pride of the farm, his best quarter horse.

Kitt caught it happening in her without doing the math, or any exam at all. He saw Lady's belly tightening up and watched her moving a little stiffly. He'd brought her in the barn yesterday, keeping her close by. She was early. The vet planned to come out in the morning to do a full exam on her, see if Kitt was correct in his guess. He couldn't wait though for her to give birth, and for the first time in two days his heart lightened. He felt it in his bones, her new little colt was going to be something special. The first of four something very special's coming to the farm; two colts and two fillies if the sonograms held true. They were all sired by the year's Triple Crown racing champion. Surely to God, they would sell in the tens of thousands on the open market.

Their sire came in at twenty-to-one odds and blew his competition away at all three derbies. Kitt had gotten his sperm a couple of years ago; way before anyone even knew the horse's name. In college, he'd tutored the owner's son through Organic Chemistry before they had any idea what the pony had in him. With the Triple Crown title on their heels, these yearlings should sell easily come spring, maybe even before then. Besides these four, Kitt saved four of the eight vials he got as payment. If he could do this same thing again, he might be turning a solid profit this time next year. Wouldn't it be something to actually have money in the bank instead of all this debt hanging over his head?

Kitt perched a leg and both arms on the gate to Lady's stall. Their eyes met and she turned away. It caused him to chuckle. She only did things on her terms, making Kitt lucky she seemed to like him. This mare was his favorite, she had a way of seeing inside him. They connected for a minute as she turned back to him before walking over. He wiped his oil stained hands on his jeans, knowing she was expecting a good rub. He opened the gate, went inside and gave her one. Before he turned away, she did her signature move and knocked his ball cap off his head.

"You think you're pretty smart, don't you? Well, I guess you are," he said, grinning as he picked up his ball cap and put it back on his head. He hadn't stepped far enough back because she was right back on him again, knocking it off his head.

"Good night, girl," Kitt laughed, picking the cap up again. The grin stayed with him as he cut off the lights and made his way back to his truck. Another deep yawn started and lasted as he got inside his truck and started it up. It was completely dark outside and seemed like he was very much alone. He wondered if Austin's people still watched him, or if they had they stopped since Austin wasn't around?

Kitt drove the trail home with the windows rolled down. The cold night air hit his face, making sure he didn't nod off. His phone sounded off at the same time his mind went fully back to Austin. He thought about ignoring the call, but it was almost morning. Rarely did anything good come from a call in the middle of the night. Kitt couldn't help the confused smile tugging at his lips when he saw Austin's name on his screen. Even with all the lecturing he'd just given himself, Kitt was too tired to resist, and answered on the third ring.

"Everything okay?" Kitt asked, bypassing the standard greeting.

"Are you awake?" Austin asked.

"I am now," Kitt teased, the smile still on his face. Austin's voice soothed his soul and calmed his nerves like nothing had before.

Silence.

"I'm kiddin'; I'm up. I couldn't sleep. How are you?" Kitt pulled the truck to the front of his cabin. He turned it off, but sat in the cab waiting for Austin to answer.

"Why couldn't you sleep?" Austin asked, his voice weirdly quiet.

"I don't know. I guess I just have a lot on my mind right now," Kitt said resting his arm out the window. He kept the phone to his ear and leaned his head back against the head rest. It was worse than Kitt had realized. He was so edgy because he missed Austin, and just his voice put everything back to right in his world.

"Am I part of what's on your mind?"

It took a second, but Kitt finally answered somewhat honestly. "Maybe a little."

"Hmm... I like that. You're on my mind, too. I couldn't sleep. One night tucked away in a sleeping bag with you, and now my body thinks your arms need to be around me in order to get some rest." Austin chuckled as he said the words Kitt felt so deeply in his heart. There was another pause before he spoke.

"How're things there?" Kitt asked.

"We had our little intervention, then a big clearing of the air between us all." Austin's voice was weary. "Cara's finally up and getting dressed, and we're going to be heading out soon. I think if everything goes like we planned, Cara and I are going to publically break up in the next couple of days. I've found out Cara and Seth developed a thing between them, and all this hiding's messing it up for them, or her, or something like that. They told me they've hooked up a couple of times. They have lots of emotion about it all. That's what drove her to this round of...well, whatever it is she does when she gets like this."

He was silent for a moment. "I don't really know, I couldn't wrap my head around it. I just kept thinking about you the whole time they were talking."

"So it was good you went back?" Kitt asked, trying to follow it all.

"Cara needed it," Austin said.

"How will this affect you?"

"I don't see how anything will change. It'll keep me at the top of the newsfeeds for a little longer, but the faster we break up, the faster I'm off them," Austin said.

"You haven't liked bein' back? Didn't miss it all?" Kitt asked, his voice a little quieter. It was his ten million dollar question, and he braved up to ask.

"Hell no! They spotted me almost immediately. It's such bullshit. The ride from the airport to my house is like a thirty minute drive, but it turned out to be three hours of hell trying to get here. I told the driver just to run the bastards over, but he wouldn't do it. Wimp!" Austin chuckled at his last sentence and then there was silence between them. "You still there?"

"Yeah, I was listenin', thinkin'," Kitt said pulling himself from the truck. He walked up the steps to his house completely relaxed now. He made his way to bed, stripping with one hand as he went.

"Sometimes you get so quiet," Austin said, and there was another pause between them. "You haven't been responding much to my texts or calling me when you say you will. You know it kills me waiting to hear from you."

"I'm sorry. I just keep thinkin' it's pretty boring here compared to there." Kitt pulled the blankets to his bed back.

"I never want to be back in this mess again, Kitt, and I haven't been bored one time since I moved back there," Austin replied. There was silence again and Austin went a different direction. "How's your sister?"

"Good, at least as far as I know. She's going back this morning." A yawn slipped out from Kitt, and he hoped Austin didn't hear it. He wasn't quite ready to end this call yet.

"I liked her. What're you doing today? Getting ready to start baling?"

"Yep. So you do listen…"

"Of course I do. Sucking and fucking aren't the only things that interest me about you. Am I buying hay from you?" Austin asked quieter.

"I think so." Kitt wasn't a hundred percent sure, but he figured it was a pretty safe bet. This time his yawn was louder. Kitt scooted further down in bed and turned over on his back. His dick was hard just from hearing Austin's voice. Kitt anchored the phone on his shoulder and grabbed a couple of tissues. It wouldn't take much to jack off once the call ended.

"Good, I'll make sure with Mike. What're you doing now?"

"Just talkin' to you." Kitt thought that if he was quiet, he could close his eyes, and think of Austin here with him…he gripped his dick and shoved the covers down. He put the phone on speaker, and laid it on the pillow beside him.

"I miss you, Kitt. While we were all talking, all I could think of was how badly I wished I was spending this time with you." Kitt let Austin's words coat his heart and give him the emotional support he craved. He'd become a little fragile in that area since meeting Austin.

"This quiet thing you do is hard on a guy's heart. I can't read your reactions over the phone, and you pull so deep inside yourself," Austin said.

"Hmm…" It was all Kitt managed. He'd already started the slow back and forth motion with his hand. His eyes closed, and he pictured Austin in his mind. He listened to the melody in Austin's deep rich voice.

"You just aren't gonna give me a break, are you, Kitt Kelly? Well, that's okay. I'll fight for it. It'll make my winning you all that much better in the end," Austin said, making Kitt chuckle, or groan, in the phone.

"When are you leavin'?"

"I don't know. They're in the bedroom now supposedly getting dressed. I guess she needs him to help her button her blouse. Apparently, at twenty-five hundred dollars an hour, the plane can just sit and wait," Austin said dryly. Kitt did the groaned chuckle again, increasing the pace, moving his hand faster tip to base. He reached his other hand low and gripped his sac. A deep moan escaped his lips.

"Are you jacking off without me?" Austin asked, still quiet, but amused. "You sound sexy as hell. Why didn't you tell me, I would have joined in."

"Goddamn your voice does it for me, Austin. I'm close." Kitt's breathing got heavy, and he arched his back stroking faster and harder.

"I need you, Kitt. My dick's so hard for you, baby. I'm shoving my hand inside my shorts now. My office door isn't locked...I don't care..." Austin's voice got breathy as he continued on, "I don't wanna find a pool boy to take it out on. Let me just catch up. Baby, I wanna suck you right now so badly...right there on your bed. Me between your thighs...damn, have I told you how much I love your dick when it drips? I love knowing I can do that to you. It's my dream... sucking you..."

"I'm comin'," Kitt groaned out, thrusting his hips forward, arching his back as his hot seed shot straight out onto his stomach. His breath panted, his head spun, and he shouted out into the room, "Goddammit, I miss you, Austin."

"Ahh, yes! That's it," Austin said quietly. They were both silent for a minute or two. Kitt let himself float back down to earth before he turned his head toward the phone. He was sated, relaxed, and ready to sleep his orgasm off.

"Did I hear you say you have pool boys?" Kitt asked still in the fog as he reached over for the tissue and slowly began to clean himself off. Austin gave a breathy chuckle, and it was a second before he answered. His voice was now deeper, more relaxed, than earlier. It seemed they'd both needed it.

"Yeah, but they're little guys, and even from the back, I couldn't close my eyes tight enough to believe it was you," Austin said. Kitt could tell he was on speaker now. Austin moved in and out of hearing range, probably cleaning himself up too. Kitt had no idea what to say to that, so he tossed the tissues in the trash, covered up with his blanket, and took the phone off speaker. He lay it on his ear as he turned over, tucking the pillow under his head. Another yawn slipped out. He was totally in that after sex place. He could sleep so easily.

"Quiet again. I like when you said '*I miss you, Austin*'. I came instantly. Baby, I don't want to be with anyone but you right now. It's just...I'm already feeling like a more honorable man since I met you. It's dirty here. I feel dirty being in this house. I want it to be just you and me. You're enough for me until we both decide on something else."

"Like a third?" Kitt asked on a yawn. His eyes were closing, but opened at the thought.

"I don't know. It'd be hard to share you. Maybe many years down the line. Do you add thirds in?" Austin asked.

"I haven't since college," Kitt confessed. "I've never had any emotion in my sex before. It's just been whenever the opportunity presents itself, however that deal played out."

"Me, too. I'm glad to hear you admitting the emotion. These are good first steps for you, Kitt Kelly. I hear you're tired. Go to sleep. I should be home some time tomorrow, and I'll text you, because I know you won't text me."

"I'm sorry about that. I don't know why I get like this. I'm not sure I believe you'll actually come back," Kitt said, his eyes fully closed now. He was snuggled up in the blanket, the ceiling fan blowing, and between the hand job and Austin's voice, he was lulled into sleep.

"It's okay," Austin said. "I'm pushy enough to stay in front of you." Kitt never heard the words. He was already fast asleep, dreaming of Austin wrapped in his arms.

Chapter 16

This new budding love between Cara and Seth was such a pain in the ass. Austin's dedicated, strong, reasonably level-headed assistant slash future wife turned frail and weak. Cara leaned on Seth to be her rock through the turbulent emotional storm of admitting her into the rehab facility. The results of Cara's devotion and need made Seth an emotional concerned wreck who rejected leaving her there alone. They were sickeningly sweet with one another. The only complication came with the cloak and dagger deal required in Austin's life.

It forced Cara to be dropped at the hospital door as inconspicuously as possible with Austin and Seth hitting the road, putting as many miles as they could between the rehab and themselves. Cara just wasn't cooperating.

She refused to leave Seth, clinging to him like he was some sort of life preserver in the deep dark haze of her life. They coerced Austin into flying across country, giving Cara a little more time and throwing the paparazzi off their trail. They were seen together in New York, walking into the National headquarters of one of his corporations. They walked in the front doors and straight out the back garage door. From there, they were immediately driven to a new charter jet registered under another fictitious name.

It was now three entire days since he left the farm, and the three of them flew overnight to the Arizona rehab waiting for them. It was a full twenty-four hours since Austin had talked to Kitt on the phone. He'd told Kitt he wanted to be home yesterday, but as the day wore on his last nerve, Austin texted Kitt and just like their apparent pattern, Kitt began the all day process of distancing himself from him. The space Kitt put between them aggravated the hell out of Austin, making everything just a little more difficult. He was edgy, angry, and trying hard not to snap.

During the plane rides, Cara wrapped herself around Seth, letting him play the hero. Austin didn't begrudge them, he just resented a life where Kitt couldn't do things like this with him. The realization that day might never happen hurt his heart. His mood plummeted, and the need for Kitt to respond to a simple message became so much greater. If all they were ever going to have together were secret moments and hidden conversations, Kitt couldn't continue to hide from him any longer. It drove Austin to a mental place where he swore he texted Kitt about every hour trying to get him to respond.

Seth stayed with Cara for as long as he could while Austin would have rather been in and out of there in about five minutes. If he could have found a way to shove her from the plane and onto the doorstep of the rehab without causing her too much bodily injury, he would have taken the option. Instead, they rode with her in the back of an ambulance with full sirens blaring overhead. It felt incredibly ridiculous and extreme to Austin. He got the no windows deal, but the sirens and stopping traffic as they rushed to the facility...yeah, no. It felt like a very bad, real life action movie with him starring as the bumbling lead detective. Austin also couldn't figure why he couldn't just stay on the plane and wait for Seth's return. For some reason, he was needed, or the tears would start back again making Cara far too emotional to deal with.

Seth decided to come to the farm for a few days of recuperation before they hit the press with the split of Austin Grainger and Cara Collins. Afterward, Seth would be needed back in LA to help field all the calls and questions coming their way. As it stood now, their publicists were concocting a plan to say Cara asked for the split, requesting her privacy and time off from filming. Austin would be unreachable for comments. He prayed he was able to stay hidden until the whole thing blew over.

Austin scheduled a third private jet to fly them from Arizona to Texas after they got Cara safely admitted into the rehab facility. This time, they flew into Houston, and went straight from the plane to the waiting car. They drove the five hours to Austin's farm by themselves. Austin had promised to be home twenty-four hours ago. He could only imagine what Kitt let himself believe about him not returning on time.

Last night, or early that morning, Austin had stayed on the phone for close to two hours, listening to Kitt breathe as he slept. He'd kicked back, just thinking about what Kitt looked like while he slept, and the sweet sounding apology he gave right before he fell asleep. It was at those moments when Kitt was tired, Austin found he fully let his guard down. Those were the best moments of them all. Austin had hung up when he heard Kitt's alarm sounding off. He didn't want to be caught doing something as girly as listening to the object of his desire sleep. That would just never hold weight in keeping his mancard strong and in good standing.

Austin drove most of the way home with nothing more on his mind than Kitt. Seth was zero company. He was on his smart phone doing business or writing messages to Cara the entire way back. Austin could have used the distraction. After several days of contemplating Kitt's on again, off again attitude, Austin had come to the conclusion he wasn't quite sure where he stood. It seemed so easy for Kitt to distance himself, and that scared the hell out of him. When they were together, Austin really felt like they were together, but when they were apart, it was like Austin didn't exist to Kitt at all.

As he drove, his thoughts strayed to a memory of Kitt's dad, something from his youth. It was wrong to think so badly of a dead man, but Austin hated the stories Kitt would tell. This one faded memory wouldn't fully form in his mind, and he reached for his phone to call his father.

"Dad, it's Austin," he said on the simple *yell'ow* his father gave.

"I know, Son. Caller ID's a great new tool." His dad chuckled at his own joke.

"Listen, I won't keep you, but do you remember the story with the Kelly's when I was younger?"

"Okay Son, that's vague even for you... There were many Kelly stories. He was always stirrin' something up," his dad answered back.

"I can't really remember. It was the one with the ice cream and Kitt," Austin said trying to dig into the recesses of his mind.

"Yeah, that's a bad one. I don't know how he didn't ruin that boy. I heard the Kelly boy went off to college and did alright for himself. We all thought he'd turn out to be a complete wreck with a father like his."

"He isn't at all. He's a good man, very respected down here from what I can tell." Funny how the need to defend Kitt superseded the need to know whatever memory his mind tried to come up with.

"Well, that's a total surprise. Kitt, right? Kitt had a lot against him growin' up," Austin's dad said.

"Tell me the story I'm thinking about." Austin tried to speed his father up.

"Let's see…Mr. Kelly, none of us were allowed to call him anything other than Mr. Kelly. He was so full of himself, which was nothin' but full of shit. He'd be so proud to take his son out and discipline him in front of everyone. Said it made him a man, and we needed to learn from him. It was like he was tryin' to teach us how to raise our own children. At least, that's what your mom always thought. This one time, he bought Kitt an ice cream and himself lunch. He sat the ice cream in front of Kitt, who couldn't have been older than five. So, Mr. Kelly ate his lunch. Every time Kitt went for that ice cream, he got smacked hard, and then Mr. Kelly would encourage Kitt again to eat the ice cream. It went on like this for the entire lunch. The kid never got the ice cream, but got beat up pretty bad. When he started cryin', he got spanked in front of everyone for embarrassing Mr. Kelly and sent to the truck. You know back then you didn't get in the way of a parent disciplinin' his child, but if I remember correctly, several of the mom's in the area still called the sheriff that day."

"That's how he was raised his whole life?" Austin asked.

"Yeah, the best I remember. It didn't matter what the kid did or thought, he was always wrong, and Mr. Kelly had a temper. His dad would whip him wherever they were and Kitt took it. One time on the football field, Mr. Kelly got mad at a play Kitt called. He stormed out on to that field, jerkin' Kitt around by the face mask until he shoved the boy down on his knees right there in the middle of the field, in front of everyone. He kicked him and stormed off, tellin' the coach to pull Kitt if they wanted to win. It wasn't right."

"Kitt's a good guy," Austin said quietly. His heart did more than hurt for the little boy and now the grown man. Kitt deserved so much better than he got.

"You've seen him?"

"Yeah. What happened to his mom?" Austin had always wondered why she was never talked about.

"Mr. Kelly married some city girl. She came down to the ranch. It lasted about two years before she was gone. Young and pretty, but not a dime to her name. She couldn't stand up against Kelly. He kept the boy, she left. As far as I know, it broke all contact between them."

Austin listened to his dad and drove thinking it all over. It helped explain a lot.

"Dad, I'm gonna buy a couple of quarter horses. I might need them to come up to you," Austin said.

"Whatever you need, Son."

"I'll draw up the paperwork. Get the offers made. I'll be paying more than they're worth, but I think they have racing potential. You'll need to get a good look at them. See about a trainer when it gets time," Austin said.

"Are they to know it's you?"

"Not on the front end, but I think eventually it will be unavoidable. I love you Dad, tell Mom 'hi'," Austin said.

"You too, Son."

Austin ended the call. That story he just heard had stayed with him through the years, but he'd never associated it with Kitt. After a few more miles passed, Austin called Mike.

"Hey, do we buy our hay from the Kelly ranch?" He asked, avoiding the polite pleasantries

"It's the plan. Unless you want it changed," Mike said back. "We'll bale our own next year."

"I want you to buy more than we need," Austin said. "Figure out whatever's left and buy it. I'll ship it up to my dad or something, or there has to be an organization to donate too. Maybe a school or something?"

Mike gave a moment of pause before a simple, "Okay… Yeah, the schools around here'll take it."

"What's up with everybody getting so quiet on me? Buy extra hay for us, but figure out what he's going to have left. Do I need to contract it now, or something like that?"

Mike was silent.

"Kitt's become a good friend to me. They're struggling and I'm not. No need for that. Also, there'll be a couple of new arrivals. They'll need room in the barn until I can get them up to my dad's. It would be better to keep these two close, and again, let me remind you of the very strict confidentiality agreement you have."

"Okay, I'll take care of it." Mike voice grew more serious. Austin heard the confusion in it, but he didn't ask any questions which Austin found he liked the most about Mike.

"Cool, I'll be home late tonight. I'll see you tomorrow."

"Ten-four, boss, and I'll call Kitt now. It'll help him out."

"Thanks and be convincing! Figure what's gonna be left, I'll take care of getting someone to contact him for it. He's not overly receptive to help, so keep it on the down low. I'm bringing my agent with me for a few days. We'll be down at the barn in the morning. Bye." At that, Austin disconnected the call.

Austin decided then, regardless of Kitt's stubborn, hard head, he was helping the Kelly ranch. He'd buy whatever services Kitt offered, and he'd pay him over the asking price. Buying hay, some of his show animals, and using his AI program on the farm was all he could think of right now, but more would come to him. One thing Austin had to offer Kitt was money. He had more money than he could ever spend in ten lifetimes. If money would ease Kitt, then he'd make sure that was one less thing on his plate to worry about.

Chapter 17

Damn it, but Kitt was tired! He forced his exhausted, gritty eyes to stay open. He sat on the sofa in his cabin, dressed in his starched Wranglers and freshly ironed button down. Austin's last text message said they were headed back hours ago. Kitt assumed Austin intended to come by the cabin since his agent came back home with him. Clearly, he got that assumption wrong. Maybe he should have gone over to Austin's. Maybe they wouldn't be spending time together until the agent left. At this point, who knew for sure, but as the hour grew later, Kitt finally gave in to the lack of sleep over the last few days and undressed.

He worked his clothes off slowly, walking through his small place blowing out the candles he'd lit, and put the iced bottle of Austin's favorite wine back in the refrigerator. He turned off the burner warming dinner. Whatever, he'd tried for a little romance.

As he stretched out on his bed, Kitt kept his phone close to him, ignoring the ache in his heart. Austin had texted him every few hours for the last three days, but he hadn't heard anything for hours now. It was late, too late. Maybe Austin got home and just went to bed like he should have done. Damn, he wanted to see Austin tonight. The late, late, late show came to an end as Kitt's eyes closed completely. Too many days of burning it at both ends caught up with him. He fell asleep with the lights and TV on, and his phone in his hand.

~~~~~

Seth didn't get much more than a *'the door on the left is the spare bedroom'* before Austin hightailed it out of the rental car and to the barn to jump on his four-wheeler. An unexpected traffic jam from an eight car pileup slowed them for hours on a highway in the middle of Nowhere, Texas. And Nowhere, Texas had no cellphone signal at all. It was after midnight before they were routed to the back roads off the highway, making the already long trip much longer.

Security had stayed vigilant, watching the property the entire time he was gone. Nothing changed in their responsibility to his sanctuary. He drove the four-wheeler out of the barn, darting straight to Kitt's cabin, a hundred percent certain they were watching him right now. His anxiety levels spiked off the charts, and under the exhausted state he currently maintained, there was no choice but to go see Kitt. As he got closer, it occurred to him that Kitt might be in the barn. He seemed to spend an extraordinary amount of time there over the last few days. Austin saw some back lights on in the house, but no activity. Kitt's truck sat outside. He slowed his ride, pulling to the fence, not caring about the noise he made.

Austin climbed the fence before jogging the distance between the fence and the house. He didn't knock. Kitt always left the door unlocked. He slowly opened the door and waited, listening. He heard the faint sounds of a soft snore coming from Kitt's bedroom. The lights were off in the main part of the house. Austin snuck in seeing two wine glasses sitting out, a set table and a plate of food on the stovetop. The other plate lay empty in the sink. Relief flooded him, Kitt had been waiting for him!

Austin walked silently through the living room toward Kitt's bedroom. Just the television and night stand lamp were on. Austin toed off his shoes, and then carefully and quietly tiptoed his way to the bed, shedding his clothing as he went. As he passed the television, he turned it off and watched Kitt who never stirred. Odd for the usually light sleeper. Austin decided to leave the lamp on.

Kitt stayed sleeping with small soft snores coming from him every minute or two. Those were the times Austin moved. He kept his eyes trained on the handsome, beautiful man lying on top of the covers, sleeping in his tighty whities. A depth of emotion Austin had never experienced before hit him hard. It caused him to stop in his tracks as he started to slide onto the bed. His heart hammered, and he stared hard at Kitt. The emotion welling inside him was real and complete. Austin knew immediately what was going on, but he also knew Kitt would want no part of it. Which didn't seem to change anything inside his heart.

Kitt finally stirred as Austin lay on the bed, coming fully awake with a startled jerk when he realized he wasn't alone. "What the—"

"I tried not to wake you." Austin paused as he lowered, but kept going, wanting to hold and be held by Kitt.

"You scared the crap out of me," Kitt said, lying back on his pillow. He absently ran a hand over his heart. Austin scooted over, not quite touching Kitt, but close enough to lean in and give him a slow chaste kiss.

"I missed you and I'm exhausted. It took forever to get home. I wanted to sleep in your arms for a few hours, and then maybe make love to you before you made me go face the entire day without you." Austin kept his tone light, hiding his feelings while giving his most sorrowful expression. Kitt narrowed his eyes.

"I saw that exact same look in your last movie when your pup died…it was so sad." Kitt rolled his eyes before he scooted over, kicking at the covers with his feet as he held his arms open to Austin.

Austin reached down to bring the bedspread up, covering them as he went to lie on Kitt's chest. He angled himself where he laid with his head in the crook of Kitt's neck. "You snore," Austin whispered simply.

The comfort of being in Kitt's arms erased every bit of anxiety, leaving just the exhaustion behind. It occurred to Austin, this was another new thing for them. They never lay in bed unless they were fucking. Before tonight, it hadn't been allowed.

"I've heard that before," Kitt said dryly, running his fingertips up and down Austin's back. Their legs tangled together. Austin could feel Kitt was half aroused, but the need to hold the other seemed viably more important.

"Did Fisker complain about it?" Austin let his obvious jealousy out in the words and Kitt chuckled.

"No, Mr. Looking for Pool Boys to Fuck. My sisters tell me. It's one of the reasons I'm down here. I can get loud during sinus season apparently," Kitt said and kissed the top of Austin's head. He wrapped Austin tighter in his arms, turning partly to face Austin. They shared a pillow and he yawned.

"You'll enjoy that immensely, I'm sure." Kitt reached over and pushed the button on the lamp to turn the light off.

"Mmm…is this the first fault I've found in Kitt Kelly?" Austin moved with Kitt's body as the light turned off.

"I don't think it's the first," Kitt said quietly into the dark.

"I do." Austin lifted his head. He rose fully to place a light kiss on Kitt's lips. "You need to sleep."

"I think it's you that needs to sleep. I can't see where you've had much in the last few days. You messaged me like every two hours."

"How can I sleep when your lips are so close?" Again, Austin leaned in and kissed Kitt softly, this time adding a small amount of tongue. The kiss lingered until he rested his head on Kitt's shoulder and sleep took them both.

~~~~~~~

It took a second for Kitt to realize the vibration that woke him came from his phone lying under his pillow. He automatically turned to check the time on his alarm clock. Four minutes before the alarm was scheduled to go off.

Austin slept with his head on Kitt's chest, and his breath warmed his skin with every exhale. Kitt dug underneath the pillow until he found the phone as it vibrated again sending another message. He'd missed four incoming calls. His phone must have silenced at some point during the night, but the vibration worked. It took time for his eyes to adjust to the bright light of the lit screen as he read the message. He reached over with the other arm to turn the alarm off so it didn't wake Austin.

Jose thought Lady was showing signs of birthing. Well, of course she was! Today was one of the busiest days of Kitt's year. They'd start cutting hay, and it required every one of his hands to help in the fields. Of course, she would pick today. Kitt carefully pulled out from underneath Austin who only stirred awake long enough to hear Kitt say he was going to the restroom. Kitt stuffed a pillow back in his place watching as Austin took the bait and pulled the pillow against his chest, instantly falling back asleep. Kitt grabbed his clothes and boots and left the bedroom, shutting the door behind him. He dressed quickly, not bothering to brush his hair or teeth. He penned a quick note to Austin and grabbed a ball cap.

The ride to the barn was a quick one and several of his regular ranch hands were already there. He pulled to the front, barely getting the truck in park before jumping out. Kitt all but jogged inside the barn doing the math again in his mind on her delivery date. She was too early. Even with the signs of her tightening and her udder dropping, Kitt still thought they had a week, and even that would have been a couple of weeks early.

It being her first birth, they had no history with this mare. Horses foaled early all the time, but three weeks – it concerned him.

"Shit," he muttered opening the barn door. He mentally checked off his men trying to decide which one would be best to leave behind for the day and keep an eye on Lady. Nothing changed as he went through the list, Jose was the only one he trusted enough to stay behind, but he was also the only one who could put in a double day's work in eight hours.

"How she doing?" He asked as he met Jose halfway to her stall.

"It's just startin'. She should have a while," he said, pivoting on his feet. Jose wasn't a tall man, but kept Kitt's pace, double stepping each of his steps.

"Did you call Doc? Have him on standby?" Kitt asked opening the gate.

"Yes, sir." Jose stayed back with all the other men staring over the stall gate watching Kitt adjust his ball cap for her.

"Good. Thanks for callin' me," Kitt said absently, his tone getting softer as he entered. He walked the few steps to Lady. He held her attention since she heard him in the barn, nodding her palomino head at him as he entered, as if she'd been expecting him, waiting for him to get there.

"Hey sweet girl, you gettin' ready for your big day, or is this one of those false starts that gets us all worked up?" Kitt asked as he began to rub her gently. He petted her down to her swollen belly, gently touching her udder before moving toward her front. He could feel her tighter, but there was no sign of her milk. The foal moved a little under his touch.

"Yeah, you're close. You know you could've waited until your due date. It would've helped me out a lot," Kitt said, still in the calm sweet tone he used with her. He was right in her face now, looking into her eyes, rubbing her head, and she bent into him knocking his ball cap off his head.

"She's close. So here's the change for the day. Jose, I'm gonna need you to stay with her. Get Doc out here to do an exam. Call me when's he's done, or if anythin' changes. I'll stay with her tonight. Maybe by tomorrow, we'll have a newborn. Her momma's records show she was in labor for a full forty-eight hours before she was born. Let's see if that holds, but I don't want her left alone." Kitt said it all carefully, keeping his tone calm. He rubbed her down as he spoke, picking up his ball cap. He angled it on his head as he rose and let her knock it off again before he rubbed down her nose one last time.

"Lady, you still got jokes even now, huh? You wait until I'm here to have this little guy, you hear me?" Kitt asked. He patted her belly one last time before he left the stall.

"Boss, are you sure? I can help you today," Jose asked. Kitt lifted his ball cap and scrubbed his head thinking over the possibilities.

"No, I can't take the chance. She needs someone who knows her. You stay." Kitt looked around at all his men waiting for him to begin. "Let's get goin'. It's gonna be a day. I need coffee."

"Yes, sir!" His newest, least experienced, field hand said.

Everyone scattered as he started toward the small break room in the back of the barn. He moved through the men lifting an arm to his nose. Kitt could smell Austin on him, his cologne lingered, and it wasn't a bad thing.

He poured his coffee, bent his head down to smell his chest, smiling when he thought of Austin sneaking in to sleep in his arms. No matter how he fought it, it wasn't just about sex with them anymore. Austin was comfortable enough in his home to sleep. Actually, Austin left his own bed to come sleep in Kitt's home. Austin still slept in his bed, and for whatever odd reason, it felt deeply gratifying.

He took a long drink of the coffee and left the break room. For the first time since leaving his house, he felt the chill in the air. They kept the barn reasonably climate controlled, but the doors were open, and everyone was preparing to leave. Jose stood at the front, giving out directions, speaking Spanish to most of the men. It was times like these Kitt wanted to hug Jose. His foreman was worth every dime of his salary. Kitt had taken Spanish in school for years, and although he understood most of what was being said, he still sounded like a complete dumbass trying to talk to the guys himself.

"Okay, boss, Jesus is bilingual. He's staying close by you. You tell him when you need something done, and he'll get it done for you. Jorge's and his crew are taking the other cutters out. Half the crew's going with him over to Smith's place."

"Thanks, man. Call me if anythin' changes," Kitt said, walking out the door Jose held open.

"Boss, you should let me do this, and you stay with her." Jose followed him out the door, closing it behind them. Kitt never slowed until he put his Styrofoam cup on the hood of his truck and climbed inside the driver's seat, digging around the truck for his jacket.

"Keep a close eye on her and take care of things around here. You can go tomorrow. I'll stay. I'm thinkin' we have time, but call me when Doc gets here. Tell Lily we'll be back at lunch."

They had ten fields scheduled for today and hundreds and hundreds of acres to cover in the next twelve hours. The sun was just starting to rise, and they needed to be in the first field by the time daylight hit full on. Kitt shrugged on his jacket and grabbed his coffee. He took another big gulp, letting the scalding brew burn its way down and warm him up. He headed for the tractor with the cutter ready to go.

It was a slow drive. The tractor topped out at thirty miles an hour. The men followed behind him. It couldn't have been much past six in the morning, and as Kitt pulled off the road making a wide turn into the driveway, his phone rang.

"This is an awfully long bathroom break. You left me sleeping, and I was so hopin' for a little good morning sex this morning," Austin said with a distinct whine in his tired voice. "Where are you? I can come to you, do you, and then leave before anyone sees me." The last part was said on a deep yawn. The engine to the tractor churned so loud Kitt turned the speaker on and the volume up as loud as it would go, and he still needed to shove the phone inside his ear to hear.

"I got a call. Lady's just beginnin' to foal, and I'm already pullin' into the Henderson's to start cuttin'. Hold on." Kitt yelled into the phone over the sound of the engine. He pulled to the far right of the Henderson's property line and came to stop, letting the tractor idle. He watched in his rear view mirror as the men lined up beside him positioning themselves to work behind him as he cut. One ran forward to get the gate opened for his entry. Every so often, a movement caused Austin's scent to drift up and an involuntary smile formed without him even realizing it was there.

"I'm back," Kitt said, again shoving the phone in his ear to hear.

"Is she okay? Does it mess up your day?" Austin asked.

"I think I have to watch her tonight. Jose stayed behind with her. Today's gonna be longer without him out here, but I need him to keep an eye on her," Kitt said. He saw everyone behind him waiting for him to start, but he missed Austin and loved knowing he was talking to him right now while still lying in his bed.

"Anything I can do to help? Mike can come over so Jose can help you today," Austin offered.

"Nah, Jose knows her as well as I do. She needs someone she knows and who knows her. Jose's just a worker. He can outwork anybody, but I'm staffed up. Actually, overly staffed. It should be fine," he said. "I'll call if I can't get it done. I gotta go."

"I'll be thinking about my missed opportunity. I should have jumped you last night when I had the chance," Austin said.

"Stay longer and get some rest. You need it." Kitt was just as unwilling to end the call as Austin seemed to be. They sat there a minute quietly, not saying goodbye.

"I might do that. I can smell your cologne all over these pillows. I might have to take one of these home with me," Austin finally said.

Kitt didn't respond. He'd been smelling Austin on himself all morning. He mentally weighed whether to say it out loud or not, but decided to keep quiet, not able to find the very simple words to say.

"I love it when you get quiet, Kitt. I'm beginning to understand it happens when I unnerve you...and that feels really good."

"I'll talk to you later," Kitt said simply.

"Goodbye, be careful today. Let me know if you need us."

"Bye." Kitt forced himself to drop the phone in the cup holder next to the coffee. His eyes darted up to the rearview mirror, and he rolled his eyes at the blush on his cheeks and the smile on his face. His cock throbbed in his Wranglers. Dear God, did he have it bad. Kitt picked up the coffee cup and carefully took a drink, and then smelled the cologne lingering on his shirt.

"Damn, it's gonna be a long day!" Kitt positioned the tractor and adjusted himself in the seat as he pulled forward starting to cut the miles of overgrown hay in front of him.

~~~~~~

"You're in love." Seth declared as Austin came through the back door. "You've been making fun of me for the last forty-eight hours, and here you're grinning, whistling, acting like life couldn't get any better in this aloneness. In the desert. Texas is a dust bowl, so not the heaven you've made it out to be." Seth sprawled out on the sofa with the television on and the laptop in his lap. It was noonish, and Seth already looked bored as hell.

"As per normal, you have no idea what you're talkin' about." Austin quipped, walking through the house, deciding Kitt should be the first one to hear he carried that emotion, not anyone else.

He'd stayed at Kitt's most of the morning. Made himself breakfast and just stayed in Kitt's stuff until he forced himself out. He only did a little bit of pillaging through Kitt's belongings, and only because he found an interesting stash of his photos and movies hidden in the bottom drawer of Kitt's night stand. At some point, Austin would definitely be getting some kind of explanation about those. Of course, it would have to come after he figured out how to say he'd seen them under the stacks of hunting and fishing magazines, and still buried further under the accounting folders of the farm.

"It's either love, or a long night of great sex confusing itself as love," Seth said, watching Austin closely. After a second, his eyes narrowed, and he bent his head to the side to watch Austin closer as he made his way to the coffee pot.

"I didn't have sex at all last night. I slept until about ten this morning and just hung out alone until a little while ago. Ever think I need a break from your love sick ass? I haven't spent this much time with you in years. And now I remember why..." Austin waggled his brows at Seth and poured himself a cup of coffee.

"Huh. You're already starting to get your accent back." That caused Seth to put the laptop down and turn completely around, eyes fully trained on Austin. "How'd I miss this?"

"What?" Austin asked, cocking a brow. He leaned back against the sink and concentrated. He was an accomplished, award winning actor, he needed to find his '*you're wrong face*', but he really didn't want to hide it.

"At first I was giving you shit, but now...it is more than a regular fuck, isn't it?"

"Yes, it's more than a regular fuck. I told you that when we were sitting with Cara," Austin said, nodding his head and pronouncing each word distinctly. He took a drink of his coffee; his eyes stayed on Seth trying to gauge his reaction. For everything Austin had said about someday coming out, talking about it now made him nervous. Seth was one of the only people on the planet he'd actually told he liked doing guys.

"I didn't really pay attention. Is it love?" Seth wasn't going to let it go.

"We haven't gone there, and I've known him a long time, but not really, if that makes sense. I just re-met him when I moved back." Austin moved into the living room.

"And this is the cowboy all over the security reports? He lives close?" Seth tracked Austin with his eyes as he came to sit down in a chair near the sofa. The TV was muted, and all of Seth's attention focused on Austin.

"Yes." Austin couldn't get a read on Seth, and he felt like Kitt with these one word answers.

"Did you know he was gay before you moved here, or is that why you chose here?" Seth looked like he was piecing together a puzzle that Austin didn't even know existed.

"No, not at all. It was just a happy coincidence." Austin waggled his brows again and took another drink of his coffee.

"Convenient," Seth finally said.

"Tell me! I haven't had this much sex since...well, ever," Austin said, crossing one leg over the other. He perched the mug on the side of the chair, waiting for Seth's next comment.

"I didn't think rednecks were so open-minded about these sorts of things," Seth said after a minute's silence.

"They aren't. You can trust me on that one." Austin shook his head, chuckling a little.

"So he's in the closet?" Seth asked.

"He's buried."

"Huh...then how did you figure it out so fast?" Seth pulled his laptop back in his lap. He looked a little relieved as he turned away from Austin.

"His underwear." Austin gave his truthful response and hid his smile with another drink.

"Huh?" Seth cocked his head back to Austin.

"It took me a couple more days, but he wore a pair of *Andrew Christian* underwear. I watched him work. They showed through," Austin said with a chuckle. Seth just stared at him, the puzzled look back on his face. "You asked..."

"First, I have *Andrew Christian* underwear, and second, it's really getting serious? Like this guy's gonna be around us for awhile?"

"I think we've been over this part," Austin said.

"Humor me." Seth's attention was fully back on Austin, his laptop forgotten.

"I see the manager slash agent hat coming out. I see it in your eyes, Seth. I told you I'm done. I'm retired."

"I didn't believe you," Seth replied instantly. "I thought you'd get tired of all this nothingness. Seriously, how have you not?"

"You should've believed me. I'm not going back into that crazy ass mess. These last few days confirmed it for me. So done with all that."

"So you're thinking about really settling down here, making this your life." Seth waved his hand around the living room.

"You need to believe me when I tell you I'm not thinking about it. I've done it, and I don't want a bunch of bullshit from you right now. I'm happy. You're going to be happy with Cara, and I've made you a fortune over the last ten years. You're so tight I know it's all saved up so you have nothing to worry about," Austin said.

"It's not that. You're a great actor. It's a shame to think you'll never act again." Seth's words sounded sincere, and even though Austin had always considered him a good friend and not just his agent, hearing those words eased something inside him.

"I appreciate that, but if I do act again, it's years down the line, and it'll be a pick and choose kind of deal. I don't want that life anymore. I couldn't wipe my ass without someone taking my picture and all those rumors...no, I'm out, done! I can't even imagine what's being said about me being seen out in public," Austin said.

"It's your own damn fault. It's because you're so good looking. Gain weight or grow out your nose hair." Seth focused back on his laptop. "So where do you see this going?"

"With Kitt?" Austin asked. Not only had he missed Kitt while he was gone, he found he missed this farm. He rose, taking his empty coffee mug to the sink. He needed to get out to the barn to see what was going on.

"Yeah." Seth stayed glued to the sofa.

"I don't really know. He won't come out, so I guess I'll keep hiding until he's ready. However long that might be. You coming to the barn with me?"

"So you're really thinking long term about this guy." Seth didn't move but did cock his head back to watch Austin head to the back door.

"Yes! I think I've said that over and over." Austin strode to the back door. He brought his Southern accent out in full force. "You comin'?"

"Huh." Seth turned back to the laptop.

"Huh back, and what the fuck ever. I'm done with this conversation. You'll be meetin' him soon. He has a horse about to give birth. We're going over there later. Get changed, I'll be takin' you on a tour after I go check on things at the barn."

Chapter 18

About dark, Austin and Seth drove up to the Kelly horse barn. Austin purposefully waited until the field hands left for the day. Mike came over earlier and made regular visits for most of the afternoon to help watch Lady until the vet could free up and stop by. Mike also kept Austin posted on how things were going, even when the place started clearing out. Mike gave Austin the green light to come over. As a precaution, Austin still wore a ball cap he could pull down low and a high collared jacket he could pull up if need be.

Seth knew the drill. He'd been part of several duck out situations in the past. They walked into the barn together, Seth first, but he stopped soon, having no idea what to do or where to go. It gave Austin the second to look around, make sure the coast was clear before he guided Seth to the horse stall everyone stood around.

They walked side by side. Seth was clearly out of his element as a disinterested sneer splayed across his face. Seth's only concern seemed centered on dodging the dirt and other possibilities lying on the barn floor. Seth so wasn't feeling this ranch life like Austin had hoped he might. There was just way too much city boy in his agent, and it was something he'd never realized about Seth until right now. Over the years, they had always been in sync with one another, Seth being the peanut butter to Austin's jelly. But, by the end of the ranch tour, Seth was past the fun of the four-wheeler and ready to be back on his laptop, looking for messages from Cara.

Austin's gut told him he didn't see Seth sticking around the farm too much longer, and Austin couldn't seem to want him to stay. Their lives were different now. Austin's one hundred percent different, and he was happy with the change.

Austin picked a darkened corner and perched a leg on the bottom rail. He looked over the side of the stall. Seth came in beside him. No one paid any attention to either of them; every eye was on Kitt who stood in the stall with Lady.

Based on Mike's last call, Kitt had only been back about half an hour. He'd worked a fourteen hour day and looked a sweaty, dirty mess, which was interesting because at the same time Kitt looked hot as hell bent over rubbing Lady down. He spoke directly to her in soft soothing tones. Austin couldn't hear the words he said, but he watched every move Kitt made. Kitt handled the horse with such tenderness Austin yearned for those hands to be rubbing him down just the same way.

Before his dick grew too hard, Austin noticed the vet stood close by in the stall, watching everything Kitt did. Mike, Jose, and Lily were like he and Seth: on the outside looking in. Austin pulled his ball cap a little lower on his head, and stayed in the dark. He turned his full attention back to Kitt. It was so easy to see this was where he belonged. Kitt had some innate understanding here, and this horse responded to him on a level of which Austin had no knowledge. The man and the animal watched one another closely, and Kitt rubbed her down until he got close enough for her to move her head and knock his ball cap off. Austin realized Kitt got in the position intentionally to let the horse do the move.

"So you aren't so sore that you can play games? I think that's a good sign, big girl." Kitt nuzzled her head, rubbing behind her ears. He scooped his hat up and ran a hand down her nose as he rested the ball cap back on his head. Austin could see everything great about this horse was due to the tender loving care Kitt gave her. Based on everything he'd heard, she was most comfortable with Kitt in there with her.

"We can see what's goin' on in there, Kitt. Make sure he can come on his own, but it's risky. I'm not sure it's needed," the vet said.

"Nah, he's facin' right. I don't wanna risk it. Let's give her time. If we need that exam, I'll do it," Kitt said in that same loving tone. He spoke to the vet, but looked at the horse.

"What's going on?" Austin asked Mike quietly trying to get caught up.

"They're talkin' about maybe needin' to turn the position. She's in full labor and they're just eliminatin' he may be breech. They don't think he is. The last ultrasound showed him in the right position,"

Mike said equally quiet, keeping his eyes on the horse. Seth stood beside him with horror in his eyes as the doctor shoved a long plastic glove back in his bag.

"Can Kitt do things like that?" Austin's voice was barely above a whisper.

"Yeah, he's done it for us quite a bit. He knows what he's doin', Lady would respond best to him," Mike said.

All eyes stayed on Kitt who positioned himself behind the horse rubbing from high on her belly to her back legs. He kept a steady stream of conversation going and ran his hands over her udder. Kitt looked totally absorbed in what he did, as if it were just the two of them and no one else in the barn. The vet stayed back and let Kitt work. The horse whined a little, nodded her head, but stayed still. Kitt never stopped the flow of conversation with her. His tender, gentle touch never changed.

"That's it. Her milks droppin', he's comin' soon," Kitt said to the vet seconds later.

"I'm guessin' a couple of hours," the vet replied, his eyes trained on the horse.

"I don't know. She's too early for this. It could still be a day."

"You know it's an estimate." Doc nodded at him. "She's close. It'll be tonight."

"It's an estimate when it's not an absolute firm date. Hers is a firm date," Kitt challenged back. The horse turned to Kitt as he stood talking to the doctor. His body faced her, but his head was cocked to the side, deep in thought. She took a step or two toward him, and Kitt reached out to rub her as he spoke to the vet. She had other plans. She lifted her nose and knocked his hat off again.

"You have all these jokes tonight?" He turned back to her. Austin saw it then. He gave all his attention to his animals. They were most comfortable with him, because he was most comfortable with them. Kitt didn't hide anything from his animals. Kitt reached down and grabbed the cap, but kept it in his hands.

"After this, you'll know she foals early. Besides, you suspected this outcome from the beginnin'. I don't think it's a long labor for her. I think he'll be here soon. We'll see. Watch her tonight, call me when you need me." The vet patted the horse and left the stall.

Kitt just rested against the rail. The stress of the moment was clear on his face. He hadn't acknowledged or even seen Austin or Seth as they came in. He was completely absorbed in his horse, keeping his eyes on her as he absently put the ball cap back on his head.

"You can do this, big girl. I know you can." Kitt nuzzled her. The horse responded to him, again knocking his ball cap back down, causing them all to laugh. It was then that Kitt lifted his eyes to Austin. They exchanged something in the gaze before Kitt's eyes cut to Seth. He intently stared at him for a long moment before looking over at his stepmom. The vet was already out the barn door. If he noticed Austin, he never said a word.

"Austin, it's good to see you again," Lily said before Austin could introduce Seth. "Hi, I'm Lily, Kitt's mom."

"It's a pleasure to meet you. You certainly don't look old enough to be his mother." Seth pointed in Kitt's direction.

"Well, that's good because actually I'm his Stepmom," Lily said with a laugh.

Kitt cut his eyes back to Austin, letting his gaze linger for a second or two, before turning them back to Seth. His focus stayed on Seth until he finally turned to Mike and Jose. "I'm gonna go home and shower, and then I'll be back to sleep with her tonight. I'll call you if anythin' changes. I won't be longer than fifteen minutes. Jose, can you stay that long?"

"Yes, sir. I'll cut tomorrow. This here's way too stressful. You stay here with her!"

Austin chuckled at the sincerity on Jose's face. It was said in jest, but it was clear it was a serious thought. As Kitt came from the stall, he stuck his hand out in Seth's direction, not waiting for an introduction.

"Kitt Kelly." His introduction was a little curt compared to the tenderness he just displayed with the horse, and it was only because Austin was so in tune with Kitt he even picked it up. Tension shot between Seth and Kitt, and Austin got the impression it was just the deep rooted Southern manners requiring Kitt meet his agent. The attitude in both men surprised Austin, and he narrowed his brow watching the exchange a little confused.

"I'm Seth Walker."

Kitt shook Seth's hand and nodded. It was all he gave before turning away. The action was monumentally clear: Kitt hadn't acknowledged Austin at all.

"Kitt, this is my agent and good friend," Austin said to Kitt's retreating back. All Austin got was a simple look over the shoulder and a curt nod with a tip of Kitt's ball cap before his eyes cut back to Seth. Kitt just dismissed Austin, and this time it sure wasn't sitting well with him at all.

"It's nice to meet you. We'll have to have you over for dinner in a few days. Get through this with Lady first," Kitt said.

It was all Austin got as he watched Kitt strut through the barn to his truck. He never looked back as he stepped up inside his cab, started the truck and pulled away.

"Thanks for the help today, Mike." Jose was left with them all in the barn. "Mr. Grainger, thank you. Kitt will for sure be thankin' you soon. He's just stressed tonight."

"No, no problem. I get it. We'll get out of your way. Anything Mike or I can do to help, just let us know." Austin tried to keep his eyes on Jose and not the dust cloud forming behind Kitt's truck as he drove away.

"Thank you, sir," Jose said, walking them out to Austin's truck. As if he had no other choice, Austin finally cut his eyes in the direction of Kitt's cabin and looked out where the trail to Kitt's house lay. The dust was already settling. Kitt didn't waste a minute in his getaway.

~~~~~~

"So that's your cowboy? He's good looking enough," Seth said as he climbed into Austin's pickup truck.

"He's hot as hell!" Austin started the truck and waved at Jose as they drove away from Kitt's barn.

"If you're into guys."

"Which I am." Austin shot back immediately. How could Kitt never acknowledge him? He couldn't be in the same room without getting a hard-on for Kitt, no way he wouldn't at least say hello.

"Austin, what's going to happen if you're ready to come out and cowboy Kitt isn't?" Seth asked. "Isn't that what this is all about? You're here to get your life back, stop hiding and by your own admission, he's buried deep in that closet."

"That's still years away." Austin pulled out on the main road for the quarter of a mile until his entrance began.

"It'll be a huge problem. I know you. You're the touchy, feely type. You don't do well with a bunch of rules. Clearly, you don't.

You've up and left a job paying you twenty million dollars a film in order to be who you are." Seth kept his gaze straight, staring out the front window.

"Look, who knew I'd find him so quickly. Besides, it'll work out like it's supposed to. I don't wanna talk about it anymore. Only time'll tell how this works out. But, I'm unbelievably happy with him. It's not something I'm willing to just give up because I don't know the future in our deal."

That seemed to stop Seth, and they drove the rest of the way in silence. Austin pulled up to the back of the house, put the truck in reverse and let the truck idle.

"You aren't coming in?" Seth asked when he realized Austin wasn't turning the motor off.

"Nah, I'm going back over so Kitt doesn't have to stay there alone."

"Did I miss something? Does he know you're coming? Does he even care?" Seth stepped from the truck, but stood with the door open waiting for an answer.

"No. But it's where I want to be. Now shut the door so I can go, and tell Cara hello for me." Austin tried not to let Seth's negativity work its way in. Kitt hadn't acknowledged him, hadn't given him the time of day. That was bad enough on its own before Seth dumped his line of thinking on top of it.

"Austin, are you sure he's as into you as you are him?" Now that was the one million dollar question Austin couldn't answer.

"It doesn't matter..." Austin shook his head, his frustration clear. "Seth, what's your problem? I was happy for you and Cara. It's weird to me how you two got together after all this time, but whatever. Just back off some and shut the fucking door."

"You're right." Seth grinned at him.

"Shut the Goddamn door." Austin started backing away. Seth was going to have to move or be hit.

"Okay, okay! Goodnight!" Seth still didn't lose the grin as he shut the door.

Austin never looked back as he drove to the Kelly's. Only Kitt's truck sat out in front of the barn. Austin jumped out and went through the front doors, looking down at Lady's stall. He saw Kitt's head was bent over the gate. Again, he was talking to her, but now wearing clean blue jeans and a t-shirt. His work jacket slung over the side of the gate.

Not much need for it with the mild temperature back in the area. Kitt's voice was soft and light, and Austin knew he hadn't heard him come in.

"Will this be the colt you keep?" Austin asked as he walked down the aisle to make his presence known.

"I don't know, we'll see." Kitt looked up, surprised to see Austin.

"I couldn't stay away. Is it okay I'm back?" Austin came to stand close to Kitt at the stall gate. The horse nodded her head at Austin, causing him to smile. He reached out to rub her long nose. Kitt looked all around the barn before he spoke.

"All the trucks are gone?"

"Yeah, it's just mine and yours out there." Austin turned his eyes back on Kitt. The ends of his hair were still wet from the shower he'd taken. Austin stood there, tucking his fingers in his front pockets to keep from reaching out to touch his hair. "You were incredible tonight. She's lucky to have you."

"I'm lucky to have her." Kitt watched Lady until he finally lowered his hand from where he stroked her. He stayed with one booted foot on the bottom rail. Kitt cut his eyes back to Austin. His gaze was somber. Neither one of them said anything for a minute.

"Are we okay?" Austin asked simply getting straight to the point.

"It's weird seeing you with another guy," Kitt said after a long minute. He looked down as he spoke, but forced his eyes back up. He nodded as he got to the end of the sentence as some sort of affirmation to his statement.

"Seth's been my best friend and agent for fifteen years, nothing more." Austin wanted to make his relationship with Seth absolutely clear to Kitt. After another long minute, Kitt spoke.

"I have coffee going, want some?" Kitt lowered his foot, and pushed away from the stall. Austin grabbed his arm, keeping him there.

"Seth's straight. He's the one Cara's all crazy about."

"He isn't crazy about me, is he?" Kitt shot back.

They stood so close he could feel Kitt's breath slide across his face, and he barely resisted the urge to lean in and kiss Kitt's closed lips. This moment was one of those rare relationship moments that needed to be worked out before anything else could happen. But, dear God, Kitt's lips were perfectly made. Austin couldn't resist anchoring an arm around Kitt to pull him closer.

"All that matters is that I'm crazy about you," Austin said. He gave up on trying to work it all out in his head. Instead, he crushed his lips to Kitt's. Kitt didn't hesitate, immediately opening to him, pushing his tongue out, swirling and sucking it around Austin's. Their kiss was perfect. Any concern or worry Austin had melted away as Kitt opened wider for him. It was only the need to breathe that broke them apart.

Kitt locked onto Austin's neck, whispering as he trailed kisses up to his ear. "Come to the break room. Have some coffee with me. I need to hold you and do more of this. It's too open out here. The room'll give us privacy."

"You have to be exhausted. I can leave, let you get rest or stay out here with her while you sleep." Austin leaned his head back, giving Kitt better access to his neck.

"It's gonna take time to wind down. Besides, I'll be staying out here with here on a cot. I have to keep an eye on her so there won't be much sleeping. Unless, you need to leave. Is your agent at your house alone?" Kitt asked, pulling away a bit when asking about Seth. Anger shot across his face before he schooled his features, and Austin grinned. Kitt was jealous.

"Yeah, but he's fine. He's just here catching his breath," Austin said, tucking his hand in Kitt's. He began to walk toward the break room, tugging Kitt along with him. It took a second for Austin to realize he had no idea where the room was located.

"Come on, this way." Kitt took over the lead and took them down the long barn to a room by the back door.

"Are you jealous?" Austin asked.

"No! Not at all, not really." Kitt flipped on the light as they entered the small room. There was a sink, refrigerator and cabinet along with three large tables with chairs. The smell of coffee filled the air as it was filling the pot. Kitt let go of Austin's hand to reach around inside the drawers pulling out packets of cream and sugar.

"Of course not, because if you were jealous it would indicate some sort of feeling, wouldn't it?" Austin came up behind Kitt and ran one hand up Kitt's chest as he slid the other down over his hard cock. Austin grinned and ducked his head, breathing in Kitt's scent when he found him already rigidly ready. Austin rolled his hips into Kitt's backside while rubbing his equally hard dick against Kitt's blue jean covered ass.

"I guess I didn't expect him to be so young or good lookin'." He leaned back against Austin, laying his head back on Austin's shoulder.

"Baby, he's completely straight." Austin murmured lowering his face toward Kitt's as he placed a simple kiss on Kitt's lips.

"You've never been with him?" There was worry in his eyes, and it made Austin feel like he conquered some major war all by himself. It showed that on some level Kitt shared all this emotion with Austin and that caused him to involuntarily roll his hips and rub his rigid length against Kitt's ass.

"Not once."

"Good," Kitt said the simple word and turned in Austin's arms. He wrapped his own arms tightly around Austin, kissing him deeply. Both men ground against the other. It felt like months since he'd been with Kitt. Austin slid his hands down, gripping Kitt's ass cheeks as he tugged him closer until he was grinding Kitt harder against his aching cock. As Austin ripped his mouth free, his hips rolled in constant motion. He hadn't stroked himself off since their one time together on the phone. Austin had saved it for Kitt, and he was already too close to release. His plan was to be buried inside Kitt's ass when it happened. Austin just hadn't worked Kitt there yet, he needed to slow this down some.

"It doesn't matter. No one seems to have existed before I met you," Austin whispered the words while he trailed kisses along Kitt's jaw. Kitt leaned his head back to give Austin better access a second before a chuckle slipped from Kitt.

"You said that exact line in your movie, Last Chance, when you were trying to get in her panties," Kitt said still laughing. That did it for Austin, his immediate need slowed and he laughed too.

"And it worked if I remember correctly." Austin loosened his hold, and grinned back at Kitt. He loved that Kitt had watched his movies close enough to know his lines. "I have to admit something, I found a stash of magazines and photos at your house this morning."

Kitt pulled back from him and Austin let him, but not far enough to break his hold. Austin stayed close, followed the movement and leaned into Kitt as he leaned against the counter. The slowing down thing was working, but nowhere in his plan did it require Kitt to leave his arms. Austin raised his eyebrow and gave a crooked grin. "Could my heart be right? Could they be a jacking off stash?"

"You did not just 'find' those. No way! Those were hidden." Kitt started to move away, but Austin wouldn't let him. Instead, he braced his hands against the counter as Kitt tried to get distance.

"No, no, no…stay here with me. I did do that terrible thing and look through your stuff, but I'm telling you so it shouldn't count against me. Besides there was nothing for me to find! You like to read hunting and fishing magazines, and you apparently hate bookkeeping, but that's all. Well that and you seem to like pictures and movies of me…" Austin latched on to Kitt's neck, kissing up to his ear. He felt Kitt tense in his arms. No way was he going to let that happen. Slowing them down didn't mean stopping. No plan in Austin's mind included them stopping anything they were doing.

"I'll tell you a secret about me to help make it better," Austin whispered in Kitt's ear as he brought one hand forward, rubbing it down Kitt's hard-on. He never stopped the rhythm his hand created as Kitt leaned his head back to look at Austin. Any embarrassment he may have had was gone, curiosity clear on his face. Austin closed his eyes and tightened his grip, rewarded when Kitt rolled his hips forward into his hand. "Yeah, well…I used to jack off to the image of you in the shower. Actually, 'used to' means I still do. Anytime I need to get aroused, or finish, I pull the image of you standing under the shower up in my mind. The water dripping down your dick…I love that image in my head."

"No way, you're lying!"

"No, I'm not. I swear to you, I'm not lying. I want you, Kitt. I want you bad. I love the idea that you kept track of me over the years because I sure thought about you. I just didn't realize how much until we got together like this." Austin dug his wallet from his back pocket. He had a condom and a small packet of lube inside.

"Austin, we can't here." Kitt rejected him as Austin tossed the condom and lube on the counter in front of the coffee pot. Kitt's words said they couldn't, but his actions said something else. Kitt leaned in, gripped both sides of Austin's head and thrust his tongue forward, kissing him like he'd never been kissed before. Kitt dominated Austin, and it took a second for Austin to remember he planned to be buried in Kitt, not the other way around.

He shoved Kitt back. It was only an inch or two and never broke from the kiss, but the move gave him back control. He managed to unbutton Kitt's blue jeans as he deepened the kiss to a frenzy. Austin moved quickly. He reached out for the lube and shoved Kitt's pants down below his ass. He managed to get his undone, just enough for his cock to spring free. In one swift motion, he tore open the oil, dropped it on his dick and flipped Kitt around. Mere seconds after losing the feel of Kitt's lips pressed against his, Austin was buried fully inside Kitt's sweet ass.

There was no preparation and Kitt's tightness felt so damn good, better than any other time in his life. He pulled out as Kitt hissed a breath. Austin dropped more lubricant on his cock as he pushed back in. The lube packet fell to the floor as pleasure exploded across his body. Austin gripped Kitt's hips and fucked him. It wasn't a hard pounding. Austin moved with gentle purpose willing Kitt to enjoy this as much as he did. Austin moved his hips, finding Kitt's spot, stroking him from the inside out, loving every single second.

Kitt reared back, moaning deeply as he pushed his pants further down. Austin thrust forward, arching his back and closing his eyes. Kitt braced himself with his arms against the counter.

"Goddamn you've never felt so fucking good!" Austin almost yelled the words as he began the inevitable pistoning of his hips. Kitt pushed back further and bent in when Austin reached around to grab his cock.

"Spread your legs. You're coming with me," Austin groaned. He lifted Kitt by the chest, laying him back against his body. He kept his hips moving and stroked Kitt with a tight grip from tip to base. Austin kicked at Kitt's boots trying to spread them further apart. He was only semi-conscience of keeping Kitt's release on the ground, not on his clothes.

They were both close. Austin gathered the beads of moisture dripping from Kitt broad head and slicked his hand with the liquid as he continued to stroke Kitt's cock faster. Kitt's hands snaked up the side of Austin's shoulders, his fingers diving in Austin's hair. Those strong arms helped hold them together. "You feel too good back there. I can't hold it...I'm close."

"Me too." Austin breathed out the words panting in Kitt's ear. His hand lost the rhythm of his hips, and Kitt reached down and gripped his cock on top of Austin's hand, stroking himself.

"I'm coming," Kitt panted, dropping his chest on to the cabinet.

"Me—" Austin never finished his sentence. He came violently into Kitt. This was the best fuck of his life. Kitt was everything he ever wanted in a mate, and he was shocked he held his orgasm for as long as he did. Austin's knees buckled with the force of his release, and he fell forward on to Kitt's back. His breath sawed in and out while his heart thumped wildly out of control. Sweat coated them both. Several minutes ticked by as Austin floated. His dick stayed hard. It still twitched with small bursts of come inside Kitt as reality slowly settled back in.

"Damn, that was good," Kitt said, his strength held Austin up. Kitt leaned against the counter, legs as far apart as his jeans would allow. Austin managed to look over Kitt's side to see his release dripping down the cabinet and onto the floor.

"You came?" Austin asked seeing the answer for himself.

"Yeah. We should go without every few days. That was the best fuck of my life. God Austin, where have you been hiding that?" Kitt asked, and lowered his head onto the counter, shifting positions with his legs. Austin went with him. His cock was still hard, but empty. He tried to decide if it wanted to go another round or deflate and rest.

"You were incredible." Austin declared after another long minute. He wrapped his arms around Kitt's chest. Austin was back to supporting his own weight, but unwilling to let this moment go. Kitt looked up and Austin looked down, both their eyes landed on the untouched condom packet lying in front of the coffee pot.

Chapter 19

"Shit! Fuck, Kitt, I'm sorry. Shit!" Austin slipped his cock out and tore his t-shirt over his head, sliding it between Kitt's parted thighs. His release was already spilling out of Kitt.

"I never forget the condom! Shit, that's why it was different." Kitt's movements were slower than Austin's. He reached a hand over to pick up the wrapped condom as if he'd never seen one before.

"I've been tested. I'm clean, but fuck, Kitt I'm sorry!"

Kitt was still staring at the condom wide-eyed, and Austin tried to clean the signs of their passionate lovemaking off Kitt when suddenly a soft knock sounded from the door. As in slow motion both their heads turned to see it open and Mike stood just outside of it, ready to step in.

"You already asleep buddy, or could you use some company? I saw Austin's truck out there…" The shock of the scene registered on Mike's face, and all he could do was blink until he forced his gaze down and stumbled back a step.

"Shit…I'm sorry…" Mike's eyes never came back up as he stumbled a step back and turned away. His cowboy boots clicked hurriedly on the concrete barn floor as he hightailed it to the front.

"Damn it!" Kitt shoved away the t-shirt and started toward Mike. He pulled his pants up as he went. It was awkward, but he never stopped running as he headed out into the barn.

"Mike, come back here!" Kitt yelled as Mike disappeared through the front door of the barn.

"I never saw anything, Kitt." Mike's muffled yell came as the barn door swung closed. Kitt ran toward him, but came to a sudden halt when Lady gave a strong whine. Austin ran past him.

"Let me go after him. Take care of her," Austin said, as he went for the front doors.

Kitt had a moment where everything earthly centered directly into him and he could feel Austin dripping from his ass. Lady pulled him out of his fog with another throaty whine. "Shit, she's already foaling!"

Austin ran out the front door and Kitt pivoted on his heels, heading to Lady's stall. She was lying on a bed of straw, birthing her colt. He quickly darted inside with everything else forgotten. Kitt helped the new colt out, trying to keep Lady soothed and as comfortable as possible. He talked her through it until the colt lay to the side. Mike was behind him, handing him the suction tube.

"Is he breathing?" Mike asked. He was down on his knees beside Kitt. Mike didn't touch either horse, Lady wouldn't have wanted it. Instead, he worked alongside Kitt, handing him a towel and laid other equipment out beside him just in case it was needed. Kitt worked the new colt, going through the steps, making sure he was fine, fit and breathing properly and then he worked on Lady. After a few minutes a smile ripped across Kitt's lips.

"Good girl! I'm so proud of you. He's perfect, Lady!" Kitt grinned so big he turned to Mike who gave him a good hard whack on the back. Kitt looked over his shoulder to see Austin there. They smiled at each other before Kitt's eyes darted back to Mike.

~~~~~~~

Austin stood back and let the men work. The awkward moments were long gone. Lady became the only thing important to everyone inside the barn. Austin stayed close, but out of the way as relief flooded through him. Mike was needed here. He knew exactly how to help whereas Austin knew nothing. He would have been at a total loss at helping Kitt bring the colt into the world.

At some point through the birth, Austin saw Kitt's jacket hanging on the stall and put it on so he didn't have to resort to putting on the come stained t-shirt he'd shoved up Kitt's ass when the vet got there. All the tension of earlier was now completely gone, in its place an exuberance. Kitt's smile wouldn't leave his face.

Austin didn't know for sure how this was going to play out, but he prayed for a simple end. He decided he'd promise to never come back to the barn again. He'd swear on his life he would stay at the cabin or his house waiting on Kitt there in the future. He'd also remind Kitt of Mike's confidentiality agreement. Surely, Kitt would be able to see reason. And yet, Austin couldn't stop the dread building in his heart.

~~~~~~

Doc deemed both mother and baby healthy and the birth a success. If you could judge anything on a newborn colt, this one looked good; strong and big, a perfect match to his father. His legs were already longer than his mother's, a good sign of the size he would be. Kitt named the colt Hooch.

A yawn formed inside him, and Kitt cut his eyes up to the clock along the back wall. He was on an adrenaline high with exhaustion just under the surface. It surprised him that only a couple of hours had passed since this whole thing got started. The new little colt should try to stand in the next hour or two and he wanted to stay close by, making sure Lady was able to feed Hooch like she should. Doc left and Lady was already urging her colt to his feet. Kitt, Austin and Mike stood on the outside of the thoroughly cleaned stall, looking in.

The start of the night seemed a far distant memory. What Mike walked in on; it was funny how Kitt pushed the memory so far back in his mind, he almost convinced himself it didn't happen. It was only the pesky wet spot in the back of his jeans that wouldn't let him completely forget. For about the sixtieth time tonight, Kitt reached down and adjusted his t-shirt, hoping it covered the stain.

"I shouldn't have barged in like that. I'm sorry," Mike said into the quiet while they were all looking down at the horses. If Kitt was right, Mike's tone mixed confusion with a hint of anger. Kitt understood and got it. He only glanced up for a second before his gaze cut away. He could feel the heat pooling in his cheeks as he thought over the best way to respond. Luckily, Austin stayed quiet. Thank God for small miracles.

All Kitt came up with was to try and steer Mike away from the truth. He didn't know in what other direction, he hadn't thought that far ahead. He tried hard to remember exactly the moment Mike walked in the room. Was there any chance Mike didn't see everything Kitt thought he might have?

"This isn't what you think."

"You weren't having sex with Austin in the break room?" Mike asked, hooking an arm on the steel gate while looking directly at Kitt with a grin on his face. He dared Kitt to lie to him some more.

"Okay, you're right, Mike. That part's what you think, but this isn't a random deal," Austin said, from behind Kitt. Kitt could only turn and stare at Austin. Why couldn't he ever just keep his mouth shut!

"So you're gay? You've been gay this whole time I've known you? Or is it a new development since Austin moved in? You know what? It's none of my business." Mike said the words to Kitt, then shifted his gaze to Austin, and then back to the horse. For a second, Kitt thought he may have seen hurt on Mike's face, just like with Kylie. Out of all the scenarios Kitt thought could happen when people found out he was gay, hurt never crossed his mind. Why was Mike hurt?

"Now wait a minute." Austin began, but Kitt cut him off.

"I'm gay." Kitt spoke softly, and both sets of eyes landed on his. His heart hammered in his chest and his lungs paused in their normal, involuntary intake of breath as he said the words and told the truth for the first time in his life. "No one knows, but I've been this way my entire life. Mike, I don't know what this is gonna do to us, but I need you to keep this to yourself."

"It's not a problem. As a matter of fact, I'm gonna try to do everything I can to scrub that from my memory," Mike said with a harsh chuckle.

"Mike, it's not what you think. I care about Kitt." Austin piped in just as Kitt would have let the conversation be done and over with. He'd even started to move away from the stall. The words stopped him. He didn't look up, he just stopped unsure if he wanted to hear what Austin had to say or not.

"Is he why you moved here? I thought you were gettin' married. Or is that not right? Is it a swings both ways kind of kinky deal?" Mike tried for a cheeky response with a cocky grin on his face, but fell short, making even Austin pause, not sure how to answer.

"Look, I'm never breathin' a word of this out loud again. Congratulations on the new colt, Kitt. He looks awesome just like you knew he would. Good night, and I swear your secret's safe, buddy." Mike pivoted on his heel and never broke stride out the back door.

They watched him leave as he finished the sentence. Austin started out after Mike, but Kitt stopped him with a hand to the arm.

"Let him go. There's nothin' you can do. Mike's a good guy. Whatever's gonna happen, will happen, but Mike isn't a talker." Kitt tried hard to convince himself what he said was true. Mike was a good guy, but he liked a good story, and he liked to drink on occasion. One slip up was all it would take to have this spreading like wildfire.

"It doesn't matter. He can't expose you. It wouldn't be in his best interest. I'll bury him if he does," Austin said, reaching for Kitt who stepped toward him.

"Goddamn it what was I thinkin'? I've been caught twice, after never, ever bein' suspected. Fuck it, Austin." Kitt lowered his head to Austin's shoulder. Austin instantly embraced him. He ran his hand up Kitt's neck, tangling his fingers into the back of his hair and held him close, breathing him in.

"Babe…" Austin whispered in his ear. Kitt stayed in his arms, tucked into Austin's neck until Austin forced his head up. Austin planned a kiss, but once he got a look in Kitt's eyes, he stopped in mid motion.

"No. No more. You make me crazy. You make me think it's all going to be okay and it's not. There's a reason I had Sean. I could go to him when it was convenient for me. You walk into my life and screw convenience. Hell, *screw everything.* I just wanna fuck you for the world to see."

"It's the way I feel about you, too," Austin said carefully, clearly unsure of the point Kitt tried to make. Austin didn't back away from Kitt, he kept him close, tightening his arms around his waist.

"No more, Austin. I have too much ridin' on right now. I can't risk this. I don't think Kylie will tell, and I don't think Mike will, but I can't risk a third person findin' us out. Those two are the only people on the planet I fully trust. I can't risk this right now. You have no idea the debt my father had when he died, and all I've done is add to it tryin' to find a way out of it. Right now is too important to me." Kitt stepped back breaking Austin's tight hold, leaving them standing at arm's length. Kitt straightened his spine, bowed his chest, physically keeping himself strong.

"I want you to trust me and if debt's the problem, I have more money than I can ever spend. I can solve your money problems." There was a desperation laced in Austin's words.

"That's not what I meant. You aren't listenin'. You need to hear me. I'm not takin' your money. Why would you even give me the money, to sleep with you more? Like pay me to sleep with you and be around when you want me? No, Austin, I'm not that guy." Kitt let anger fill him. It was so much better than the ache in his heart, begging him to stop this right now. He stepped further away putting more distance between them.

"I never said that. It was never even implied." Austin began but Mike came through the front doors of the barn. He looked at each one for a long minute, his presence back in the barn said more than the words he was clearly trying to form.

"Kitt, it doesn't change anything and it sure as hell explains a lot. Your life's shit, man. If this makes you happy, you need to go for it. I'll keep it quiet, I swear." The words were said, and Mike was gone again.

"I can't risk this right now, Austin. We need to back off, and I need you to leave right now." Kitt never looked back as he stepped around Austin and walked straight to the break room to clean his release off the cabinets and throw away the lube and condom packets before anyone else had to the chance to happen in on him.

"What the fuck have I been thinkin'?" Kitt asked himself as he slammed open the break room door.

Chapter 20

Kitt pulled the tractor into the barn with nothing but the moonlight and memory to guide his path. It had been a solidly packed forty-eight hours since his new colt was born. He hadn't heard anything from either Mike or Austin. He'd sent Austin packing, so he got that. Pain and hurt radiated from Austin as Kitt sent him on his way. It had almost been a tangible entity on its own. So no, Kitt hadn't expected to hear from Austin. Maybe his heart hoped he would have, but his head knew better.

As for Mike, he didn't know for sure. Mike wasn't the kind of guy to be put off by things like this. But, it was a big breech in confidence to have kept a secret like this for so long. Kitt couldn't remember ever hearing a homophobic slur from Mike. He wasn't a racist, either. He was just a good, hard working kind of guy. To have him MIA for so long, especially after the colt was born, was just plain weird.

Kitt parked the tractor and headed straight over to check on the new mom and colt. He bypassed dinner and drove home to shower. Technically, if he let himself think about it, he was past exhausted. He hadn't slept more than a few hours since Austin shared his bed. Between the birth and the baling, work took up every bit of his time. Jose had a wife and kids and managed to do everything Kitt did and then some, but for some reason, he felt completely off his game.

Kitt's heart ached from the moment he woke until the moment he fell asleep. It never gave him a break, just a constant reminder of what he threw away. Regardless of being dead on his feet, Kitt knew he wouldn't sleep until he got things resolved, at least with Mike.

A cold front was expected, but hadn't made it this far south yet. It was back to being warm outside. Kitt dressed in shorts, a t-shirt and flip flops before jumping in his truck and driving around the property to Mike's trailer. He found it dark and closed up tight. He continued on his way straight to the Grainger barn where he saw the lights still on and only Mike's truck sitting out front.

Mike looked like he was alone, working with a couple of horses in the corral surrounding the back of the barn. Those had to be new, and Mike hadn't mentioned they were coming. Kitt got out of his truck while turning the ignition off. He purposefully ignored looking toward Austin's house. Instead, he kept his gaze on Mike as he walked over to the fence and anchored a foot up on the first post. He leaned against the rail.

"She looks good," Kitt called out as Mike came closer.

"Yeah, she's picking it up. She was an unexpected surprise yesterday. I'm finding the owner does things like that a lot." Mike grinned keeping the horse on task of whatever skill he tried to teach her. They were silent for a few minutes. Mike continued to work until he finally looked over his shoulder. "What's up?"

"Nothing. Just came over to see if we're cool." That caused Mike to look back at him.

"Hang on, let me put her up." Mike dismounted and walked the horse inside. Kitt followed him into the barn, coming in from a side door. He watched Mike stall the horse, and he stayed back out of the way, only bringing fresh hay over when Mike latched the stall from the outside.

"I hadn't heard anything from you," Kitt said, as he leaned over the side of the stall and laid the hay out.

"You should've told me."

Kitt appreciated the honesty from Mike.

"You have to understand why I didn't," Kitt said. They were standing at the gate, staring at the horse as they spoke. Kitt looked at the stallion in the stall to his right. "He looks good. How old?"

"I do understand, but it makes us more one sided. You know everything about me," Mike said, as he ignored Kitt's question and walked away from the stall. Kitt followed a couple of steps behind him as Mike flipped off the lights in the barn before he said anything more. "Has it always been like this?"

"My whole life." Kitt looked at Mike, but the dark made it an easier conversation.

"You know, in college, those women threw themselves at you. You were always the gentleman. I couldn't see how you didn't take advantage of the situation, but you never did. I don't know how I didn't figure that out."

"I haven't ever told anyone. You're the first person I've ever said it out loud to." Kitt followed Mike outside and now they walked aimlessly in front of the barn. No direction, they just walked and talked. They had about the same posture, hands in their pockets, eyes downcast, watching where they walked as they tried to clear the air between them.

"You told Austin."

"No, I didn't. He figured it out," Kitt said, causing Mike to stop and turn to face him.

"No way! How?"

This conversation was much harder to have face to face.

"He said he figured it out from my underwear." Kitt snorted at the memory of Austin telling him how he'd unraveled the truth. "When the waist band was outside my blue jeans that day I was throwin' a fit over the fence." Kitt couldn't hold the eye contact and kicked the grass patch with his sandal.

"Really?"

"It's what he said." Kitt shrugged. There was a long pause before they were back to walking in what seemed like a large circle around the front of the barn and their trucks.

"Austin came out and talked to me this morning. He said it wasn't just a fuck for him. Is it just a fuck for you?"

"I put the brakes on it after you left." Kitt came to a stop, giving Mike no choice but to stop too. Kitt never looked up, instead, kept his eyes trained on his now dust covered toes.

"Why?" Mike finally asked defensively. Kitt stalled, it took a minute to form the words, to find the truth and not let another lie slip through his lips. Technically, now that Mike knew the truth, he never had to lie to him again and that was monumental. The honesty of the thought made Kitt suddenly a little emotional. It felt so good to just tell the truth.

"Both you and Kylie caught us. I've never been found out before because I keep it all far away from here. At this rate, if we keep going like this, everyone in town will know by the end of the month. I can't jeopardize things like this right now." As Kitt spoke, he started walking again. This time Mike didn't follow.

"I won't tell, Kitt." Mike's voice was reassuring and he stood his ground.

"Thanks," Kitt replied, and dropped his hands in his pockets.

"How's Hooch?" The subject change was abrupt, but Kitt knew it was intentional. They'd talked about it, Mike was okay, and they were good.

"Good. Super good. So far, he's everything we hoped for and Lady's nurturing, she's a good little momma. They're good."

"I was gonna stop by after I finished tonight," Mike said.

"It's all good. Jose's there. I'm goin' out there at midnight to check on the little guy, but I think it's fine. We aren't really needed around the clock, it's just precautionary. Doc came by today and gave him a thumbs up." Kitt turned back to his truck.

"Cool." Mike was silent for a moment before his voice rang from behind Kitt's back. "You should go talk to him."

The words stopped Kitt in his tracks and his heart leapt. "I think we need to give it a rest. I need to apologize, but it needs to chill between us." Kitt shook his head slightly and started back to his truck.

"Goddamn, Kitt. You spend your entire life alone. He's a good guy. And, I noticed you seemed happier over the last few weeks, and it doesn't make me a girl that I noticed. You're like a brother to me. It's probably not a bad thing to have someone sharing your life after you've been all alone for the majority of it. I get it's probably hard as hell to allow someone in. There has to be a lot of fear in that, but I still think you should go talk to him. I would if I were you."

"Is his agent still here?" Kitt asked.

"I think so, but he's leaving tonight. All this isn't his thing," Mike said. Kitt came to a stop at the back of his truck and Mike walked up to him. "How's the cuttin'?"

"A little behind."

They stared at one another for a long minute.

"I can come in the morning," Mike offered.

"Nah, we'll catch up with Jose back on business. I'll call you if it gets more behind."

Mike nodded and climbed into his truck. He started the ignition and rolled his window down.

"You should've told me. It wouldn't have made a difference. You gotta know that, somewhere deep inside you." Mike put the truck in reverse and drove past Kitt. "Now go talk to him. Bye."

Kitt watched the taillights of Mike's truck disappear. The relief was staggering. Now there was just a hole the size of Texas in his heart where Austin was concerned. He ran his fingers through his hair, and then tried to pat it down, knowing he caused it to stand up in every direction. Kitt forced himself to the house. His heart pounded in his chest with every step he took. He deserved nothing less than to have Austin slam the door in his face, but he needed to try to apologize.

As he got to the steps of the front porch, he heard laughter. Austin's agent was laughing, or at least Kitt assumed it was Seth. Hell, it could have been his own replacement in there laughing with the both of them. Or, even worse, the agent could be his replacement. Anger shot through him at the thought and jealousy took its hold. Part of him wanted to turn and forget making amends. If Austin could be so happy while Kitt suffered beyond reason…yeah, the other part of him won. That part wanted to tear the shit out of whoever Austin laughed with right now. His arm reached up and knocked hard on the door on its own accord.

Seth answered, took a step back and opened the door wider. His eyes narrowed as he looked at Kitt. That look kicked Kitt's heartbeat up that much more. He clenched his fist thinking how easy it would be to right hook the guy in the open doorway. He could drop Seth straight to his knees. Wouldn't that send Austin a message about their future? Hell, maybe it would send Austin packing, and Kitt could finally get on with his life.

As Kitt warred within himself, Seth looked over his shoulder toward Austin. The door was open enough to see Austin sitting at the table eating a bowl of cereal. Their eyes collided, and the smile Austin wore left his face. He stood, concern spread across his brow.

"Kitt? What's wrong?" Austin asked moving toward him.

"I'll leave you two alone." Seth darted to the side of Kitt as he looked back at Austin. He made a wide sweep around Kitt and jogged across the porch, taking the steps down to the yard.

Kitt didn't move from the spot he stood rooted in. He just stood there looking at Austin who stood in front of him. His heart settled, and the aggression of his deep breath turned more to a pant. Austin was about the best looking man Kitt had ever seen. He had no hard edges, he was just smooth and captivating. Kitt's dick grew hard.

"What's happened?" Austin asked again.

"Nothing...there's nothing wrong. I came over and talked to Mike, and I just..." Kitt stopped and stared for one full minute before he continued, "I'm sorry, Austin. I was wrong. Is it too late?"

"You're angry." Austin was clearly confused.

"I'm not angry." Kitt shook his head to affirm his declaration and forced his face to relax.

"Then what's this?" Austin asked, moving his hand toward Kitt's stance.

"Nothing, it's nothing." Kitt took a step back and breathed in deeply, hoping oxygen would somehow find its way to his brain. He had to get a hold of himself and quick. His eyes searched the dark and spotted Seth a few hundred feet away, walking aimlessly in open pasture.

"There's nothing between us, but friendship." Austin came outside to stand behind Kitt. Not close enough to touch, but close enough that Kitt could smell his cologne.

Those were hard words to hear. They said it all and were very clear. His heart fell to his knees and he closed his eyes. He should leave, but didn't. He'd come this far and wasn't opposed to begging for a second chance.

"I don't want just friendship. I want so much more than that. I was wrong to send you away. Are you tellin' me it's too late?" Kitt asked, still facing the pasture. His head hung low, his eyes were closed and seconds felt like minutes as he waited for Austin to answer.

"What? No, I mean Seth and I. It's just friendship between us."

This time he felt Austin's breath on his neck. Austin's body brushed against Kitt's. It took a full minute for him to understand the words with the way his body reacted to just Austin's slightest touch. He forced himself to calm down, to register each word Austin spoke. It was only as Austin stepped completely into him that he got what Austin tried to say.

"I miss you, Kitt." Austin finally turned Kitt around, and they stood chest to chest, both with their hands in their pockets.

"I miss you, too."

A smile lit Austin's face, but he didn't reach out to Kitt.

"I spoke to Mike this morning. He's not gonna say a word."

"I was wrong. It was fear talkin'. I'm sorry I hurt you. If I haven't ruined it, I'd like us to keep going. If I have, just tell me and I'll leave. At least, I tried."

"I must not be clear. I've had years of communication training, yet, I can't get through to you. Kitt, yes please, let's keep going. I want to. I've prayed for the last two day that you would come around. If you hadn't, I couldn't have waited much longer." Austin murmured and reached out to wrap an arm around Kitt. "I missed you. I gave Seth my phone to hide so I wouldn't call you, and he hid it too well. I tore the house apart trying to find it and couldn't. It's what he was laughing about when you walked up. I was coming to you tonight. I missed you."

"Come to my house," Kitt whispered as Austin brought his lips forward for a soft kiss.

"Oh God, that sounds good." Austin swiped his tongue forward, turning the kiss aggressive. Kitt met each bold stroke Austin made with one of his own. It had only been two days, but it felt like years since he kissed this man. The thought caused a primal groan to escape. Kitt wanted Austin and wanted him badly. The sooner they made it to his house the better off he would be. Their moment was interrupted by an alarmed yelp.

"There's something out here with me. *On four legs!* I can't fucking decide if staying out here with it is better than getting my ass kicked on the porch!" Seth was walking backward, taking big steps back toward the house. A few yards from the house, he turned and ran up the steps, straight past Kitt and Austin back into the house.

"How the fuck do you do this? Shit, I'm so out of here." Seth slammed the door and then opened it again, digging a hand in his sweatpants, producing Austin's cell phone. "It was in my underwear. The one place you would never think to look, ass."

"Wait! Let's start this over. Kitt, this is Seth Walker, my agent. And he's leaving tonight. He doesn't quite see the wonderment of being out here." Austin turned in Kitt's arms to lean back against his body.

"No offense, this place sucks. The bugs are crazy big. Spiders in my fucking bathroom, dust everywhere. It's a million degrees even in the winter, and slinging cow shit out of the stalls isn't my idea of a good time!" Seth slammed the door in Austin's face.

"We've been waiting for the cover of night to help keep us hidden. I have a plane ready to take him back to LA. Do you wanna ride with me to Dallas?" Austin asked Kitt while turning back in his arms.

"I have to be at the barn at midnight." Kitt lifted his hands to cup Austin's face as he bent in for another soft, lingering kiss. He loved to kiss Austin. This was exactly where Austin needed to be, right here in his arms, kissing him like it mattered.

"It's probably not the best idea I come there," Austin said, seconds before he swiped his tongue across Kitt's bottom lip. Austin rubbed his aroused cock against Kitt's who jerked at the simple touch. Kitt's hips involuntarily rolled forward, begging Austin to continue the simple move. Austin smiled into the kiss, but something abruptly changed. Austin's body tensed, and he stepped back a step, taking Kitt's hand.

"Come over tomorrow night whenever you can. I'll be waiting no matter how late it is." Austin guided Kitt down the steps toward his truck. They walked hand in hand in the moonlight, but Austin kept them about a foot apart. Kitt was desperate to be back in Austin's world, and he forced Austin closer, wrapping an arm around him.

"I'm really sorry," Kitt said. Austin's body stayed tense, and he never broke stride as they headed toward Kitt's truck.

"I get it. We have to be more careful. It's my fault. I should've stayed away. I just missed you, and then you gave me the best fuck of my life. Kitt, I'm not gonna let you go that easily, but you need to be in this with me. I don't want to keep going through this every few weeks." Austin's words were simple and clear, but his actions were still very specific. He pulled Kitt's truck door open. Once Kitt got inside, Austin held out a hand, pushing at Kitt's chest keeping him there as he shut the door. Kitt was so confused as he watched Austin walk around the truck and open the passenger side door, sliding inside.

"You won't be alone in this—" Kitt began only to be silenced by Austin with a raise of the hand.

"See? I just proved I'm learning. I wanted to drop to my knees on the porch, but instead, I walked all the way to your truck before I went down on you." Austin grinned, cocking his brow as he spoke. His aggressive actions were directly the opposite of the words he so casually spoke. He slid across the seat, lifting the center console. He shoved one hand down the front of Kitt's shorts, rubbing and massaging his cock as he unfastened his shorts with the other hand. Kitt lifted the steering wheel and Austin's head went down. In one swivel of the tongue, Kitt's cock was sucked deep inside Austin's mouth. It was no effort to Austin, he deep throated Kitt on the first try.

Kitt hissed in a breath and jerked his hips up, going deeper down Austin's throat. Austin's head moved up and down, sucking Kitt in and out as he worked his sac out of his shorts. The action was so hot, all Kitt could manage was a few throaty breaths as he tangled his fingers in Austin's hair. His eyes rolled in the back of his head and his head dropped back on the headrest.

"Baby... you're so good at this." It emerged more of a moan, Austin knew all the right moves as he rolled Kitt's balls in his palm. Austin only broke from the deep suction to whisper his warm breath over Kitt's aching cock.

"Come in my mouth when you're deep. Jam it down my throat. I like that the best." Austin was back on him, licking, sucking and bringing Kitt to an almost automatic climax. He came hard as he shoved himself down Austin's throat. His tangled fingers pushed Austin's head further down on his cock until the orgasm took him over the edge, and he forgot everything.

When he opened his eyes, Austin's face was in his, wiping the back of his hand over his lips, clearly proud of himself. The grin was too much, and Kitt smiled a lazy grin back as Austin spoke. "You were perfect. I like it just like that. That minute of not being able to breathe as you shoot your load down my throat. I like that a lot."

"I remembered." Kitt kept the grin on his face and lifted his hand, stroking his thumb across Austin's cheek and jaw until he threaded his fingers into Austin's hair. He loved the excitement Austin so obviously experienced at giving him a blow job. He cupped Austin's head, bringing him forward and swiped his tongue across Austin's lips, loving the taste of himself that lingered there.

"I swallowed you all and cleaned you up," Austin said against his lips, and waggled his eyebrows.

"So I'm guessin' we're at the point of figurin' out exactly what the other likes...you like me to rim you. It makes you come every time. I could do it now for you if you would come to my house..." Kitt tried again, still sated from his climax. Austin laid his head and upper body down along Kitt chest, snuggling up as Kitt held him there tightly. The angle was perfect to keep them face to face.

"It's an incredibly tempting offer. One I'm going to so regret missing out on. Seth's driving me crazy. The plane's waiting, and I have to get rid of him. You can't see from this direction, but he's flashing the porch light at me now. He's ready to go. Are you sure you can't ride with me? We could get a little room in some rundown motel. Maybe there will be an old vibrating bed."

"I have to stay." Kitt smiled at the thought of Austin Grainger in a roach motel somewhere along a Texas highway.

"I want you to want me." Austin said the sweet confession so plainly. "I wanted you to come for me. It's the only reason I wasn't at your door last night."

"I do. I want you so bad." It was dark outside. Kitt could make out Austin's face, but the dark helped hide some of the emotion those simple words stirred inside him. Kitt lowered his head, kissing Austin thoroughly until there was a rap on the window of the truck.

"I'm coming. Get in the truck, Seth." Austin sweet tone turned hard. Austin didn't move, nor did he break eye contact with Kitt. "You'll come over tomorrow night?"

"Absolutely. You keep this hard-on waitin' for me." Kitt slid his hand down, gripping Austin tightly.

"I don't think that's gonna be much of a problem." Austin ran his hands over Kitt's face, looking at him closely. "You're such a handsome man."

"That's exactly what I thought about you when I saw you sittin' at that table tonight."

"You mean something to me, Kitt," Austin said, and leaned in again for another kiss.

"I feel the same way." It was the truth, Austin did mean something to him.

The kiss didn't end until a pair of bright headlights flashed into his truck. They were blinded as a horn sounded off.

"See what a pain in the ass he is? It's the only reason we aren't in your bed right now. I need to get on the road." Austin shot Seth the finger into the bright headlights. He kissed Kitt again before crawling out the passenger side, and adjusting himself with the light of the cab.

"Be careful out there. Text me when you get home," Kitt said.

"I don't want to wake you." Austin shook his head and shut the door. Kitt started the truck, rolling down his window.

"I'll be up. Text me," Kitt pulled Austin in by the t-shirt for another smoldering kiss. Right there in the headlights for Seth to see.

"I feel perfectly marked." Austin grinned, pulling away. "I'll see you tomorrow night."

Chapter 21

Winter ~ three months later

"The fuckin' check came from the same company that bought my land!" Kitt almost yelled as Austin opened his back door.

"Hmmm…that's a coincidence. Why don't you come in, and we can try to sort out how something like that could've happened. Go over theories, investigate, get down to the root of the problem." Austin waggled his eyebrows as he turned away from the door, needing to stir the boiling sauce he'd set on the stove. It was his turn to cook tonight. The romance of cooking for another was gone, and Austin opted to reheat the spaghetti his housekeeper made a couple of days ago.

"So, I went to your barn, and you have two new horses!" That Kitt yelled, still standing outside the back door.

"Interesting. The pieces do seem to be falling together. Kitt, come in, it's cold out there!" Austin tried for reasonable as he turned down the heat on the stove. His head stayed cocked far enough over the center island to keep an eye on Kitt still in the doorway.

"Why did you buy my horses?" Kitt demanded. Clearly, he was angry as Austin knew he would be. It was only the beginning. Just wait, Kitt was going to be ballistic when he found out Austin also bought the other two who were still too young to wean from their mothers.

"Per you, who everyone says is an expert at all of this, they're the best. I want the best on my farm. Come in and start the fire. You've let all the warmth out of the house while being your normal hardheaded self." Austin finally looked down to dump the contents of a pot of boiling water in a colander in the sink. He flipped the cold water on before rounding the corner. Kitt still stood outside his back door.

"They aren't the best. I never said *the best*. They're close. If someone who knows what they're doing works with them, they could be valuable."

Austin narrowed his eyes as he walked to his back door. Kitt's head looked close to exploding which was technically what Austin knew would happen when he got the check in the mail.

"I bought wine. Baby, come in. Talk to me inside. Let's talk about it over dinner. Come in, it's cold," Austin said it all while stepping out on the porch and guiding Kitt inside. To give Kitt credit, he did walk forward. Not in the circle of Austin's arms, but at least now he was in the house which was a great start.

"Why did you buy them? Stop buyin' my shit, Austin! First the hay, now my horses. Why?"

"Do you ask everyone who buys something from you why they're doin' it? Isn't it safe to assume I wanted them so I bought them? And my animals need hay, Kitt." Austin tried to come off as if the answer was more than obvious. He even shook his head and rolled his eyes at the absurdity of Kitt thinking his animals didn't need to eat.

"Not at those prices. Those prices were inflated. I'd have just given you the damn hay. Wait a fuckin' minute, did you start the price war over them? You did!" Kitt solidly yelled the last sentence and Austin could see the real anger. It was time to stop being flippant and be truthful. He didn't want his sexy boyfriend leaving him tonight. Last night, Kitt had promised he'd spend the entire night with Austin. This was their night to celebrate the selling of the horses. Austin needed to get a hold of this quickly before Kitt stormed off.

"Kitt, you're only selling those ponies because you need money. The way I see it, you need time with these horses. And Hooch is yours, no one else's. It's clear to everyone who watches you two that he's yours. You can make something out of him. Out of all of them. It's an investment, nothing more. This gives you time with them. Besides, you were selling them too cheap. I'm not gonna cheat you or watch someone else do it." Austin spoke plainly, his voice stayed even, and he never took his eyes off Kitt.

"I can make somethin' out of them, but sellin' them is a normal way to progress. It was fair market value, Austin. You let me be all excited about makin' so much money when it was you trickin' me!"

Kitt's voice was lower now, he wasn't quite as angry, but clearly still upset.

"I loved seeing you so excited. It's a special memory I'll always cherish and now you see how much it means to me that I was able to make you that excited. I don't want to talk about this. I bought a couple of horses, and it was still a very good deal. I took an opportunity to keep the horses in the family. Now come sit down, eat dinner and let's talk about how terrible you're being to me, and how much attention I'm gonna need to get past all this." Austin tried to lighten the mood as he reached across the table and poured Kitt a glass of wine. Kitt took it, drained the glass and poured another. It gave Austin hope, and he worked quickly making two plates of food. Austin didn't keep his back turned away for too long. Kitt was very good with a weapon.

"Whatever, Austin. I don't want your money. I'm not cashin' the check," Kitt declared as he sat at the kitchen table with a thump and poured himself another glass of wine, draining that one too.

"You are cashing the check, Kitt. I bought a couple of horses. I'm also buying hay to feed mine and my dad's animals. Why can someone else buy them, but I can't?" Austin asked proud of this argument as he set Kitt's plate down in front of him.

"I don't like takin' your money. It makes me feel like I'm kept. I don't like it at all." Kitt sounded more dejected than Austin ever heard him sound.

"Get over it. You took it when you sold me this land, and if I remember correctly, it was *way* more overpriced than those horses." Austin took his seat and dug into his plate of spaghetti with more gusto than he felt. He just wanted things back normal between them.

"That was before I knew you." Kitt sat there looking at Austin.

"Get over it!" Austin's mouth was full of food as he spoke. "They're announcing my separation from Cara tomorrow."

"They think she's strong enough now?" Kitt asked. It was the perfect diversion to take his mind off the horses as Austin had hoped it would.

"Yup, Cara's supposedly doing well. They're planning a pretty immediate wedding to help draw some of the attention off me, per the publicist email."

"And you're not sad?" Kitt watched Austin closely.

"Nope, not at all. I'm actually incredibly happy for them and me." Austin taped Kitt's plate with his fork. "Eat babe, I have plans for you tonight."

"You say that every night," Kitt said with a chuckle. Austin supposed that meant they were over the argument, at least until the next sell.

"Because it's true. It's my most pressing issue of the day. You know what occurred to me? We've never had sex in my laundry room, and I have a side loading machine. How have we let that one slip past us?" Austin grinned big at the thought.

"You're a mess, Austin Grainger. My plan was to come here, tear the check up in your face and leave for the night," Kitt said, taking his first bite of food.

"I like my plan so much better."

~~~~~~

Kitt was pushed up on the washing machine. His feet hooked up around Austin's shoulders. The washing machine was in full spin mode with a purposefully lopsided load. Austin was buried deep inside his ass. All in all, it was great sex. The spin cycle did add that extra vibration and thrust. It even made the control panel digging in his back bearable. Austin looked like he was in heaven. He gripped Kitt's thighs tightly, keeping him right in that position as he fucked him hard, in perfect time with the spin on the machine. Austin had even talked him out of their required condom wanting to feel that moment they shared in the break room all those months ago.

"Fuck, it feels so good. I want it to last forever," Austin groaned from between clenched teeth. His eyes were closed tightly, his breath panted and pleasure was clear on his face.

"Harder, Austin. Make it harder." Kitt watched Austin move faster, trying to go deeper. Austin always wanted to please Kitt. It seemed its own kind of aphrodisiac for both of them and made the orgasm a little better in the end. Kitt reached down, gripping his cock and stroked. Having Austin over him like this was enough to have him come. It wouldn't take much more than a few strokes to get Kitt off.

"I'm coming. Fuck I'm coming. I can't hold it..." Austin slammed into Kitt, over and over until Kitt felt Austin's release filling his ass. Austin jerked a couple more times, digging his fingers into Kitt's legs until he finally fell forward with Kitt's legs and chest underneath him. Kitt barely finished his own release before his knees were shoved to his chest. Kitt's body wasn't this limber and the washer cut off finishing the load as if declaring all three of them were done with this session.

"Baby, you're hurtin' me." Kitt moved, trying to free his legs. Austin moved, but not in a good way and a spasm struck Kitt's calf. He jerked forward in pain, and they both landed hard on the laundry room floor. Kitt pushed at the cramp in his leg, trying to work it out.

"God, that was good." Austin lay fully back on the tiled floor, his eyes closed, totally sated. "Jesus, I love doin' you bareback."

"How in the world did we go from me from tearin' up your check, to you fuckin' me on a fuckin' washer with no condom?" Kitt asked, all that calm goodness gone as he walked out the cramp in his leg. He put a hand on his back where the washing machine knob scraped straight up as they fell to the floor.

"Kitt, I'm clean. I just got checked again. I got the test back like three days ago," Austin said watching Kitt as he walked around the laundry room.

"Was that when you were off signin' my check to mail to me? Why didn't you just bring it with you, save the postage," Kitt asked, and grabbed a towel in a laundry basket to clean himself up. Austin was dripping out of him, and running down his leg.

"I thought about it, but decided if I brought it home, you'd figure it out faster." Kitt walked out of the laundry room door toward the bathroom. Austin could see *Kenmore* pressed into his back. "Where are you going?"

"To shower, I'm a mess. My back hurts," Kitt called out, walking farther away from Austin. It took a second before he heard Austin running barefoot across the tiled floor toward him. He smiled, figuring he wouldn't be showering alone.

~~~~~~

Close to midnight and after another round of hot shower sex, Austin lay with Kitt wrapped in his arms in Austin's bed, just like he liked. This time Austin bottomed, and Kitt made sure Austin knew who the real boss was in their relationship. It didn't seem to matter how many times he'd been with Kitt, or how often they were together.

It never quenched the thirst Austin had for Kitt. Lucky for him, Kitt seemed to feel the same way. After a minute of searching Kitt's handsome, sleeping face, Austin ran a finger down his nose and across his lips as he slowly woke him.

"Babe, wake up for a minute," Austin said quietly. Kitt's eyes fluttered open, and Austin turned them to where Kitt could see Austin's face clearly. "I don't like it when you get so angry at me over something as silly as buying some horses. I don't like to fight with you."

"Me either, I'm sorry." The response made it clear Kitt was tired, still groggy, probably half asleep. Austin smiled down placing a soft kiss on Kitt's slightly parted lips.

"Kitt, I want you to keep and work those horses. No, now, I see you waking up. Listen to me. I want it to be an investment. I'm investing in your ability. It's not a loan. Look, if it doesn't work, then you're not out a thing, and you sold the horses like the farm needed you to do. No harm, no foul. And, I'll get two really good horses to have on my farm. If it does work, you keep the primary share in the horses, and we both make a lot of money. Actually, it does have a downside. You'll have to work them for no payment. We can hire a trainer. You can pick him, I'll pay him, but it's you that needs to work them. If they turn out like shit, it's wasted time for you, but this money gives you breathing room to try and make something of Hooch. So no matter how it all turns out, I win in this investment. And, at some point, what I want has to matter."

Austin kept his eyes locked on Kitt's as he spoke. There was a rawness there between them. Kitt was fully awake, but still relaxed in Austin's arms. His eyes scanned Austin's face for several moments before he responded.

"Every day I wonder if this is the day you're gonna wise up and realize what you left behind. If you start feelin' obligated to me, that's just gonna speed that day up faster." Kitt spoke quietly, staring straight up at Austin. It was an honest, true answer. One that was completely unexpected, and Austin could see Kitt's heart in his eyes.

"It's two different deals...there's you and me, that's one deal, and then we'll also be business partners in another deal. But baby, I'm not going anywhere, no matter what. I like this between us. You've healed my soul. There's nothing I miss from that old life that I haven't found a hundred times better here with you." Kitt started to speak but Austin stopped him, placing a finger across Kitt's lips.

"I see the doubt in your eyes. I hate it because I can't remove it no matter what I do. Only time will prove that I'm here to stay as long as *you* want *me*. You're so hardheaded, Kitt!" Austin took a deep breath and stared at Kitt. "Honestly, as for the investment, I need them. I made twenty-three million dollars off my last dumb movie and that's before it's gone to DVD. I have money, too much money. I pay people to search out investments for me. What I'm gonna love is when you pay out more than any of those stockbroker or investment firms have ever made for me."

"I'm not ready to take your money. It's not a separate deal for me. It's all personal," Kitt said quietly.

"I get that, but since I'm defining all the areas of our lives together, you need to know, I love you. It's completely personal for me, too. Let's do this between us all the way." It was the first time Austin declared his feelings. Certainly not the first time he'd felt it, but the first time either one of them said it out loud. Austin hadn't risked much, he thought Kitt felt the same way. But, the silence, although normal, wasn't helping his nervous heart. When the silence continued, Austin panicked a little.

"You are my boyfriend, right? I'd hate to lose my wife and not have a boyfriend..." Not the funniest thing Austin could have said, but he tried to lighten the mood between them. Kitt was perfect at being quiet. Now, his declaration was beginning to feel like a major faux pas on his end.

"Okay, well I see maybe I oughta have asked you to be my boyfriend. Be my boyfriend, Kitt. You'll be my first boyfriend ever." Austin shouldn't quit his day job to become a comedian, but worse than that, his heart was breaking. A boyfriend didn't require love. Why was that asking too much? Hell, they'd spent the better part of the last four months together. Why was it so out of line for Austin to ask Kitt to be his boyfriend? It wasn't out of line at all. Kitt had to share these feelings. The guy hadn't really slept since Austin moved here, surely that meant he wanted to spend time with him.

"I love you. But I still think you're gonna go back to that other world someday. Leave here behind. I'll be your investment partner. I'll train the horses for a while. If we see potential, I know a trainer I want to hire. She'll cost a lot, but she's worth it if the talent's truly there."

Austin stayed focused on the '*I love you',* not really hearing more than bits and pieces of the rest of what Kitt said.

Austin bent to whisper in Kitt's ear. "Say it again."

"I love you." Kitt stared straight in Austin's eyes. "Why does that surprise you? I've been in love with you since the beginnin', you know that."

"I didn't," Austin simply said.

"What? That's crazy. You knew. How could you not know?" Kitt asked and Austin didn't have an answer. He started to speak, then closed his mouth not sure what to say.

"Austin, I risk everything I have every single night to spend time with you. How does that not say I love you?" Kitt asked clearly confused.

"I guess I just needed to hear it. I don't know. Stop looking at me like I'm dumb. I didn't know!"

"Of course, I love you. I've honestly probably loved you since I was fifteen years old and watched you play ball. Hell, I was in the truck when my dad caught you and Wanda at the pond. That memory's etched in my mind forever. I was like twelve or thirteen. I've loved you since then. You were so beautiful in every way to me. I loved to listen to you talk when we were in school. I'd wait for hours in the locker room just in case you walked through. You're the reason I worked so hard to make Varsity my freshman year. Just so I could be near you. You've always had my heart. It's never belonged to anyone else." Kitt said it all with such truth and honesty in his eyes Austin was stunned speechless. Kitt laid his heart out and rolled from Austin's arms. It took a second for Austin to even comprehend Kitt was leaving the bed. Why was Kitt leaving his arms? Austin reached for him not letting him get too far away.

"Come back here. Where are you going? You can't say all that and leave my bed," Austin said, but Kitt shrugged free.

"I should get home. I'm tired, but more so, you're tired. Sleep wouldn't kill us."

"Nooo…don't try to get out of it. You said you would sleep here tonight until five when your alarm went off. You promised that last night. Kitt, get back here and tell me you love me again. Tell me how you loved my voice." Austin had a distinct whine to his voice as he wrapped his arms tighter around Kitt from behind. The bed covers were all messed up, tangling around Austin and Kitt sat on the side of the bed.

"My ass and back hurt. I need Advil." Kitt laid back a little to kiss Austin's upturned face.

"I have it in the kitchen, and you should be more careful of the knobs next time. How do you tell a man you've loved him for most of your life and talk about ass pain and Advil all in the same tone of voice?" Austin asked. He rolled off the bed to his feet.

"I'll definitely be more careful next time because it'll be you on your back hangin' on for dear life," Kitt said, following Austin out of the bedroom.

Chapter 22

Spring – three months later

Cara crawled back on top of Seth who was sprawled out naked across the king sized bed of the Dallas Omni Hotel's penthouse suite. She grinned as she straddled his hips, but didn't sit on his rigid length. Instead, she continued to stroke his hard-on as she rested back on her heels.

"Tell me the truth. Did you do this on purpose so you didn't have to go back to that farm?" Cara let her perfectly shaped silicone breasts lay on Seth's chest as she bent in for a tender kiss.

"Inside is better than outside," Seth whispered into her kiss, arching his back and thrusting his hips deeper into her hand. She rose and lifted her hips, but sat back again, teasing him unmercifully. She wanted real answers, and Seth looked like he wasn't paying attention to much more than the movement of her hand. Cara stopped it and lifted a perfectly arched brow, waiting for his answer.

"What? Don't stop…" Seth moaned and reached for her. Cara quickly rolled away, laughing as she ducked out of his arms.

"Tell me the truth, Seth. I totally wouldn't put it past you to call in those sleazy, stupid photographers to keep us from going out to see Austin. Now did you do it or not?" Cara accused Seth while standing at the end of the bed. Seth lunged for her, but she backed out of his hold. "Answer me…"

"No, I didn't do it…but only because I didn't think of it!" Seth said, lying on his side, stroking himself, his head in his hand. Actually both heads were in his hands, and his eyes were on her breasts.

"Hmm…you sound believable. But, if you didn't do it, that means they might be getting close. Maybe we shouldn't go out to the ranch, but I really want to see Austin personally and thank him!" Cara said, stomping her foot and worrying her bottom lip. After a second, she flipped around and walked to the window. At twenty-three stories high with protected window glass, no one would be able to see in, but Seth was a protective new husband. He came up behind her, moving her from the window before he took hold of her breasts. They were big, too big, and spilled over his hands just the way he liked it.

"Sweetheart, we're going to the ranch first thing in the morning. I've had them followed for two days. They're following us, nothing shows they know anything about Austin, I promise. Now come back to bed. Babies don't get made without diligence." Seth never let go of her breasts and walked back toward the bed, pushing her forward.

"I don't know, Seth. Something's wrong if they're still looking for him." Cara bent her neck a little further to the side for his kisses.

"It's Rich and Mercedes. They can't find their asses even if they have a roadmap, and you know Austin's been their primary focus for the last ten years. They're totally being watched as they watch us. We'll know if they move one foot, then we can act accordingly."

"Do you think Kitt will like us?" Cara asked as she crawled on to the bed and looked over her shoulder with a grin and a wiggle of her hips. He grabbed her, holding her right there and eased his hand between her slightly parted thighs.

"He might like you."

"He'll like you now that we're married," Cara said on a small moan.

"We'll see. Now, no more talking and a lot more…Ah, yes! You're very wet. Good girl."

~~~~~~

"They look good!" Mike yelled from his perch on the side of the corral fence. Austin was beside him, with Micah, his two boys and Lily all there with him. Kitt walked Hooch through the gates in a newly fenced area of the pasture. Jose adjusted the hydraulics on their brand new horse walker. Kitt held on to Hooch's reins while talking to him as he attached his halter to the walker.

None of them paid too much attention to the car pulling up to the barn. Austin kept his eyes trained on Kitt, but stepped back a couple of steps until he forced his eyes to the Prius now parked next to his truck. He saw Cara hop out from it, a giant smile on her pretty face. She ran to Austin, jumping right up on him, and wrapped her long legs around him as she gave him a giant hug. Seth sauntered over a little more sedately.

"You look so good!" She squealed. Austin had no choice but to wrap his hands around her thighs and ass to help hold her up. Her long legs and arms stayed tightly wrapped around him, and she kissed him all over the face.

"Seth, you let your wife do this to everyone?" Austin teased his agent who came to stand in front of him.

"He's got a point, Cara," Seth said dryly. Austin still had Cara by the ass, but lifted one hand to shake Seth's hand.

"I don't care at all. I missed you, Austin. And it's so good to see you looking so good. You do like it here!" She kissed him one last time and dropped her legs. She was tall, and didn't have far to drop.

"I never thought I'd see you here again." Austin laughed while looking at Seth's not so happy expression. Cara stayed glued to Austin's side, and he wrapped an arm around her.

"Me either." Seth wasn't laughing.

"And I love it out here. I want us to buy some property out here for a little private vacation home. Wouldn't that be great, Austin? We could be neighbors!" Cara smiled big, ignoring the grimace her husband gave as she left her hold on Austin and wrapped herself around Seth. Cara was just that way. It was the reason Austin picked her from the beginning. She was comfortable no matter where she was or what she was doing.

Austin had the sudden feeling of being watched, and he turned around to see the entire practice came to a standstill. Well, all except for Kitt and nothing ever stopped him from working. The rest of the crew stared openly at him, Cara and Seth. Okay, everyone but Micah's boys. They only had eyes for Cara.

"Lily, Mike, Micah, this is Cara and Seth. That's Kitt and Jose in the arena. These are Micah's boys Rusty and Brent." Austin did quick introductions, pointing everyone out. They all put those polite Southern manners to good use and came forward to shake hands, welcoming them to Texas.

"I have dinner cookin'. My girls don't know about Austin, but both are gone tonight. I want you all over for dinner," Lily said graciously, before calling over her shoulder to Kitt. "And that means you too."

"Yes ma'am." It was the only indication he even knew what was going on around him. All eyes turned toward Kitt as he held tight to Hooch's halter. He walked slowly with the horse and never turned or looked up, but kept his free hand rubbing on Hooch with each step they took.

"Lily, you didn't have to go to any trouble for us," Seth said, after a minute of silence.

"I didn't at all. I'm headin' home to finish things now. Kitt, they look great," Lily called out, and for the first time, everyone watched Kitt turn toward Lily and acknowledge the others.

"Oh, Austin, he's yummy! I see why you like it here so much!" Cara said, linking her arm in Austin's, moving them to the fence. Austin covered her words with an ease only achieved by years of hiding from the public.

"He's Hooch, the oldest of the horses, but only by a few weeks. Or about a month, right Mike?" Austin asked. Cara stepped up on the fence and laid her chin in her hand watching Kitt work.

"This is the colt you guys had while I was here?" Seth and Mike followed along behind them.

"Yep, big isn't he? He's like his dad, really pretty fast already. Getting faster every day," Mike said. Seth came to stand behind Cara. Everyone else was back to watching Kitt work with the chestnut.

"Huh. Well that's something else," Seth said, dropping his hands in his pockets.

"It is. He and Kitt are like one," Mike added.

"He's beautiful. Can I see them all?" Cara shaded her eyes with her hands from the bright sunlight. She stood on the bottom rail and Micah's boys were standing off to the side. Austin looked back at them, catching them stare at her ass. All he could do was chuckle. He totally got where they were coming from, he was still as transfixed with Kitt's ass.

"Boys, let's get home. Cara, it was nice to meet you, Seth, good to see you."

Hands were again shaken as Southern manners required. The boys looked so regretful to be leaving, but listened to their father without any outward protest. Their slow moving feet said it all.

"Come on, I'll take you on a tour," Austin said.

"You guys go. I'm going to check email," Seth said.

"Baby!" Cara whined. "It's our honeymoon, we're supposed to be together twenty-four-seven!

"You should've read the fine print, honey. It said unless we came here. Go have fun. Come get me when it's time to eat." Seth ignored her whine, and kissed her pouty lips. He grabbed his briefcase along with a suitcase from the backseat of the Prius and went straight for the house.

~~~~~~~

Kitt sat in a darkened corner of Austin's porch and waited for the chatting to end in the barn and for Austin to come back to the house. The best he could hear, Cara and Austin were in the barn doing another walk through and Seth was in the house, staying hidden away from any of the scary farm things that might go bump in the night. Kitt rolled his eyes at the thought.

Austin made him promise to come over tonight and spend time with them, but he hadn't wanted to, not even a little bit. He'd suggested Austin get some quality alone time with his friends because even after all these months, Kitt truly wanted nothing to do with Seth at all. Jealousy ran thick in his heart over the guy. It didn't matter that he was a married man, a married *straight* man, with a brand new beautiful wife or that Seth seemed overly afraid of his own shadow. Kitt never managed to get the image out of his head of Seth and Austin walking up to Lady's stall all those months ago. It set his heart on fire every time he thought about it.

Most people knew of the Kelly temper, but Kitt tried to always be cool, calm and collected. He wanted to come off like there wasn't much more on his mind other than work. Those were defense mechanisms he learned years ago when dealing with his dad. Any sort of awkwardness and Kitt would pull deep inside himself, outwardly appearing to focus on nothing but the task at hand. His dad's backhand had taught him to keep an eye on everything. You never knew when the proverbial or literal fist might be coming out of nowhere to punch you in the gut. Keeping your head down helped keep the attention away from you. That fist came out of nowhere and punched Kitt hard today, squarely in the chest.

When Kitt watched Cara with Austin this afternoon, so many of those old feelings of thinking Austin would eventually leave and return to Hollywood came rushing back. Austin and Cara were so pretty together. They fit with one another. Seth fit with them too. That polished pretty world had a place for Austin. How had Kitt let himself forget that? So, instead of going in, trying to make amends with Seth or interrupting Cara and Austin on their tour, Kitt sat outside and waited. For what, he didn't know for sure.

"They're so perfect, and I love the idea of you all racing them! Did you always plan that when you bought this place?" Cara asked, walking beside Austin. This time she held Austin's hand as they walked slowly from the barn to the house.

"No, not even a little bit. I just stumbled on it, and Kitt let me get involved." The lights were all turned off. The night was quiet. Kitt could see and hear everything said between them.

"I wasn't sure you were as happy as Seth kept telling me, but I can see he's right. I'm glad for you, Austin. I can't see how no one knows about you and Kitt, it's so obvious," Cara said. It perked Kitt's ears right up. Any worry he felt about eavesdropping just came in second to worry they were being too blatant to the people around them.

"Kitt's better at it than me. I'd come out today in order to quit hiding." Austin looked down at the ground as he spoke, still holding her hand.

"You're in love." There was a smile in the way Cara said the words.

"I'm so in love. So forever and ever until death do us part in love. He's everything to me." Austin words made Kitt's heart lurch from his chest. It was exactly how he felt. Forever and ever until death do us part...exactly like that!

"Oh Austin, I'm so glad! You deserve that! And, he's hot as hell. I mean seriously, Austin, you're good looking, but he might give you a run for your money. I can't wait to see you two standing next to each other!" They were walking into the yard now. Austin had installed a gate around his back yard to fence in the swimming pool. Some of the cows had found their way back there and stumbled into the pool. Several fell in, and it was a nightmare trying to get them out.

"I can't tell if he doesn't know how good looking he is, or if he doesn't care, but regardless, you should see his body. It's as good as his face. Every single muscle's toned. His chest makes me lose my mind, and his ass...I wish he'd get over here. I want him to get to know you guys." Austin walked up the steps and stopped, turning back toward Kitt's house.

"Seth thought he was jealous of him," Cara said, following Austin's gaze, but looking all around.

"I might've been a little jealous." Kitt stepped up from behind. He walked the distance separating them and Austin opened his arms like it was the most natural thing in the world. Kitt never hesitated as he slid into the embrace. Austin hadn't ever said those things to him. All the worry of the afternoon faded away after hearing what Austin just so casually said.

"Ah...you are here. Yay!" Cara said. She stepped up to join them in the embrace. "I'm so glad you came along, Kitt. You saved our boy!" She hugged Kitt tighter, making him startle and look up at Austin's serious face.

"I tell him that all the time, Cara, but he doesn't believe me." Austin seemed fine with Cara right there with them. He leaned forward to kiss Kitt's lips again. Cara stayed with them, smiling big in their faces.

"Well, you can believe me then, Mr. Kitt Kelly! And what a great name! Where'd you get such a name?" Cara asked.

"My parents..."

They were laughing as Seth opened the backdoor. "Rich and Mercedes were standing watch outside the Omni waiting for us to make our move. We got past them no problem. Apparently they're still there watching."

"Yay! We got away from them! Rich is just creepy and Mercedes...I mean seriously, what's wrong with his face? Can you believe they followed us to Dallas on our honeymoon? What did they think was gonna happen?" Cara left the circle of Kitt's and Austin's arms, to stand with her husband, circling her arms around him.

"I can't believe no one's thought to look out here," Austin said.

"I can't believe no one out here has said anything." Seth's tone was very matter of fact.

"No one's even talking about me anymore. I'm finally off the radar. Thank God." Austin's breath tickled Kitt's neck as he spoke.

"The mosquitoes are eating me up, come inside," Seth said.

"Seth, you're a serious pansy. Go in, we'll be a minute." Austin kept a tight hold on Kitt, not moving.

"How long were you here?" Austin asked as Seth shut the door behind them. Kitt answered the question with his silence.

"I meant everything I said, and I don't want you to be nervous about it. I've wanted to say it to you for so long. I've just been trying to give you time. This is forever for me, and you're so very hot…just one kiss…" Austin wrapped Kitt tightly in his embrace and grabbed his ass, tugging Kitt tighter against him. Right as Austin's lips descended, Kitt looked over to the right to see Cara and Seth standing in the window. Cara bubbled with excitement at their kiss. Austin's tongue bounced off Kitt's cheek as he realized he'd been denied.

"Get a room you two!" Seth yelled. Austin reached up to turn Kitt's face back to him, and thoroughly kissed him regardless of who may be watching.

Chapter 23

"Stop fidgeting, you look great," Austin said from behind Kitt who stood in front of his dresser's mirror adjusting one of the two silk ties he owned. Austin watched him from the bed which made him feel a little more self-conscious wearing the formal clothes he had on. Kitt stepped back, surveyed the knot, and then looked back at his hair before pushing the front pieces back. He hoped he looked the part of a fill-in father for his littlest sister's Spring Queen nomination.

"Really, you look good." Their gazes connected in the mirror and a faint blush sprung across Kitt's cheeks. "Put on the suit jacket. Let me see the whole look."

"Shouldn't you be gettin' up, and goin' home? You have company at your house." Kitt shrugged on the suit jacket. He stood back in front of the mirror, fixing the collar, as Austin rose from the bed, naked and came to stand behind him.

"I'm glad you went with the black tie. I like this black and white look you've got going on. No talking to strange men tonight, and absolutely no secluded bathroom runs with anyone. You know what just occurred to me? I'm thinkin' I might need to go out tonight. Show up there so I can keep my eye on you." Austin looked at him in the mirror, making Kitt roll his eyes as he shoved the short pieces of his hair back off his forehead.

"She cut it too short." Kitt picked up the hair brush on his dresser.

"No, come here. Let me gel it." Austin didn't wait for Kitt to agree, he padded over to the bathroom. Kitt didn't follow.

"Get over here and trust me." Austin stuck his head out the bathroom door a minute later. "Hello? Remember what I did for a living...come on!"

Kitt heard his bathroom drawers opening and closing as he pulled off his jacket and went as far as the bathroom door.

"No weird crazy messed up hair. I just want it off the forehead," Kitt warned.

"Got it. Sit on the toilet, it won't take but a minute." Austin had gel in one hand and a hair dryer in the other. Reluctantly Kitt moved forward to do as he was told, and Austin went right to work.

"I just don't understand why you can't come over after you're done tonight." Austin started right in again. It was the same argument that brought Austin over earlier, even though Cara and Seth were left alone at his house. Austin hadn't gotten the response he wanted from Kitt by phone, so he'd brought the argument face to face.

Kitt tried to remind Austin of the importance of the Spring Football game and the naming of the Spring Fling Queen during half time. Bryanne was up for nomination, thereby forcing Kitt away from the farm to escort her out on the field as her father figure. Then after the big game, he would be obligated to attend a district wide school dance as a chaperone. It was Cedarville's big night out. Everyone went, dressing up in their finest, and Kitt wouldn't be home until the early morning hours.

Besides all that, Cara and Seth were on their second and last night at the farm. Seth had taken the whole stay about the same as he had the first time, making it clear he needed to get the hell out of Dodge, or they would all be miserable. Kitt thought Austin should spend some quality time with his friends. It all seemed perfectly reasonable and clear to Kitt why Austin couldn't come over tonight. But, Austin's hard head wasn't having any of his line of thinking. Their argument ended up in bed just like everything else they did together. Austin tried to persuade him the entire time they made tender sweet love, but Kitt wouldn't give.

"You're a difficult man, Austin." Kitt looked up at Austin who stood working on his hair.

"Don't move! You messed me up! First rule of hair and makeup: no moving!" Austin slapped Kitt's head back down. Kitt gave a deep sigh, and then realized his eyes were the perfect level to stare at Austin's cock. It was rare Kitt got to see it sated and hanging freely. After a moment, he lifted his hand and cupped the sac, bring the cock up for a better inspection. He could see it hardening in his hand and he smiled at the response.

"You know if you get me hard and leave, that's just plain mean. You'll have to come over afterward. It won't be a choice anymore."

"Like it ever was a choice?" Kitt replied, this time lifting only his eyes to look up at Austin, not moving his head at all.

"Good, you agree to come over." A grin spread on Austin's face.

Before he could reply, the dryer flipped on. Kitt rolled his eyes at Austin's tactics and focused back on the now hard cock lying in his hand. He watched it for a second or two before lifting his other hand to cup Austin's sac, rolling the balls in his palm. He debated on moving his head. Austin was brushing his hair with the blow dryer on. After a minute Kitt gave in and moved, sucking Austin deep into his mouth.

He wasn't as good at giving a blow job as Austin, but he was getting better. Kitt took him deep with the first suck, gripping the base with his hand. He moved back and forth, sliding Austin's cock against his tongue, his hand following the movement of his mouth. Kitt worked Austin's cock deeper and deeper until he finally had Austin hitting the back of his throat. The effort wasn't lost on Austin. The dryer dropped to the floor and his fingers tangled into the short pieces of Kitt's hair. Austin's hands helped Kitt move fast as the taste of pre-come filled his mouth.

"Damn," Austin muttered, his hips rolling with each thrust of his dick in and out of Kitt's mouth.

"Open wider, baby." Austin urged and Kitt closed his eyes tight, gripped harder than he should at Austin's sac and forced his throat open. It was exactly what Austin wanted. Austin fucked his mouth, stopping his breath, and Kitt fought the urge to panic. Instead, he let his heart hammer as Austin's sac tightened and he punched his hips forward spewing his seed deep down Kitt's throat. It was exactly the move Kitt loved for Austin to do to him, and finally, he gave it back. It didn't matter spots were forming in his eyes and his lungs were about to burst. Austin was getting something he loved and just like that, he released Kitt and air filled his lungs.

Austin was on his knees, digging his fingers into Kitt's hair, pushing his tongue forward for a deep thorough kiss. Austin lapped at the taste of himself in Kitt's mouth. It was another move Austin did every time Kitt sucked him off. Austin told him he loved to know Kitt tasted of him. It took Kitt some time to understand some of these moves his boyfriend made, but now that he did, it filled his heart with pride. Kitt loved that Austin loved him.

"I have to breathe." Kitt finally pulled from the kiss to take large gulps of air. At the same moment, he heard his sister in the living room.

"Kitt, come on! We've been waiting for you to go, and I have to be there early. I have to be the first one there because I'm head cheerleader." Bryanne's voice sounded louder the closer to Kitt's bedroom she got. Kitt pushed Austin over trying to slam the bathroom door closed.

"Bry... I'm dressin'. Y'all go without me!" Kitt called through the now closed door.

"You're a pig. Why are all these clothes layin' all over your house? And your bed's a mess, it looks like you never make it. I'm tellin' mom you don't make your bed. You know how she hates that." Bryanne's words came right from the other side of the door.

Both Kitt and Austin stood staring at the door. Austin nudged Kitt, moving his hand in front of his mouth, trying to get him to say something. Nothing came out because Kitt's heart was pounding so badly in his chest, he couldn't hear to think.

"Kitt, open the door! I want you to see my all white, head cheerleader uniform. I look good in it! You need to tell me how pretty I look! Besides I've seen you in just a towel. Open up!"

"Bryanne, go on, I'll be there in a little while. I'll see you then," Kitt said lamely, and as an afterthought, he threw out. "Of course you look beautiful. You're the prettiest girl in school."

That one earned Kitt a silent double high five from Austin.

"Yep, that's true! Okay, hurry! Don't be late! I don't want Margaret Hines' dad to get all the attention because then everyone will be lookin' at her. And don't wear your hair stupid. Look good Kitt!" The bells on Bryanne's sneakers made it clear she was walking away.

After hearing the front door close, Kitt stuck his ear to the bathroom door and listened to see if she might still be inside ready to jump out and scare him. After several long minutes, he heard nothing.

"Just go out there and see if she's gone," Austin whispered.

Kitt's heart slammed so badly he couldn't think how to move, little alone do anything else. Austin stepped back and opened the door, letting the door hide him as he pushed Kitt forward.

He kicked into action, scanned the house and looked through the front window. There was dust on the trail. Austin came to stand behind him, and he jerked at the sudden touch. Austin laughed, but Kitt couldn't return the gesture. It was times like these that always hit home with him. Just when he thought everything was going smoothly, that he and Austin were safe and doing a good job at hiding, something happened to prove him wrong.

"You aren't supposed to be here in the day light hours," Kitt said in a stern voice, pointing a finger in Austin's face.

"Aren't you getting tired of that rule? We could just be friends. No one knows what we're doing in here. Or, the few people that don't already know what we're doing could think we're just friends, Kitt. Guys do hang out with each other."

"No, we start breakin' our rules, then we get relaxed, and it slips out more. No daylight hours." Kitt ran his fingers through his hair and stopped, patting his head. "It's all messed up now, isn't it?"

"It's my fault. Come back to the bathroom, let me redo it." Austin pivoted on his heels. "Besides, if you would just have followed the rules and agreed to come over tonight, I wouldn't have been forced out in daylight hours to come talk to you. Ever think of that?"

"Wear these," Kitt said, sitting down on the toilet handing Austin his pants.

~~~~~~

Mirror balls and colorful flashing lights spun in time to the music blaring in the high school's gymnasium. Kitt sat with some of the other parents at the designated chaperone's table listening to whatever Taylor Swift song was now playing. The kids danced closely together under the hanging twinkle lights that represented some theme Kitt was sure he wasn't getting. What Kitt did know, Bryanne danced too close to her current boyfriend, but he didn't need to get involved. The principal stood ready to pounce, separating any dancing couple who actually got close enough to touch chest to chest.

Regretfully, they served no beer. Kitt knew how that sounded in his head, but after two hours of the Spring Fling dance, Kitt sat at the small table past ready to hit the road. Even at this point, spending the evening with Seth and Cara sounded preferable to this. Micah sat in the seat next to Kitt, looking pretty much just as miserable. His wife, Heather, came to the table and sat down in a huff. She looked exhausted as she plopped her feet up on an empty chair.

"Kitt, I have someone I want you to meet, and you can't say no. She's one of those Dallas girls you like so much. I met her when I was buying the decorations for tonight. I got her phone number. She's smart, pretty and single. Here, look at her picture. I told her I'd be calling to set up the date. When's good for you?" Heather fired out word after word, working with her phone and shoving a picture of a pretty woman in his face. If this was Heather exhausted, he wondered how Micah kept up.

"I told you not to do this," Micah said. "I'm sorry Kitt."

"And, I told you he needs a wife and kids. It's time he got one." Heather shot right back at her husband.

"Kitt, I've been meanin' to talk to you, buddy." *The Future Farmers of America* Agriculture teacher came up to the table, taking the empty seat next to Kitt, effectively saving him from any answer he needed to tell Heather.

"What's up?" Kitt asked, hoping the relief wasn't showing on his face.

"No Henry, wait! I need to get this done tonight." Heather interrupted them, typing on her phone. "Kitt, when's good?"

"Heather, leave him alone. Kitt, don't answer her." Micah took the phone away from her which started a whole new argument, leaving Kitt free to focus on the Ag teacher.

"The cattle drive runs next week. Tuesday through Thursday, during spring break. I need parent volunteers. Got any time to go with us again this year?"

And, that's when Kitt remembered why he dodged the FFA teacher. All of a sudden, he wished he was scheduling a date with Heather's girl rather than sitting here talking to his high school buddy.

Kitt had done this run every year since he was in high school. It was hard, treacherous, and absolutely zero fun from an adult point of view. They ran two hundred head of cattle around in a big circle, all on horseback doing an authentic, old school cattle drive. It was three days of pushing teenagers to act like grown men and women. Some got it, but most didn't. Last year, he'd told the old teacher he was done. No more trips for him, but now as he looked at his high school buddy his heart plunged.

"Is it already that time of year again?" Kitt asked lamely. Micah chuckled at him. Of course, Micah was going. He had two boys involved.

"Yep, same time every year. Can I count you in? The boys learn a lot from you, Kitt. Nobody but you can put modern agriculture education to practice. We sure would appreciate it if you'd head out with us again."

Henry's enthusiasm had Kitt backed into a corner. If Austin didn't like him being gone one night, how would he feel about two or three nights? As if on some sort of cosmic cue, his phone vibrated in his pocket.

"Let me just make sure Jose's gonna be around, but okay…yeah, I'll go." Kitt finally committed as the second vibration came through on his phone. Then a third. Austin thought tease texting was hilarious. He sent message after message and Kitt felt sure they all said the same thing, '*COME OVER'*.

"Thanks, Kitt. That means a lot to me. Micah, we all still meetin' at your place?"

"Whatever works." Micah chuckled at the look on Kitt's face. "Buck up, buddy, Mike's goin' too."

"Kitt, now answer my question! When's good for you to drive up to Dallas and take this girl out?"

"Whenever you want, Heather," Kitt said, as he rose. He palmed his cup and excused himself, heading across the gym to the punch bowl. Damn, he hoped somebody had spiked it by now.

~~~~~

It looked like Big Dick's Tavern was hopping after the school social. The place was packed, drawing Kitt and Micah in as they drove through town together. Heather had stayed behind on clean-up duty giving Micah the out and a few minutes alone. Kitt didn't even ask as he pulled his pick-up truck off the highway into the gravel parking lot. He skimmed the place looking for a spot to park.

"It's because no one spiked the punch. It's too politically incorrect now to do shit like that. Too bad. It made the place more bearable," Micah said as he looked around at all the vehicles in the parking lot.

"Yeah, we're gonna have to work on that next year." Kitt tugged at his tie, loosening it as he followed Micah inside. It was somewhere after one in the morning, but the place was packed solid. The juke box blared an old Willie tune. The dance floor, pool tables and bar were all loaded full of people.

"See if you can get us a table," Micah called out over the music. Kitt wound his way to the tables, nodding his head or shaking hands with people along the way. He knew everyone here. There wasn't anyone in the place he hadn't known for most of his life.

"Hey man! I haven't seen you around at all!" Jimmy shoved out of a booth, shaking Kitt's hand before taking the seat next to JoLynne. Kitt heard rumors they were dating. From the way Jimmy's arm reached around her, pulling her into his side, the rumors seemed to be true. Apparently, they'd hooked up back months ago, the last night Kitt had been in the bar. Right before he met Austin. It was funny, Kitt used to come in here at least once a week, and for the past several months it hadn't even occurred to him to come in before tonight.

"Been busy. Hey, JoLynne," Kitt said, nodding at her across the table.

"Hey yourself, Kitt Kelly. Where you been hidin'?" she asked.

"Workin'." The one word response was all he was willing to give. Micah came up to the table and Kitt pushed himself over and took the offered beer. Micah and Jimmy did quick fist bumps as another song began.

"He's sold his horses." Micah yelled across the table.

"No kidding, all of 'em?" Jimmy yelled back. "I saw the semi's movin' the hay out. You're doin' real good, man. I'm happy for you." Kitt got the same fist bump as Micah.

"It's not that big a deal." Kitt shrugged it off because technically was it considered doing well when Austin bought everything he sold?

"Whatever, man. No one thought you could dig out of your daddy's hole." Jimmy paused, his eyes darting up to Kitt's. "No offense."

"None taken. I wasn't sure I could either." Kitt lifted his beer, tapping the long neck with Jimmy's. "Any chance on a table? The quarters look stacked."

"Not tonight. The old timers got some competition goin'. It's a fund raiser or somethin'. It lasts until four. Next week's poker. I won a hundred bucks last week! You should come play!"

JoLynne stayed weirdly quiet, watching Kitt closely. Kitt ignored it for as long as he could, but finally cut his eyes to her.

"You're in love, Kitt Kelly! Who is she?"

Every head at the table turned to Kitt. Hell, every head within hearing distance turned to him. After a minute, it felt like every pair of eyes in the bar was trained on him just to see what everyone looked at. He knew his cheeks brightened under the stare, and he had no idea how to answer that question.

"It's true!" JoLynne sat up a little straighter, clapping her hands. "Who is it? Is she from here?"

Kitt started shaking his head, but the words weren't coming. Of course, his phone picked then to vibrate in his pocket. Jimmy narrowed his brow, Micah looked shocked, and JoLynne beamed.

"There's no she in my life. You're way off base." Kitt denied. Not exactly a lie, but it did feel very much like one. Why was he struggling with lying about his sexuality now? He shook his head again. "You don't know what you're talkin' about, JoLynne."

"Whatever Kitt! Tell us! You can't hide her forever!"

"Heather has him set up with some Dallas girl. I don't think he's lyin'." Micah's eyes narrowed at Kitt.

"He hasn't left the farm for months." Speculation was clear on Micah's face.

"Honest to God, I haven't. I've been workin'. It's been too busy for any of that." Kitt drained his beer, resisting the urge to drain Micah's too, just because it sat in reach.

"Last call for everyone but the pool players!" The call came from the bar.

JoLynne kept her eyes focused on Kitt. "Say what you will, but I know a man in love."

~~~~~~

Verne sat forward at the bar, downing his eighth, tenth, twelfth, or whatever number beer. He stayed hidden, close to the juke box, away from everyone since Kitt and Micah walked in the door. That little mother fucker fired him. He'd helped raise that boy to manhood. He'd been Mr. Kelly's foreman, his right hand man and lover since before Kitt was born, and the little fucktard fired him for standing up for the Kelly legacy. Something that little fucker should have done all on his own.

No one knew how bad Verne hurt at losing Kelly. He still mourned him every single day. The only official Last Will and Testament anyone could find made it clear Kitt was to keep Verne working on that farm for as long as Verne wanted, but Kitt with his big fancy ideas tried to come in and take over. Kelly cared for Verne, told him he loved him more than any other person he ever fucked, and Verne believed that with his whole heart.

Since he left that ranch, Verne tried to get in Kitt's way. He stopped the sale of everything he could. He used all his past contacts to work against Kitt. He'd set up rumors about Kitt using anabolic steroids and other performance enhancing chemicals. Verne thought it worked, but to listen to them talk now he could see Kitt was selling something to somebody. Besides, he'd seen those semi's with his own eyes, rolling through town with the Circle K hay bales strapped on.

He'd have to get more crafty. No way Kelly would go for this happening on his land. The Kelly ancestry would all have to be turning over in their graves. Artificial insemination? It just wasn't right. Farmer's made a living off their land. Not other people animals, doing God's own work. That was stealing, and Kitt was clearly stealing from everyone.

"Verne, I think you're done for tonight," the bartender said. Verne was too far gone in thought to reply. After a long pregnant pause, Verne moved his glassy eyed stare and focused on the bartender.

"I'll make sure he lives on!" With that, Verne wobbled off the seat, fell forward, but stayed on his feet, and kept his back to Kitt.

His rented one bedroom was a five minute walk from the bar. Perfect amount of time to plan. He stepped out into the cool night air, saw the Kelly truck parked right up front and dug in his pants pocket for his pocket knife. He palmed it and never stopped walking. He mumbled as he jammed the knife in the front tire, then he went to the back tire. It didn't matter the parking lot was full of people, or Kitt's truck was directly under the only light in the parking lot. Verne was oblivious to everything but the plan formulating in his head.

~~~~~~~

Kitt slid from the back seat of Jimmy's crew cab pick-up truck and gave another quick thank you before absently shutting the door. The clouds covered the moon, and it took a minute for his eyes to adjust as he walked up the front porch steps to his cabin. It was somewhere around four in the morning. His truck was still out front of the bar, two tires were flat, and by the time he found out about it, the sheriff was involved. Verne sat cuffed in the back seat of the squad car, and Kitt went through twenty questions with the officer who brought him outside for a statement.

A formal statement of what? Kitt didn't know. Verne stared him down the entire time he talked to the officer which was pretty much the same look he'd gotten from Verne for most of his life. Verne hadn't ever liked him. He gave Kitt that crazy eyed stare, and Kitt assumed all this meant Verne still hadn't gotten over being fired.

This wasn't the first time Verne did something stupid like this, but it was the first time he'd done it so publically which meant his anger must really be festering. Lily mentioned seeing Verne in town a couple of times totally smashed, very early in the day. Gossip had Verne the town derelict. He couldn't find more than a day job and drank pretty much all the time. Kitt also heard Verne went through every bit of his savings and regularly spouted claims to Kelly land, but never had it been this malicious before. Hell, he hadn't even seen Verne inside the bar tonight.

Once Verne got carted off to jail, the debate started on whether to change the tires there or leave it until tomorrow. He had a spare, so did Jimmy. They rolled up their sleeves and changed one tire with his spare and then the other tire with Jimmy's spare which immediately went flat.

The entire time they worked, a tipsy JoLynne sat outside, chatting with everyone about how 'in love' Kitt looked. How did she see that? What was even more odd and totally uncomfortable, most of the women agreed with Jojo. It was like an unseen radar every female in the place possessed. Kitt was so ready to get the hell out of there he couldn't work those tires off his truck fast enough. The only good thing going Kitt's way, Austin finally stopped texting about one forty-five in the morning, saying he was going to bed.

Two hours from the time the bar gave last call, Kitt and Micah loaded in Jimmy's truck and got a ride home. They owed Jimmy big since neither had to call for a ride.

Kitt opened his front door to see his television casting shadows from his bedroom door. A smile tugged at his lips, and Kitt realized again, for about the millionth time since meeting Austin, he had no say in his own life. Austin slept soundly in his bed, waiting for him to get home. Kitt dropped his suit jacket and tie on the chair, toed off his shoes and a groggy Austin opened his eyes.

Kitt undressed and stopped by the bathroom to wash the black marks from the dirty tire off his hands. Austin moved in the middle of the bed, the covers were lifted and Kitt slid in, taking Austin in his arms.

"I'm so glad you didn't listen to me." Kitt ran his nose along Austin's neck, and into his hair, breathing him in.

"I wanted you to be happy to see me." Austin's voice was laced in deep sleep as he nuzzled into Kitt. They lay in their normal position, Kitt on his back, Austin spread across him.

"It's been a night," Kitt said, yawning loudly.

"You smell like dirty rubber."

"That would be the double flats," Kitt said, and Austin stayed quiet.

"Did she win?" How did Austin so easily pickup that he didn't want to talk about the flats?

"Absolutely! Miss Spring Fling of the ball. I didn't see her again until it was time to leave."

"Good for her! I got Mr. Spring Fling four years runnin'. Great honor indeed." Austin chuckled, his breath tickling Kitt's chest.

"I knew you had to remember Spring Fling even though you acted like you never heard of it before!" Kitt said into the dark room.

"I missed you tonight. Good night, I love you."

"I love you, too."

Chapter 24

"They aren't here! Where the fuck are they?" Rich screamed into the walkie talkie. He'd swiped a hotel bell hop's uniform and followed maid service inside the room. Three days of constant surveillance for nothing. Cara Collins evaded them! How the hell did she even know they were following her? They were stealth and she was blond, for God sakes!

"What? Are you sure?" Mercedes responded back with a hiss. They'd been there for the better part of seventy-two hours watching for any sign of the pair. Cara and Seth had checked in through the front lobby. Being in open sight was one of the very best ways to hide. It was only because he and Rich followed them so closely from the wedding that they were even able to track Cara and Seth to Dallas. No one believed Cara and Austin could still be friends after such a public break-up, but there was no public acknowledgement showing Austin dismissed or fired Seth as his agent. It didn't add up. If an agent stole a guy's wife, surely, the guy would fire his agent. Except Austin hadn't. So that had to mean something, but what?

Since the only conclusion was to follow the honeymooners, they did. They switched out, guarding the front and back doors of the hotel waiting for Cara to make her move. A honeymoon in Dallas didn't make sense. It wasn't a romantic draw kind of place. Actually, it was March and already getting hot outside. Besides that, there was nothing to do here. No sights to see, no ocean to draw you in. Why would they come here if not for Austin? Texas was his hometown no matter how much he bashed living here as a child.

"This has to be your fault! How did you let them slip by?" Rich stormed from the room, the maid's eyes wide at his sudden outburst. He slammed the door and stalked down the hall toward the elevator.

"You wait till I get my fucking hands on you! I should've called in Keefer! He has a fucking brain in his head!"

"My fault! It's your fault! You were the one with the connections here. You trusted those guys we hired to watch them! " Mercedes hissed into the phone.

"Fuck you! I trust him better than you! Fuck! What was I thinking calling you in on this. You wanna know what? Half of nothing's what you're worth. Which is exactly what we have right now, *because of you*!"

The elevator doors opened and the two men stood staring at one another. The entire lobby turned, looking at them, and Rich resisted the urge to tackle Mercedes right there. That would surely land them in jail. He needed to think, get a plan and find Cara Collins.

"They had to know we were watching. I'm done playing with them. How much money do you have?"

"I'm not giving you any more money." Mercedes dismissed Rich by turning and walking away.

"I'm calling in Dunc," Rich said quietly. That stopped Mercedes in his tracks. He pivoted on his heel, awe on his face, and stared at Rich.

"No way, we can't trust him." Mercedes gave a half-hearted protest.

"I can; he owes me a favor. Now, how much money do you have? It's gonna be expensive." Rich palmed his phone and dialed. Three calls later, he was connected with an ominous sounding voice, covered with a voice over machine. Rich's heart began to pound rapidly in his chest as he realized he was speaking to Dunc.

"We need any information you can find on Cara Collins, Seth Walker and Austin Grainger." Rich blurted into the phone.

"Five thousand a day, two day minimum." The electronic voice said back.

"That's crazy!" Rich almost laughed at the absurdity of the cost. "That's the deal," the voice said.

"*Okay*! Okay but I want some guarantees. This story goes nowhere else." Rich was completely frazzled. Ten thousand dollars. Was it worth it? If they found Austin, it would be worth that times one hundred percent more.

"Deal! Paypal, Dunc666. I'll begin when the cash hits my account. You have thirty minutes. I'll contact you when I find something. Do not make contact with me." The phone went dead.

"We need ten thousand," Rich said, looking up at Mercedes

"*Ten thousand dollars!*" Mercedes went nuts, and again the lobby was back to staring at them.

"Shut up! Just think of what we'll make if we find Grainger," Rich hissed, grabbing hold of Mercede's arm, pushing him through the hotel and out the front doors.

"Damn it! That's my life savings," Mercedes said back. "No!"

"We have twenty-six minutes, come on!"

~~~~~~

Kitt pulled the cinch tight on the saddle, mentally going over everything to make sure he was completely packed and ready for the cattle drive. The route they were taking would drive them to the far reaches of the local reservoir. They would round it, and then back home along the National Forest. There would be no cell phone signal, no electronics, and nothing for the entire length of the trip. If Kitt forgot anything, it would make the trip that much more torturous.

"I'll keep an eye on the horses. The Grainger farm has tons of men employed, but they don't know shit about ranchin'," Jose said, following along behind Kitt, making sure all the packs were tied down properly on his horse and nothing could come loose.

"They're Austin's security. Keep an eye on Hooch, even if you have to bring him over here, which is actually probably the best idea. Get 'em all and bring them over here." Kitt locked his rifle in the saddle before he lifted his foot into the stirrup, and climbed on Bullet. Jose looked up at Kitt, shielding his eyes from the early morning sun.

"Are you sure? I don't want to get arrested as a horse thief. That's still a hangable offense here in Texas," Jose joked.

"I'll tell Mike when I get over there. Keep things under control here until I get back." Kitt turned toward the Grainger farm where Mike waited for him.

Kitt kicked Bullet into a trot until they reached the other property. There was a gate now between the property lines with remote control access making it easier to get from one side to the other. Kitt opened

Bullet up to a full run heading straight for the gate. He was behind this morning and knew as much as he wasn't looking forward to this cattle drive, the kids and teacher were double time excited. He and Mike needed to get over to Micah's and quit throwing the whole thing behind schedule.

Mike stood outside the barn, cinching his horse. Austin sat on the porch, drinking a cup of coffee, watching Kitt closely as he rode up. Kitt tried hard to ignore him. Austin was just so good looking with the sun hitting him just right. As he rode up closer to the barn, Mike pointed Kitt toward Austin.

"The boss wants to see you before we go. I'm gonna be a minute, I'm still loadin'." Mike never stopped packing his saddles. Kitt slung a leg over his horse and looked over at Austin. He hadn't moved since he rode up. Kitt hesitated. He didn't want go over there. They'd said their goodbyes not three hours ago, and it hadn't gone well. Austin couldn't understand why he was going away for three days and wanted Kitt to back out. He'd made the mistake of telling Austin he hadn't planned on going this year, but felt obligated. Austin jumped on that one. It even got to the point, Austin demanded he not go, or at the very least, come home after the first night. He declared he never left Kitt for more than one day at a time, but Kitt didn't budge. He'd obligated himself, and it meant he must go. Austin wasn't without power. He could get underneath Kitt's skin faster than anyone, and if Kitt walked over there now, it would just make the leaving that much harder in the end.

"If you don't come over here, I'll come there!" Austin yelled out across the yard. He stood at the edge of the porch, closest to him. "I don't think you want that."

Kitt didn't. After another pause, he rolled his eyes to the heavens and did the walk of shame across the yard, through the gate and up the steps. Austin had gone inside when he hit the gate and Kitt followed him in.

"Austin..." It's as far as he got before Austin was wrapped around him, thrusting his tongue forward. Austin kissed him as if there was a threat of never seeing him again. After a minute, Austin pulled away, leaving Kitt stunned, wanting more, and pulling Austin back to him.

"Stay...please stay. I'll leverage the washer in and I'll bottom. I know it doesn't seem like it, but I like to bottom. I'll bottom from this point out. Stay here Kitt...I'll miss you too badly, and I have a bad feeling about this." Austin leaned his head against Kitt's forehead.

"Austin, please don't do this again. I'm having Jose come get the horses. He can keep a better eye on them over at my place. Do you have a problem with that?" Kitt eyes stayed focused on the lips just inches from his mouth, and he leaned in for a soft, lingering kiss.

"Kitt, stay here, please." It was the third time in a matter of days that Austin mentioned a bad feeling, but when he asked about it earlier, Austin couldn't place it. It was just a gut level instinct.

"You go over there with Jose and keep our horses working, every day. I'll be back in three days. I'll call you immediately. Don't jerk off! Be ready for me." Kitt lifted a hand to Austin's head and cut off whatever he was about to say by kissing him deeply, holding him in just the angle to delve deeper into the kiss.

"I have to go, miss me. I'll miss you." With that, Kitt left. Mike was waiting, mounted and ready to go. Kitt didn't pause, but climbed back on Bullet, and they rode off together toward Micah's place.

Chapter 25

"Boys, watch your flank!" Kitt yelled, keeping his eyes on the herd. Bullet moved instinctively with Kitt's simplest body movements. This time, they moved toward the stray wayward cattle leaving the herd as the two boys bolted from the huddle they were talking in. They weren't super steady in their saddles, their horses jerked, but luckily, it was enough of a commotion for the cows trying to make their escape. They rushed back together with the others, and it didn't cause too big a problem.

Kitt pulled back on his reins, guiding Bullet back to his designated position of bringing up the rear. And, the irony of it didn't get lost on him. From this angle, he was forced to cover all sides, helping the kids whose cattle ran astray. It was taxing and Kitt was past exhausted. When he was a kid, he loved doing the cattle drive. He and his buddies took it so seriously. Kylie loved to go every year when she was in school. She was the whole reason why he always volunteered to chaperone. He wanted to be there for her if she needed him. Now, it was different. Outside of Micah's boys and a few others, Kitt didn't see too many of these kids truly interested in making agriculture their life after high school.

Besides the immediate fatigue that set in under these kinds of conditions, Kitt hadn't talked to Austin since he left a day and a half ago. It made him edgy. No matter how he tried, Kitt could never find cell phone signal during breaks, or where they camped for the night. Last night, he'd even gone out and up a small mountain and still couldn't get high enough for signal coverage. Kitt missed Austin. If they were a normal couple, Austin could be here now. However, if they were an outted couple, no way the school would have either of them here. He couldn't see two gay men being allowed to escort the kids out like this. Which, at this point, didn't seem like such a bad thing. Damn, but he was past ready to get home.

"Jonathon, watch ahead!" Kitt yelled. He knew he couldn't be heard. He kicked Bullet into gear, tugging the reins to the left and galloped after the cows leaving the pack. The teenager never saw it, just kept looking completely dazed and confused out toward the miles of nothing to the side of them.

~~~~~~

With a swipe of his t-shirt sleeve, Austin wiped the sweat from his brow. His breath panted, his chest heaved. Both he and Jose had been working the horses for most of the afternoon, just as Kitt instructed them to do. Jose carried the same ways about him as Kitt did with these animals. They responded to him with a simple gentle touch or voice. They connected on a different level. As for Austin, not so much. Every move, every instruction, was more difficult and caused him to have to do twice the work to get them to do what they were supposed to do.

"We need to let him run. He's getting antsy," Jose called out to Austin motioning toward Hooch. They were building a make shift track between their properties. Just dirt and a chain link fence, but something to get the horses familiar with. Hooch was a pistol. The colt was still young, but huge, growing bigger every day. And damn, he could run. He regularly left the others behind.

"Let's do it then." Austin pushed away from the fence. He'd do anything to exhaust himself and hopefully, get some sleep tonight. It had been a solid two days without any word from Kitt. And, there had been no sleep because apparently, all of a sudden he couldn't sleep without knowing Kitt was safe or tucked in beside him.

As he rummaged through the tack room for a stop watch, he heard a noise outside. Austin smiled and busted through the barn hoping Kitt had come home early. It was gonna be hard to contain the nonchalance and not run straight to him. He'd have to force himself not to jump on Kitt right there and kiss him with all the missing in his heart.

He rounded the corner and saw one of Micah's oldest mounted, dirty, and looking tired. He spoke quickly to Jose before kicking the horse in the direction of his house. "What did he say?"

"They're a day behind. Its goin' slower than it should. They'll be home sometime day after tomorrow." Jose continued to work the animals and didn't pay any attention to Austin. That was a good thing. He wasn't sure he was hiding the emotion he felt from the few simple words said to him. *Another day? Really?*

"Which one do you wanna clock?" Jose called out from behind Austin. He still stood rooted in the spot, watching the dust settle from the horse.

"You take Hooch." Austin finally turned, ducked his face and pulled his ball cap down firmly on his head. It was a normal move, but today it was more than that. It was to hide his eyes. Austin honestly felt like he wanted to cry. He had to fight back the tears. In all these months, he hadn't gone more than a few hours without talking to Kitt. It was such a girly response to missing your mate, but he couldn't shake it. He climbed on his mount and grabbed Hooch's reins. Austin managed to head toward the track before the tear slipped down his cheek.

"Damn it! Get a hold of yourself! God, I like it so much better when I'm the one leaving!" He muttered at himself, wiping the tear away.

~~~~~~

"*Mom, shut up*, I'm working!" Dunc aka Glenda yelled across the basement of her parent's home.

"I have to do the laundry!" her mother yelled back in a raspy voice. A voice hardened by age and years of smoking. She never stopped smoking the cigarette perched between her lips as she loaded the thirty year old washing machine that sat ten feet from Dunc's computer equipment.

"God, Mom! You're such a fucking pain in the ass!" Dunc screamed although her beady little eyes never left one of the three monitors in front of her. Her fingers skimmed over the keyboard like only a person who had spent their entire life on the computer could. Dunc had just about gained entry into the hacked Facebook account of Austin Grainger's parents. She'd been working on it for hours and finally figured out the password. She'd read on Google that no one ever strayed from the standard birthday format. It was just trying to figure out which birthday it could be. This one was Austin's himself, not very original of the proud Grainger papa.

"Yes!" Dunc was in! She'd hacked into a Facebook account!

Damn, she'd been trying to do this for years. Her reputation as a badass computer genius was pretty much made up by her herself. She'd put it out there in her online groups that she was a man and the most worthy of anyone in the groups. By God, if she couldn't have accolades in the real world, she'd force it in the made up world of the internet.

Glenda searched the Facebook account. She went through the messages and all the groups he belonged to. She didn't know what she looked for except something to feed Rich and Mercedes about Austin. Just enough that she could toss it back in their court and not look like she just stole their money and left them high and dry. Rich was a staunch online Dunc supporter, she didn't need him on her bad side, upsetting the balance of her group.

Biting at her fingernail she stared at the screen. It had taken hours to break in and there was nothing here! On a backward thought, she went to the account settings and pulled up the email address used to log in. Perhaps there was a secondary account that might mean something.

A grin spread easily along her cracked, dry lips when she found a company email address. She swiped the information out of the system and quickly turned to another computer pulling up a search and find database. Dunc plugged the information in, and through her advanced gold membership, she found the address belonged to a company Austin Grainger owned with his father. Okay, now she was getting somewhere. The company's headquarters were based in far northern California. It looked to be a ranch.

She let the system run and watched the screen. Cigarette smoke drifted her way.

"God, Mom, you're gonna kill me with that second hand smoke!" Her eyes never left the screen.

"You're fifty-five years old and never go outside. Lack of sun is gonna kill ya!"

"Die already!" Dunc bellowed.

"Get a job!" Her mom yelled back moving up the steps.

Dunc lost all interest in her mom, and another grin spread across her lips. She'd typed in the same login information she'd hacked from the Facebook account and Daddy Grainger's company website took it. Now, all she had to do was take a look around. Not that she had a clue what any of it really meant. First, she'd go through the business side of things, and then the emails, because it looked like it was all tied together. If Austin was anywhere in here, she'd find him and hand the information over to Rich. If it was any good, he'd be paying double to get it. Twenty thousand dollars would buy one hell of badass computer. Hell, she could even get a new server and still have money left over.

Maybe there'd even be enough money to get someone to bump off her pain in the ass mother. How had she not died yet?

Hours ticked by as Dunc went through every little detail.

~~~~~~

Working the horses on the track did loads to help Austin's exhaustion, but little in the ways of helping his heavy heart. They worked Hooch without tiring the young colt, but they gave him a good run. Austin rode his own horse, holding the reins to Hooch and one of their fillies, Little Lady. They headed back to Kitt's stable. Jose rode beside him holding the reins to the other two horses, and they kept at a slow trot until they came over the ridge by Kitt's cabin. The small hill gave them a perfect angle to see something was going on at Kitt's barn. Austin's security team was involved. Several of them were in a standoff surrounding a man and Austin's heart plummeted. Had he been found out? Maybe this was the bad feeling he'd had hanging over him for days.

"Son of a bitch!" Jose yelled and brought his horse to an abrupt halt, effectively breaking Austin's train of thought. His first instinct was to barge down there to take care of the problem. The paparazzi didn't need to harass the Kellys to get to him, but he brought his horse to a stop at Jose's words and action.

"Do you know him?" Austin called out.

"Stay back. It's Kitt's dad's son of a bitch old foreman. The one that blew out Kitt's tires the other night!" Jose yelled and Austin narrowed his brow. He hadn't heard that story, or anything about this guy.

"Stay back, I'll handle it. If he sees you, the whole town's gonna know." Jose didn't wait, he tossed his ponies reins to Austin and kicked his horse into a gallop rushing toward the altercation.

~~~~~~~

"Verne, you know you aren't supposed to be here." Jose dismounted his horse about three yards from where the old foreman swayed on his feet, surrounded by Austin's security team. They never quite left their undercover position, but showed way more brute strength and aggression than a normal everyday run of the mill cowhand. The drunk old man looked angry and agitated, his eyes crazier than normal as they focused on Jose.

"This is mine! This place is mine! He was gonna leave it to me, not that panty waste son of a bitch!" Verne stumbled on his feet, but caught himself before he fell on his face.

"A fuckin' wetback foreman...that's fuckin' bullshit!" Verne tried to spit at Jose, but did little more than drool down his jaw. He was way too drunk to even form a proper spit.

Verne kept his hands in the pockets of his filthy jacket even as he stumbled around. The movement was odd, and Jose watched Verne's hands closely, trying to see if it was possible there was a weapon inside.

"Verne, you need to leave before I call the law in on this. The courts say you shouldn't be here. I'll get someone to take you back to town, but you need to leave."

Jose took a step forward. Verne kept swaying heavily on his feet, lurching around. The security team stayed right on him, and Jose could tell it was hard on them not to just handle this situation themselves. One of the security guards held a weapon in his hand, right alongside his leg, pointing it down toward the ground. Had they been on Grainger land, Verne would be lying face down on the ground, begging for his life.

"You're a fuckin' wetback, cock sucker. Does he make you suck his cock? Is that part of your job?" The question came off so ludicrous it caught Jose completely off guard. The hesitation seemed to piss Verne off that much more, like he'd got something right. Anger flared in his eyes. Jose was completely unprepared when Verne snapped the gun from his pocket, aiming it as best he could in Jose's direction. The Grainger security guards didn't hesitate. Multiple shots were fired.

~~~~~~~

Austin turned the horses, holding on to all four of the young ones and moved slowly back to his barn when he heard the sound of gun shots. He came to an abrupt halt, tugging hard at the reins of his mount. He flipped around, dropping the reins to Hooch and the others as he took off toward the Kelly barn. He hadn't gone far and it didn't take long as he pounded forward in a full gallop, barreling up on the scene. His men's weapons were drawn. Jose was holding his left arm, and the old foreman lay spread out on the ground. Austin didn't stop until he got to Jose.

"What the fuck happened?" Austin yelled toward his guards. Three were down on the ground with Verne. Austin jumped down and ran to Jose who held the side of his arm, blood dripping down. "Are you alright?"

"It just grazed me," Jose said. A cowhand ran to them carrying several towels. Austin's eyes were back on Verne as he stalked forward.

"What the hell happened?" Austin called out to Sam.

"He came on the property while you two were gone, saying all kinds of shit. We narrowed in on him as he went toward the barn. He told us to get out of the way, he was setting the place on fire."

Two guards kept their weapons aimed at Verne, but Sam was bent down on his knee. He checked the guy's pulse as the other two performed CPR. He tried a couple of spots and shook his head toward Austin and Jose.

"He was breakin' a restrainin' order. Has anyone checked on Lily?" Jose forgot about the arm and palmed his phone dialing her immediately. Her truck pulled down the trail from the main house as he put the phone to his ear. She must have heard the shots.

"Are you sure he's gone?" Austin dropped down on his knees next to the security guard who pumped Verne's heart. Another bent down, tearing his t-shirt over his head, holding it to the bullet wound at his shoulder. "Call 911."

"We're too far from any hospital out here," Jose said.

"I heard the shots." Lily came running for them, her phone in hand. "I already called the sheriff. He's headin' out here."

"See if he can get a paramedic." Austin took hold of the t-shirt, pressing down, trying to stop the blood flow. Another guard bent Verne's head back and began mouth to mouth. They worked on Verne for several minutes, counting off, pumping his heart until they finally got a faint beat.

"There's no time! Load him up, put him in the back of my truck. Lily, call the sheriff back. See if he'll meet us on the road, escort us in." Jose kept his tone normal, but his actions were anything but. He moved quick, giving clipped instruction to the guards. Three lifted Verne, while three continued to work him.

"Jose, your arm." Lily forced the minute's pause, tying a clean towel around his upper arm. One of Austin's guards was in the driver's side of the truck, Jose jumped in beside him and they were off. They wasted no time, speeding down the trail before either had their truck doors closed. Lily stood watching the truck, back on the phone with the sheriff. His siren screamed in the distance.

Chapter 26

The grainy, gritty feeling in Dunc's exhausted eyes didn't stop the clicking of her right finger, tapping the mouse of her computer. Nothing more than pure self-preservation kept her looking. She'd been awake for a solid forty-eight hours, and Rich never stopped calling. He proved to be the pain in the ass she knew he'd be. She needed something, anything, to give back to him. Rich was too loud and could cause too big a stink online, jeopardizing everything she'd worked so hard to achieve.

Surely, Austin Grainger's parents hid something she could use. Hell, maybe she should go back to her original idea and make some shit up. Lead Rich on a wild goose chase and blame him for not closing the deal. Ten thousand dollars was ten thousand dollars, and there would be no way to prove she didn't find the information about Grainger. With that much money, she could get a new server, maybe a new computer, but damn, the thought of bumping her mom off was way more appealing than she thought it might be.

The biggest problem in her way, the Grainger's hung on to so much crap in these files. Grainger's parents were boring as hell and straight as arrows. Their little Farmville accounting of the company was solid. The purchases, the payroll and all its accompanying documentation all catalogued in nauseating order. Nothing looked out of place, and nothing indicated Austin Grainger participated at all in this company.

Eight email accounts were associated with the website. So far, she'd been through six of them, dating back over the last ten years. She'd done the obvious searches. Tried for the quick finds and was now going file by file, and dear lord, did these people lead boring lives.

She opened the seventh file with a big jaw cracking yawn. She kept going, not wanting to lose access, because at some point some system software would have to alert them she was digging around. There was no chance she could sleep even a few hours and hope to get back in as easily as she had the first time.

Dunc went months backward when an IP address from Texas caught her eye. She'd seen some purchases in Texas coded in the accounting, but it wasn't really a surprise. Austin's parents were from that area, but to have an active IP address in Texas where Cara and Seth were also vacationing... Dunc slapped her face and downed another five hour energy shot from the mini refrigerator at her feet, trying to gain a little more clarity in her head. Of all the places in the world, why would Austin go back to his home town? He wouldn't, it was too easy. The place would be swarming with reporters and photographers. It was too obvious of an answer. Maybe this was a brother or sister, maybe a cousin, but it was someone close to the family. The conversation flowed too easily between them all. It was also someone who made decisions for the company. They were never told no, just how much or how big.

"Goddammit! Glenda, you fucking stink. Get off that thing and go to bed!" A voice sounded from the basement door. The smell of cigarette smoke wafted down as Dunc kept staring at the screen, trying to ignore her mother.

"Keep smoking hag, maybe you'll die. *Shut. The. Fucking. Door!*" Dunc yelled, but as before, her eyes stayed on the screen. She clicked file after file, reading the contents.

It was very clear this person ran the business. Ranch hands reported to him as well as security. This person would lead her to Austin if he was in this company. Dunc kept going. Cara's name was mentioned, intervention, flight schedules, and a string of files from an overnight security watch. The IP address never faltered, and Dunc opened the only picture files in the email. They were of a naked man. Well, a half-naked man. He was having his picture taken in the dead of night, walking out of some log cabin. The whole right side of his body showed. He was good looking if you liked tall, handsome men. Dunc didn't. Dunc preferred the ladies, but she could see where someone would find that picture hot. Dunc saved the file on her computer, planning to sell it later.

From there, every shot showed this guy until he was bending down, kissing another man. It wasn't Austin, but the car was expensive and the license plate showed. Dunc sat back, looking at the screen.

Why would this be here? The fucking Fisker was from Texas. These were taken in Texas. After a minute, Dunc kept going through the messages, paying closer attention. Cara, Texas, gay men kissing. It wasn't three emails later Dunc found a series of emails from Cara, addressed to Austin. None of them made sense to Dunc, and it didn't look like Austin ever responded to any them. They were from months ago, but about the same time the photos were taken.

As the pieces came together in Dunc's mind, she opened the photo again and ran a scan on the face. Thirty seconds later she had a name, Kitt Allen Kelly. Austin had photos of a naked man in his email. Those were the only photos in all of his email. She didn't follow entertainment news because it wasn't about her, so Dunc quickly opened a browser and did a quick search of Austin's name and the word *gay*. The results filled up the page. She opened story after story. There were too many rumors swirling about Austin's sexuality for this to be a coincidence. Now, all she needed to do was pin it down.

The cell on her desk rang. Rich. Enabling the voice altering device, she answered on the fourth ring. "I said I would call you when I found something."

"Your time's coming up and we're out of money. What've you found?" There was fear in his voice, and Dunc smiled. There was that internet group reputation at work.

"Fuck off! You've wasted my time." Dunc disconnected the call and scrambled the number. As she sat staring at the screen, her heart began to pound. She had what every other news agency wanted on the planet, a link to Austin Grainger being gay. No way was she giving the information up for a measly ten thousand dollars. Try ten million dollars.

Dunc worked faster now, the drink and adrenalin kicking in. She narrowed in on the IP address and pulled up Kitt Allen Kelly's background in a few keystrokes. As the pieces fell together, a smile tore across her face. Now, what tabloid would pay the most for what she had?

~~~~~~

The stars twinkled as Kitt lay on his sleeping bag, trying to get some shut eye before his midnight shift of watching both the cattle and the kids began. He tucked himself away from everyone while he tried for sleep. It was their last night out. He was dirty, gritty, and still fully clothed.

He dropped his cowboy hat over his face, but quickly punched it off when only images of Austin appeared behind his closed eyes. Austin smiling, sulking, angry, disappointed. It didn't matter which look, they all clouded his mind. *He was so in love with Austin.* The hiding made everything harder. It was a depth of love he felt deeply in his soul. Austin proved every single promise he'd ever made to Kitt. He stuck around. They were solid, and it sure did seem their futures were tightly woven together.

Kitt crossed his arms over his chest and adjusted his body, trying to get comfortable on the hard ground. The smile formed easily. His life couldn't be any better than it was right now. A shooting star shot across the night sky, and as Kitt closed his eyes to sleep, he sent a wish to the heavens. No matter what happens, let Austin stay just like this in his heart forever.

~~~~~~

After so many months of pulling off this secluded, private, and secret home, Austin couldn't believe he stood on his front porch with the local law enforcement, Sheriff Wilson. A man he'd apparently gone to school with. Sheriff Wilson was a few years older than Austin, and he stared hard trying to pair the right kid in his memory to this man.

Wilson grew into a full-fledged old man. Despite his age, he'd apparently been sheriff of this community for quite some time. He was balding, with deep gray in his hair and didn't take too kindly knowing Austin lived here and he had no idea.

It was early in the morning, the day after Verne's hospital run and a full investigation began. Austin supposed by the time the sheriff made it to his door, he'd known Austin lived in the area. Wilson didn't seem surprised when he opened the door, but the sheriff also wouldn't come inside the house. The entire interview took place on the front porch. The sheriff asked the usual questions. What did Austin see, what occurred from his perspective, how he helped in getting Verne to the hospital.

Jose stopped by last night to let him know Verne survived, but was in very critical condition. It didn't look good. His blood alcohol levels were high and that tied the hands of the hospital staff on treatment options. Per the sheriff's update this morning, Verne was still in about the same condition. Life support kept him alive, and they were trying to find any next of kin while hoping for a miracle.

"So how it's all looking from here?" Austin asked, his arms crossed over his chest, his stance matching the officer in front of him. He was concerned about his men. None were detained last night, but he'd called his attorneys preparing to fight any charges filed against them.

"Every story's holding together. Your ranch hands all have proper ID and up to date permits to carry concealed weapons. Right now, it looks like Verne brought it on himself, but it's still under investigation. Verne was intent on causin' harm, and Jose could've been killed. Texas law allows for this kind of thing. Besides, Verne wasn't supposed to be within thirty miles of the place. If Kitt had been there, this might have been a very different story. Off the record, it's a good thing your men were watchin' the place. I try to keep my men close to here," the sheriff said, dropping his eyes back to the pad and finishing up his notes. He flipped the small spiral closed and tucked it back in his pocket. The sheriff didn't make any movement like he planned to leave, and Austin stood there watching him.

"Being the sheriff around here, it would've been common courtesy to notify me of this many armed men in my county." Wilson continued, his eyes trained on Austin.

"It was more of a stayin' completely hidden kind of deal, Sheriff. We never intended to do more than keep unwanted attention off my land." Austin never broke the direct stare. He wasn't going to apologize for being here, or the last few months. They were the best of his life.

"I should've been warned of anything unseemly trackin' the area." The sheriff added as he pulled his cowboy hat from under his arm and tugged it down on his head.

"I need this to stay quiet. We've had no trouble here. If I get some, I promise you'll be the first to know. I'm stayin' hidden, and no one's talkin' about me anymore. Pretty soon it's not gonna matter. I'll be just like every other citizen around here."

"I guess that's about it for now. Thank you for your time, Austin. Tell your parent's hello for me." With that, the sheriff retreated down the steps and headed back to his patrol car.

On so many levels, this was the exact reason why Austin had chosen here to hide. No one treated him any differently because of his celebrity status and certainly not the sheriff who'd just walked away from him.

As he walked back inside his too quiet house, Austin looked around with nothing to do. It had been three very long days since Kitt left, and the cattle drive still wasn't over. The sheriff had made it clear, in his prediction of what could have happened if Kitt had been around. Did Verne have it out for Kitt? On top of everything else Kitt dealt with, he had a focused enemy intent on destroying him? How had Austin never known about this in all these months he and Kitt spent together?

Austin wanted Kitt home, tucked away safely, never to walk outside again. The sheriff said it was a good thing his men were keeping an eye on the Kelly's place. He didn't like that at all. Verne had come after Kitt. If his men hadn't been there; if Kitt had been at the barn alone...Austin's heart seized in his chest at the thought. Kitt always carried his rifle in his saddle, but what if it hadn't been close at hand when Verne pulled up? Did Kitt know the severity of Verne's intentions? Verne could have easily pulled the trigger on Kitt. The pain of potential loss crushed his soul, and it took a full second to push it aside.

Reminding himself it didn't happen that way, Austin forced himself to do something functional today. What could have been didn't matter right now. He needed to get his mind off the *what if's* until he could get Kitt safely home. Both ranches were pretty much in lock down, only doing the minimum needed.

Austin decided he could kill a couple of hours doing some checks on his market reports and checking in with his dad. He ended up talking to his mom and all of his brothers and sisters trying to kill more time. Even in all those conversations, Kitt stayed foremost in Austin's mind.

About noon, Austin went to feed the animals. All the yearlings were locked up tight in Austin's barn. Even hurt, Jose felt better about keeping a close eye on them himself. He dropped hay in the feeding troughs, and then drove the property. An unknown call came through on Austin's cell. At the same time, several messages popped up on the screen of his phone. He bypassed the unknown caller opting for the messages, hoping they were from Kitt, that he'd gotten signal somewhere along the way. He smiled running a finger over the screen and brought his pick-up truck to a stop in the middle of the pasture. He didn't want to miss a minute if Kitt had time to talk. The phone number of the message he'd opened came up as unknown, but the image that greeted Austin wasn't. It was a picture of Kitt. It was one from his email, the one where Kitt stood partially nude outside his log cabin.

For a long second, Austin sat there confused looking down at the photo. Sliding a finger across the screen, Austin pulled up the next message. It was the picture of Kitt bending down to kiss Fisker. Jealousy raked his heart and for a minute more, he wondered why he'd put these on his phone. The next message was the deed for the land he lived on. Clarity came crashing in as he saw the New York area code on the phone number. He opened the next incoming message as his phone alerted him of a voice mail from the same number.

The message was simple: '*This is Chrissy from Enquiring Minds Entertainment News. We know you're in Texas. We know you live next to Kitt Allen Kelly, and we know these were in your email. You have until the morning to agree to an exclusive interview to set the story straight before these hit every major market around the world. Even if you can stop us in the States, you can't stop us worldwide, but it's your choice how this plays out. Call me.*'

Austin's heart physically stopped in his chest. *They knew.* They hacked his email and they knew.

Seth's call broke the image on Austin's phone. Julie, his publicist called at the same moment. Both must have gotten the same message. He answered one, then the other, putting them on conference as he sat in his truck right in the middle of the pasture, his heart at his knees. The cattle made their way to his truck, eating the hay from its bed.

"Where's the breech?" Seth asked.

"My email." Austin's heart now hammered in his chest. It wasn't just that they'd found him. They'd found Kitt too. "Goddamnit!"

"Austin, we ignore it and let it happen. They have no real proof. A couple of pictures of another man naked, none of this implicates you. They have no proof you're involved. It's two men who aren't you, kissing. We can get you off the property."

Seth stopped her flow seconds before Austin could. "That's his boyfriend."

"So? It changes nothing. There's no proof in any of this that Austin's involved. We'll get you across the world and make this a lie they're trying to put on you."

Austin could hear Julie typing away as she spoke, already outlining everything just said.

"Kitt's still gonna be outted," Austin said lamely.

"He looks like a big boy. A real big boy." Julie chuckled. The typing stopped and he could feel her eyes staring at the picture he'd secretly snapped. There was absolutely no proof, but he knew in his heart she stared at his Kitt.

Austin's tone turned hard. "I'm not hangin' him out to dry. This will ruin him, and it's my fault those pictures were taken. He doesn't even know I still have them." Dread filled his heart. He stared out his front window, but saw nothing other than Kitt's life being ruined, and in return, Kitt pulling completely away from him. And that was the very best case scenario in this deal he came up with.

"Austin, this is easy enough to sweep under the rug. Pay this cowboy off. He'll be fine," she said. Austin stayed silent for several long seconds. "Austin, you still with us?"

"He won't take my money. Seth, get me a car and a flight to New York. I'll take care of it," Austin said, ready to end the call.

"From where?"

"Good point. Change in plan. Get me a helicopter here on my property in thirty minutes. I have to try and find Kitt. He's helping the school out. I wanna leave Dallas within the next ninety minutes." Austin put the truck in gear and drove slowly through the cows surrounding his truck.

"I'm advising you not to do whatever you're thinking of doing," Julie said.

"Don't respond to Chrissy or anyone, period. I'll be back in touch." Austin disconnected the call and dropped his head to the steering wheel. What was he going to do? Was this the best plan? Nothing else came to his mind, and he'd have the entire flight to consider every option. Palming his phone, he quickly dialed a number.

"Well it's about damn time you returned a phone call!" Donnie Cliffs of the *Late Show* answered on the first ring.

"I need to be on the show tonight, but it has to be on the DL. I mean, *way* down low. No one knows I'm on until you call me out. If you do it, I promise tomorrow's gonna be a boom for you."

"Alright, can you get here by six?" Cliffs asked.

"I'm gonna try." Austin popped his head up, driving again.

"See you then."

Austin dialed Kitt's number, not allowing himself to think about his actions. The call immediately went to voice mail. "Baby, I'm so sorry. I'm leaving a note on my kitchen table explaining more. I'll keep you posted as I go. I just wanted you to know that I'm here for you no matter what. Even if you never wanna see me again, I'll make sure you're taken care of and everything's yours, Kitt. The horses, my land, the farm, it's all yours. I love you beyond anything reasonable, more than life itself. You're everything to me, and I'll regret this for the rest of my life. I'm so sorry for what I've done and what I'm about to do."

Austin disconnected the call and drove straight back to the house. He'd have no more than twenty minutes to shower, dress and get to the helicopter. He got ready in ten, and took the other ten to write his note.

The helicopter landed close to the house. He was out the door, running to the copter with his head ducked low before his security team could even surface to find out what was going on.

~~~~~

A plane waited for Austin as he landed at Dallas Executive Airport. There was little time to spare. Seth, who was the most metro sexual, most uncowboy kind of guy, arranged for a stylist to be on the plane, along with a hairdresser and make-up artist. When Austin questioned it, Seth's exact words were, *'Have you looked at yourself in the mirror lately? You need this'*. The entire time they worked on Austin, he was on the phone with Seth, Julie, and all of his attorneys trying to find any other feasible alternative out of this mess.

No one came up with anything to stop the pending photo campaign from going worldwide. Immediate injunctions would stop the United States publications, but it was a global world now. Kitt would be plastered all over the entire world. It would easily seep into the United States even without a United States entertainment company featuring the story.

None of Austin's staff, other than Seth, could understand why this had Austin so worked up. To them, this was nothing more than another round of the same rumor that had plagued him for years. No one got how much Austin changed since meeting Kitt. He'd become honorable. This landed squarely on Austin's shoulders, and he wouldn't slink away from it. He should have deleted those pictures.

Hell, he shouldn't have even taken them, and no way would he leave Kitt to deal with this on his own.

Once it became clear that no amount of talking would sway Austin, Julie became a dog with a bone helping him with exactly the right words to say as he spoke to Donnie Cliff tonight. Austin's whole game plan came down to him getting the word out first. Maybe no one would care about Kitt's photos if he was honest with the world. If Austin was lucky, it might only be a passing interest as to who the guy was that finally caught his eye.

After a four hour flight, and a whirlwind of activity, Austin was back to having solidly blond hair again. His dark tan didn't need any sort of spray refresher, but he was plucked, clipped, cut, manicured and pedicured all before being outfitted in a tailored, classically cut, modest, yet expensive as hell, suit.

Austin ran late getting to the *Late Show*. Donnie stood on stage, already doing his opening monologue as Austin arrived in studio well after eight. It gave Donnie's staff very little time for edits before the program aired. Donnie held the show as long as he could, well past the point of anything safe, just to get Austin on as his guest tonight. There was no time for them to talk first, or for him to prep Donnie before he took the stage. Tonight, they'd wing it.

It wasn't ten minutes after Austin came to the theater that he walked out on stage, waving his hand to the audience, his sexy signature grin in place. He casually shook hands with Donnie, waved at the band, and then the audience again. They went wild having had no idea he was planned for the show tonight. Several minutes passed with the audience standing and applauding just for him. He waved, bowed, smiled, and Donnie stood beside him trying to get a hold of the audience. Nothing worked until they got it out of their system and were ready to sit again.

It was the standard late night talk show set-up: a desk for Donnie with a couple of chairs to the side for the guests. Austin took a seat to Donnie's right. He sat casually, hoping he pulled off the calm exterior of a man with easy confidence, not showing the reality of his heart frantically hammering in his chest. Internally, his focus centered on Kitt, but he kept the outward calm like he'd been trained to do. After the first couple polite pleasantries, Donnie just looked at Austin, not sure what to say. Donnie was a trained comedian, his timing perfect, and he got a big laugh from the audience as the two of them sat in silence, staring at one another.

"So...whatcha been up to since we last saw you, oh, eight months ago?" Donnie finally asked.

"Well, I've been farming. I bought a farm in Texas." Several Texans from the audience hooped and hollered at the mention of their home state. Austin could tell Donnie hadn't been expecting a truthful answer, and was now trying to piece the right questions together to get to exactly why Austin sat before him.

"Really now? Farming. Aren't you from Texas?"

"Yep. I bought some land in the same area I grew up. It's a little secluded out there, but about the same area." Austin crossed his leg over the other, making a show of getting comfortable. He looked at Donnie like he was a simple, simple man. It caused another round of laughter from the audience.

"And after all these months of looking for you, no one thought to look out there?" Donnie asked in his way of making the press and media look like a bunch of dumbasses.

"Nope, haven't had a single incidence."

"Those paparazzi aren't nearly as smart as they think they are. Wish they couldn't find me. So is that the reason you and Cara broke up. She wasn't into becoming a farm girl?"

"No, I think she took to the farm really well. Seth hasn't at all, but Cara enjoys her time there." Austin nodded, understanding he was being purposefully vague.

"Okay. Since this is only an hour long show maybe after this break you could fill us in," Donnie said and waggled his eyebrows, turning to the cameras. He made another comment, something Austin didn't pay attention to, and they went to commercial break. He was off the spotlight, both figuratively and literally, for only two minutes. Austin took a long drink of the vodka, not water, sitting behind his chair. Donnie leaned in whispering to him as the cameras panned out.

"I don't know how far you want me to take it." They were both smiling, giving the audience a visual they were sharing something personal as they spoke.

"Just lead me into how my life's goin', and I'll tell you. You won't need to fish around for it." The camera crew counted off again and Donnie sat back to take his position and to reintroduce Austin to the show. After a moment he turned back to Austin. "So, have I asked, whatcha been up to on that farm of yours? Raising chickens?"

"Mainly horses and cattle. It's a cattle farm, but dabbling in some purebred horses."

"And you're just on the farm playing old McDonald?" Donnie asked and the audience laughed, even Austin laughed. He supposed he'd done everything Julie told him to do. He'd drawn out the speculation, come off as relaxed and as in control as he possibly could. Now he needed to get to the point.

"A little more than that…Donnie, I came out here tonight—"

"It's about damn time you got to the point!"

"—I've decided on putting something out in the world on my terms for a change. Not let the media spin it out of control. I'm just gonna be truthful. I've met someone—"

The audience cut him off as they stood and gave him applause. Austin grinned, waved his hand and bowed again, but Donnie got a hold of them quick.

"Sit down! I don't think he's finished. Sit. Down!" Donnie stood using his hands to lower everyone back in their seats. "Now go on. You've what?"

"Like I said, I've met someone who I want to spend the rest of my life with." Austin grinned at the more sedate, yet still very sincere clapping.

"Well that's great, Austin." Donnie said it more as a joke, rolling his eyes as if that wasn't really a big bomb to drop, certainly not big enough to rework his entire show around. Again, the audience laughed, and finally, Austin lifted a finger silencing everyone.

"Well, I think your scoop comes in the fact that I'm gay. My forever love is with a man. A man I've known most of my life, but just recently reconnected with. It's him that drives me here now. He's an honorable, good, hard working man who wants his privacy just as badly as I want mine."

Donnie stared at him in silence. Austin had no idea if the audience clapped, if they made any noise. His whole focus centered in keeping his features passive as his heart hammered violently in his chest.

"Well, good for you! I've known you for many, many years, and I couldn't be happier for you, Austin." Donnie seemed genuinely sincere in his words and actions, and Austin let out the pent up breath he was holding. "Is he here?"

"No, and he doesn't know I'm here. He's a real farmer, working with the school this week. It's gonna be a surprise to him I'm here."

Austin finally came back into himself and had no way to judge the audience except they were quieter now.

"Well, we all know how much people like surprises..." Donnie leaned back in his chair, tucking his hands behind his head. "How's he gonna feel about all this?"

"Not too happy, I suspect." Austin grinned, looking a little sheepish at the laughing his response evoked.

"Then why're you here? Probably not the best relationship move to go against your partner."

"I've been ready to shout it from the highest mountain for so long. I'm so in love, but he's kept me quiet. I had my private email hacked last night. I wanted to get my side of the story out before they can make it something ugly and sinister, because it's not that at all. I love this man with my whole heart. He's everything to me, and I believe he feels the same way about me."

A small grin spread across Austin's lips, and he looked down for a second thinking about Kitt. All the worry and negativity left him as thoughts of Kitt filled his soul. His smile grew bigger as peace settled in. A moment of silence followed. The entire studio audience sat quietly. This was the freest moment of Austin's life, and it felt great. The only thing that might have made it better would be for Kitt to be here with him. He wanted to share this moment with him.

Looking up, Austin realized he'd even silenced the seasoned pro Donnie Cliff. "I've lived for years with the paparazzi and tabloids trying to twist and turn everything in my life. There's nothing to manipulate here. I love this man with all my heart. He loves me. That's it. There's nothing more to say."

"I'm glad to hear it, Austin. We need to take another break. Will you be able to stick around, answer some questions?" Donnie asked. "We might even be able to take it out to the audience."

"Sure, I'm always ready to talk about my Kitt."

With that, Austin said Kitt's name to the world. Relief was strong as he realized he'd taken the story away from the tabloids. He'd come out, done it on his own terms, and he refused to let the worry about what Kitt might think concern him right now. He'd worry about that after he left this stage. For now, it needed to be game on. Happy go lucky, man in love wanting to tell the world. But, he did say a little prayer as he took another long swallow of vodka.

Chapter 27

A driver took Austin from the studio to the Ritz Carlton in downtown New York City. Apparently, the buzz of his announcement had already made it through the gossip mill. It didn't seem to matter the *Late Show* was in overdrive, trying to get the editing done before the ten thirty broadcast. It still leaked, but that was fine. It just meant more people would watch the show tonight to see if what they heard really was true.

Austin pulled to the back of the property to the side entrance secluded from the general public. He palmed his phone, checking his messages to see if anyone had heard from Kitt. After he'd landed in New York, he'd sent Sam and his guys out to try and find the cattle drive. It was a shot in the dark, but he felt he had to try.

Kitt's reaction was his only concern, and now the worry set in. It stayed foremost in his mind. His phone rang and Austin gripped it tightly, looking down at the screen. He answered on the second ring.

"How do you feel?' Cara asked.

"Good. Nervous. I don't know. I wish I could've talked to Kitt before I did it," Austin said as he came through the door to his suite loosening the knot of his tie. The little panic in his heart was growing. He could hear Seth talking in the background, and Cara recited what he said. "*Good Morning America*'s booked you at 7:30. They don't know why, except you want to be on the show."

"Good, then back to Texas, right?" Austin asked tugging the tie over his head. "Did you stop them from booking more? I have to get back to Kitt. I don't know when he'll be home, but it'll be tomorrow and I need to be there." He'd shrugged off his jacket, the tie now gone, and he rolled up his sleeves. He put Cara on speaker as he stalked across the room to the mini bar. Austin pulled open the cabinets, found a bottle of vodka and opened it. He did little more than pour it in a glass before he took a big swallow. His brow furrowed as the liquid burned its way down his throat. He could feel some of that long standing old anger at this world filter in, but he pushed it out. He only had himself to blame for how this happened.

"Austin, do you want me to go there tonight? I can wait for him. Either at his house or yours... And someone has to tell Lily and the girls," Cara said.

"Shit, I forgot about that. Kylie's away at college. If she can come home for a little bit, that would be best. Get her a ride home. If she can't, get security on her. Shit, Cara, can you go there until I can get back home?"

"Yes, I'll leave right away."

"I'll call Lily myself right now. I'll tell her you're coming there. I've got security tight around them, but let me see if I can get Kylie home tonight. Cara, handle anything that comes your way. Use anything you need, but get them all taken care of." Austin abruptly stopped speaking as room service entered, carrying a tray of food. "Let me know when you get there."

Austin disconnected the call and stood silently watching the waiter set his dinner on the table. He'd been a part of too many situations where room service wasn't really who they said they were, and left with photos of him or some story of what they saw in his room. Austin wasn't taking any chances tonight. He signed the ticket and walked the waiter out, handing over a twenty as he closed the door behind them.

Lily was a speed dial away.

"Lily, it's Austin. I need to talk to you."

"Is Kitt okay?" she asked, sounding a little panicked.

"Yes, I think so. Look Lily, I need to tell you some things, and I need to ask you to please keep them to yourself. Well, at least for the next few hours." He actually gave a harsh laugh at what he just said. He thought the bubble of laughter might sound a little hysterical and grabbed the vodka before strolling across the living room to sit on the sofa and kick his feet up on the coffee table. This was going to be the first of many conversations just like it, and he needed the practice.

"Lily, let me start from the beginning..."

~~~~~

The cattle ran easily through the back fence of Micah's pasture. It seemed like they were just as tired of this little exercise as the rest of them. The excitement of the trip was drained, leaving a bunch of exhausted, irritable teenagers and even more irritable adults. Over all, it turned out to be a good exercise for the kids. It let each and every one of them know how hard life used to be for a cowboy, and in Kitt's opinion, it taught the importance of an education. He'd spouted that thought over and over during the trip, hoping it would sink in.

Kitt got every head inside the fence. Micah's boys stayed back there with him, helping to guide the herd in. The others scattered, trying to find their parents who were scheduled to pick their offspring up.

Micah's land sat off the road. This gate was several miles from the main road, and Kitt weighed his options. He could easily sneak out the back, loop around, and be home in about fifteen minutes, or he could go tell everyone bye and help get the kids off. As he made the decision to sneak off, something caught his attention. He saw Austin's security guys close by. There were four or five of them on horseback riding straight toward him. Mike was leading their way. They were all in full gallop, driving their horses with a hell bent purpose. It took a second for him to realize they were riding to him.

"Rusty, get the gate!" Kitt yelled. He would have dismounted, but the concern of seeing them all headed his way had him riding Bullet around the cattle, causing a bit of a stir. That's when Kitt saw Micah. He was on horseback, a few hundred feet behind Mike and the security team. The look on Micah's face said it all. Kitt instinctively knew, they'd been outted.

"Kitt, go out the back way! Lily and the kids are at the house and safe! Austin's outted, you're outted, and the press's swarming the place!" Mike yelled out, barely slowing down as he rounded the herd to the back gate. Micah came from the other side and Kitt did little more than follow as Austin's security did their best to surround him. Micah was off his horse and unlatching the gate, opening it wide. As Kitt got closer Micah held a tabloid up for him. Kitt grabbed it as he rode by. The front cover was a full body shot of him in the nude, his privates blurred out, his robe billowing around him. Kitt's heart fell from his chest. His eyes looked directly into Micah's who stared straight back at him.

"Go!" Micah reached out, slapped Bullet on the flank, kicking Kitt into gear. He urged Bullet on, driving him forward in a burst of power. The exhaustion from just a few minutes ago was gone, and adrenaline fueled both man and horse. They rode hard, circling back around several miles until Mike finally motioned for them to stop, hidden in the dense forestry surrounding Micah's property. Sam, the security guard Austin talked to the most, stayed right beside Kitt the entire ride.

"He left you a message on your voice mail and this on his table. I brought it with me because I'm not sure it's safe to go back to his place right now. Austin has all of us on your place," Sam said. Mike just sat quietly staring back at him. No one else said a word.

Kitt pulled his phone from his pocked. The battery was low, but there was a weak signal. He dialed his voice mail. There were so many messages from reporters it took a minute to get through them. Kitt was in shock, he felt numb, a little disjointed, and his thought process faltered as his eyes focused back on the tabloid picture. When had this picture been taken?

Finally he got to Austin's voice mail. He listened to the whole thing, and then restarted it, listening to it again. Austin's voice was desolate. His words were sad, and Kitt's heart hammered too badly to hear everything clearly.

"Where's Lily and my sisters?"

"They're at the house, protected. We've kept everyone off your land. The horses are secure, Jose's with them. We've put all our energy into your place, per Austin."

"Where's he?" Kitt looked around at the men as heat scorched his face. They were all on horseback, riding like pros, and every one of them knew about their relationship. But, the evidence in his hand had him blushing like a school girl.

"In flight back here."

"What happened?" Kitt asked.

"It's in the note he left for you, sir."

Okay, the sir was new, and it somehow made Kitt more anxious than he already was. He looked up at Mike who quietly stared at him, quiet. Kitt tore open the envelope and pulled the letter out to see Austin's handwriting.

It's completely my fault. I should have deleted those pictures. I thought the email account was secure and have no idea how anyone found out it was mine. I'm doing the only thing I know to do, and that's to get it out in the world before the tabloids throw you under the bus. And they would do just that, Kitt.

I'm so sorry. I wish I could speak to you before I do this. Please do what my security tells you to do. They're trained in this. I'm so sorry.

All my love,

A

It still didn't provide any answers except Austin knew about the photo of him on the front of the magazine. Kitt looked down at the magazine again. He didn't know exactly when it had been taken, but the entire right side of his body was bare and he was standing at the front door of his cabin. If it was possible, even more heat rushed to his cheeks and he looked up again at Sam.

"When was this taken?" The caption on the tabloid was clear: *Austin Grainger's Cowboy Lover Cheating, Up Close and Personal.*

"When we first moved in. There's more inside. It was the night the guy driving the sports car came. Austin had us delete the photos. I don't know how they got them."

"Austin's email," Kitt simply said. He thumbed the magazine like it was a noose he was slipping around his neck. A nude picture was humiliating enough, but if Sean was in there, Kitt was completely outed. It took a second, and his hands started to shake as shame hit him hard. It was right there for everyone to see, Kitt bent down to kiss Sean who sat inside his car. Dread filled his soul as his now numb heart allowed him to toss the magazine to the ground.

"Where did Austin go?" Fear set in, making him grow cold inside. Kitt was completely shamed for the entire world to see.

"He wants you to call him to explain." The guard handed Kitt a cell phone to use.

"No, you explain it to me." The famous Kelly anger spoke for Kitt. The anger he'd tried most of his life to hide now became the most dominant emotion pouring through him. It would make Kitt unreasonable and unstable, but would definitely replace the hurt coursing through every vein in his body.

"I don't know all the details, sir."

"Cara's at the house with Lily and the girls. She's been there since Austin asked her to come out last night. I'm gatherin' Austin thought if he spoke first it would take the focus off you. He's gone to New York,

I think," Mike said it quickly and efficiently. He'd been Kitt's friend too long, he knew how Kitt worked.

"There was no clear evidence the email account was Austin's. They were trying to flush him out through you. He wasn't going to let you go like his PR team wanted him to do. I was on the call, Mr. Kelly. He drew the attention off you. This isn't the big news of the day, as bad as this looks." Sam pointed to the tabloid now lying on the ground. "It's all about Austin Grainger being gay. He made the announcement last night before this was printed. We have a man waiting at the bend, making sure we're clear. We need to get you home, sir."

Kitt didn't hesitate. He kicked his mount into action and moved quickly toward home. The anger never left, nor did the firm set of his jaw. This was the very worst thing that could have happened to him. Nothing compared to this, and to top it off, Austin planned to leave. He was giving Kitt everything. Kitt had allowed his heart to become involved while it was always just as he'd thought, he was a kept man. Austin was giving him the land, the horses, everything. They weren't partners. Kitt was a kept toy, and yet, he'd fallen in love with Austin. Kitt loved him so completely that at this moment it wasn't the fear of what was to come, but the fact that Austin planned to leave that made him drive his mount harder, barreling toward home. Fuck whoever was there. Fuck everything. Kitt had lost it all.

~~~~~~

Three hours later, Kitt finally shut the door to his cabin. Fatigue from the trip allowed his temper to settle. That, and the knowledge Lily and his sisters were okay. When he'd walked into the main house, Lily grabbed him up, hugging him tight. So did Kylie but Bryanne wasn't quite as receptive. She was angry. Her date for the night was cancelled because they were on lockdown. It made her so angry he could see some of that fired up Kelly temper in her. She didn't care whether Kitt was gay, straight, or dropped off the edge of a cliff, it was all about her.

Cara had been kind. She'd tried to explain what she knew of the situation, but Kitt didn't want to hear any of it. He stayed quiet, turning into himself. If he didn't want to hear any of it, he wanted to say even less. From the front windows of the main house Kitt saw several news station vans from Dallas and Austin out front. He'd been told Austin's gate swarmed with them. Several snuck around back. All of Austin's security resources were here and focused on the two farms.

Kitt returned to his cabin, pleading exhaustion. He needed time alone. He picked up his phone charging on the night stand. He had thirty-three missed calls, all from Austin. He silenced it and laid it back on the night stand, ignoring it and his heart's need to hear Austin's voice. It took him a minute to rationalize the rudeness of his action, but then he remembered the voice mail. If his heart needed to hear Austin he could play the message Austin left earlier. The one where Austin told him he was leaving, giving him everything. The exact one where Austin somehow managed to make this so much worse in those few short sentences. Yeah, when Kitt missed Austin and needed to hear his voice, that's what he would play, reminding himself of what an idiot he'd become.

For now, Kitt decided on food and then sleep and then a plan, all in that order. At some point in the near future he'd have to turn on a TV, get a good grip on what was happening, and where he stood, but not now. Kitt was too hurt to do much more than exist.

Kitt stood in front of the microwave warming the plate of food Lily sent over when his front door burst open. It wasn't the quiet, stick your head in the door, are you home, kind of greeting. It was a solid shove open, slam against the wall. Kitt turned quickly reaching for his rifle, chastising himself for not locking the door in a situation like this. But, as he turned his eyes to see who had come in, he found Austin standing in the doorframe.

The sun shone in around him. For a minute, they just stared at one another. Kitt was completely taken off guard by the angel standing in his doorway. Okay, he needed to amend that, the angry angel standing in the doorway. Kitt turned his back on him to pull the hot plate from the microwave, carrying it carefully to his kitchen table.

He did it all just to hide his runaway heart, and the emotion at seeing Austin in his house. Kitt was in survival mode. Instinctively, he calmed and began working with his hands. He never said a word to Austin as his heart hammered in his chest. Where was that damn anger when he needed it to help him get through situations like these?

"You can't pick up your phone to let me know you're okay?" Austin glared at Kitt who purposefully ignored him. Relief flooded Kitt as he felt the first stirrings of anger building back up. It would help stamp out some of this intense hurt. Maybe even help him not cry in front of Austin.

Kitt stalked back the few steps to the kitchen counter and grabbed a water bottle, silverware and a napkin and took a seat at the table. All of a sudden, he was no longer hungry. Austin always fucked him up.

"I had to call Mike to find out you made it back. Cara said she talked to you. You couldn't answer any of my calls?" Austin said again when Kitt ignored him. The palm of Austin's hand slapped down hard on the table, jostling the plate. That caught Kitt's attention. The anger licked at his soul, and his eyes cut up to Austin's.

"I'm ruined, but you should know that. What else do you want me to say? Thanks for my land back."

"You aren't ruined. I can take care of us if you'd get that through your thick skull. What was I suppose to do, let them run those pictures of you and hide? Let you take the brunt of it all? Fuck no, I wasn't gonna let that happen. I love you. I love you so Goddamn much. I meant every fuckin' thing I said on *Late Show*. You're everything to me." There was so much anger in the way Austin said it, he looked like he might burst into flames at any given moment.

"You told me there were photos of Sean, never of me nude, or of us kissin'. You said they were deleted. How many more are there of me like that? Is the price of the photo my fuckin' land back?" Kitt demanded an honest answer. He'd shoved his plate of food back and gripped the sides of the small table. Kitt fought the need to tackle Austin who stood there indignant over something as simple as Kitt not answering the phone.

"That was my fault. I told you that," Austin said, but Kitt's words had him taking a step back. Finally, it was about something other than him not answering a fucking phone. "I only took the picture that one time. I had them deleted, all but the ones on my computer. You were so hot, so beautiful. You turned me on so much...I wanted you so badly. I didn't delete them. I'm sorry, I should have, but I love that picture so much." All the riled anger left Austin's face, and now, he was moving around the table toward Kitt who quickly moved around the table the other direction.

"So they found the pictures by what, hackin' your computer?" Kitt asked with the table between them. He grabbed a hold of his anger and held it in place. It was the only thing that would get him through the next few minutes.

"Please don't move away from me. I haven't slept in days. Kitt, I'm sorry. I can take care of us until the horses are ready to compete. I ruined everything, but I can take care of us. I can take care of Lily and the girls. Please let me do it." They circled the table as Austin talked to Kitt.

"I thought you were leavin'? You said I could have it all," Kitt fired back.

"If you don't want me anymore, if I ruined us, I'll leave you everything. I'll still take care of you and the girls. I promise, but damn it, please stop moving away from me, Kitt. And stop toying with my fucking heart. How badly have I fucked this up?" Austin stood at the head of the table as Kitt moved out of the small kitchen to the far side of the living room, placing the coffee table between them.

"You look all Hollywood again," Kitt said instead of answering Austin.

The answer was so clear inside Kitt. His heart sang because nothing was as bad as Austin leaving him. He'd let the world run over him as long as Austin gave him the time of day. Austin followed him, stepping up onto the coffee table and over it to move closer as Kitt backed away. Austin wisely stayed a foot away from Kitt backing him toward the bedroom.

"It's because I hit the circuit again. I thought if I got it out there before the sleazy tabloids, I could spin it in the right direction. My PR firm says the focus groups are thirty-two to one in our favor. I couldn't stop the pictures, Kitt. I tried to file injunctions, but I didn't have time. All I knew to do was to bring it out. Tell the world I love you." Austin voice cracked a little at that. Kitt stopped, staying very still. Austin gave him room to digest it all.

"You said that on *Late Show*?" Kitt asked. He crossed his arms over his chest trying to hold his heart together.

"And *Good Morning America*. Haven't you seen the television today? It's being played over and over." Austin took a small step toward Kitt, but right before they touched, he pivoted on his heels, stalking out the front door. He was back in a minute, laptop in hand. Kitt still hadn't moved.

"I have it on my laptop. Please sit down. Watch what I did. Please." Austin sat the laptop on the kitchen table and pulled up a file. Kitt could hear Donnie Cliff's voice announce Austin, and the cheers erupted from the audience. Austin shoved out a chair and Kitt came forward to take it. He watched the screen closely, his arms still crossed securely over his chest so they wouldn't reach out to Austin.

It was an emotional experience to see the man he loved beyond reason turn back into his actor mode. Austin looked so handsome up on that stage, and stayed calm, cool, and collected during the entire interview. Even when he took questions from the audience, something Kitt had never seen on *Late Show* before.

The last question from the audience to Austin was *'What made you finally come out?'* Austin didn't hesitate, he never looked away, he just stared at the woman and answered easily. *"When you find the person you know you're supposed to spend the rest of your life with, things that mattered before him just don't matter anymore. I've been gay my whole life, Kitt makes me okay with it. Actually, he makes me proud to be gay because I get to spend the rest of my life with a man as good as he is."*

Kitt let himself reach his hand over and take Austin's who stood beside him as the video played. It took a moment longer for him to look up at Austin because tears were swimming in his eyes. "Did you mean it, or was that the actor talkin'?" Kitt asked.

"I meant every single word." Austin gripped Kitt's hand tighter and dropped down to his knee to be closer to Kitt's level. "Tell me I didn't ruin it between us. Tell me we're gonna be okay. I can handle any of this if I didn't lose you."

"No more pictures," Kitt said.

"No more pictures." Austin nodded.

"I love you like that, too." Kitt looked deep in Austin's eyes. Austin reached in to kiss Kitt's parted lips.

"I don't ever want to lose you. I was so afraid." Austin's voice broke again as he pulled Kitt to him.

Chapter 28

A horde of people descended on Austin's farm. Publicists, public relations people, attorneys, managers, and Austin's agent were all there ready to strategize. This was too big a story and too important of an outcome not to guide as best as they could. Kitt sat through hours of meetings during which he generally stayed quiet. The team also met with his stepmom and sisters who were stuck in the house going over well rehearsed statements about Kitt and their knowledge of Austin once it was safe to go out in public again.

No part of their small community was left untouched. Reporters were everywhere. The public high school was bombarded with photographers, interviewing anyone and everyone they could get their hands on. Old teachers of Austin's in high school, Kitt's college professors were all interviewed. It didn't matter what they said, hell, most people's story stayed the same: Kitt was a good man and the entire town was in shock; they'd had no idea. It wasn't until yesterday that anyone mentioned Kitt's dad. It was an off-handed comment by the local restaurant owner that had his dad now headlining the news. It went from Kitt being the love of Austin's life to Kitt being abused as a child. Stories Kitt had completely forgotten were surfacing. Speculations grew to a frenzy, having analyst's on split screen piecing together exact moments in Kitt's life when he could have turned gay.

As Kitt sat through about the seventh hour of meetings, he was lost to it all. He stared out Austin's back window, into the pasture, thinking over the last few days. He'd lost three of his ten full time ranch hands. Two more were showing signs of abandoning ship. Jose was solid. He stood by Kitt's side, giving them all a firm talking to. It was business as usual for Jose, and he'd run the farm pretty much by himself since this all fell down on their heads. With Austin's security still posing as ranch hands, and Mike helping out, they were able to make do without the three men he'd lost. But, it was double the work watching both farms and taking care of every animal on them.

Austin came to sit beside Kitt. They held hands openly. It was something Austin pushed on him from almost the beginning. It gave Kitt strength so he didn't fight it. Austin handed him a beer with a smile. That smile always seemed to ease Kitt's heart. As he sat, Austin intertwined their fingers back together, but Kitt moved his eyes back to the window. Micah's pick-up truck pulled up to the barn, and both he and Jimmy got out.

Kitt didn't hesitate as he rose. His movement interrupted the meeting, but he gave no explanation as he went straight outside. Austin followed on his heels. They made it down the porch steps and across the fenced back yard as Micah and Jimmy came through the gate.

"For the record, I knew it," Jimmy said.

"Me too," Micah said as an immediate follow-up. All three of them came to a stop about two feet apart. They all stood in about the same stance with their legs apart, fingers tucked in the front pockets of their jeans. Austin was still a couple of feet from them. He broke the pattern, walking straight up behind Kitt, putting his hand on his back until it slid to the side of his waist. It took everything Kitt had not to move away from the hold, to stay there and let Austin prove himself and their relationship to these men.

"It's weird to see you two together like this, but we talked it over, and we're standin' by you. I don't like what's bein' said. We called Jimmy's cousin. He's an attorney and said he can try to stop some of it. We can pay him out," Micah said looking from Kitt to Austin as he spoke. A dirty, dusty Mike came to stand behind Jimmy and Micah.

The show of solidarity caused emotion to well up in Kitt. He didn't speak for a long moment fighting back the relief. He'd been so afraid of losing them all. For his entire life, he'd feared being left completely alone if anyone ever found out the truth. When Kitt stayed quiet, Austin spoke up, helping him out. He stepped up against Kitt's back and slid his arms completely around Kitt's waist, holding him tight.

"It's what we've been inside talkin' about for most of the day. There's no reason to waste your money. I'm gonna stop as much of it as I can. The best thing you guys can do right now is get the people to stop talkin', no more interviews. No more tryin' to take up for Kitt, no defendin' him. The press's gonna twist and edit their words until what they said comes out completely different. They're just makin' it worse. Can you do that for me?" Austin asked.

"We can try. I'll get Heather on it and head into town."

"Me too. JoLynne can get on the girls," Jimmy said. There was no messing around with this group of guys. Once given the job, they were on it. Before they ever hit the gate, all three were dialing their cell phones.

Within an hour, the town was silent. Kitt and Austin watched the local news and then national news. All were still in town covering the area, but no one was talking anymore.

It didn't stop the reporter's speculations or the nude shots of Kitt going viral, but after a few days Austin started teasing Kitt. He'd say if Kitt wasn't such a good looking guy, no one would care. Those times always caused Kitt to blush, and he would duck his head down grinning at the suggestions that always followed. The whole interaction became their own kind of foreplay, and the end result always had them in bed, Austin trying hard to make Kitt blush again.

Within a few weeks the frenzy in town slowly came to an end. Being out allowed Austin to stay with Kitt fulltime, there was no need to hide. They worked together during the day and slept together every night. Austin kept Kitt with him, by his side pretty much twenty-four-seven and for some reason for a guy who lived his life in virtual solitude, Kitt didn't mind having Austin with him.

"I was thinkin' about takin' you into town tonight for dinner. I have something I want to talk to you about." Austin finally said a little over two weeks after everything came out.

"Do you think it's too soon?" Kitt asked.

They were standing in Austin's bathroom, both just showered from a particularly dirty day of running cattle. Austin's suggestion caught Kitt off guard, causing him to stop drying his body in mid-wipe and look up at a shaving Austin's reflection in the mirror.

Austin lifted his eyebrows. "Embarrassed to be seen out with me?"

"No, I didn't say that." Kitt slowly began drying himself again. His eyes narrowed in speculation.

"We need to get out as a couple if this community's ever gonna accept us." Austin spoke as he finished shaving.

Kitt brushed his teeth and shaved himself. Austin stayed in the bathroom after he was done and stood with his butt against the counter. He was still completely nude, his arms crossed over his chest watching Kitt. After a few minutes of Kitt staying quiet, Austin continued on. "Look, I've wanted to take you places. It's reasonable to have dinner out, it's what couples do. We need to think about travelin' together, weekends away, goin' out into the world together. It's reasonable, Kitt, but the first step's gonna be tacklin' this town. Just because they supported you doesn't mean they're comfortable. We need to get them there. Plus, I've been thinkin' about something. We could have a nice little dinner, talk, and then go over to that bar, have a drink or two, shoot some pool and come home."

"Okay." Kitt didn't move his eyes from his reflection in the mirror to look at Austin as he patted aftershave on his face.

"Okay? That's all you have to say?" Austin asked clearly surprised he didn't have to fight this out.

"No PDA. Zero! None at all," Kitt said as he turned to the closet. He had clothes here now. Not lots, but some. And, Austin had bought him a set of all his toiletries to have on hand.

"Alright. I can live by that rule for tonight. We can go as buddies so we don't freak anyone out too badly." Austin followed Kitt into the closet.

They dressed quietly. This was a big step for Kitt. Austin had already tackled this one by going on *Late Show*, but for Kitt this was his voluntary public coming out and it scared the crap out of him. After all the times of never being seen together, they were going into town for dinner. Would the photographers be gone? How would the townsfolk take them? The questions never stopped running through Kitt's mind, and he was nervous as hell. Kitt chose his clothing carefully, feeling like a cold beer, maybe a shot or two of something would be in his very near future.

~~~~~~

It looked like there were two agreements Austin made for the night. One, no public touching, and two, being the designated driver. Austin stood back, busying himself in the living room as Kitt downed a beer in a couple of deep gulps while standing in the opened door of the refrigerator. The outward calm of dressing must have been a façade, Kitt was obviously uncomfortable.

When Kitt realized Austin planned to drive, he grabbed two more beers for the road. Austin took it as some sort of encouragement that his sexy boyfriend needed to be drunk to be seen with him in public. Well, maybe it wasn't that, but the thought did cross Austin's mind, and he chuckled. If Kitt needed a good buzz, it was fine. Austin didn't say a word, he was just relieved he kept the refrigerator stocked with the required Bud Light for times just like this.

Austin had made plans for this outing a couple of days ago, but hadn't had the nerve to suggest it until tonight. Even when he'd brought it up, his heart thumped in his chest, and he had his face covered in shaving cream to hide any reaction that might show. He knew from experience, the more they shied away from this, the more people would speculate. They needed to be out as the couple Austin told the world they were.

The no touching thing would be hard. They needed to act like a couple. There was a fine line there, but Austin needed to walk it tonight, and so did Kitt. If Kitt needed to get tipsy to help make it happen, then Austin would DD it tonight, and maybe get in a peck or two in front of the others, claiming this man as his. Because without a doubt, Austin knew the reporters and photographers were still incognito in this town. This night out would be front page tabloid news tomorrow morning.

"Babe, what constitutes as a PDA?" Austin asked driving down the dirt road leading to the main highway into town. He turned on the local country classic radio station, the one Kitt liked the most. Kitt drank the beer down in one gulp before answering.

"No touchin', no kissin'. Stay an appropriate amount of space from me." Kitt answered clearly and efficiently, reaching over to search the stations. The move confirmed how nervous he was as he went through station after station, not really listening to the music, just pushing buttons. After a minute more of eternal scan, Austin stopped him by entwining their fingers together and pushing the radio button back to Kitt's favorite station with his index finger.

"If I can't touch you all night, at least let me hold your hand now." Austin brought Kitt's knuckles up to his lips and placed a soft kiss on the back of his hand. "I love you. It's gonna be alright. I promise."

"There's no way you know that." Kitt turned to look out the window into the night as they drove along the darkened highway. Austin could see a small smile on Kitt's face through the reflection in the dark window. The smile didn't match the statement, and Austin hoped it was a possible joke.

"I do because no matter what happens tonight, I'm bringin' you home, layin' with you in my bed, makin' love to you and wakin' up in the morning with you in my arms. So no matter what happens, it's all gonna be all right in the end."

Kitt didn't say another word. The smile stuck, so did the quiet, but he was calmer even as Austin pulled into a front parking space. "You ready?"

"As I'll ever be." Kitt got out and looked around the parking lot. Austin came to the front of the truck and waited, watching Kitt take the full minute looking at the other vehicles parked around them. Finally, perhaps a little reluctantly, Kitt came to stand in front of Austin.

"After you, babe."

"No name callin'," Kitt said, immediately amending the rules as he stepped past Austin to walk straight inside. As Kitt hit the front door, slowly every head in the place turned his way. The jukebox played, but other than that the noise in the room slowly died off as Austin came in the front door to stand directly behind Kitt. He gave Kitt no PDA, but he stood as close to him as he could without touching, and stared back at everyone. He pointed at a table and touched Kitt on the back.

"How about that booth in the corner?" It broke the silence, but not the focus. People openly stared. Austin vaguely remembered some of the faces they passed from back in the day, but Kitt had to know them all. Yet, no one acknowledged him. It was like they didn't see him while staring directly at him. Austin on the other hand was treated like the celebrity he was trying not to be. Every girl in the place was beside herself watching him walk through the restaurant. Much to their clear vocal regret, Kitt took the side of the booth facing them and Austin sat with his back to the room.

"Well, that wasn't so bad." Austin grabbed a menu from behind the napkin dispenser.

"Whatever. I think that was about the most awkward thing I've ever done in my life." Kitt stared at Austin as if he'd grown another head as they walked in.

"You haven't been in my shoes the last ten years, that felt almost normal," Austin said, reading the menu. He looked up and saw Kitt still staring at him and reached over to hand him a menu. Kitt took it, but laid it down, not looking at it. A perky little waitress came over to the table, handing Kitt a beer with two waters.

"Hey, Kitt. I talked to Kylie. She says she's back at school now and everything's calmed down. I'm glad all that died down. It was crazy around here, but the tips were *great!* What can I get you to drink, Mr. Grainger?"

Austin wanted to jump up and hug this waitress. Whoever she was to Kylie, Austin was forever in her debt for approaching the table like a normal, reasonable human being.

"Call me Austin, and I'll have Bud Light, please," Austin said, looking her directly in the eyes. He gave the grin he'd been taught to give. It didn't matter the grin felt awkward on his face. He'd been told the ladies loved it, and he loved this waitress, so she got the grin.

To her credit, she did stare at him for a long minute, smacking her gum, before she began to fan herself. "Whew, you sure are good lookin'. Do you know what you want for dinner yet?"

Austin looked over at Kitt, but the waitress answered for him.

"He always gets the t-bone, medium, baked potato, no sour cream, green beans. Right, Kitt?"

Kitt gave a nod, and Austin smiled bigger.

"I'll have the same, but add his sour cream to mine. I love the stuff." Austin dropped the menu back behind the napkin dispenser, grinning at Kitt.

"Alright then, I'll be back with your Bud Light in a bit."

"Bring me another." Kitt lifted his beer. She raised her eyebrows but stayed quiet, nodding once before she left them alone.

"The décor hasn't changed much over the last fifteen years. Still very nineteen-seventies up in here. You come here a lot?" Austin asked.

"I used to. Before you moved in." Kitt's eyes left Austin's, and he scanned the room. Austin had no idea what Kitt was seeing, but his expression grew harder, and Austin didn't like it at all.

"Babe, pay attention to me, no one else. I'm your date," Austin said, pulling Kitt's attention back to him.

"No 'babe' tonight, Austin." Kitt immediately responded, looking directly at Austin.

"I'm sorry, but stay focused on me. Ignore everything else, okay?" Austin nodded his head trying to get Kitt's agreement. "Trust me, if you get comfortable with this, so will they. They're pickin' up what you're puttin' out there, and it's tension and judgment. Let it go. We're a couple. Couples eat together."

Austin worried about Kitt. He didn't let him too far from his sight, and anytime anything was brought up about them, Austin dodged it and moved Kitt away from the question. He also kept Kitt too busy at night to watch the news or surf the net. He didn't want Kitt stumbling across all the gossip and accusations being flung around about him. It was clear the world thought Kitt had cheated on Austin with Fisker. It was absurd, but the only way the reporter had to spin the story without looking like a sleazebag for exposing Kitt.

It concerned Austin so much, he'd even reached out to Sean to make sure he was good. That had been one of the most interesting conversations he'd ever had. Austin went into the conversation jealous and testy, but Fisker was loving all the attention of his new fame. Fisker was fine being considered the man Austin's lover cheated with, and his social life couldn't have been any better.

What bothered Austin the most was Kitt's staff. A little more than half ended up walking out. It took a couple of days, but six out of ten left the farm. Kitt also got a few cancellations on scheduled insemination gigs he'd had set up in the area, and two of the largest farms pulled their hay baling from Kitt. No matter how Austin tried, he couldn't shield Kitt from those kinds of things, but Mike worked his magic and got Kitt focused on Austin's farm.

They were going to become a shorthorn breeding farm. It would definitely require Kitt start an artificial insemination program through the new cows and heifers arriving. Mike also moved his range cattle over with Kitt's, combining them, helping to keep the integrity of the new breed stock intact. Every bit of this was done to prevent Kitt from being able to take a minute to breathe and realize everything he'd lost because of Austin.

The beer was put in front of him, and Austin smiled a thank you. Kitt drank his first one down, and a replacement was put in his hand.

"I've been thinkin' about something for a few days now. Actually, for a couple of months, but really hard the last few days. I think we should combine the farms. Make it one large one again. Run them together. Heck, we're already doin' so much of that now," Austin said, and then took a long drink of his beer, watching for Kitt's reaction. The reservation he knew was coming hit Kitt's brow, and Austin hurried on with his plan.

"We already run the horses together. The track's across both our properties. The range cattle are mixed together on your back property. The shorthorns are gonna be partially yours for the insemination work you're doin'. I just think it makes sense," Austin said trying again. "We could remove the fence I put down the middle, open that pond back up. Mike could manage the cattle, he's good at that, and Jose could run the horses. They could share duties on crops, or whatever you think." Austin stopped because he rambled and Kitt just sat there quietly for a full minute.

"I don't know. I never thought about it before."

What did that answer mean? And the reservation still lingered. Austin had been watching it all week, and for that matter, most of their relationship.

"It makes sense," Austin said into Kitt's silence. Kitt's full focus was on Austin.

"We've only been together eight or nine months," Kitt whispered, leaning in across the table. "Don't you think that's a little soon to be movin' everything together like that?"

"We've been together almost every single day out of eight months, two weeks, and four days, Kitt. That makes us more than just together for a little less than a year." Austin said it, and Kitt stayed quiet because he didn't need to say what was clearly on his face.

"Ba…. Kitt, I'm here to stay. Haven't I proved it yet? I love it here with you," Austin said quietly, not wanting to be overheard. He leaned across the table toward Kitt who was already leaning on his elbows staring at Austin. The reservation was gone, his face just intense now. It gave no clue what was going on in that head of his.

"They still want you for movies. Nothing's changed since you came out. You thought it would, but it hasn't," Kitt said in almost a whisper. Austin could see he wasn't quite as effective as he thought at keeping information from Kitt. A small amount of hurt snuck into Kitt's eyes, and that landed squarely in Austin heart. He'd caused everything about Kitt's world to be dramatically turned upside down, changed forever. Austin could tell by the stares Kitt got tonight that things had also changed in how this community saw Kitt. But for Austin, he was still a coveted commodity, maybe even hotter than before. The movie deals were rolling in at least one a day.

"Maybe someday I might do another movie if *we* agree it's right for *us*. You won't let me reach across this table and take your hand, but I want to so badly…I would love to have you on set with me on some tropical island for six weeks, just me and you. The international community can be much freer with their bodies than we are here in the States. You'd be so hot on a nude beach. I can just see it in my mind…" Austin took a second to look off, thinking about his nude Kitt walking on a private beach, playing with him in the crystal blue ocean. They'd make love as the water lapped over them. The grin spread across his lips as he turned back, momentarily forgetting they both weren't sharing the same thought, and he gave a laugh.

"And, I can see that you don't understand its greatness. For right now and the foreseeable future, I'm right here with you, Kitt, until *we* decide something different. And when I'm gone away on business, I'm still right here with you for as long as you want me. This is where I want to be. *You're* where I want to be. Our focus needs to be on our farms. Combinin' them makes sense. I can give you controllin' interest if it makes you feel more comfortable. But it'll make us stronger. I want us to be a breedin' farm. You can get us there, Kitt."

"Here's your dinner, and can I say that everyone's just tryin' to hold off before comin' over here and askin' for your autograph, Mr. Grainger. You're quite the buzz in here," the waitress said, setting each plate in front of them. "The steak sauce is by the napkins up there. Is there anything else I can get you? How about a couple more beers?"

Kitt gave a nod to her question. Austin shook his head no.

"Alright then, Kitt, you're weird tonight. Are you sure you want another beer?" She looked confused and directly at Kitt.

"Yeah, he's drivin' tonight," Kitt said, absently looking up at her.

"I think it's for courage," Austin added.

"What? You don't need courage, Kitt, we love you here. You've been through a lot, but we're like your family here, and we respect you. I know I do! I'll get you another beer, but promise me you two will stick around and let everyone get Austin's autograph and get reacquainted with him again." She didn't wait for an answer, but turned on her heels, done with the conversation.

"Not shy is she?" Austin asked

"Not at all. She's been my sister's best friend since birth. If Kylie told anyone that she found us, it'd be her." Kitt reached for the steak sauce.

"Ah, maybe that's why she's so comfortable with us. Well that's good. We need people on your side, Kitt. Now, say 'yes' to me before you put that bite in your mouth." Austin waited and watched Kitt with his fork mid-way to his mouth. It lowered, but rose again and he ate the bite, nodding his head.

"We can try it. See how it works. Open up parts of that fence dividin' us. It would make it easier to run the cattle in the back pasture." Kitt cut another bite. Five beers seemed to make him more amicable, and the sixth just plain made him relax. Austin needed to remember that in the future. He'd never seen Kitt drink this much of anything, and it looked like Kitt was a happy tipsy man. Maybe if Austin kept the beer coming they could go parking after they left. Have some truck bed sex on the way home.

Austin smiled at the thought and realized Kitt was still talking. He forced his mind back trying to catch what he missed. "Do you agree?"

"Ask me again." Austin looked up at Kitt.

"If this doesn't work for either of us there's no harm, no foul, and it goes back to normal."

"Okay, if you'll agree that the surveillance fencing goes around the entire property. It'll make it easier for my team to look over everything." Austin began cutting his steak.

"Is that what this is all about? You want to keep a better eye on things?" Kitt stopped eating.

"No, not at all! It's easier to have the farms run as one. We're too invested in each other, but it would make it safer for everyone if the fence was around the whole place. It would catch any breeches." Austin spoke with his mouth full.

"Here, Kitt. Is there anything else I can get you?" The waitress appeared with another beer for Kitt.

"No, we're fine," Austin said. Kitt seemed more relaxed and was back to just eating with Austin like they had done almost every night for months and months. "I have the papers drawn up at home. You can read and sign them, or I'll tell you what's in them and you can sign them."

"Pretty sure of yourself." Kitt swallowed down a gulp of the beer. There was humor in his tone, and his eyes stayed on Austin.

"No, that's one thing I'm not when I'm dealing with you, Mr. Kelly, but I was hopeful. I've had these papers for a week trying to man up and find the right time to ask."

"Now I see why you're getting me drunk." Kitt pushed the plate in front of him aside, but kept the beer in his hand. He sat back in the booth, his eyes stayed on Austin, and the grin on his face had Austin growing hard just watching him.

"I think that's you gettin' yourself drunk, but keep goin'. I like it when you agree with me." Austin waggled his eyebrows, and Kitt chuckled. They were back to normal, at least through the length of the meal.

~~~~~~

Kitt let out a loud, jaw cracking yawn as Austin drove them home. It was well after midnight. Kitt's favorite radio station played quietly in the background. Kitt had kept drinking, but slowed it down some when they went over to the bar. Even slowing it down, Austin estimated Kitt had consumed at least a twelve pack over the last few hours. Not too drunk, but drunk enough for what Austin had in mind.

"Tonight turned out pretty good, don't you think?" Austin asked. The pickup cab was dark, Kitt's head was rolled back on the head rest, his eyes closed.

"It stressed me out to do that tonight, but everyone got less weird as the night went on." Kitt gave another yawn and Austin lifted the console and patted the seat.

"Come sit by me." When Kitt didn't move, Austin reached across and grabbed his hand. "Sit next to me. Put your head on my shoulder. Sleep if you want."

Kitt finally slid across the truck, straddled the hump in the floor board with his feet and came right up against Austin's right side. He laid his head on Austin's shoulder.

"I didn't know you could dance like that. All the women wanted to dance with you all night. It was hot as hell watchin' you dance. I even got a little jealous." Austin kept one hand on the steering wheel, the other slid between Kitt's thighs, tucked under his leg. Kitt wrapped his arms around Austin's and Austin leaned in to kiss the top of his head.

"I like to dance. I've been dancin' with those girls since we were in school, but you kicked my ass in pool. You kicked everyone's ass. How much did you make tonight?" Kitt asked, lifting his head to look at Austin.

"Fifteen bucks! I tried to give it back, but no one would take it. It's a good group of people up there. Old man Howard used to scare me a little when I was a kid. He was real nice tonight."

"Yeah, he's a good man. I swear though people must have called each other. That place was packed for a Tuesday night." Kitt leaned in to kiss Austin's neck as he spoke.

"I had a good time." They were quiet the rest of the way home. Austin pulled the car to the front of the gate in his back yard. Not to the barn where he usually parked. When Kitt realized what he'd done, he turned a questioning gaze at Austin as he found a newer country station on the radio. "I want to dance with you on the porch. We can leave the truck doors open, turn up the radio. Dance for awhile. I might have you dancin' with me every night now that I know you like it."

Kitt didn't say a word. He slid out behind Austin on the driver's side. Austin left the ignition on, rolled down the windows and shut the door. It was dark, the music easily reaching the porch. The porch light was on, but Austin turned it off, letting the moonlight shine down on them. It took a minute to move the patio furniture around, but they did it and Austin took Kitt in his arms.

"You're everything to me," Austin murmured as he pulled Kitt completely against his body. Both men had immediate hard-ons that brushed against the other as they began a slow Texas Two Step around the porch. Kitt led, Austin followed, but they stayed close together through the entire first song and most of the second. It was Kitt breathing Austin in, running his nose along Austin's neck and nibbling at his ear that caused Austin's footing to finally falter.

"You undo me, baby," Austin said, angling his head back. Kitt had a tight hold around his body, his arms anchored tight at Austin's waist. As Austin leaned his head back, Kitt pushed both hands down on Austin's ass, gripping him while tugging him even closer.

"We're out now," Kitt whispered in Austin's ear. "I never thought that was ever gonna happen." Kitt bent back, capturing Austin's lips with his own, thrusting his tongue forward. Kitt ground his hips into Austin, rubbing and massaging while keeping their feet moving in slow steps.

"I'd dream of this…kissin' you…makin' love to you while on the dance floor…." Kitt turned them in a slow circle and never released his hold on Austin's ass. Austin returned the kiss with as much passion as Kitt gave.

"All night tonight, all I could think about was you out here dancing with me until you made love to me here on this porch." Austin whispered in Kitt's ear and caught Kitt off guard as he shoved his pants down, freeing Kitt's cock. Austin started to drop to his knees in Kitt's preferred position, but Kitt was having none of it. He grabbed Austin's arms, turning him around. He bent Austin over the rail on the porch. There was little prep as Kitt tugged Austin's blue jeans down. It wasn't a second before Kitt pushed two fingers through Austin's tight rim, scissoring his fingers to work Austin quickly open. Austin shouted rearing back and gripped the rail for support.

"I want you," Kitt grumbled. He gripped himself, rubbing his broad head against Austin's tight opening. Kitt pushed forward and Austin's body resisted.

"Damn it, I need lube." Kitt started to spit in his hand.

"I have it." Austin dug in his jean pockets, pulled out a small packet of lube and handed it to Kitt.

There was no time wasted as Kitt ripped it open with his teeth, dripping it on his cock before he pushed forward, easily breeching Austin. Tonight, Kitt conquered. His cock was huge and Austin wasn't ready to take all of him. He stood straight up as Kitt pushed all the way in. As a rule, they both liked it a little rough and Kitt didn't disappoint. Kitt fucked Austin like he had the right to do it, right there on the porch rail.

Kitt worked Austin from behind, moving as fast as his thighs would go. Kitt was his perfect lover. The exact height, perfect position; Kitt instinctively knew just how to move to keep Austin on the edge. Austin gripped a hand on Kitt's hip and the other on the post holding the rail in place. Austin held off, not touching his own cock, knowing it would be all it took to come. Kitt kept up the pace from behind, and Austin dripped in anticipation. Austin's cock begged him to finish the job. He gritted his teeth, and held on for dear life.

"You feel so fuckin' good! Goddamn you were made for me...for this... " Kitt ground his teeth together as he grunted out the words. Austin was so tight. This was so perfect. He gripped Kitt, milking him until nothing else mattered.

It was their sacs hitting against one another that undid Austin. He came on a shout, not even stroking himself off. Kitt never stopped moving, but Austin couldn't hold it. He fell forward, wrenching free of Kitt's hold as his legs buckled out from underneath him. The rail caught him as his orgasm exploded from his body. Austin felt Kitt reaching for him, trying to bring him back to finish the job.

"Noo…" Kitt moaned, but Austin could do nothing more than breathe. It was Kitt's very first time to go without a condom, and Austin smiled. It made them one during these times, nothing separating them, and it was shocking at how good it felt to finally make love with a trusted one, skin to skin.

Austin anchored against the rail, not more than a minute had passed, but Kitt seemed to have none of it. Austin heard movement behind them. He forced one eye open and looked back to see Kitt's shirt coming over his head. He wiped down his cock.

Kitt moved quick. He lowered Austin to the porch floor with the moonlight in perfect position for Kitt to see Austin's face. He straddled Austin's chest, working his plump, erect cock. "I'm not done. Suck me."

Austin wasn't given a chance to respond. Kitt shoved his dick down his throat.

He deep throated Kitt on the first thrust. Kitt slid down his throat on the second push. Kitt leaned forward, landing on all fours and fucked Austin's mouth. He pistoned his hips back and forth. Austin was completely relaxed and able to open even further than normal, willing himself to take all of Kitt, and just breathe when he could. The deep moans Kitt made had Austin lifting his hand to massage his ass and sac, running the balls through his palm. When he slid a finger in Kitt's ass, massaging the gland, it was all it took. Kitt tightened and roared, shoving himself as far down Austin's throat as he could. His release jerked and spewed from his body.

Apparently, Austin just rocked Kitt's world. Kitt fell to the side, slipping from Austin's mouth. Austin took a deep breath in through his nose, swallowing down everything Kitt left behind. The timing worked out perfectly, breathing was as important to him as sucking Kitt off, and now, he had both.

"Goddamn, how do you do that?" Kitt asked. He was laying on his back now, his arm thrown over his eyes as if the moonlight was too bright to look at. Kitt was panting, his chest heaved, and he had already begun to drift off to sleep.

Austin grinned, wiping at the side of his mouth. As much as he loved Kitt's taste, he loved to kiss Kitt after they sucked each other off to share the taste. Austin pulled up, climbing up on Kitt and did just that. He kissed Kitt thoroughly, holding his head in place with his hands, his tongue swirling and suckling, tenderly making love to Kitt's mouth.

Both missed the car lights pulling in next to Austin's truck.

"For God's sake, the house was like three steps from where you're lyin', couldn't you have made it inside?" The sheriff's voice ripped them apart as it came through the night over a loud speaker.

"I'll give you one minute from right now to get up and get your clothes right before I come up there. Don't make me see anything that might permanently scar me for life, Kelly. I've seen enough of you recently. I might arrest you just for that."

They bolted up, moving quickly. Both Austin and Kitt were dressed in a matter of seconds. Austin had no idea what this was about, or why the sheriff was here, but it couldn't be good at this hour of the night. They were down the steps as the sheriff met them in the backyard.

"I'm sorry to come out so late. I figured you might be here. The town was buzzin' tonight, and I heard Austin drove," the sheriff said.

"Yes, sir." Kitt responded and Austin followed with a nod because it was the only thing he thought to do. "Is everything alright?"

"Son, they took Verne off life support this evening. He died almost immediately. Part of my job was to notify next of kin. I also went and got his belongings from the room he rented. I found this." The sheriff held a shoe box and he handed it to Kitt.

"As best as I know, no one else saw it, but I can't be sure of that. I'm breakin' the law, but I just figured you'd been through enough, and Lily and the girls didn't need any more stress." The sheriff said it, trying hard to hold eye contact, but finally lost the battle. He lowered his head and nodded.

"Sorry to bother you two so late. I'd say I'm sorry about Verne, but he caused you lots of bullshit for no reason. Maybe that'll show you why." The sheriff turned on his heels with a simple goodnight and took off without another word.

"Come inside, let's see what's in there," Austin said, putting an arm around Kitt.

~~~~~

Kitt followed Austin up the steps, lifting the lid to the shoe box. It was too dark to see much, but he could make out some old photographs of his dad. As Austin opened the backdoor, the images struck Kitt hard, causing him to stumble a bit as he walked inside. Austin went through the living room, turning on the lights, and Kitt shuffled a hand inside the box, moving the contents around. There were photos of his dad as a younger man, even before Kitt was born. Kitt dumped everything from the box on the table.

There were so many pictures of his dad and Verne together, taken like they were on vacation. They posed at different monuments, state signs, arm in arm. There were also letters, all bound together with a rubber band. Kitt's heart began to pound as he realized what he held. He looked up at Austin who'd sat down at the table, just watching him. Kitt sat down and pulled the rubber band free and opened the first letter. It was a love letter to Verne from his dad.

Hours passed by as Kitt read each letter. They were full of emotion, of love, of everything his dad had felt for Verne, and all the wishes he had had that some day they could be a real couple. Kitt's father had been gay. As he and Austin sat at the table, Kitt read everything, seeking out the photos that matched each letter's date. Kitt let Austin look at each one before he put them together in chronological order. Apparently, his dad had met Verne in high school. They'd been lovers since the beginning; Verne had been his dad's first lover.

Through the letters, Kitt learned his dad's history. The battles he'd had with his family. His dad had paid Kitt's mom to be his wife. She'd been young and poor, just a pawn to him, much like Lily must have been. They'd both been too young and in too much need to know better. Both had been there to help his father hide and keep his standing in the community.

For over the forty years Verne and his father were together, Verne had broken up with his father more than once, needing more of a commitment. And, his dad had promised Verne the farm if anything happened to him. It was right here in black and white. His dad hadn't had a proper will when he died, just something he'd scribbled down a long time ago on a piece of paper to their family attorney. Verne could have fought it and won, but he'd have to bring forward a relationship no one had known they had.

Verne never fought Kitt in court, keeping his father's secret. Instead of battling it out in public, Verne fought him every day until Kitt had no choice but to fire him. Kitt never knew all that aggression stemmed from Verne being a grieving lover, deeply in love with his father.

Austin stayed quiet, making coffee, keeping Kitt's cup filled well into the night. Neither of them said much. Some of the letters his dad sent before he died showed he feared Kitt was gay and hiding. His father talked about trying to beat it out of him, not wanting Kitt to live a life of lies like he did. With the letters spread out across the table, along with the photos, Kitt looked across the table at them all, then at Austin.

"I never knew him." Kitt felt small, insignificant. This one hurt Kitt.

"He never let you know him."

"But that's what I've been doing, too, the one thing I never wanted to do...I'm living my father's life."

"Not anymore. You broke free where your father didn't have the nerve to." Austin pulled his chair right next to Kitt. Austin took Kitt's hand and brought it up to kiss his palm.

"It's only because of you that I'm out. I didn't do it on my own."

"That's not true. You went out tonight. You didn't have to, but you did."

"My dad died a bitter angry old man, and it was because of this. He could never be with the man he loved. That would have happened to me if I hadn't met you." Kitt turned in his seat to face Austin, threading their fingers together.

"It would have happened to me too, but I met you." Austin tightened his hold on Kitt's hand and leaned forward for another light kiss. They sat there a minute more until Kitt turned and carefully placed everything back together inside the box before putting the lid back on it.

"I don't think Lily should ever know, or my sisters. We need to keep this hidden." Kitt nodded to confirm his decision. "We need to find a safe place for this."

"I like the *we* part of that."

"No more hidin'." Kitt nodded again. The beer he'd drunk, and the emotion pouring through had him a bit frazzled. Austin smiled at him and came in for another kiss.

"Agreed, no more hiding. Now, come to bed. You have to be exhausted." Austin pulled Kitt back to their bedroom.

"I love you, Austin." Kitt followed behind him, bringing the box with him. No chance he wanted it left out.

"I love you, too, baby."

Epilogue

One year later

Austin pocketed his phone as he stepped up into the driver's side of his pickup truck. Kitt was on the passenger side waiting for him. Austin smiled at him.

"That was my attorney. They found the guy that hacked my email. He's a she named Dunc. They're arrestin' her in Mexico as we speak. Ironically, it was my nemesis who helped find her. Rich and Mercedes filed charges against her for stealin' their money. She's apparently livin' it up, not stayin' discreetly hidden. She'll be expedited back to the U.S. to stand trial."

"Dunc's a girl?"

"I guess, who knows, but jail time should be fun for her." Austin reversed the truck until he got a clear path to head out into the pasture.

The land immediately behind theirs had come up for sale, Austin bought it, and now they had a combined twenty-five thousand acres together.

They did officially join the farms, operating as one now. Kitt moved in with Austin at his house. They gave Kylie his cabin for when she came home for the summer or Christmas breaks. Then once school was out, she'd have a place to live for as long as she wanted it. Both their lines of breeding cattle and quarter horses were coming along better than expected. Hooch and Little Lady were entering the racing world this next season.

As Kitt expected, Austin started a new project, another film. It's one he decided to produce, as well as star in. It was filming primarily in Texas, mostly here on the ranch in the furthest back pastures on the newly purchased land. It was a remake of the Great Gatsby. Austin decided to build a replica of the house here on the ranch. He wanted them to live in it after the filming was complete. Austin was constantly asking for Kitt's input. He listened incessantly to all the details on the movie and house. Okay, it was more like Kitt pretended to listen to all the details. Austin wanted Kitt happy there. It would take years to film correctly, but he wanted the home perfect for Kitt.

As they drove to check out a problem with a back fence, Austin was already back on the list of actors he planned to take various roles. For the most part, Kitt kept his nervousness to himself. Austin was just so excited about acting again, but it concerned Kitt. They were together now, and he needed to live in the now for as long as he got the opportunity. It's what his father and Verne's relationship had taught him, so he sat in the truck, watching the fence line, letting Austin talk.

It was already dusk outside. They needed to get a move on it to see the fence line properly. Kitt started to say something, but Austin kept the flow of conversation going every time he opened his mouth to speak. Austin kept taking his time until he diverted from the path heading out into the open pasture. The move caused Kitt to narrow his brow, and he looked over at Austin, who continued the steady stream of talking, not letting him interrupt. Out of nowhere Kitt saw lights. It looked like maybe a small fire until they drove closer. There were candles burning. A smiled spread across Austin's lips and he sighed.

"I was afraid I was gonna have to start talkin' about the declaration of independence...Surprise!"

"What is it?"

Austin laughed at Kitt's confusion.

"It's the house, honey. See it roped off?" Austin stopped the truck, turned off the ignition, but left the lights on and jumped out. "This is the first floor. Come on, I'll give you a tour."

The first floor was huge, it took Kitt a minute to even comprehend the size of the place, and there were two more floors in the plans. Austin made a production of walking them through the front door, stepping into a huge grand entrance with a stairwell separating the living room. The kitchen and guest rooms were at one end, their bedroom at the other. It was the part Austin had sectioned off with candles. In the middle of the room was a sleeping bag, pillow and an air mattress. To the side of it sat a picnic basket, champagne bucket, and a fire pit was close by. Austin slowed a little, walking to the bed. It was getting darker outside, not quite night, but it took a minute to see the small black velvet box and envelope in the middle of the bed.

"Marry me." Austin simply said, bending down to take the box and the envelope. "Kitt, I can sometimes see the anxiety of all this in your eyes. This is the only way I know how to relieve it. Marry me and honeymoon here with me."

Kitt opened the envelope as Austin opened the box for him to see a simple gold band sitting on the dark velvet. Austin used his cell phone for light and Kitt got the gist of what was in the envelope. Their honeymoon would be at the Kentucky derby with a signed contract from the trainer Kitt had wanted, agreeing to come work with their horses.

Kitt's smile must have said it all. Austin grabbed him up, wrapping him in his arms.

"Thank you. Thank you, I love you! Now let's get Hooch ready to race!"

The End

About the Author

Best Selling Author, Kindle Alexander, is an innovative writer, and a genre-crosser who writes classic fantasy, romance, suspense, and erotica in both the male/male and male/female genres.

Send me a quick email and let me know what you thought of Texas Pride to kindle@kindlealexander.com.

For more information on future works check out the website at: www.kindlealexander.com

Other Kindle Alexander Titles

From **Phaze Books**:

Up in Arms   Blood Bonds (A Bonds of Love
                              novel)

From **Red Rose Publishing**:

Eligible Bachelors (Reality with a Twist Series)

Printed in Great Britain
by Amazon